"IT'S GOING TO

His voice was low and s̶ ̶ ̶ ̶ ̶ ̶ ̶ ̶ ̶
hers, her pulse kicked u̶ ̶ ̶ ̶ ̶ ̶ ̶ ̶ ̶ "We're going
to be okay."

We? "You don't know that," she whispered.

"I know that you'll do your best and that's all anyone
can do." His fingers slid sensuously over her arm.

"But my best—"

"Your best is passionate and strong. Your best is
better than anyone else's I know," he insisted, the
searing heat in his eyes melting her. Then his mouth
closed over hers. She let out a soft gasp and parted her
lips. While she knew friends didn't kiss like this, she
made herself stop thinking. She wasn't going to think
about anything painful, not when she could lose herself
in his kiss.

With an aching deep in her heart, Cael trailed her
hands over his back, his neck, and into his thick hair.
Goddess, she adored kissing this man who could be so
tender and hot all at the same time.

Kissing him was oh-so-much better than any dream
she'd ever had. His kisses made her feel cherished,
special, and most of all, for the first time in her life,
desired . . .

"Fast-paced and sexy otherworld adventure."
—**LINNEA SINCLAIR, RITA award-winning author
of *Hope's Folly***

*Please turn this page for more
praise for Susan Kearney . . .*

PRAISE FOR
SUSAN KEARNEY

"Kearney is a master storyteller."
—*New York Times* bestselling author
VIRGINIA HENLEY

"[Kearney] combines sexy romance with spaceships, laser guns, psychic powers, and time travel."
—*Tampa Tribune*

"Susan Kearney takes you on a wild ride, keeping you guessing until the very end."
—*New York Times* bestselling author
KAREN ROSE on *Kiss Me Deadly*

"Out-of-this-world love scenes, pulse-pounding action, and characters who come right off the page."
—*USA Today* bestselling author
SUZANNE FORSTER on *The Dare*

"Looking for something different? A futuristic romance . . . *The Challenge* gave me a new perspective . . . love and sex in the future!"
—*New York Times* bestselling author
CARLY PHILLIPS

LUCAN

THE PENDRAGON LEGACY

SUSAN KEARNEY

FOREVER

NEW YORK   BOSTON

Copyright © 2009 by Hair Express Inc.
Excerpt from *Rion* copyright © 2009 by Hair Express Inc.
Excerpt from *Jordan* copyright © 2009 by Hair Express Inc.
All rights reserved. Except as permitted under the U.S. Copyright Act of 1976, no part of this publication may be reproduced, distributed, or transmitted in any form or by any means, or stored in a database or retrieval system, without the prior written permission of the publisher.

Book design by Giorgetta Bell McRee
Cover design Diane Luger
Cover art by Don Sipley

Forever
Hachette Book Group
237 Park Avenue
New York, NY 10017
Visit our website at www.HachetteBookGroup.com.

Forever is an imprint of Grand Central Publishing.
The Forever name and logo is a trademark of Hachette Book Group, Inc.

Printed in the United States of America

First Printing: September 2009

10 9 8 7 6 5 4 3 2 1

This one's for Amy Pierpont, editor extraordinaire!!!!!
Your insight's amazing, and I've thoroughly enjoyed
working with you. You've not only made this book
so much better, you've made me a better writer.

ACKNOWLEDGMENTS

There are so many people who work behind the scenes whom I'd like to thank for their efforts on my behalf. This is my first book for Grand Central Publishing, and I have yet to meet everyone, but I know that without editorial help, art, promotion, marketing, production, and sales, this book wouldn't have made it to the shelves. This is such a team effort, and without everyone's help, I wouldn't be able to write the books I love. In particular, I'd like to thank Diane Luger and Christine Foltzer for my beautiful cover, Anna Maria Piluso for the book's production, Giorgetta Bell McRee for book design, and the Grand Central Publishing department.

I'd also like to thank Julie Leto, Charlotte Douglas, and Jeanie Legendre for their critiquing efforts. Thanks for making the book so much better.

LUCAN

The precious myths of our heritage are our way of understanding things greater than ourselves. They are tales of the inexplicable forces that shape our lives and of events that defy explanation. These legends are rooted in the spilling of our life blood, in the courage of brave hearts, in the resilience of humanity's tenacious spirit.

— ARTHUR PENDRAGON

PROLOGUE

In the near future

S low down, Marisa," Lucan Roarke warned his twin.

They were deep inside the cave he'd discovered in the Welsh countryside in the shadow of Cadbury Castle, and his helmet light had settled on a gaping crack in the compacted clay of the cavern's floor. "Don't step on that—"

"What?" Marisa looked back at him just as the ground opened beneath her feet. Falling, she flailed her arms and clawed at the cave wall for a handhold, but the loose earth crumbled beneath her fingertips, and gravity dragged her down through the crevice into the darkness below.

Lucan lunged to grab her, but the unstable earth lurched and dipped under him, throwing him off balance, and his fingers missed her by inches.

"Marisa!" The sound of splashing water drowned out his cry.

Lucan had brought his sister to Cadbury Castle for a vacation, and he'd been excited to show her this cave—his latest discovery in his quest for the Holy Grail. Although many dismissed the Grail as mythical, his years of exploration and research had convinced him the vessel actually existed.

Lucan peered through the gloom into the chasm, but his helmet light couldn't penetrate the blackness. Even worse, the earthen sides of the hole made a steep vertical descent. Reaching for the heavy-duty flashlight he carried in his back pocket, he yelled, "Marisa? Talk to me, damn it."

Nothing but silence answered him.

Closing his eyes, Lucan inhaled deeply and concentrated on linking his mind with hers, a telepathic communication the two had shared since they were little.

Marisa. Where are you?

In the water. Help me. I'm cold.

Heart racing, Lucan shined the flashlight into the darkness and spotted her head above the rushing water.

"Lucan. Here." Smart enough not to fight the powerful flow of water that tried to sweep her downstream, Marisa swam for the wall at an angle and clung to a rocky ledge.

"Hang on."

She coughed and sputtered, then shot back, "If I let go, it won't be on purpose. Hurry. It's freezing."

Lucan reached for the rope in his backpack and cursed himself for bringing his sister into the bowels of the cave. He'd sweet-talked her into coming along, desperate to break her out of her funk. Since her latest miscarriage, she'd been fighting off depression. He'd hoped this excursion would take her mind off her loss, at least for a little while. He hadn't intended to distract her by risking her life and scaring her to death.

He uncoiled the rope, then leaned over the hole to see her lose her grip on the ledge. The current pulled her under. "Marisa!"

A split second later, a pale hand broke through the water and clutched a rock jutting from the wall. Marisa pulled her head and shoulders above the torrent, spat water, and forced her words through shivering lips. "I knew . . . I should have gone . . . to Club Med."

He looped the rope around the biggest boulder within reach. Then he tossed the line down the narrow shaft. "Grab on and I'll book the next flight to Cancún."

Marisa stretched for the rope. And missed. Water surged over her head. Again she swam to the surface, but the current had carried her too far downstream to reach the lifeline.

With no other choice, Lucan jumped into the dark shaft. He fell about twelve feet before frigid water closed over his head and ripped away his glasses. His flesh went numb, but he managed to keep a grip on his waterproof flashlight. His lungs seized and his vision blurred. Forcing his shocked limbs to move, he kicked for the surface. And heard Marisa's scream. Turning around, he swam in the direction where he'd last seen her.

Already his teeth chattered. He struggled for breath, and his waterlogged clothing and boots weighed him down. The raging current swept him under, but his concern was for Marisa. She'd been in this icy water too long. Clenching his teeth, he kicked harder until he was finally close enough to grab Marisa's shoulders. They had only minutes to find a way out before hypothermia set in.

He pulled her close. "I've got you."

When she didn't reply, fear poured through his system. Fighting to lift her head above the surface, he shined his light around the cave in search of a shoal or a shallow pool.

Marisa lifted a quaking hand. "There."

Just ahead, the river forked. One side widened, the other narrowed.

Using most of his remaining strength, he steered them toward the wider fork, praying it wouldn't take them deeper underground. His prayers were answered when they rounded a bend and the water leveled out onto a dirt embankment.

He pulled Marisa out of the river, and together they lay on the bank, panting, shivering, and exhausted. When she didn't speak, he aimed the light on her. Her eyes were closed, her face pale, her lips blue. He wrung some of the water from her clothing, then rubbed her limbs with his own freezing hands.

Her eyes fluttered open. "One word . . . about my hair, and I'll s-smack you up side the head."

"You look good in mud."

She slapped at his shoulder but didn't have the strength to land the blow.

He smoothed her hair from her eyes. "Save your strength. I don't want to have to carry you." She needed to walk to keep the hypothermia at bay.

"W-wuss." She crawled up the bank until her back rested against a dirt wall.

Lucan focused on survival. "We've got to get moving or we'll freeze."

"You wrung the water from my clothes. What about you?"

"I'm fine."

"Of course you're fine. J-just like when y-you were in Namibia and that black mamba bit you?"

"I lived."

"Barely." Marisa took his hand and tried to stand, but her knees buckled. She grabbed the wall behind her for support and it began to collapse on top of them.

Lucan lunged and threw his body over hers, shut his eyes, and prayed they wouldn't be buried alive. Clumps of cold mud cascaded over them and bounced aside.

"You okay?" Lucan asked.

"Oh, now I'm really having f-fun." Marisa spat dirt. "So glad you s-suggested"—her teeth chattered uncontrollably—"th-this little vacation."

Lucan shoved to his feet. "Think what a great adventure story you'll have to write."

"I don't want to *be* the story." She rolled her eyes and sighed. "But you love this shit. You're probably getting off on—"

Wow. Her telepathic thought interrupted her words midsentence. And her amazement came through in waves— surprising waves that peaked with astonishment.

"What?" He spun around to see exactly what had shocked her, and he froze. He focused his flashlight on the unearthed urn, hardly believing his eyes or his luck. The intricate design made dating the piece easy. "It's Tintagel ware."

"Tinta-who?"

"Tintagel ware is an ancient indigenous pottery. Fifth or sixth century. More evidence that Cadbury Castle really was King Arthur's home base."

They both jumped aside as another slice of wall and more pottery crashed down, revealing a hidden room. At the sound of breaking terra-cotta, Lucan winced. An ancient scroll poked from the shards, and he dashed to pull the paper from the muddy earth before the dampness reached it.

Old and fragile, the antiquity had survived in amazing condition. He balanced the flashlight between his shoulder and chin, unfurled his find, and squinted, wishing for his lost glasses.

Marisa peered over his arm, her reporter's curiosity evident. "What is it?"

Lucan stared, his pulse racing in excitement. The astrological map revealed the Sun, the Earth, planets. And many stars. But what had his heart battering his ribs was the line drawn from Earth to a star far across the galaxy. He was looking at an ancient map of the heavens. His mouth went dry. "This is a star map."

"Why do you sound so surprised? Even the most ancient cultures were into astrology."

"Astronomy," he corrected automatically. "I'm no astronomer, but this looks . . . far too accurate for its time. King Arthur, remember. The Age of Chivalry."

"Yeah, right."

Lost in thought, he ignored her sarcasm. "This map has details the Hubble telescope might not pick up, yet it's thousands of years old. It's unbelievable."

"So it's a fake?"

"I'll have to perform tests . . ." He squinted at the map. His gaze moved on to the distant stars and their planets. "Hell."

"What now?"

He pointed to the map. "This moon is named Pendragon."

"Wasn't that King Arthur's last name?"

He nodded and squinted. "And written right under Pendragon is the word *Avalon*."

"Avalon? Is that significant?"

"Avalon was a legendary isle ruled by a Druid priestess called the Lady of the Lake," he answered. "She helped put Arthur on the throne. And according to the stories, Avalon was also where King Arthur left the Holy Grail."

"The Holy Grail?" Disbelief filled her voice.

"The powers of the cup are legendary. If the myths are true, the cup might cure physical ills—cancer, heart attacks, and . . ." He hesitated before breathing out the word. "Sterility."

Though neither his sister nor her husband was officially sterile, like most of Earth's population, they couldn't have children. Her recent miscarriage had been her second in as many years. If the cup truly existed and he could find it, his sister—and hundreds of thousands of others—could finally carry a child to term.

"Throughout the ages," he continued, "many men, including Arthur's own Knights of the Round Table, have searched for Avalon and the Holy Grail. Legendary stories of the Grail's healing properties exist in many cultures, yet no one has found it." He pointed to the small moon on the ancient map. "Maybe that's because Avalon wasn't on Earth."

"You've lost your mind." She sighed, but the catch in her voice exposed her wishful thinking that after all this time despairing, she might be able to hope again.

"A search for the Holy Grail might be the most exciting thing I'll ever do."

"It might also be the last thing you ever do. Didn't you learn your lesson when you went in search of Preah Vihear antiquities?"

"The golden statue of the dancing Shiva I found in the Khmer temple was worth—"

"Ending up in a Cambodian jail?"

"Just a little misunderstanding. We got it squared away."

She cursed under her breath. "You sure you don't have a death wish? Or are you just an adrenaline junkie?"

She was fussing only because she loved him, so he ignored her rhetorical questions. Besides, he wasn't the only twin who took calculated risks. As a reporter for the *St. Petersburg Times,* Marisa had placed herself in danger often. They were some pair. She wanted to report the present to change the future. Until now, he'd believed humanity was headed for extinction, and he had studied the past because the future looked bleak. But if he could find the Grail, the past just might offer hope.

Marisa sighed. "We need to dig out of here."

He carefully rolled up the parchment and placed it in the dry sample bag he'd pulled from his backpack. Then he shined the light on the broken pottery. Kneeling, he began gathering as many shards as he could carry.

He reached for a particularly large piece, covered in an array of signs and symbols, when he spied daylight glimmering through a tiny opening on the far wall of the hidden room. A way out. "Time to go."

"Now you're in a hurry?"

"Don't you want to find out if this map's authentic?"

She sighed. "I'm more interested in warm, dry clothes."

"Do you realize what we may have found?"

"We? Just you, my brother. Avalon? The Holy Grail? A cure for cancer? The idea is more than crazy. It's nonsense. But knowing you, you'll find a way to follow that map to Avalon."

"If the star map pans out, you'll want first dibs on the story—don't deny it."

"You're a restless, adventure-seeking fool. That stupid map is going to take you straight to outer space."

He could only hope.

As they deny the world, not only in the spirit realm but in the material plane, the world will cease to exist.

—THE LADY OF THE LAKE

1

Eight years later, half a galaxy away

Cael was going to die. Not with the dignity a High Priestess was due. Not even with the respect afforded a physician.

And it was all her own fault. When she'd thought she'd seen her owl, Merlin, flapping frantically in the cooling conduit, she'd foolishly attempted a rescue. That had been mistake number one. Instead of calling maintenance for help, she'd grabbed a ladder, yanked off the outer grid, and crawled into the ductwork. Mistake number two. She'd forgotten to take a flashlight. Mistake number three. And now she was stuck in the dark conduit, half frozen, her hair held firm by the intake valve, her hand caught in the mesh screen meant to keep out rodents.

She'd shouted for help, of course, but no one had heard. With her robes and feet dangling into the hallway, she would have been hard to miss, but her coworkers never came down the hall to the High Priestess's office.

Being High Priestess wasn't all it was assumed to be. Yes, she lived in a magnificent residence, free of charge, and her people revered her, even enacting a special law to allow her to be both priestess and healer, but the average Dragonian wouldn't think of stopping by for a chat, never mind asking for her medical opinion.

While she believed her empathic ability was a gift that enabled her to use her healing skills wisely, her people too often looked at it as a curse. A curse that might blast them if they looked at her the wrong way . . . so most preferred not to look at her at all.

To her regret, she'd treated only a few patients since she'd joined the Avalon Project's team of specialists, which included astronomers, archeologists, physicists, engineers, geologists, and computer technicians. Unless they had an emergency, her coworkers preferred other, less daunting healers. And if she didn't turn up for work in the lab tomorrow, she doubted anyone would search for her. They'd assume she was attending to her High Priestess duties.

So she was stuck. Alone as usual.

And Merlin wasn't even here. Mistake number four. Had she imagined that the owl had needed her help? She should have known better. The bird was crafty. He wouldn't fly into a conduit that had no exit. He wouldn't get stuck as she had. It would be just her luck if she died here of dehydration.

"Damn it." She pounded on the metal wall with her free hand and yelled. "Just turn off the cooling coils, hand me a knife, and I'll cut myself free."

No one answered. The suction from the intake valve threatened to snatch her bald. Again she wrenched her wrist, but the mesh held her fingers in a clawlike grip. Tired, cold, she closed her eyes and dozed.

"Lady?" Someone tugged on her foot.

She awakened with a jerk and almost yanked her hair out by the roots. Teeth chattering, her side numb, she figured she must have been dreaming of rescue.

Then she heard the same deep and sexy yet unrecognizable voice again. "Are you stuck?"

What did he think? That the High Priestess slept here because she liked being frozen into an ice cube? "Please, can you get me out?"

A warm hand grasped her ankle, and an interesting tingle shot up her leg as he tugged.

"Ow! My hair is caught in the intake valve, and my hand got stuck in the mesh when I tried to free myself."

She was about to ask for a pair of scissors or a knife, when she heard the duct metal creak and a thud. Then a man's chest was sliding over her legs. And his movement was tugging up her gown.

Holy Goddess.

She'd never been this close to someone before. No one dared touch the High Priestess.

Yet he'd crawled right into the duct with her and was inching his way past her hips. Both her hearts jolted as if she'd taken a direct electric charge. His heat seeped into her, and the feel of his powerful, rippling male muscles had her biting back a gasp of shock.

It was impossible not to feel the heat pulsing between them. Studying the signs of arousal in a medical book was one thing. Experiencing them was quite another.

The stranger was edging up her body, and her senses rioted. Never had anything felt this indescribably good. She wished she could see his eyes and his expression. Even her empathic gift was failing her. Her own excitement was preventing her from reading him. Was he enjoying the feel of her as much as she was him? Did he have any idea that her hearts were racing? That her skirt was above her knees?

Ever so slowly, he crawled to her waist and his head slid between her breasts, his warm breath fanning her flesh. His mouth had to be inches from her . . . oh, sweet Goddess.

"The air duct really isn't made for two," he joked.

Her pulse leaped. Her nerves were on fire. "There isn't enough air," she gasped.

"It's fine." He wriggled until his cheek pressed hers and she could feel the fine growth of a beard one day past a shave. His broad chest warmed her. Her hips nestled his, and she felt him harden against her.

She stiffened. So he wasn't unaffected, and that fact secretly pleased her. Although it shouldn't have.

Apparently not the least embarrassed by his physical reaction, he chuckled, his breath warm and tantalizing in her ear. "Don't worry. It's not like we have enough room in here to get any closer."

She squeezed her eyes tight. "You don't know who I am."

"You feel . . . beautiful." He reached above her head and ran his hand along her hair, his fingers strong and gentle. "I'm going to remove the grate so we don't have to cut your hair."

His muscles flexed, and he popped the vent from the duct. "Now let's free your hand."

He skimmed his other hand up her body, lightly teasing her waist, the side of her breast, her cheek. She sucked in her breath as a ripple of pleasure washed through her.

"I'll be happy to do more of that after I get you out of here," he murmured and ran his fingers up her arm to her trapped wrist. "Hmm. I've got a screwdriver in my back pocket. Think you can reach it?"

She licked her bottom lip and moved her free hand across his firm hip to his curved buttock. Her fingers itched to explore. After all, she had to find his pocket, didn't she?

"Try a little higher, sweetheart," he urged, his voice amused.

"If you want to live, don't call me that," she said in her best High Priestess voice. But instead of sounding authoritative, her tone was breathy and light.

She fumbled her fingers over his buttock, enjoying the hard muscle and the sensuous curve, and finally found and unsnapped the pocket. Oh . . . my. The material inside that pocket was so thin she was almost touching his bare, warm flesh. At the thought, her breasts tingled and, certain he could feel her nipples hardening against him, she flushed.

"What should I call you?" he teased.

She hesitated. If she told him her name, he might not finish freeing her. "I'll introduce myself once we're out of this mess."

"Honey, we're way beyond the need for formal introductions—not when your sexy little hand is grabbing my ass."

She snatched the screwdriver from his pocket. "Got it."

He gave instructions with an easy self-confidence that told her he was enjoying himself. "Reach up my back, over my shoulder, and place the screwdriver into my hand."

She did as he asked and found herself admiring his broad back, the muscular shoulders. She was wrapped around him, and the feel of his hard male body had her trembling. She hadn't known a man could feel so good.

His maleness was erotic, exotic. Exciting. Her blood rushed though her veins with a heat that made her feel more alive than she'd felt since she'd first taken to the skies in flight.

"You're awfully quiet." The rough texture of his words was almost as exciting as his muscles straining over her. "Am I too heavy?"

Too heavy? He was perfect.

She swallowed hard. "How much longer . . ."

"Until we're done unscrewing? Now, there's a question I haven't been asked before." She could hear the grin in his wry tone and was grateful when he changed the subject. "How'd you get stuck in here, anyway?"

Every time he turned the screwdriver, his pecs tensed against her breasts and his erection pressed hot against her thigh.

She tried to distract herself by talking. "I thought I heard a bird trapped in here."

She expected him to tell her she was silly, but he paused in his handiwork. "So you're the adventurous type?"

Was she? She had no idea. From the moment she'd been born, her destiny had been set. The Elders had trained her as High Priestess. It was her duty to perform religious ceremonies, to bless babies, to mediate high-level disputes. But she'd wanted to connect with people, so she'd insisted on becoming a healer, too. That was the reason she worked on the Avalon Project, hoping to find the Holy Grail and cure her world of all illness. Was that the same as adventurous?

He popped out the last screw, and she tugged her hand free. Her fingers landed in his thick, soft hair. "Sorry."

"Don't be. I'm not."

"You might be really sorry—once we get out of here."

"Why's that?" He began to wriggle down her body. "Are you married?"

"I'm never getting married." The High Priestess wasn't allowed to wed. Even if it wasn't forbidden, who would want a woman who had the strength to kill her own mate?

"You have seven big protective brothers who'll want to beat me up?" he teased.

"There's just me and my two sisters." She couldn't keep the wistfulness from her tone.

"No husband. No brothers. And you don't want to marry. Honey, you're ideal," he said, his tone soft and husky. Finally, he jumped down, and she found herself missing his warmth. Then his strong hands slid up her legs.

"I can get out . . . by myself." She tried to wriggle away but couldn't, of course, with the duct restricting her movements. "Is anyone else out there?"

"No one. It's past midnight."

"Thank the Goddess." His large hands almost spanned her waist. He lifted her from the conduit and set her down on her feet. Her skirts dropped to the floor, and she smoothed them while avoiding his gaze.

As the ceremonial robes swished around her legs, her customary decorum returned. "Thank you. You saved my life. But I won't tell anyone, so please don't worry . . ." She raised her head and met his eyes.

"I'm not worried." Cocking his head to the side, he'd spoken as if he found the idea absurd. He smiled as if he was seeing Cael the woman, not the High Priestess, and it charged her with intense awareness. Of him.

In the dim light she recognized him. Lucan Roarke.

The new archeologist on the team had dark hair, compelling blue eyes, and a sculpted jaw. And he wore glasses. Obviously he needed a new prescription, since he didn't seem to recognize her.

"If anyone learns that you touched me, the State will execute you."

"Really?"

"The only exemptions are during my healing duties or for blessings bestowed in religious ceremonies."

She expected him to back away, tremble, even grovel as others in his position would have. Automatically, she braced for the normal blast of fear, but instead he leaned toward her, his voice seductive. "Lady Cael"—obviously he *did* recognize her—"I wouldn't mind if more than my fate was in your hands."

LUCAN HAD SCREWED UP. So much for keeping a low profile. He knew better than to flirt with any woman . . . much less Pendragon's High Priestess. So much for taking an inconspicuous walk around the complex to clear his head. What had he been thinking?

That she was soft and toned. That her hair was like silk. And her scent . . . her scent reminded him of summer rain. Lucan had seen some unusual things during his thirty-two years, but nothing as unsettling as Cael's irises, which he could have sworn had flared with tiny golden flames.

"Get back to work," he told himself.

He couldn't let the experience sidetrack him. It didn't matter that she was the most fascinating woman he'd met . . . ever. Or that every time he closed his eyes the memory of her soft curves pressing against him made him forget how much work he had to do. And how little time he had left to do it.

His career had taken him to dozens of ancient archeological sites and thrown many puzzles his way. But Lucan had not spent five years flying across the galaxy, then three more learning a new language and establishing himself as a respected Dragonian linguist, to settle for anything less than the Grail. He'd endured years without the companionship of his friends and family, the taste of spicy Buffalo wings and cold Corona, the smoky sounds of hot jazz and the smooth roar of his Classic Harley, deprivations he'd tolerated, all for the sake of finding the Grail.

He shifted his gaze to the large observation port that filled one side of the lab. Just beyond the wall of glass and illuminated by floodlights, Avalon punched into the night sky, an alien gray marble obelisk. Only a third of the massive structure was visible above ground, and the entire edifice was shielded by a mysterious energy that allowed no one and nothing to penetrate its secrets. Lucan was certain the Grail lay behind the shielded wall.

"The answer to breaking through that shield has to be right here in front of me." He scowled at a copy of the ancient, alien glyphs that the Avalon team had discovered on the obelisk's wall earlier the previous day.

These same glyphs were on the star map he'd found on Earth, suggesting that there had been travel between Earth and Pendragon over fifteen hundred years ago. According to Arthurian legends, King Arthur left the Grail in Avalon. But this Avalon was across the galaxy from Earth. The idea seemed outrageous, yet Lucan couldn't ignore the facts. This moon bore Arthur's last name. And the ancient Dragonians had named the imposing obelisk Avalon.

Coincidence? Lucan didn't think so.

"Think." He glared at the symbols, willing them to respond. Was he looking at an alphabet, or did the glyphs stand for individual sounds? "What are you hiding? What's your secret?"

"If only I had a coin for every time someone asked *me* those questions."

Holy hell. He'd assumed Cael had left for the evening. How long had she been in the lab? What had she seen?

Like an idiot, he'd left the star map in plain sight. Had she seen enough to recognize the parchment hadn't originated on this moon?

Forcing his mind out of a tailspin, Lucan leaned over his desk and deliberately knocked over his mug of tea. Then he whisked the damning star map into a drawer while the dark, hot liquid oozed into papers of much lesser value.

Lucan forced a smile at Cael, as if he welcomed her interruption. "*You* have secrets?"

"Doesn't everyone?" She strode across the lab, her steps graceful, her bearing regal. "Maybe I can help." Cael spoke with casual confidence, and Lucan couldn't pull his gaze from her. The light danced in her eyes in a way that mesmerized him. He saw not only intelligence, but a vibrancy, a mystery. "Or do you prefer to work alone?"

He shrugged and wiped at the mess on his desk. Lucan wasn't a loner by nature but by necessity. The less he shared with his coworkers, the less chance he had of slipping up, blowing his cover story and fake résumé, and revealing his true identity. And if these Dragonians figured out he wasn't one of them, they'd make sure he never got within a thousand yards of Avalon. They wanted the Grail as badly as he did. For Cael and Pendragon, finding the Grail would be a boon that would eliminate disease and suffering and the need for hospitals, medical research, and drugs.

"Right now I need to decipher these glyphs," he said.

She glanced at the symbols. "You think they're the key to breaking through the shield?"

The Dragonians had been trying for centuries to bring down Avalon's outer protective shield so they could search inside for the Grail. Modern technology, bulldozers, acids, and blasting had failed to win them access.

Lucan threaded his fingers through his hair. "If I could translate the glyphs, I could answer your question."

He poured more caffeine-laced tea and offered her a mug.

"No, thanks." She eyed the almost empty pot, and her hair brushed her shoulders. With the two of them alone in the lab it was impossible not to recall her hair in his hands, or her fresh-rain scent, and his pulse raced as she raised her eyes to his. "You think going without sleep will help?"

He sipped the tea, and over the brim of his cup he read concern in her eyes. And female curiosity that he couldn't afford to encourage.

He was so aware of her, it was almost as if pulling her out of that vent had ignited something between them. "I can't waste time sleeping, not when that subsurface cavity might open up and swallow Avalon tomorrow."

Last summer's drought had created a massive water shortage. The Dragonians had pumped water from the subterranean aquifer into their cities until they'd emptied the underground reservoirs, leaving a vast sinkhole beneath Avalon, one that grew larger and more likely to collapse the ground above it by the day.

"The latest estimates say we have weeks, maybe months." She hesitated as if she didn't want to say more but then continued, "But even if the ground holds, General Brennon's newest satellite data show that the expanding sinkhole has weakened the area so much that it may be dangerous to bring down the shields."

"How dangerous?"

"The shields are reinforcing Avalon's stability. If the ancient walls collapse, the adjoining part of the city might fall into the cavity."

Lucan's eyes narrowed. "So what's he want us to do? Give up?"

"We won't." Her curious gaze settled on his desk and the copy of the runes. Her eyes, a startling mix of old soul and pure innocence, drew him in. "Are you any closer to an answer?"

He set his cup aside and chose his words carefully. If he gave Cael a reason to report anything suspicious, Sir Quentin, Avalon's chief archeologist and head of the government's Division of Lost Artifacts, would take her seriously.

"I'm no closer to translating the glyphs than when we uncovered them yesterday afternoon."

Despite years of study in ancient runes and hieroglyphics, he hadn't been able to make any sense of the connection between his map and ancient Avalon.

"You might want to give yourself more than a day to solve one of our moon's ancient puzzles." With an encouraging raise of her brow, she moved aside several of his books, and together they finished mopping up the spilled tea. When their hands accidentally touched, his flesh tingled in response. Her violet gaze jerked toward his in surprise. "You're driving yourself too hard."

That was so not his problem. The only thing too hard around here, suddenly, was his dick.

Damn it. Not now. He needed to play this cool. He bristled, then tried to hide his reaction. But a telltale flicker in her eyes told him she'd noted his irritation.

The lady was perceptive. Too perceptive? He raked back his hair to give him time to cool his jets. The last thing he needed was her ordering him to come in for a checkup. "I'm sure I look like hell. But a shower and a shave should—"

Cael placed her hand on his shoulder. "Relax." What was she up to? She seemed to be deliberately touching him now, and it occurred to him that she was scanning him with her empathic ability.

He prayed to God she couldn't read his mind, then forced himself to relax. She read feelings, not thoughts. For now, his real identity was still safe. And if she was picking up any of his lusty yearnings, she was pretending otherwise.

Cael knelt, scooped the rest of his books from the floor, and placed them back on his desk. "I won't send you to the medical bay—"

"Thanks."

"If you promise to sleep for a few hours—"

"Agreed."

"In your bed. Not at your desk." She smiled, perhaps to take the sting out of her words.

He cocked his head to one side and shot her his most charming grin. "You want to come tuck me in?"

Damn it. He'd been keeping the conversation on a

professional level, and then he'd blown it again. He kept forgetting Cael was not just a colleague. No Dragonian he knew would venture such an innuendo with the High Priestess, even in jest. But then, he doubted any other man had shared an air duct with her, either.

When she placed her hands on her hips and frowned, he thought she was offended. Then the corner of her mouth quirked to form a saucy grin. "Will that be necessary? My tucking you in?"

Necessary? *No.* Pleasurable? *Oh, yeah.* He envisioned her leaning over him, her eyes widening as he tugged her into his arms for a kiss.

Stop. He had to stop fantasizing. Stop looking at her.

He cast his eyes down to his desk. "Maybe if I hit the sack, the answer will come to me in my dreams." Fat chance. He was going to toss and turn. And think about her.

"I'm glad you're optimistic. It's terrible to think these glyphs might be our last chance . . ."

She looked worried, and not asking what was on her mind took all his willpower.

He cleared his throat and put the remaining items on his desk to rights, willing her to step away so the rainy scent of her hair didn't flood his lungs, so the light in her eyes didn't dazzle, so her lips weren't close enough to tempt him.

Too much was at stake to think about anything but his mission. He must have been more tired than he'd realized. But exhaustion was no excuse. What the hell was wrong with him? And what was wrong with *her?* He might have admired her long, long legs and flowing blond mane since he'd arrived at the lab, but she'd never shown him more than a passing glance.

When she spoke, Cael's voice was low and silvery, threaded with sorrow. "You know, finding the Grail means . . . everything . . . to me, too."

Looking away, perhaps deliberately avoiding his gaze, she fingered her necklace beneath her tunic's collar. "My nephew . . . is sick. He's"—her voice broke—"only five."

The hint of desperation in her voice revealed a deep, black agony. One he knew all too well. "You can't heal him?"

She shook her head, her fingers rubbing the necklace. "I shouldn't have said anything. The last thing you need is more pressure. I'm sorry."

Lucan nodded in understanding. "My sister's unable to have a child. All her life she's wanted to be a mother, and her dream was ripped away. I'd hoped the Grail . . ."

Marisa's doctors had eventually declared her barren after the last miscarriage, and watching her be torn apart by grief was almost more than Lucan could handle. More and more people on Earth were being given the same diagnosis. Infertility was reaching epidemic proportions. Without a miracle, people on Earth faced extinction.

That's why the Vesta Corporation had funded his mission. That's why Lucan had crossed a galaxy to achieve his goal. Always in secret. Always alone. Always hiding his real past from everyone around him.

Cael touched Lucan's arm, infusing him with an awareness he was certain could be his undoing. "Then you understand," she whispered.

Reluctantly he pulled away from her touch. "More than you'll ever know."

Legends are born when life soars into the heavens or falls to the earth.

—Merlin

2

After only a couple of hours of fitful sleep, Lucan was back at his desk in the lab, staring at the glyphs, praying for a breakthrough, and trying without success to ignore Cael, who worked several desks away. Only a few other members of the Avalon Project team manned their stations at this early hour.

"We've accomplished nothing!" Sir Quentin, the team's head archeologist, burst through the door and headed toward Sir Shaw's desk at the front of the lab.

"That's not true," Sir Shaw countered. An esteemed professor who was currently on sabbatical, Shaw was lending his expertise to the Avalon Project as the field-work supervisor.

Lucan couldn't recall the last time the two leaders had agreed on anything. Perhaps Sir Shaw believed the un-verified reports that the Division of Lost Artifacts was a secret arm of the military under direct control of Sir Quentin and General Brennon. Perhaps it was simply a difference in basic scientific theory. Either way, the hypothesis that arguments spurred new ideas wasn't working at Avalon. Lucan couldn't help but wonder how long it would take for them to come to blows. If events led to a brawl, he'd bet on Shaw. Although older, shorter, and heavier, his passion came from the heart, whereas Quentin was a by-the-numbers kind of guy.

Glancing across the lab at Cael, Lucan checked her reaction. To her credit, she did a damn fine job of hiding her annoyance, but the slight narrowing of her eyes and tightening of her mouth gave her away. Apparently, she, too, preferred to work in peace.

Other scientists had begun to file into the lab and head to their work stations. Men and women alike tripped over themselves to stay out of Cael's way, and he spotted a flicker in her eyes. Irritation? Pain?

Sir Quentin brandished his clipboard. "I have nothing to report to my superiors."

"You're worried about the government response, or General Brennon and his Lost Artifacts Division?"

Never before had Lucan heard Shaw openly accuse the other scientist of a secret military connection. For a moment, even Cael looked shocked before she quickly masked her expression.

Quentin waved his clipboard in Shaw's face. "How dare you question my loyalty?"

Shaw slapped the clipboard away and its papers fluttered to the floor. "We've made progress of sorts. We've learned what doesn't work."

Lucan's gaze returned to Cael. She'd stooped to pick up the scattered forms. The task might have been beneath her, but she moved with such an effortless grace that Shaw and Quentin didn't notice her.

Lucan found himself holding his breath, sensing that Cael appeared to be waiting for the right moment to intervene. Despite himself, Lucan edged closer. If Shaw and Quentin came to blows and she stepped into the fray, she was the one who'd need protection.

Quentin slammed his fist onto the nearest lab table. "With the sinkhole expanding, it's time to take more drastic measures."

"Not yet." Shaw shook his head. "The shield's technology alone is priceless. If you rush, you risk destroying it. And if the military's Division of Lost Artifacts takes over, they'll get inside first."

"The military has no intention—"

"Don't kid yourself. They want the Grail as much as the government does," Shaw insisted. "But scientists need to control the contents."

"We all need the technology and the profits it can produce."

Cael set the papers on the lab table and placed herself between the arguing men.

"This isn't about profit," Shaw raged. "Whatever we find inside Avalon is our heritage. These gifts from the past must not be sold, but should be *given* to everyone to share." Shaw took a breath and visibly tried to calm himself. "If we can duplicate the shield and use it to protect our buildings from pollution, we could improve productivity. Maybe create domes over our cities, so we can once again breathe clean air."

Quentin's voice turned icy. His meaty hands closed into fists. "You're dreaming. Naive. Foolish."

Lucan tensed. He used every measure of control to stop himself from interfering.

"I'm in charge of the dig," Shaw insisted. "I'll decide—"

"Sirs," Cael interrupted without raising her voice, but

immediately the air stilled, and as she spoke, her words seemed to drain the tension from the lab. "I suggest we table this discussion for another time. We have yet to figure out *how* to get inside Avalon. Please, everyone, take your seats."

She was simply amazing. They all listened and obeyed. Shaw looked a bit sheepish. Quentin's eyes flared with fire he was too angry to hide. The rest of the team settled in seats behind their desks and computer banks. Again Lucan saw tinges of fear in the team's faces, as they waited to see what Cael would do next.

Shaw faced his team. "Our situation has become critical. We have only one week until we must turn over the facility to General Brennon and his Lost Artifacts Division." He glared at Quentin. "I also have no wish to see the military take over. Soldiers have no respect for scientific research or preserving artifacts. I can't imagine what the politicians were thinking, turning over Avalon to the military's control."

Lucan wondered if Quentin and Cael would stay to help the military. With tensions high over the Grail's potential powers and who would control them, the Dragonians had excavated Avalon in a series of stops and starts for centuries, barely avoiding a civil war in the process.

"Perhaps you can negotiate more time for us?" Shaw asked Cael.

She shook her head, her hair swirling around her shoulders, her voice musical but firm. "Satellite data support Brennon's claim that the underground cavity is growing. Time is running out."

Shaw grimaced. "Then I suppose we shall have to move on, as Sir Quentin suggested, to more drastic measures."

Finally. At last some action.

Lucan looked across the room at Rion, an astrophysicist with a reputation for innovation and a man whom he would have liked to call friend. Rion had seemed certain their latest efforts were about to pay off, and he had an uncanny reputation for knowing how matters would turn out. Some chalked up his ability to luck, others to clairvoyance. Rion himself was mum on the subject. The two men exchanged a look, and Lucan nodded.

Rion cleared his throat, drawing all eyes to him. "We could attack the shield with a high-level laser burst."

Although laser technology was common on Earth, on Pendragon the device was still theoretical.

"Did you computer-model it?" Shaw asked, immediately interested.

Rion cast a glance at Lucan. "Actually, the prototype was finished yesterday. Seems our linguistics expert has a wicked talent with cutting-edge technology."

Lucan opened his desk drawer to retrieve the prototype, placed the device on a work counter, and set the control. By building the laser, he'd taken a risk of blowing his cover, but only a small one. Language experts weren't expected to have the knowledge to build a highly sophisticated laser, but Lucan's fake résumé claimed that his Dragonian father owned a robotics plant, and Lucan dabbled at inventions.

While the other team members surrounded him, ohhing and ahhing at the laser, Rion and Cael spoke quietly. Lucan found it interesting that Rion didn't seem to fear Cael as the others did. Taller than Cael by a foot, Rion had to bend down for them to put their heads together. Her blond hair contrasted against Rion's darkness, reminding Lucan of when he'd freed her from the vent. How soft she'd felt against his hardness.

"The beam's stable?" Shaw asked, leaning over the device.

Lucan moved a rolling display board to reveal a gaping hole in the lab's wall. "I tested it last night."

"Are you certain there are no harmful side effects?" Quentin asked.

Lucan shrugged. "Ninety percent certain."

Shaw nodded. "With the military breathing down our necks, that's good enough odds for me. Let's try it, people."

Quentin turned to Lucan. "If the laser works, you'll have to turn over all rights to the device, since you constructed it while under government contract."

"Understood." Lucan raised his voice. "Everyone don eye protectors."

Cael moved away from Rion, their conversation over.

Lucan placed safety goggles over his glasses and attached power cords to the laser. The device hummed. "Ready?"

"Go ahead," Shaw ordered and pointed to Avalon's shield. "Open the observation port."

Lucan prayed this would work. Because, short of detonating a nuclear bomb to access Avalon, they were out of options.

"Fire when ready," Shaw said.

"Initiating a two-second laser burst." Lucan threw a switch. Pure blue light lanced from the device, through the observation port, and struck the shielding dead center. The clear sparkles of Avalon's shield flashed a dull orange.

Someone cheered, but the reaction was premature and died on a hollow note.

One orange blink in the shield was all the laser had achieved. As if in defiance, the shield returned to its normal clear, multi-sparkled hue.

Lucan tensed, waiting for Shaw's orders, willing the man to increase the burst.

"Hit it with a longer burst," Shaw ordered, impatient now that he'd made the decision to blast away.

"Upping the burn to four seconds." Lucan made the adjustment and fired. And held his breath. This time the shield absorbed every damn atom of energy he threw at it. Almost as if, after the initial laser burst, the shield had self-corrected.

Was the shield's technology capable of learning? Interesting. Aggravating. He gnashed his teeth with frustration, but he really wanted to smash his fist into a wall. Apparently, Rion had been wrong about the laser's capability. Strangely, he didn't look disappointed.

"Close the port," Shaw ordered, discouragement threaded through his voice.

The team descended on the laser. Arguments ensued regarding how to increase its potency, and the engineers who'd grabbed the specs from Lucan's desk began to theorize on different angles they should try to penetrate the shield. In the mad chaos, Lucan made eye contact with Cael. She sent him a sorry-it-didn't-work look, hesitated, then approached him.

With the team still speculating on the new tool, no one noticed as he stepped back from his desk to meet her. "You're disappointed," he said. "I really thought the laser—"

"We're all disappointed," she corrected. Her smile widened, and the effect made his pulse quicken. "But in science, failure often leads to success. Look how you've stimulated them." She indicated the scientists, who were busy examining the laser and discussing the design. "Have a little faith."

"Faith?" When it came to Cael, his thoughts were anything but spiritual. Reminding himself that he had to stay neutral and ignore the heat and pull of his attraction, he tore his gaze from her very full, very tempting mouth to look her in her eyes. "I'm a man of science. I know that shield can be breached. I just wish I understood how it works."

"The Goddess says to choose our wishes with care, because once we attain our wishes, we may not be pleased with the outcome."

Usually it took a lot more than a pretty smile—okay, a dynamite smile—and an encouraging word to gain his attention. But Cael's presence packed a feminine punch that rocked him to the core. Once again, he was instantly, insanely, inexplicably hard.

She raised an eyebrow. "What about legends? Do you believe in them?"

Legends? He'd always been a sucker for a legend. Ever since he'd arrived on Pendragon, he'd been on the lookout for tales of King Arthur and his Knights of the Round Table, but he'd found only place names that teased his imagination.

"Tell me a legend."

As if sensing his keen interest, Cael perched a hip against the nearest desk and settled in for a conversation. Her unique scent, sweet and crisp, broke through the odor of recycled air. He had the sudden urge to bury his nose in her hair and inhale deeply, but he squelched the instinct.

"Perhaps *legend* is the wrong word. Haven't you ever heard of the *Book of Jede*?"

"Nope."

"The *Book of Jede* is a fairy tale." She laughed, a warm, enticing sound that cascaded over him like a warm shower. "I heard it first from my grandmother when I was about three."

"I've never heard the tale." He tried to imagine Cael at the age of three. Curly-headed. Tiny. Curious. But he couldn't do it. The vibrant woman she was now dominated his thoughts.

"You want me to believe in fairy tales?" Lucan grinned.

Cael scooted her cute little backside onto the desk and crossed her exquisite legs. "What kind of childhood did you have?"

"The usual." He shrugged, keeping his voice down and glancing around the room. Rion was deep in discussion with a biologist. Quentin and Shaw were still arguing, albeit less heatedly. The rest of the team continued to pore over the laser's schematics. Nevertheless, Lucan still didn't want to speak about his false past and counterfeit identity.

Cael peered at him, a stare that tried to pierce the soul. He held her gaze, a tad bit longer than he should have. "We need to get back to work." Now, that was lame. But damned if he could think straight with her drilling him with that I-want-to-know-what-you're-thinking look.

She ignored his suggestion. Instead she stroked her throat, parting her tunic. He got an eyeful of her graceful neck and a flash of a metal choker with strangely familiar markings before her fingers blocked his view again.

"When the universe formed," she began, "there was darkness. Only darkness. Blackness from here to eternity. But then the Goddess seeded the universe with stars, bringing precious light and life."

"And what does that have to do with—"

"Hush. I'm getting to that." She shifted on the desk, her skirt rising to just below the knee, and as she slid off her shoe and rocked it on her toes, her calf tensed. The sight of her smooth, tanned legs made his mouth go dry and he swallowed hard.

"Go on," he urged.

The sooner she finished the story, the sooner she would leave. And she most definitely had to give him some room.

If he'd eaten recently, he would have suspected his food had been drugged, because every sense in his body had gone wacky. If he'd been alone, he might have sought release from the sexual tension and taken matters into his own hands. If he'd been on an uncivilized world, he might have thrown her over his shoulder and carried her straight to his bed.

Lucan did none of those things, of course. But as Cael spoke, her words didn't simply tell a story, they coaxed the blood in his veins to race double time. The seam in his pants had grown so tight he feared he might suffer a permanent indentation. And stranger still, he couldn't have stood and walked away to save his life.

"After the stars lit the heavens, the blackness faded. Worlds warmed, life grew. Animals and people evolved. But the blackness never lost to the light. The blackness only retreated. On Pendragon, a woman named Jede claimed to honor the Goddess, but in truth, in the search for immortality, she practiced the dark ways. To teach Jede a lesson, the Goddess sent her two gifts."

"Gifts are punishment?" He frowned.

"The first gift was eternal life. All Jede had to do to live forever was to obey the Goddess. The Goddess told her never to open the second gift."

"But she did?" Lucan had heard similar legends in many cultures. Strange how often that happened. Earth had the story of Pandora's box. Pendragon had the *Book of Jede.*

"Jede lived long enough to bury her husband, her children, and her grandchildren. She remarried, had another family, and buried them, too. After many thousands of years, she had wealth, comfort, all the things she'd always believed were so important, but she still wasn't happy. She grew bored, lonely. She decided the Goddess hadn't given her a gift at all, but had cursed her. The pain of outliving those she loved ate away at her soul. Believing death would end her pain, she opened the second gift, assuming death would be the punishment for disobeying the Goddess."

"What was inside? Did she lose her immortality?"

"A Goddess never takes back her gifts. She kept her promise of immortality, but she wasn't cruel. Inside the box was a spell that turned Jede into a dragonshaper."

"A dragonshaper?" He frowned again. "I don't understand."

"According to the legend, as a dragon Jede wouldn't suffer the loss of those she loved. Because as a dragonshaper she'd never be allowed the kind of love and family she'd enjoyed as a woman."

"Why did you tell me this story?"

"I believe that like Jede the dragon, who got her wish, we will eventually get ours and break through the shielding. I just fear that, like Jede, when we get what we thought we wanted—"

"We won't like what we find?"

"Now you understand."

He supposed he did. Yet her fairy tale would not deter

him. He'd come too far to back off because of a children's story.

She angled her head, and her collar parted, revealing the choker necklace he'd glimpsed earlier. The spectacular gems in a multitude of sparkling colors had to be worth a fortune. But it wasn't the stones or their value that made him suck in his breath.

The stones were embedded in metal.

And holy hell. The metal was engraved with an Anglo-Saxon alphabet, runes.

Lucan stared at the necklace, his mouth gaping. He couldn't be certain from a glance, but it looked as if someone had inscribed other symbols beneath the runes, symbols that reminded him of the ones he'd seen on the star map, as well as on Avalon's exterior wall. It was as if he was looking at two languages. Runes from Earth—which meant he'd be able to decipher them—and the glyphs from Pendragon.

Please . . . God. Let Cael's necklace be the key he needed to read the code. Frantic, he reached for a piece of paper and pen. "Don't move, Cael. Please let me draw—"

"Drawing my likeness is not permitted."

He sketched with fierce, swift strokes. "I'm not drawing *you*. Just the symbols on your necklace."

She reached up to her neck. "I don't understand."

"Please, don't talk. Don't move." Lucan sketched what he saw. But with every line, every rune, his excitement mounted. He stared at her necklace, then the paper on his desk, making sure he'd made no mistakes, and then he darkened the runes—making the glyphs stand out in stark relief. "Where did you get that necklace?"

"It's ancient and has been passed down from High

Priestess to High Priestess for centuries." Cael shot an odd look at him. "Are you reading those symbols?"

"Give me a minute." Ignoring the runes, he stared at the glyphs, alien glyphs that were so close to the ones on Avalon's walls his heart battered his ribs with agitation.

Picking up the paper, he sprinted to the port that looked out on Avalon. He held up the paper, placing it against the glass so that it appeared next to the glyphs on the obelisk. "They match. Exactly. They match."

Cael peered over his shoulder. "I don't understand."

Lucan shook the paper and grinned. "There are two languages on your necklace. When I removed one, it left me with the other, glyphs, which are exactly the same symbols that are inscribed on Avalon's walls."

"Can you translate them?"

Damned if Cael's necklace hadn't turned out to be his Rosetta stone. "Now that I've separated the two languages, I can."

The team of scientists, drawn to the port by the excitement in Lucan and Cael's voices, surrounded them and stared at the drawings Lucan had made. "What does it say?"

"Tell us," Quentin demanded.

"Please do," Shaw agreed.

Rion slapped a desk, and, as usual, his action commanded everyone's attention. "Settle down, people. Let the man think."

Lucan waited until the team quieted, then studied the runes. "Drinking from Avalon's cup is a shield against death."

Holy hell.

"You did it." Cael's eyes brightened.

Rion shot him a thumbs-up. Quentin gave him a bear

hug. Shaw embraced him. Other scientists clapped him on the back, their faces lit with enthusiasm.

"Look!" Rion's shout echoed through the lab. "The shield's morphing."

Lucan turned to see. The shimmering sparkles vanished. The shield was down.

Gone.

Cheers again broke out around the lab, and Cael's eyes teared with happiness.

"What about the nearby buildings?" Shaw asked. "Any sign of a cave-in?"

One of the geologists checked his instruments. "The topography's stable."

The team breathed a collective sigh of relief. The shield was down. And the city was safe.

The Priestess of Avalon is from another realm where the sun shines differently. But the magic of Avalon never changes.

—THE LADY OF THE LAKE

3

Cael stared hard at Avalon, searching for a remnant of one tiny sparkle, but the shield had truly disappeared. As Avalon's High Priestess, she could not show uncertainty or dread. Or fear. Straining under the burden of her position, she called on inner strength to appear serene and joyous. And, indeed, a part of her was full of joy and hope.

If the Holy Grail was inside, as the glyphs Lucan had translated certainly implied, it could cure thousands of her people, including her nephew, whose condition was worsening by the day. Just yesterday she'd spoken to Jaylon, and he'd sounded so weak. He'd made her promise to visit soon and to bring the Grail. She prayed to the Goddess that she could keep both promises.

Outside the window, Avalon dominated the view, a dark, massive stone building of mystery. The momentous occasion had upset her equilibrium and had her mind whirling, her nerves rattled. For so long she'd yearned for the healing powers of the Grail. So why were her feet rooted to the floor, reluctant to move? She should have been elated.

Maybe it was natural to worry. As long as Avalon's shield had stood, Cael could hope that someday they might find a way inside. Someday they might find the Grail.

Someday had turned into today.

And now she feared Avalon would be empty, that the Grail would not be inside, that finding the holy cup would prove as impossible as taming the wind, and her dreams would end. Then she'd have to go to back to the city of Feridon, where Jaylon was dying, and tell her nephew she'd failed. That not only couldn't her healing skills cure him, but that she hadn't found the Grail. Then he'd live out his last few weeks without hope.

She stroked the sacred choker she wore to conceal the dark purple scales that twined around her neck. At her touch, those marks, the ultimate symbol of what she was, fluttered as if asking for release.

Not now.

The seemingly magical disintegration of the shield had the team buzzing, consulting their instruments and speaking quietly among themselves. From across the room, Cael could see that Lucan looked baffled, mystified, excited.

He was an intriguing mix of intellect and physicality, a man who could argue his point as well as fight for it. A fitting helpmate for a priestess. Frightened by how much that thought appealed to her, she squelched it, even as she admired Lucan's height, his shiny black hair that almost touched his collar, his blue eyes emphasized by his glasses. Sharp cheekbones added to his intensity and attractiveness. She had to keep a grip on her emotions. Desiring him was way too dangerous.

As if he could sense her thoughts, Lucan looked at her

and began to cross the room. "I'm going outside to take a look." Lucan spoke softly in her ear, his breath fanning her neck. In the celebration, she hadn't noticed his approach, and the warmth of his breath on her neck almost made her jump.

To other women the implied intimacy of his whisper might be a small thing, but in all Cael's years, no male had ever sought her out, whispered in her ear, or shared secrets with her. No one. Suddenly, she was all too aware of Lucan, his powerful shoulders, his corded neck, his chest that was as broad as the Dumaro desert.

What was he thinking? Didn't he have any regard for proper behavior?

She should have admonished him. Instead, she kept her voice low. "You want to go now? What's your rush?"

"How can you be so patient?" he countered, his eyes twinkling.

The scales on the insides of her wrists began to tingle, and she didn't have to be an empath to read his eagerness.

"This is an historic moment. It mustn't be hurried." She smiled to take the sting from her words. "The president will make a speech. Video crews will come in so the public can witness the event. Would you deny everyone a chance to be part of—"

"We don't know how long the ground will remain stable. And we don't know what made the shield come down," Lucan said, daring to interrupt her. "Suppose the shield raises again just as suddenly? Or the obelisk collapses? We could miss our opportunity."

"Or be trapped or crushed inside." Quentin came up behind them. His tone was firm. "No one's going into that building until the engineers clear it."

Shaw joined them. "Why not?"

Quentin stared down at Shaw. "I won't have needless deaths on my watch."

From the rising tension in Lucan, Cael thought he might explode. Instead, he placed his hand on the small of her back and guided her away from the debating leaders.

Lucan was touching her. Absurdly, she wanted to lean closer into him and had to remind herself that he could lose his life for that gesture.

Cael glanced over her shoulder to see if anyone had noticed. Luckily, with the lights dimmed and all gazes on Avalon, no one paid them any attention. Except Rion. Out of her peripheral vision, she thought she saw him watching them, but when she turned to look, he glanced away.

Warm and firm, Lucan's touch shot tingles straight to her belly. The last time anyone had touched her . . . she'd been five. Until her fifth birthday, her parents had adhered to the law and treated her like her sisters. She'd been held and touched and loved, as if she was a normal little girl. But once she'd reached the age where she could practice dragonshaping, she'd lived apart from her sisters and parents and the Elders took over her education, teaching her about her dragon blood. A blood that made her stronger than her people. A blood that made it difficult for her to rein in her temper. A blood that made it possible for her to kill with dragon fire. For their own protection, her people were forbidden to antagonize her, to encroach on her space. Or to touch her.

Cael didn't want to be different. She didn't want to be feared. Or revered.

Of course, what she wanted didn't matter. She was a High Priestess, sacred. Destined to walk through life alone. It was her fate.

For Lucan's sake, she should pull away from the warmth of his hand. But she couldn't summon the will-power to step aside. Especially after they strode through the exit and into the hall, where no one was around to see this breach of protocol. She was amazed that such a simple touch, such an ordinary connection between two people, could feel so extraordinary.

By the Goddess, he felt good.

Her blood raced too fast through her body. She couldn't seem to draw enough air into her lungs and had to force words past her breathlessness. "Where are we going?"

"Outside." He dropped his hand and headed for the door. "To Avalon."

"But Quentin said we couldn't enter—"

"He didn't say we couldn't *look*." His voice sounded husky, coaxing, conspiratorial.

All her life Cael had done what her people expected. She'd followed the rules that had been set long before she'd been born.

But when Lucan stepped outside, she followed him. Immediately she felt a shift in the air. Three decades ago, a Dragonian had invented air scrubbers that cleaned some of the pollutants from the skies. But factories had increased production and the scrubbers never seemed to keep up. Pollutants often fogged in the cities, and the air tasted bitter. But today the wind was fresh, the air almost clean.

"Come on." Lucan took her hand, entwining his fingers in hers. She found herself matching his pace, running beside him toward the obelisk.

Lucan halted before Avalon's shadowed entrance. The ancient bronzed doors beckoned. Without the shield to block them, they looked more solid, yet luminous, and her pulse simmered with excitement.

She placed her hand on the door, and it felt cool and smooth. A slight tingle skimmed up her arm—undoubtedly her imagination. She grasped the ancient lever that would tumble a lock. If she pulled, would the doors open?

"Don't." Lucan tugged her back.

"What's wrong?" The urge to go inside was so strong her stomach drew into a tight knot.

He spun her around to face the laboratory they'd just left. "Fire. Look."

Flames lit up the far perimeter of the lab. Already the blaze on the north side crackled, shooting hellish sparks into the sky. Red and orange flames raced along the rooftop.

She gasped in horror. "It's spreading fast along the roof."

"We have to go back and warn them." His expression was set. "If the fire reaches the flammable chemicals stored there, the lab could explode before the team even realizes there's danger."

He was right. And yet . . . she didn't want to leave Avalon. She had to force her feet toward the lab, her stride keeping pace with his as he pulled her along.

Hand in hand they sprinted toward the building to warn Shaw's team. Outside the lab's door, a whirring in the sky made her pause. She heard the engines of machines, skimmers, hovercraft, and choppers. "Listen. Help's coming."

Lucan tilted his head back and peered at the smoky sky. Flames silhouetted his bronzed face, his square jaw and determined eyes. Above, a squadron of aircraft loomed above the flames and dropped powder onto the fire.

Lucan's eyes narrowed. "Are those firemen?"

"That's the military." Could General Brennon's satellites have picked up on the fire that quickly? She held her breath, praying the powder would douse the conflagration. Instead, the opposite occurred. "By the Goddess. The fire's burning faster."

"That powder is an accelerant."

She shuddered, her gut swirling with fear. "This fire . . . it's no accident . . ." She met Lucan's worried gaze. "I think it's an attack. The military must have learned we dropped the shields."

"They want the Grail," Lucan muttered.

"Or they don't want *us* to have it?" she suggested as he pulled her deeper into the shadows. "They may have even started the fire."

"Hell, they may have caused the sinkhole."

She peered over his shoulder at the airships, noting how he shielded her with his body.

Lucan twisted the handle to the door of an annex to the lab. "This fire's their excuse to take over."

"We have to warn Shaw."

"The door's locked."

She removed her communicator from her pocket and watched while Lucan slid a screwdriver from his boot and attempted to jimmy the station door. She tried contacting Shaw, then Quentin. When neither answered, she swore under her breath. "The military must be jamming signals."

"This way," Lucan said. "Once we find Shaw, we'll tell him that the scientists have been betrayed. Then we'll find a way to protect Avalon."

Betrayed? Of course. General Brennon must have had a spy on the scientific team. Someone must have notified him the minute that they'd eliminated the shield and now . . . the flames were spreading like the wind.

Why hadn't the alarms sounded? Had the military

jammed those, too? Did that mean the fire units wouldn't respond? With the fire starting on the north end of the complex, the scientists inside still might not know what was happening.

When the lock gave, she shoved past Lucan, entered the building, and took stock of their situation. The lights were out, so the backup generators hadn't kicked in. She sniffed but didn't take in so much as a whiff of smoke. Either the internal air scrubbers were independent of the backup generators and removing the fumes, or the fire hadn't reached this far.

"This way." Taking Lucan's hand, she led him down the hallway. How easy that small gesture of reaching out to him seemed. How natural. She could easily become used to touching. And being touched.

"You can see in the dark?" He was squinting through his glasses.

His question stopped her cold.

He had no idea what she was.

There was no other explanation.

"I've always had great eyesight." She spoke lightly, but a shiver ran down her spine. The Priestess of Avalon, a dragonshaper, could see in the dark and possessed keen hearing. Everyone knew. But not Lucan, apparently. No wonder he'd placed himself between her and the military airships. No wonder he held her hand and whispered in her ear. No wonder he didn't fear her. He didn't know. But how could he *not* know?

Who in the Goddess's seven universes was he?

"You don't believe in dragons, do you?" she asked.

"You do?" he shot back.

While he'd just confirmed her suspicions, now wasn't the time for revelations and long explanations.

Even with the emergency lights down, she had no difficulty steering through the long corridors. Her second set of lenses activated, lenses that expanded the pupils of her eyes. If Lucan could see her now, he would see no white around her irises—just dark purple. Very few people had seen her in this state, but those who had, even doctors who'd studied her vision, had been repulsed. But as she led him around water coolers, a file cabinet, and boxes of supplies, she was grateful for her superior vision.

"I hear shouting." She made a right, then a left.

"It sounds as if they're heading away from us."

She frowned, and her voice rose in fear. "They're running toward the fire."

"We have to go faster. Stop them and turn them around. Hurry," he urged.

She broke into a run, then stopped at the main lab's double set of doors. Lucan placed his palm on a door, feeling for heat. He must have been satisfied, because he opened the door. Smoke billowed out.

Gagging, she stepped back. No one could breathe that smoke and live for long. "Shut the door."

"Someone may still be in there. Wait here." Lucan lifted his tunic over his mouth and nose, darted into the lab, and shut the door behind him. If he got lost in the darkness, he'd die in there.

Moments ticked by.

She should have gone with him, but he hadn't given her the chance, and if she went inside now, she'd never find him in that thick smoke. How long could he hold his breath? Should she go inside and shout to him? Should she flee?

Damn it. Where was he?

She took a deep breath and cracked open the door.

Flames lit parts of the lab. Smoke burned her eyes, and tears trickled down her creeks. He had to be insane or the bravest man she knew to rush in there. "Lucan!"

Blindly, he lumbered into her and she backed away. As soon as he passed through the door, she slammed it shut against the smoke and heat. Lucan crouched over, coughing, Sir Shaw draped over his shoulders.

Shaw's clothing reeked of smoke. The material was smudged with soot. He had several deep cuts. Blood soaked his back, and the handle of a knife protruded between his shoulder blades.

In search of a pulse, she placed a finger at Shaw's neck but found nothing.

Lucan gently eased the man facedown onto the floor. Papers spilled from Shaw's lab coat pocket.

"Son of a bitch," Lucan cursed when he spied the knife, and his rage almost knocked her flat.

As an empath she could easily be swamped by sensory overload, and she'd had to become adept at blocking human emotions. But as Lucan's anger pounded her, her temples throbbed. She couldn't block out his fury and could absorb only so much pain. The urge to reach out to him was so strong, she lifted her hand to his face.

"Who would do this?" she asked.

"Don't know." Still coughing, Lucan grabbed the hilt of the knife as if to withdraw it.

Cael placed her hand over his. "Leave it. He's lost too much blood. He's gone."

"In the smoke . . ." Lucan's words came out a harsh croak. He'd clearly breathed more fumes than he should have. Sweat poured over his face, and smudges of soot blackened his forehead. "I didn't see the knife. If I'd known . . . maybe I could have stopped the bleeding."

She shook her head. "You did what you could. Did you see any of the others?"

Lucan shook his head and placed his palm on the door. "It's getting hotter. We have to leave."

She closed Shaw's eyes and stood, a lump burning her throat. She hadn't known the scientist long, but he'd been a fine leader. A decent man.

Lucan's anguish enhanced her own sorrow, until she felt as if she were drowning in despair. She had to regain control. Now was no time to let her empathic senses override her thinking.

Lucan bent to pick up the body. Blocking his emotions while cornering and corralling hers, she stopped him. "We need to leave. Now. Shaw wouldn't want us to die with him."

Lucan slowly straightened, suppressing his own grief. "You're right."

Praying there weren't other scientists trapped in the lab, she turned back the way they'd come. Already the hallway had grown uncomfortably hot.

Still, she spared a few seconds to gather the papers that had fallen from Shaw's lab coat and stuff them in her pocket. Had the man died protecting those papers?

So many questions spiraled through her, but the fire was spreading, and the floor outside the door had begun to burn. She grabbed Lucan's hand. "Let's go."

They made their way toward the exit as explosions thundered around them. Flammable chemicals had begun to heat and burst from their containers. If Cael and Lucan couldn't escape, they would die.

Although his breath sounded labored, Lucan kept pace as she sprinted to the door. When he stumbled, he regained his balance. She tried to head back in the direction they'd come, but smoke and flames blocked her path, and she diverted to a different route.

"We have to get off the site. And hide until we figure out what to do." Lucan's voice was low and harsh from the smoke.

Hiding wouldn't be easy. Everyone on the moon recognized her face.

One thing at a time.

Behind her to the right, fire flared and shot hellish sparks into the charred ceiling. Automatically, she turned left down a hallway, but the burning wreckage of a collapsed ceiling blocked the way. At her sudden halt, Lucan ran into her, grabbed her waist to keep her from falling. "Sorry."

They couldn't go right or left. The hallways were burning. The flames flaring. Fiery debris rained onto the floors. She raised her voice to be heard above the fire's crackle. "We have to backtrack."

From behind, fire roared down the hallway toward them. She tried to open the door beside her. It was locked. With nowhere to escape, no vast open space where she could dragonshape into a form that could save them, she braced for death. Prayed it would be quick.

A tremendous crash sounded beside her. Lucan had kicked open the locked door. He yanked her into the room and slammed the door shut as the backdraft whizzed past.

She gasped and inhaled the reek of old garbage and cleaning supplies. In the darkness, she made out shelving and brooms, mops, pails, and paint buckets.

She searched for an exit. Didn't see one. It was entirely possible they'd come through the room's only access. Had they merely delayed the inevitable? Not even her unusual strength could break through the steel girders that framed the ceilings and floors of this building. "We're trapped."

"Where exactly?"

She wished she could shut down her heightened sense of smell. One of the disadvantages to superior senses was that when a smell was bad, it almost overpowered her ability to think. This stench was almost knocking her out. Then the fire would . . . *Stop it*. She took short, shallow breaths. "We're in the janitorial unit."

He stepped forward, feeling his way along the walls. "Maybe there's a back door?"

"There isn't. I can see the rear wall."

He remained calm, his tone thoughtful. Even more impressive, she didn't sense even a hint of panic. He wasn't faking calm. He *was* calm, undefeated. "Tell me what else you see."

"Cooling conduits." His steadiness helped settle her claustrophobia. Usually, she was okay with the fact that she didn't have room to dragonshape, yet with her life in danger, the walls felt as if they were closing in. "Maybe if we pry off the vent—"

"What else?"

Interesting that he didn't jump at the first option. "There's a vacuum system. And a service elevator." She tugged him forward. "Over here."

Behind them the door smoked and blackened, and flames ate through the panels. Calm was a good thing, but urgency and haste were in order now.

He pounded on the doors of the service elevator. "Where does this go?"

"I have no idea. But the power's off. We can't take the elevator anywhere because it doesn't have a manual override. At least not one I can see." She turned around, searching the stacked trash bags. "But there's a garbage chute over here somewhere that might take us to the basement."

Lucan joined her search and started flinging aside bags to clear a path toward the wall. The room grew hotter and began to glow. She worked alongside him and prayed the flames wouldn't reach them.

She wasn't ready to die. Not yet. Not when she'd found a man who didn't fear her. Who treated her . . . like a woman.

Lucan worked with fast and powerful efficiency, grabbing heavy bags with each hand and tossing them aside. Sweat streaked his brow, but he didn't slow his pace. She managed to move only two bags at a time. The stench made her stomach roil. Her back ached. The muscles in her arms burned. But she dared not rest, even for a moment.

Perspiration soaked under her arms, down her back, and between her breasts. The trash bag straps cut into her palms. But the discomfort was nothing compared to what they'd suffer if the flames reached them. The crackling fire at the door behind them and the increasing heat spurred her efforts.

"Found it." Lucan shoved aside one last trash bag and pulled open the chute's door. "Get in."

Again his gallantry of putting her first made her feel feminine—even if she stank like a dead fish. But perhaps she would be the first to die. Cael had no idea if the chute would drop them into the heart of the fire.

The ceiling started to smolder. Any place was better than here. She stepped forward. Lucan held out his hand to help her climb into the chute. Without hesitation, she took his hand, wondering if this was the last time she'd ever touch him.

"You'll have to lie down. Feet first," he instructed, all business. Then his veneer cracked, allowing her to sense his deep concern about sending her down the chute.

"Cross your arms over your chest." She did as he commanded, wishing she knew what he was thinking. But she knew what he was feeling. Eyes smoldering, he looked at her mouth, leaning closer until his perfect face was a mere inch from hers. It was crazy how much she wanted him to kiss her. And then for one too-brief moment, he pressed his lips to hers.

Her first kiss. Filthy, stinky, scared, she nevertheless marveled at the sweet sensation. Her lips welcomed the pressure, and when he pulled back, she ached for more.

He grinned. "Good luck, princess."

"Priestess," she corrected automatically, but she doubted he heard.

He'd closed the chute, tipping her body downward. She began to slide. It grew so dark not even her keen eyesight could discern any light. She picked up speed, and friction began to warm her calves, the backs of her thighs, her bottom. Just as the heat became uncomfortable, her feet crashed through a hinged door and she was airborne.

Above all, have fear of traitors, for they creep in the dark, burn the cities, ravage the heart, and steal the souls of men.

—ARTHUR PENDRAGON

4

Lucan wanted to wait until he could be sure Cael cleared the chute. Around him, the ceiling buckled. Fire shot across the floor. His heavier weight would make him fall faster, but he couldn't delay any longer. He jumped into the trash chute with fire licking at his back.

He yanked the chute door closed and let gravity do its job. Was he jumping from the fire into an inferno? Would he land in the middle of a burning slag heap? Would Cael be waiting for him at the bottom, or had she been injured in the descent?

If these were his last moments, he wanted to go out with the memory of her lips against his. But even more, as he surged through the black chute, picking up speed, he wanted to live to kiss her again.

His body dropped, the friction heating his flesh, and he spread his feet, using the soles of his boots against the sides of the chute to slow his progress. There was no point to surviving the fire only to smash his bones when he reached bottom.

He went from filthy metal surrounding him to . . . midair and blackness. Falling, gut swooping, he flailed, trying to catch hold of something in the darkness. Anything to stop his fall. But his fingers grasped nothing but air.

His free fall ended in a jarring crash onto his back that knocked the oxygen from his chest. Something hard poked his shoulder. Something gooey and rank oozed down his neck.

"Lucan?" Cael's voice pulled him back from a close encounter with unconsciousness.

But he couldn't respond right away. Not until his head stopped spinning, not until his lungs drew in air. Through the blackness, he reached for Cael, but he touched only plastic bags. More garbage.

"Lucan?" she called again. "Tell me you aren't hurt. Talk to me, damn it."

Finally his chest muscles relaxed, allowing him to draw in a much-needed breath. The stench almost overpowered him, but he managed a whisper. "I'm here."

She found him in the darkness. Her hands touched his shoulder. "Are you hurt?"

"I'm fine." He shook off his grogginess. She'd taken the same route, suffered the same jarring landing. How was it that she sounded so unaffected?

"You don't sound so good."

"I'm fine," he repeated. Gritting his teeth, he shoved up from the mess onto his feet, not an easy task in the unstable garbage. "But you sound as fresh as if you just rolled out of bed."

She didn't respond to his innuendo. As usual, she didn't talk about herself and switched the conversation back to him. Concern deepened her voice. "Your neck's bleeding."

"Just scratches." Automatically, he attempted to push his glasses onto the bridge of his nose. But he'd lost them during the fall.

"Here." She shoved the glasses into his hand.

"Thanks." He put them on, but he still couldn't see beyond the blackness. "Where are we?"

"I'm not sure. Since there aren't any windows, I'm guessing we're in the basement."

His eyes teared as they strained to see, then began to adjust to the darkness until he could make out shadowy areas against inky blackness. "Let's do a perimeter check. Maybe we'll get lucky and find a door."

She stood, but a bag popped under her foot and he heard the sound of her body hitting plastic. She didn't gasp or complain—not even about the foulness. "Maybe we should crawl?"

"Good idea." He listened to her movements and reached for where he thought her leg to be. "I'm holding on to you so we stay together."

"This way." She began to creep over the bags. Some had come down the chute whole. Many had spilled. He prayed they weren't slithering through contaminated chemicals.

Girding himself, he moved forward. After what seemed like endless crawling, she stopped. "I've hit the wall."

"You still on top of garbage?"

"Yes. Apparently the entire level's one gigantic incineration bin." She sounded more weary than frightened. "There's no way out."

He refused to believe that. "There's always a way."

They circled the perimeter for what seemed like a long time before stopping. Hot, thirsty, and tired, he slumped against the wall for a rest. He would not give up. He hadn't come this far to die in a garbage dump.

"Is it getting warmer in here?" she asked, her voice rising in concern.

He wiped sweat off his brow with the back of his wrist. "We just need a rest."

"It *is* heating up."

Lucan realized it wasn't as dark as it had been before. A faint red glow was emanating from beneath the garbage. Uh-oh. "The incinerator's burning the trash."

"And us along with it?"

Sweat soaked him. Within the last few seconds, the temperature had shot up twenty degrees.

He started tearing open the bags of trash. "We need to find something heavy or sharp enough to break through the wall."

Sweat poured from his body. His lips dried and cracked. As the fluids seeped out of him, so did his strength. He tossed aside trash, feeling for something, anything, to use to get them out of here.

Cael swore and then softly began to pray to the Goddess.

He couldn't let her die.

It was hot. So hot. They didn't have time to cut their way out. The heat was cooking his brain. He reached for Cael. His arm wouldn't respond. "Sor . . . ry."

He couldn't save Cael.

He couldn't bring home the Grail.

Sorry. So . . . Sorry.

Lucan collapsed. He heard a distant crash. A roar. Fire blasted through the wall. Hot enough to melt it? He must be hallucinating.

And if that wasn't strange enough, he was scooped up and flung through the air.

Lucan awakened slowly. Why was he so groggy? Where was he? His head was pillowed in a soft lap, gentle fingers caressed his brow, and warm languor spread through his body.

Uncertain what had happened, or how much time had passed, he opened his eyes.

"Welcome back."

Had he died and gone to heaven? Was he dreaming? Was a blond-haired, violet-eyed angel hovering over him?

Angels didn't have dirt smudges on their cheeks, did they? Half awake, he reached up and brushed the soot from her face. Her skin was soft, satiny, smooth, and he found himself caressing the same spot even though the dirt was gone.

Their eyes locked.

Cael blushed, and she pulled away from his touch, then poured water between his lips. He swallowed, his eyes searching hers. Her pupils had become a golden inferno surrounded by dark purple irises that didn't look so human anymore.

His gaze moved past her to the incinerator room. The cinderblock wall had been reduced to rubble, and garbage smoldered within the ruins. How had they survived? Had the blast flung him through the wall and out of the garbage heap? Was that why he'd blacked out?

Although he hated to question their good fortune, he frowned. What had caused the explosion just when they most needed to escape? Seemed like a huge coincidence.

Cael had carried water from a nearby fountain in a cup-shaped piece of plastic. He drank more and looked around. "What happened?"

Her neck was dark with soot: she wore her now tattered and dirty pink tunic backward. When she turned to get more water, he saw that her tunic pocket, which had held Shaw's papers, was burned away, the pages lost. But from the gaping hole in her clothing, he understood that modesty had required a readjustment.

He shouldn't stare. But damn, she had a sexy back. The hollows of her shoulder blades called to him. And the sensual purple markings down her spine made him want to explore her with his tongue. A purple tattoo? Of some kind of vine?

She looked from the demolished wall to him, raised her chin, and squared her shoulders, almost as if bracing her body against an expected attack. "I broke the wall."

She'd broken through the wall? With what? "*You* broke through . . ."

"Who are *you?*" she asked, eyes wide with curiosity. "Why don't you know who I am?"

Her first question rattled him, and he ignored it. He had to choose his words with care. "I know you're the High Priestess." He breathed out a sigh of frustration. "But that's all I know. It's not like I can go to the library and look you up."

"My privacy's protected by law." She fidgeted, and he could tell there was something she wasn't saying.

He searched her face—for answers. "What are you hiding?"

"I-it's forbidden to write or speak about me without special, preapproved permission through government channels."

No wonder his research hadn't scratched the surface when it came to the High Priestess.

Perhaps she'd attribute his ignorance to confusion due the blast. His gaze moved to the giant hole she'd created, and he raised a singed eyebrow. "So how'd you break the wall?"

Unease flickered in her eyes. "I hear engines circling. They may be hunting us. We need to leave." She gestured to the parked vehicles in the garage. "Unfortunately, those skimmers are all locked."

Standing on shaky legs, he tucked his question away to ask later. He also relegated to the back of his mind the alien vision of her purple irises and her slender back with its enticing curves and taunting hollows entwined in that tantalizing vine. He would savor the memory later, along with the memory of their short but sensual kiss. Right now, he needed to get them out of here. Squatting, he opened the compartment in the heel of his boot. The hidden multi-tool and circuit rerouter had saved him on more than one occasion.

He staggered to the nearest skimmer, a flying vehicle that the Dragonians used for transportation, and slapped the device on the lock. After an audible click, he opened the door.

With a sigh, she slid into the passenger seat. "I've never stolen anything before."

"We're borrowing. Not stealing." He sat behind the controls, revved the motor, and grinned. "This baby has some juice."

"Try not to crash."

He dialed in the Dragonian equivalent of pop rock and grinned. "I'm a very good driver. Made it halfway across the city last week with only three or four fender benders."

She rolled her eyes at the ceiling. "Focus on getting us out of here."

"No back-seat driving," he replied.

She turned down the music and cast him a puzzled glance. "This skimmer doesn't have a back seat."

Damn. He needed to be careful. Sure, he'd become fluent in Dragonian, but some idioms didn't translate well.

"Hold on." To distract her, he stepped on the gas, slid out through the exit, and lifted them straight up into the night sky.

She braced a hand against the dash. "I don't have to worry about the military killing us. Your driving's going to do that for them."

He laughed, careened upward through the garage exit, and steered through thick black smoke. To avoid crashing, he relied on the sensors, veering right, then left, making steep banking turns and several dives.

She peered over her shoulder. "The military's going to pick us up on radar."

Once clear of the smoke, he could merge into one of the lanes in the traffic grid above the city. But first, he had to fly there undetected.

Lucan reached under the dash and ripped out a few wires. "There."

"What have you done?" Cael's eyes widened.

"No one can track us now." He banked the skimmer sideways and joined the high-speed lane. Zigzagging past the other skimmers, he poured on more acceleration.

"Were you a thief or a racer in your last life?" she asked.

Survival was exhilarating. He laughed. "Two of my three favorite things are tinkering and fast driving."

"And your third favorite thing?" she asked innocently.

He tried for a devastating grin. "Hot sex."

She blanched but finally found her voice. "I played right into that, didn't I?"

Damn it. What was it about her that kept making him forget his cover? Maybe it was the shared danger. Or that she'd kissed him back before he'd dropped her down the trash chute. Or the fact that it had been way too long since he'd been with a woman.

After several sharp turns and two level changes, a glance at his GPS revealed clear skies behind him and no sign of military ships following.

He gave her a sideways glance. "So how *did* you blast us out of there?"

Cael frowned, then leaned back in her seat, a resigned look in her eyes. "When you were a child, what schools did you attend?"

"What does that have to do with you blasting us out?" he asked.

"I'll get there. Just answer me, please."

"Fine." He kicked the cruiser into the stratosphere, where there was little traffic this late at night, and set the controls to autopilot. He'd eat fuel, but he really needed to concentrate on his cover story. Most of his false Dragonian identity focused on his adult years. Who would have thought anyone would ask details about his childhood? He decided to stick to the truth, modify it only when he had to. "I was home schooled."

"By your father?"

"Mom and Dad shared the task, and my aunt and uncle had a hand in my education, too. I also hit the computers pretty heavily. Why?"

"Because you're a nonbeliever."

"I am?"

"Your parents never took you to the Icons?"

Oh, Lord. What were the Icons? She must have read the blank look on his face.

"Religion?" she prodded.

Oh. "My parents believe that good and evil comes from within—although they do pray to a higher power."

"So they don't honor the dragonshapers?" she asked as they flew into a dense cloud that wrapped them in white fog.

Honor dragonshapers? That would be difficult, since they'd never heard of dragonshapers. He couched his reply in the most polite tone he could muster. "My folks never mentioned them. And although I've heard legends—"

"It's more than a legend."

"Really? You've seen a dragonshaper like in the *Book of Jede*?"

She laughed. "Actually I haven't *seen* a live dragon. But other people have."

At least she hadn't been insulted by his question. Religion was a touchy subject on most worlds.

"You should do that more often." Her face lit up when she grinned, making her look relaxed and carefree. Sometimes Cael appeared to carry the weight of the world on her slender shoulders.

"Do what more often?"

"Laugh."

"Really?" She turned toward him, her purple irises dark with a flicker of golden heat.

Damn, he could drown in those eyes. He wondered what color they'd turn if he kissed her again. Made love to her. "Oh, yeah. When you laugh, you don't sound like a High Priestess or a healer."

"But that's who I am."

"No, that's what you do." He shrugged. "There's a woman hiding behind those titles. And I like her."

At his compliment, he could have sworn her eyes glowed a soft golden color, but it could have been a glint of starlight coming through the fog.

"We were talking about dragonshaping," she prompted, but her tone was softer, relaxed.

Why did she insist on changing the subject? "I'd rather talk about our brush with death."

"I'm trying, but you keep interrupting." Her eyes narrowed again. "Are you going to let me continue?"

"Are you saying a dragonshaper miraculously knocked down that wall?" He eyed her curiously. In his experience, religion was often invoked to explain the inexplicable. Gitata, a lover he'd met on the primitive world Dron during his journey to Pendragon, had believed his spaceship was a god. And why not? Her world had not yet discovered electricity.

"I don't know about the miracle part, but yes, that's what I'm—"

The sound of the windshield cracking cut off her reply. Cael peered over her shoulder. "It's the military. They're shooting at us!"

"They don't give up, do they?" he muttered, wondering how many were on their tail and if he'd have to land to evade them.

The skimmer shuddered. Wind roared through the craft. The engine stalled. Lucan kicked off the autopilot and pitched the nose down, sending the vehicle into a steep glide to pick up speed. Beneath his hands the controls vibrated.

The military ship that slid in behind them fired off

another shot. Their engines sputtered and died, plunging them into an uncontrolled spiral.

"Our wing broke off!" Cael had to yell to be heard over the roaring wind filling the skimmer.

"We're going down."

Wind whipped his face. Hot metal peppered them. Pain seared his shoulder.

The craft began to break apart, disintegrating in the night sky. He reached for Cael's hand. If they were to die, he wanted to leave this existence holding her tight.

But the exploding craft shot him one way and her another. He fell endlessly, tumbling through traffic, miraculously missing a skimmer by inches, close enough to see the wide eyes of the driver staring at him in disbelief.

Falling, he searched the sky for Cael. A piece of burning debris seared his leg. Another piece of metal pierced his chest and agony lit up his nervous system.

The military aircraft moved in, their bright lights blinding him. From below, the Pendragon landscape rushed up at him.

He squinted against the light and tearing wind and searched for Cael, wanting to see her one last time. For a second, he thought he spied her falling amid the wreckage, but her image was swallowed whole by a massive shadow.

Draw now together to guard the realm.

—MERLIN

5

Unlike the confines of the garbage pit where Cael had managed her dangerous partial shift, the sky gave her ample maneuvering room. Her brain altered, her body expanded twentyfold, her arms extended into wings, her spine into a huge tail. Her skin thickened, turning dark purple like her flesh marks, and her bones actually became lighter, allowing her to fly.

She no longer possessed her higher powers of reasoning, but she remembered the human male. Her keen eyes picked him out amid the falling debris. With a giant flap of her wings, she soared toward him. Smelled his blood.

Too much blood.

Was he already dead? She timed her drop and swoop to come up beneath him and settled his weight on her back. *Hold. Hold on.*

His hand gripped her neck. *Who are you?*

His thoughts resounded in her brain. She almost bucked him off. Never had anyone put a thought in her head. Spoken to her mind to mind. But the man was important. Injured. Needed to rest and heal. And her dragon brain had not the words to answer his question.

Instead, she flew to safety. *Hang on.*

The shiny metal markings in the sky flew closer. They fired blasts that stung her flesh. Annoyed, she turned her head, roared her fury and rage, and incinerated the machines in one searing blast of fire.

Where are we going?

To the nest.

A beach image entered her mind. The man wanted to go to that beach. She'd flown there once. Too remote. Too hot. *No.*

Yes. He sounded weak.

She shook her head and flew to the nest. It had been too long. Much too long. She needed to go home.

During the flight, the man's grip on her back weakened. Expending much energy, she spread her wingspan and increased her speed, until the rush of wind made her hearts beat faster. The cold, thin air at the high altitude invigorated her, as did the reappearance of her old friend Merlin.

The owl had appeared out of nowhere and now flew at her wing, his presence lending her strength and reminding her that, like the owl, she was born for this climate and night flying. But the man was fragile. She must fly him to warmth. To the nest.

Hours later, Merlin still at her wingtip, she spied the nest in a remote mountain ridge, high and steep. She circled the nest twice in search of danger. Sometimes men with guns climbed here. So far none had ascended high enough to invade the nest. But now men hunted her and the human male. She had to make certain not to fly into a trap.

Exhausted from the long trip, knowing she still had much work to do, she landed in a gentle glide, careful not to spill the man from her back. Only after landing did she shrug her wings, tilting the human until he slumped to one side and tumbled into the snow. Then she humanshaped.

Naked in the freezing air, Cael did a cursory examination of Lucan's injuries. The sight of the snow, stained with blood from his wounds, filled her with despair, and her fear for his survival escalated. He was in critical condition, badly wounded in several places and close to death. Her feminine instincts urged her to care for him first, but as a doctor she knew he was better left outside. Outdoors, the cold would slow his heart rate and blood flow, protecting his body from massive trauma. And experience had taught her that if she didn't attend to her own icy extremities, she wouldn't have enough feeling left in her numbed fingers to sew his wounds. As badly as she ached to stay with him, she forced herself to enter the nest, slipped her feet into fur-lined boots, her hands into heavy gloves, and shrugged into the warm cloak she always left waiting for her. Then, pulse racing with urgency, she hurried back outside with a blanket.

While Merlin watched from his perch on a ledge above the nest, she spread the blanket over the snow beside Lucan, then rolled his body onto it. In her dragon form, his weight had been insignificant, but to her human shape, he was a heavy, muscled male, his mass difficult but not impossible to move. Praying he was still alive, alarmed that she sensed no consciousness, she dragged him indoors.

During her short time outside, her flesh had come close to frostbite from the biting cold. Lucan's body temperature had lowered even more than hers, from his time in the snow as well as the flight in the high-altitude cold. She prayed that the exposure wouldn't cause permanent damage.

But that decrease in temperature appeared to be working in his favor. The freezing chill may have helped keep him alive, and now that he was warming, he was in the most danger. Cold blood in his fingers and toes rushed back to his organs, and the severe temperature change could cause a heart attack.

She couldn't do anything for his heart, but she could staunch his wounds to stop the bleeding.

She cringed at the deep and painful wounds to his beautiful chest and broad shoulders. But she shut down the female part of her and let the physician take over. Now was not the time to fall apart, nor the time to think about how she might have made a fatal mistake in flying here. To save him, she had to focus all her skills on healing.

After tugging him into the main area, which was warmed naturally by volcanic hot springs, she slipped off her boots and gloves, then cut away his clothing. The wound on his shoulder, ragged and nasty, looked the worst. From the massive loss of blood, she suspected a nicked artery. Up here, she didn't have surgical tools to operate in the nest. Hoping he could recover on his own, praying the metal fragments had gone in his chest and out his back without damaging an organ, she cleaned and cauterized the torn flesh. The nick at his neck she covered with a bandage. The gashes on his shoulder and leg she sewed. If his heart seized or if he had severe internal bleeding, he wouldn't survive.

Through all her ministrations he didn't move. His pulse remained weak, his skin white. As she tended to his wounds, images flashed through her mind—of Lucan holding her hand, of the passionate way he kissed her right before she'd dropped down the chute.

Live. Damn you. Live.

When she finished her treatment, she again took his pulse. Although she'd stopped the external blood loss, he'd already lost too much. His breathing remained shallow. His skin was pasty and cold. But he didn't shiver—the body's way of warming itself—and his inability to do so was a very bad sign.

When she opened his eyes to check his pupils, he didn't react.

He was dying.

The knowledge crushed her, consumed her. Biting back a cry of anguish, she almost doubled over, racked by the certainty she was losing him.

He needed blood. And the only blood here was hers.

But she had dragonblood, sacred blood, a genetic anomaly. Giving her blood was forbidden by custom and law.

Giving her blood was wrong.

But he didn't deserve to die. Tormented, she rocked back onto her heels, feeling as if her hearts were being clawed from her chest. How could she not do everything in her power to save him?

It's still wrong.

Again she checked his pulse. It was slower, weaker. She gasped, succumbing to despair and frustration. Without her blood he wouldn't regain consciousness. She'd never speak with him again. Never laugh with him again. Never touch him again. He would die.

His life force was almost gone.

Smoothing back his hair, blinded by terrible panic, she felt her thoughts whirl. If he died, if she didn't do everything she could to save him, she would have to spend the rest of her life without knowing him, without the possibility of a future that wasn't so unbearably lonely.

Cael did not break customs lightly, but she couldn't let Lucan die. After letting her cloak slide to the floor, she grabbed tubing and needles. She hooked their circulatory systems together so that her blood flowed into his veins. Both her hearts, as well as his, dispersed her blood. As he grew stronger, she grew weaker and cold.

Still, she ignored the exhaustion and chills, and she gave him more. Gave all his body would take. And when his color slowly returned to his cheeks, when his pulse strengthened, only then did she unhook the tubes connecting them. Exhausted physically and emotionally, she slumped. She could do no more except share her body's warmth. Taking off her robe, she lay down naked by his side and cradled him in her arms.

LUCAN MUST HAVE passed out. When he awakened from a deep sleep, he found a warm, naked female spooned against him. He didn't recognize his surroundings, a simple cave with stone walls and rough-hewn furniture, but he identified the scent of the woman, and his nostrils flared. Cael.

In contrast to the hard floor under him, Cael's sensual curves felt velvety soft against him, and memories came rushing back. Sir Shaw's murder. The fire. The incinerator. Cael holding his hand. Cael's kiss. Her purple eyes smoldering with golden flames.

Being shot down.

Pain. Pain in his shoulder and radiating down his arm. Pain in his chest. His neck. Here the memories became more confused. He must have been hallucinating from the injuries. He recalled a shadow swooping out of the sky to save him. Somehow he'd summoned a telepathic link with the creature—a power he thought had disappeared years ago when he'd flown out of Earth's solar system and left his twin behind. But his dream had nightmarishly twisted his telepathic link with Marisa to a mind link with a . . . dragon. And an owl had flown as the dragon's wing man. Talk about bizarre.

The dragon images were intense, visceral. He recalled the frigid mountain air slicing him, the wind whipping by as he clung to the leathery scales of the dragon's back. There'd been terrible pain in his shoulder. More pain mixed with images of Cael tending his wounds.

Wounds? Pain?

He flexed his shoulder. He had no pain. No wound. None.

Could she have healed him with some miraculous drug? Something he hadn't heard about during his time on Pendragon? Legends on Earth endowed the mythical High Priestess of Avalon with all sorts of mystical healing powers.

Cael's cheek lay pressed to his chest, her bare legs entwined intimately with his beneath the robe that covered them both. His gaze wandered over her face, from her closed eyelids rimmed with long golden lashes, to her shoulders, to her lush breasts.

Suddenly Lucan had a more pressing need than finding answers to his questions. Heavy lust filled him. It was hungry and urgent, raw and primal. In that moment, he could think of nothing he wanted more than keeping Cael in his arms, kissing her, making love to her. With her palm resting lightly on his chest, her breast curving against his side, it was as if in sleep she was daring him to take her.

And take her he would. Lucan had never been much good at resisting temptation, and he saw no reason to change now. So what if she was High Priestess and touching her was forbidden? A man had to take some risks to feel alive. And a woman as lovely as Cael was worth a lot of risk.

In sleep she cuddled against him, the smooth caress of her skin on his proving there was nothing mythical about her. She was all female. And soft. So soft. Although her eyes remained closed, she was waking. Snuggled in his arms, her hair fanning the pillow, she tipped her face toward his, her lips curved in a smile.

Dipping his head, he kissed her mouth. With a soft moan, she parted her lips. "Mmm."

He nibbled her lower lip and asked softly, "Where are we, hon?"

"The nest," she answered sleepily. "It's safe." And then she kissed him again, her mouth drawing him closer, her tongue slipping shyly between his lips, feeding his hunger.

Between kisses, he asked, "How did we get here?"

She tugged his mouth back to hers. "Later. I'll tell you later."

Cael's sleepy sexiness hit him with the intensity of a summer thunderstorm. Urgency slammed him. He had to have her. *Now.*

His lust flared white-hot, and he didn't just ache with need. He was primed to explode.

What the hell was going on?

Cael nipped his shoulder with her straight white teeth, and he hissed in a breath as she licked away the sting. Wrapping an arm around her shoulder, he helped her roll on top of him until she straddled his hips. She looked like a goddess, warm, willing, and wanton, her hair falling seductively around her strong shoulders, locks of spun gold curling over her breasts. Breasts that were larger than he'd expected, rounded, firmer, with perfect pink tips.

At the sight of her pink nipples, so close to his face, he raised his head to slip a pink tip between his lips.

She tasted like ambrosia. And desire pulsed between them, flooding him with the need to make her feel as wild and raw as he felt.

He laved her flesh with his tongue and she went crazy. She bucked, her jerky reaction catching him off guard, and his teeth tugged too hard on her nipple.

"Easy, darling," he murmured.

She gyrated her hips, arched her spine, and tipped her nipple back into his mouth. "I don't want easy."

That worked for him. Every damn muscle in his body demanded he take over, thrust into her. But damn it, he wanted this to be good for her. Gritting his teeth, sweat rolling over his brow, he crushed down his wild urges.

He wasn't going to slam into her and take what he needed. He was civilized, not a savage. But at the sight of her eyes turning golden, blood roared in his ears and rammed through his system. His heart kicked in triple time. And every cell in him drummed a demand to thrust into her now. *Right now.*

With her brows knotted in fierce determination, her lovely mouth uttering tiny encouraging groans of pleasure, she seized hold of his shoulders, slamming him against the floor.

For a second, he saw stars. What the hell?

She wasn't holding him down so much as using him for leverage. Looking like a wild warrior priestess, the pagan choker around her neck her only adornment, she looked straight into his eyes. And a lightning bolt of heat fired through him.

Her voice was proud, yet silky soft and intoxicating. "Tell me you want me."

His intended chuckle came out a groan. "You have to ask?"

"Tell me."

Surely she could feel how badly he wanted her?

"Tell me," she repeated.

He couldn't speak. His mouth was too dry. His head spun from craving her. And he was fighting himself, willing his hands not to yield to his body's demand to seize her hips and plunge himself inside her.

She rubbed her breasts against his chest, creating a sensuous friction, and he lost all chance for rational thought.

When she rocked against his erection, his body went haywire. Every tortured nerve cell howled for more of her touch. More of her scent. More of her essence. And she was teasing him, rubbing her downy nether lips along his rigid sex, and nothing had ever felt this good.

God damn. He wanted to bite her. He wanted to plunge inside her. And thrust and thrust and thrust. Gritting his jaws to prevent the animalistic urge, he clamped his hands on her waist. As if sensing he might try to curb her pace, she stepped up her rhythm.

Too fast, too soon. He feared he wouldn't last long enough even to sheathe his sex in her heat. He had to slow her. He needed a second to breathe, to regroup, to gain control of the tension gripping him. But as if sensing his intent, she shimmied her hips, taking him deep inside her in one giant thrust of heaven.

Mother of God! She was a virgin. He'd felt her barrier shred. And if he'd had any sense, he would give her body time to adjust. But before he could react, she reared up and slammed down on him again. Harder.

Her hands clenched his upper arms, but her strength was no match for his. He rolled, intending to end up on top, to take control of this madness, but she was fierce, using his momentum to tumble him again. He lost count of how many times they rolled across the floor. They knocked over a chair. A table toppled. Her nails clawed his back, drawing blood, but the sweet pain only increased the pounding primal urges. He forgot civilized. Gave in to the savage urge to sink his teeth into her shoulder.

"Yes," she screamed and bit his earlobe. Blood trickled down his neck. "Yes. Yes. Yes."

He rammed into her with shocking need, and she clawed his hips, sucking him deeper, lifting her legs and hooking them around his back, so he could plunge deeper still. Every time he thrust in and out, she squeezed, and her slick heat shot him into a frenzy.

This was insane. Intense. He couldn't draw air into his lungs fast enough. Slick with sweat, with no finesse, he pounded into her. Taking exactly what he wanted. Demanding everything she had.

She lifted her hips to match his cadence, meeting him thrust for thrust. The ache in his balls tightened to exquisite pain. Grinding his pelvis, he pumped hard. Fast. Deep. The roar in his ears matched the beat of his hips.

Her gyrations added fuel and fury to the mating, her strong thighs rising to meet his, urging him deeper. And when she spasmed and took her woman's pleasure, he emptied into her with a giant roar, the bliss bursting from him in a white-hot bolt of magic lightning.

The Dragon is no different from the Serpent. Both are dangerous, cunning, and powerful.

—THE ELDERS

6

That was amazing." Cael had felt pleasure greater than she'd ever imagined possible. No one had ever looked at her in such a bold, sensual way. She had never felt more important, more desired. The closeness they'd shared had been delicious, intimate, and so very satisfying. In fact, she couldn't wait to do it again. And again.

She'd seen the way his eyes had smoldered as he'd paired with her. He seemed to want her as much as she wanted him. Just then Lucan turned to her and stared at the bite marks on her neck, his eyes widening in astonishment. He started to touch her skin, then jerked back his hand. "I'm sorry I wasn't more gentle."

She was the dragonshaper, and *he* was worried about hurting *her?* "You did nothing to my body that I did not enjoy." She said the words slowly, willing him to believe her. But she could feel he was shaken by the intensity of their pairing. He didn't understand. He didn't know she was a dragonshaper.

For her to keep deceiving him was wrong when he didn't know what was at stake. Although the idea of revealing her true nature frightened her, she couldn't go on like this. The risk was huge, yet if they were to have any chance at a future together, he had to know what she was. To believe. His people might not know about dragon-shaper destiny, but it was time he knew the truth. So this honorable man could make his own choices.

She just hoped he'd choose her.

Filled with tension, Cael found a robe for him, and after he donned the garment, she gestured toward the door. "Come outside with me. There's something you need to see."

"It's freezing out there." He glanced out to the snow-covered mountain peaks that surrounded the nest. "Just tell me."

She snorted and raised her eyebrows. "You won't believe me."

"Why not?"

"Because you have no faith."

He didn't dispute her words. "And if I go outside with you, what will I see?"

"You will see a dragonshaper." She held his gaze, feeling his disbelief war with his fierce curiosity.

Perhaps she should wait. Build a better bond with him before showing him . . . but that would be the coward's way out.

"A dragonshaper?" He stepped toward her, then glanced at his now fully healed shoulder, and clearly, he remembered other things. "How can I believe in a dragonshaper when I don't even know what it is?"

"A dragonshaper has the ability to change from human to dragon and vice versa."

"Like in the *Book of Jede*?" He raised a skeptical eye-brow. "You expect me to believe in a fairy tale?"

"Just the dragonshaping part."

"And this dragonshaping, how exactly does it work?"

"We don't know. The biological science is still a mystery."

"I see." He couldn't keep the skepticism from his voice.

Clearly, he didn't see. And he didn't believe her. Even if filled with dread over how he would react, she needed to give him the proof he sought. She pointed to his shoulder, where his jagged wound had already healed. "You don't even have a scar, but you slept for only a day and a half."

He peered at the bite marks at her neck. "Your wounds are gone, too—just tiny scabs. You must have some really strong medicines to—"

"I didn't give you any medicine." She took a deep breath and let it out slowly. "I gave you dragonblood."

"Dragonblood is an herb?" he asked.

He certainly knew how to make things difficult. "Dragonblood is blood from a dragon."

"Right, a dragon flew by and you captured it, stole its blood, and put it on our wounds."

She rolled her eyes.

"Sorry, I don't believe in magic dragons."

"Who said anything about magic?" Taking a deep breath, she reminded herself that Lucan was a scientist. A linguist who knew how easily words could be used to deceive. She could only show him and hope he could deal with the truth. And in her hearts, she braced against the possibility that he might very well loathe and fear her once he learned her true nature. "Come with me."

After pairing with him, she didn't know how she would bear it if he feared to look her in the eyes. If he cringed at her touch. The risk she was taking made her stomach clench into knots. And it took all her self-discipline not to delay the inevitable.

More determined then ever to get this over with, she marched through the entrance into the freezing air. He didn't hesitate to follow, yet kept his distance.

Cael stared at the steep rocky peaks of the mountains, breathed in the chilly air, allowed the cold snow beneath her feet to seep through her flesh, into her blood, and deeper into her bones.

"Look at me," she commanded and dropped her robe.

CAEL STOOD NAKED before him. He sucked in a cold breath. Wild energy ripped through him, and suddenly, he had a raging hard-on.

He didn't just yearn to hold Cael's soft flesh against him, he had to have her again. Immediately. What the hell was wrong with him?

Cael frowned at him. "You've got to contain your emotions."

"I don't understand." His passion was strong and building in intensity, like a brewing storm.

"Because your emotions . . . hurt."

Damn. He kept forgetting she could feel his need. "My emotions are hurting you?"

Lips pressed tight, she nodded. Even in pain she was stunning. With her shoulders squared, her chin raised, her spine straight, her breasts lifted, and her nipples tight, she looked magnificent against the jagged rock cliffs. She'd also freeze to death if she didn't—

He blinked and Cael vanished. In her stead stood an enormous purple- and green-scaled dragon with a massive tail. The dragon's head sported spikes. Its teeth had to be as long as his thumb.

He staggered backward. A dragon. Unless he was hallucinating, Cael had turned into a dragon.

Son of a bitch. The High Priestess was a dragonshaper.

He held his breath as she gracefully spread her wings, launched her massive body from the cliff, and soared into the sky. Her huge body with its heavily muscled chest shouldn't have been able to fly. Even with a wingspan three times his height, she looked too heavy to soar. Yet she flew with a grace that stole his breath away. As a woman Cael enchanted him, but as a dragon, she was wondrous, spectacular. Mesmerizing.

Lucan had seen many beautiful and amazing sites in his life: the pyramids in Egypt, the crystal caves on Isir IV, the singing coral reefs of Abicron Station, the phosphorescent jelly floaters on Sighi Meteron. But none could match the glory of Cael's flight. She was gorgeous and dangerous and wild.

Cael, High Priestess of Avalon, was a dragonshaper. No matter how many times he thought it, the fact still wouldn't sink in. But after all, this moon was named Pendragon. And Pendragon, King Arthur's surname, meant "master dragon." Was Cael's dragon-morphing ability another connection between this world and King Arthur? Or was Lucan searching for connections that didn't exist?

Lucan couldn't quite wrap his mind around the history. Not even as he followed her flight, a real live dragon soaring across the sky. Even more amazing, he sensed her pleasure at being airborne. And her hunger.

Food. The clear and direct thought leapt from Cael's dragon mind into Lucan's as she swooped to a ledge and dug into the cliff. She ate a mouthful of dirt . . . and a strange metallic taste filled his mouth.

How was this possible? It was as if he were sharing her experience. And then he remembered his surreal flight from Avalon. Apparently his hallucination hadn't been an hallucination at all. After the skimmer had exploded, Cael must have dragonshaped and flown him to safety.

While he'd had no telepathic link with Cael in her human form, he could read her dragon thoughts. Yet he could no more understand why he could communicate with Cael's dragon than he could with his sister back on Earth. But as Cael left the metallic dirt and flew on in search of meat, a dark mass among the snowbanks caught her sharp eyes.

Food?

No food. Just a tree branch.

She flew onward, her thoughts linked to his.

There. Jasbit.

He watched her powerful wings adjust and she dipped, diving toward her prey. But he shouldn't have been able to *see* her—not from this distance.

Between his enhanced eyesight and their shared telepathy, he wondered what exactly was happening. Was some force manipulating them? Or was it coincidence they shared this mental link?

Folding her legs and wings, Cael streamlined her body and dived straight for the animal she hunted. Plunging fast, her aim true, she seized the prey in her mouth, shook it hard. He heard, through their mind link, the snap as she broke its neck. And then with barely a break in her flight pattern, she opened her wings, caught an updraft, and circled back toward the nest.

With the meal clenched between massive jaws, she landed on the ridge, and he watched in fascination as her clawed feet gripped the icy ledge. She tossed her thick neck and flung the *jasbit,* a six-legged furry creature about the size of a deer, against a wall of rock.

Facing her prey, the dragon let out a mighty roar and then a burst of flame.

Once again she shapechanged, and, as the dragon folded in on itself, the mind link he'd shared with her snapped. In the blink of an eye, she stood before him naked, the blood on her lips the only sign of her predatory flight.

She shivered, raised her eyes to his, and cocked her head to one side. Lifting an eyebrow, she waited for him to speak, her expression as human as any woman's, as vulnerable as any he'd ever seen.

Lucan picked up her robe, carried it to her, and draped the fabric over her shoulders. "I now believe in dragon-shaping."

"Good." She snuggled into the warmth of the robe. He drew it tight against the wind, and her hand closed over his, her gaze challenging. "You could read my thoughts?"

"Not your thoughts. I heard what you broadcast."

"How is that possible?"

"I've always had some telepathic ability. Apparently, your dragon and I are on the same wavelength."

Her gaze searched his. "Aren't you afraid I'll roast you?"

He sensed her need for reassurance. And he didn't need to be an empath to realize that although her chin was high and her shoulders squared, she was bracing for him to reject her. As much as it would be better for his mission to do just that, he couldn't be that cruel. Not when his first instinct was to take her into his arms and kiss her from her gorgeous head to her beautiful toes.

He spoke lightly. "If you were going to cook me for your next meal, you wouldn't have saved my life. Twice."

"That's true." She stared at him, eyes still searching. He held her gaze, hoping she could read his emotions, which tended toward wonder and awe. But despite his words, she seemed uncertain and asked, "You really don't mind I'm a dragonshaper?"

"Why would I mind?"

Relief softened her features, and a smile played at the corner of her mouth. When another shiver racked her slender body, he pointed to the door. "Come on, let's go inside. Please."

"But the *jasbit*—"

"You did the hunting, I'll take care of the rest."

She shot him a long, assessing look. He held her gaze, and she slowly released a pent-up breath. Finally, she pointed to a ledge above the cave's entrance. "Make sure Merlin eats his fill."

"Merlin?" He looked up to see an owl peering down at them. According to Arthurian legend, Merlin was the king's advisor. "Did you say *Merlin?*"

"Yes." She gazed at the owl fondly. "Thousands of years ago, one of my predecessors named him Merlin."

"You're saying Merlin is thousands of years old?"

She shook her head. "Merlin is always the name of the owl who befriends the High Priestess. Over the centuries there have been as many Merlins as there have been High Priestesses."

"Are there legends about him?" he asked. Could one of this owl's ancestors have been connected to King

Arthur's human advisor? In many Earth myths, Merlin had the ability to change into either a young boy or an old man. But Lucan had never heard of Merlin changing into an owl.

"Merlin's known to be quite protective of the High Priestess." Cael grinned and headed inside.

Lucan approached the *jasbit,* and Merlin flew down from his perch to supervise. Kneeling, Lucan removed a tiny laser from the toe of his boot and made a minor calibration adjustment. The laser hummed and emitted a beam sharp enough to cut open the animal. Within moments, he'd tossed the *jasbit'*s entrails onto a lower ridge for scavengers and washed the inside of the carcass with snow. Slicing off a good-sized chunk of meat, he set it aside. "Here you go, Merlin."

The owl swooped down for his meal.

Merlin. Lucan supposed he shouldn't be surprised by another link to King Arthur or the Holy Grail. But he was. Pendragon and Cael kept throwing surprises at him.

Especially Cael. What he'd learned about her fascinated him. But he couldn't forget that his mission had to come first. Now that he was healed, he had to return to Avalon and resume his search for the Grail. He had to find that healing cup.

And once he did, he'd be heading home.

WEARING SLIPPERS AND A ROBE, Cael joined Lucan before the fire and tried to assume a casual demeanor. It wasn't easy. They hadn't spoken more than a few words since he'd witnessed her dragonshaping and they'd experienced that puzzling mental link.

Her empathic abilities told her that Lucan didn't fear

her, not even after he'd seen her in dragon form, but she didn't know what he thought about what he'd seen. What he thought of *her.*

She watched curiously as Lucan leaned over the meat, his expression thoughtful. Surely he realized she could kill him with one flaming breath? Shove him off the mountaintop with one sweep of her giant wing? Then again, he was proving himself a man full of surprises of his own. Who would have thought a linguist could actually clean, spit, and roast game?

Or cook? He brushed a sweet sauce onto the meat, a recipe he had conjured from raw ingredients in her stash of supplies. "I've never smelled anything so tempting."

His eyes brightened. "You must be starving."

"Who taught you how to cook?"

"My folks." Lucan added more coal to the fire. "When we were young, they took us camping. Dad taught my sister and me to hunt. Mom taught us to cook."

She sniffed appreciatively. "I'm glad they did."

Lucan's curious gaze had fastened on her wrists. Her first instinct was to tug down the robe, to hide the marks that made others so uncomfortable. But Lucan had seen all her marks. And he hadn't flinched. In fact, he'd licked his way up her body, cherishing the parts that made her different, bringing her such unimagined pleasures . . .

He took her hands, turned them palm up, and peered at her scales. "You were born with these?"

"Yes."

"And exactly what do you believe about the Goddess?"

"That she gives life to all things. That we honor her by honoring the world of fire, air, earth, and wind. That if we don't lead a life worthy of her principles, after death we return in a lower life form."

"Reincarnation, huh? And if you live a life worthy of the Goddess, what then?"

"We reach the highest level of existence."

"Which is?"

"Dragonshaper. Spiritual leader of Pendragon." She shrugged and shot him a wry smile. "In truth, I've never believed I am holier than any other. I don't really know why the Goddess chose to put her marks on me."

Lucan tilted his head. "Have you ever heard of the Lady of the Lake?"

"Of course. We all learn about her as children." She wondered at his question, as well as the sudden tension she felt radiating from him. "The Lady of the Lake was a High Priestess. She lived on an island surrounded by mist. One day, when the mist was particularly heavy, she became disoriented and ended up in another realm, where she lost her ability to dragonshape and her capacity to serve her people and the Goddess."

He nodded, and she could feel him fighting to get his emotions under control. "So you enjoy serving your people?"

She raised an eyebrow and tugged the robe tighter at her waist. She was used to people putting up emotional walls so she couldn't read them, but when Lucan did so, it made her anxious. "I enjoy blessing babies, safeguarding our culture, and protecting our heritage. That's why I'm involved with the Avalon Project—that and the hope that finding the Grail will cure my nephew. I am honor-bound to try to heal the rifts between different factions of society. But not everyone upholds the ideals of honor and chivalry. Some believe them archaic. The fact that we've evolved so far from our roots is disturbing."

"Honor. Chivalry," he said, as if testing the words,

tension drawing his mouth taut. "A woman like you deserves a man who can live up to those ideals. And I . . . am not that man."

A wave of pain and anguish washed over her. Lucan's pain and anguish. And she became terribly aware that he knew he was hurting her but doing it anyway.

Her gut twisted. "I don't understand."

He stood and threaded his hand through his hair. "I care about you, but I don't want to mislead you," he said gently.

Pain tore at her, but she kept her chin high. Despite her efforts at control, her voice cracked. "Mislead me?"

He tensed, the cords at his neck bunching. "I find you very attractive, physically, emotionally, and intellectually."

"But?" she forced out the word, certain that what he said next would hurt, hurt worse than any tongue-lashing the Elders had ever delivered. Hurt worse than her sisters' lack of affection.

He paced, a determined and frustrated energy in his movements. "Cael, we can't have a future together. Not the way you want."

"We can't?" Pain settled in her chest, despair seeped into her bones, but she refused to break down in front of him. She'd been so hopeful that he would accept her dragonshaping, she hadn't thought past that moment.

"My work's very important to me."

"So is mine. I don't see how passion for our work relates to our passion for each other."

A muscle ticked at his jaw, and a shadow crossed his eyes. But he met her gaze, and she saw so much emotion simmering there, resolve, sorrow, and banked anger. "I'm not ready to settle down."

Now it was her turn to be shocked. He wasn't ready?

What the hell did that mean? That their pairing had been purely for pleasure? What if she'd conceived?

Damn him.

Her motivation had been pure. She'd given her body with high hopes and a virtuous spirit. If he hadn't reciprocated, then he was not the man she'd thought him to be.

"I'm not rejecting you," he added hastily. "I'm just saying . . . your expectations are different from mine."

Her entire body began to shake. She was barely holding herself together. "You're saying you don't want a relationship?"

"I'm saying I can't *have* a relationship. Not now."

"If you only want recreational sex," she threw the ugly words in his face, her mind spinning in bafflement at how she could have made such a huge mistake, "you'll need to find yourself another woman." Her voice was so tight it trembled with her fury.

He nodded gravely, his cheeks chiseled rock. "I understand."

"So we're done." The finality left her angry, weary, and alone. Again.

She'd thought he'd wanted her. She'd felt his urgency, his hunger, and had assumed he wanted and felt the same things she did. Apparently she'd read him wrong. She knew nothing about relationships. He hadn't wanted *her*—he'd wanted only her body, pure physical gratification. During her dragonshaping, she'd felt his mindlink. But she'd confused lust and telepathy for the beginnings of something deeper.

Had she seen what she'd wanted to see, or did he have feelings for her he hadn't acknowledged—even to himself? She supposed it didn't matter.

Wrapping her hands around her waist, she tried to contain the pain whirling inside her. She felt sick to her stomach, as if she were being ripped apart. She'd wanted to be treated like a normal person. Now she knew what normal rejection felt like, and she wanted to cry.

But she was the High Priestess. And the High Priestess didn't let people see her hurting. Instead, she turned away from Lucan, and her communicator rang. The timing couldn't have been better.

Lucan jumped at the ring tone. "Don't answer that."

"Why not?"

"It could be traced."

What an odd notion. Cael had been briefed on all the newest military technology, and she'd never heard of tracing a call. "That's not possible." When Lucan didn't contradict her, she opened her communicator, eager for the distraction. "Hello?"

"Lady Cael, this is Rion." The astrophysicist from the lab, the man who'd helped Lucan build the laser, had survived!

"I'm so glad you made it out of the fire." Relief, and hope that others too had survived, filled her.

"Thanks. Is Lucan with you?"

She frowned. How could Rion have guessed that she and Lucan were together? "Yes. I'll put you on the speaker."

"Lucan?" Rion's voice was tense.

"Yes."

"Military investigators are blaming you and Lady Cael for starting the fire."

Cael looked at Lucan, expecting him to deny the accusation. He shook his head and placed his finger to his lips. Fine. She'd let him do the talking. For now.

"Why would they blame us?" Lucan asked calmly.

"You were seen leaving the lab together right before the fire. All the doors were locked from the outside, preventing people from escaping the burning lab."

Cael gasped and raised her hand to her mouth.

"Only four of us survived," Rion said. "You two, me, and Sir Quentin."

Oh, Goddess. Everyone else was dead? She blinked back tears for those who'd died. Compared to the loss of life, her personal disappointments were inconsequential. She was the High Priestess. She had to rise above her own raw feelings.

"How did you and Quentin get out?" Lucan asked, his eyes narrowed.

"That's not important. The military thinks you're holed up in Cael's mountain hideaway. If that's where you are, you have to flee. Now."

"We didn't start the fire." Stunned, Cael blurted the denial.

"Doesn't matter what you did or didn't do," Rion said. "My contact inside the Division of Lost Artifacts has told me that if the military arrests you, you won't live long enough to prove your innocence."

"What's happening at Avalon?" Lucan asked.

"The ground continues to weaken. And Shaw's suspicions about Quentin's military affiliations were correct."

"How do you know?"

"Quentin's now openly admitting he works for General Brennon at the Division of Lost Artifacts."

"You think Brennon ordered Quentin to start the fire at the lab so the military could take over Avalon?"

"As we speak, they're hiring a new team to go forward with the project."

"The shield's still down?" Lucan asked.

"Yeah. But there's another one inside. They're talking about blasting again." Rion sighed. "So far I've talked them out of it."

"I should be there." Lucan curled his hands into fists. He might not be able to commit to her, but she couldn't doubt his commitment to finding the Grail. Not when determination rained from his every pore.

"You come back and they'll arrest you. They may find you anyway. You have to get out of there."

The line went dead.

"This makes no sense. How can they accuse us of arson? If you hadn't talked me into going outside to look at Avalon . . ."

"We would have been killed, too."

Horror filled her. Eighty people had died. "My people will never believe . . . we have to go back and set the record straight."

A vow sworn before the Goddess reverberates through time and space.

—HIGH PRIESTESS OF AVALON

7

L ucan helped Cael to her feet. She looked pale, shocked, like she was about to faint. And she wasn't thinking straight. "Didn't you hear what Rion said? If the military kills us, we won't be around to clear our names."

Cael's color began to return. "You believe Rion?"

Lucan wanted to, but he also had a lot of questions. Like how had Rion gotten out of the fire? How had he known Lucan was with Cael?

"If he's wrong," Lucan said, "and we leave, what harm will it do? But if they capture us, we have no proof of our innocence, no alibi. We need to leave, right now." He could see the anxiety written on her face and, beneath it, the pain he'd caused her. Pain she didn't deserve. A woman like Cael deserved a man who could devote himself to her happiness. Perhaps once, he'd been that man. But not on Pendragon. "We need warm clothing. Do you have any to spare?"

She tossed him a unisex tunic and his own slacks, both too thin for protection from the harsh elements. But as he retrieved his socks and boots, and she thrust a spare fur coat, gloves, and a hat at him, he wasn't fooled by her practicality. She wouldn't meet his eyes. Her motions were jerky, and clearly she was very upset. No doubt the fault was his. He'd been her first lover, and he'd hurt her. While he was far from proud of himself, how could he have resisted Cael after he'd awakened to find her naked and willing in his arms?

While he wrapped the remaining meat in a pack, Cael, expression stoic, threw in a thermos and matches. She retrieved a rope harness from a niche and slipped it over her shoulders.

"Come on. We can leave through here." She headed deeper into the cave.

He followed her down a long tunnel lit by sunlight that filtered in through slits cut into the marbelite walls. "Where's this go?"

"We'll exit on the other side of the peak." Her tone was flat, devoid of all emotion. "The mountain will block their radar from spotting us."

"How do you know?"

She lifted an impatient brow. "I'm a military mediator. While I'm no expert, I'm not ignorant of their capabilities, either."

The passageway came to a T and she turned right. "I'm going to dragonshape, and I'll have to fly fast and hard." She twisted the rope, knotted it, and placed it loosely over her shoulders. "You need to tie yourself to me."

He recalled her steep dive, her powerful wings, and the speed with which she'd flown through the air. "Where are we headed?"

"It depends on whether they spot us." She turned a dark corner and continued through the tunnel. "We have to fly now. Every second counts. Those military ships are fast. If they pick me up on their radar, we'll never get away. And your bulk isn't much, but you'll slow me."

Great. He'd made love to her, told her he wanted only sex, and now he was going to slow her flight, lesson her chances of getting away.

He couldn't let his guilt get in the way. It was time to leave and return to Avalon. Following Cael, he turned his thoughts to their escape.

Lucan hoped Rion was an ally. Of all the scientists Lucan had met on Pendragon, Rion was the one man Lucan would like to believe they could trust. His call had ended abruptly. Was Rion in danger—or had he wanted to end the conversation before they asked more questions? "Why don't we fly back to Avalon, locate Rion, and find out what he knows?"

She shook her head. "It's too dangerous to go to the city. I'll need a well-thought-out plan and a place to stay before we can risk that route."

She jerked open a heavy wooden door. Following on her heels, Lucan skidded outside onto a rock ledge, where Merlin perched as if waiting for them.

Immediately the air turned frigid and his breath frosted. Ice covered the mountaintops, and ancient glaciers gleamed a dark blue, their ice crystals sparkling in the occasional ray of sunlight peeking through the clouds.

Cael removed her clothes, then stuffed them into a pack attached to the makeshift harness. On the icy cliff, her perfect pink skin looked delicate and ethereal. Hunger washed over him, and he felt an aching desire building inside him. Damn it. He didn't have the right to look at her with desire. Not when he couldn't stay, couldn't be the man she needed him to be.

Cael dragonshaped, morphing and growing scales in a mere instant. The rope harness expanded to fit the dragon, and she turned her massive head and nudged him toward her back.

He grabbed hold of the harness and climbed on. His mental link with Cael connected almost instantly.

Now! Hurry. We must go.

As he straddled her sinuous shoulders, he knew she was going to take him on a ride of a lifetime. A ride that would save their lives. Filled with excitement, he slipped his feet into the stirrups, wrapped his hand into the harness, and hunkered down. He thought he was prepared to fly with Cael, but the sudden surge of her muscles as she leaped off the cliff was pure poetry.

For a moment they hung in a perfect balance between cliff and sky. Then she plunged straight down, and a rush of adrenaline had him holding tight to the harness. Wind slammed his face. Forced to squint, he peered over her head and saw nothing but icy cliffs, snow, and Merlin keeping pace with their mad escape.

As they dived, it began to snow. Fat white flakes stung his cheeks and coated Cael's dragon scales.

Hanging on to Cael became increasingly difficult. He struggled to stay upright and centered. His arms strained, his hold on the harness precarious as he fought to stay on her back. Breathing in the freezing, snow-filled air weakened him. To protect his face from the sting of the cold, he ducked his head and tried to draw in oxygen through the fur of his cloak.

At the sudden menacing drone of machines, he risked a look over his shoulder. *They're coming.*

Be still, Cael's mental demand sounded in his head, and he crouched lower.

Fine. Cliffs whizzed by at dizzying speed. Snowflakes pelted his face. For a moment the world went gray. They'd flown through a cloud and had almost reached the next mountain, but he could hear skimmers in pursuit.

He glanced back again. The sky was clear of skimmers. If she could make it around the bend, they'd stay out of radar range.

She banked violently, tearing around a cliff face so fast he floated off her back, weightless, barely managing to hold on to the harness with one hand.

I told you to hang on. She swerved back under him.

I'm trying.

Try harder.

And she'd had the nerve to complain about *his* driving. Gritting his teeth, he settled onto her back, which was now icy and slick.

The skimmers' engines roared behind them, and the sound echoed through the mountain pass and down into the valley, so loud he was sure they had been spotted. The aircraft cleared the mountain peak behind them just as Cael careened around the last ridge.

He breathed a short sigh of relief. *I think we made it.*

Not yet, we didn't.

The valley below didn't look that different from the mountain peaks. The entire mountain range was one giant ice ball of rock and snow. But the wind here didn't cut so badly.

He hunched down, trying to warm his face. When he looked forward again, Cael was flying straight at a black mountain cliff so steep that no snow or ice clung to its vertical sides.

Cael, you need to turn!

We're on course.

The only thing they were on course for was suicide. Again Lucan heard the roar of skimmers. *They're gaining on us.*

Cael continued straight toward the cliffside. Lucan tensed. As they neared the jagged rock, he could see more details. What had appeared at a distance as a monolithic solid surface was actually a rock face pockmarked with caves, their entrances so dark they were indistinguishable from the surrounding surface, like a geological hunk of Swiss cheese.

She flew into the nearest aperture, one he hadn't noticed until they were almost on top of it. He hoped the skimmers hunting them wouldn't see it, either.

He expected Cael to slow and land, but she flew through the cave until it widened into a gray lava tunnel with luminescent walls that threaded deep into the mountain.

She flew him through the tunnel for what seemed like hours. He spied several connecting tunnels, but Cael never veered off course.

Finally, they reached what appeared to be a dead end, and Cael landed gracefully. He slid from her back onto the tunnel floor, landing much less gracefully.

She humanshaped, and he handed over her clothes, then folded the harness into the pack. He wondered if the skimmers could come roaring after them. "Does the military know about these tunnels?"

"I hope not." She dressed quickly. "Come on. After that flight, I need food."

TURNING DOWN A darkened passageway, Cael led Lucan to her storage alcove. She'd cached basic food supplies in canisters, along with communicators and blankets.

"Do people come after you often?" he asked, glancing around at her fully stocked array of supplies.

"This is a first for me." The first time the military had chased her. The first time she'd been accused of arson. The first time she'd made love. The first time she'd been rejected. The first time she'd felt as if her hearts were shattering.

Lifting a hatch to a tiny cellar where she stocked frozen vegetables and fruit, she peered at her choices. But her mind wasn't on meal preparation. Or how the supplies the Elders had instructed her to stock throughout the mountains were coming in so handy.

Ever since Lucan had rescued her in the air duct, her life had been spinning out of control. She felt restless, edgy, and excited to be in the company of a man who treated her like an equal, but she hadn't forgotten how much he'd hurt her. That he wasn't ready to make commitments.

Cael had been hurt many times in her life. When she'd gone to live with the Elders, and later, when her parents died, she'd cried herself to sleep every night for months. Even back then, she'd always wanted a friend. But everyone had feared her. She'd always been alone.

Uncertainty hit her. She didn't want to be alone again. Wouldn't she be better off salvaging some sort of relationship with Lucan? They could be friends. Nothing more.

Drawing in a deep breath, she corralled her swirling emotions. She looked up to see Lucan watching her and was acutely aware of the way his shoulders strained the fabric of his borrowed tunic.

His steady gaze took her measure. "Are you all right?"

"Of course. Why?"

"For a moment there, you looked angry enough to blow smoke out your ears." His mouth twitched.

He was teasing. Sometimes he said the strangest things. But he'd also lightened the mood, and she laughed. "The smoke comes out of my nose."

He smiled, and she could sense he was relieved that she'd momentarily put aside her hurt feelings. Too bad his inherent kindness also cut deep, reminding her how much she yearned for more.

He pulled the *jasbit* from the pack and lit the kindling in the woodstove, his movements unhurried, efficient. To keep from staring at all his rippling male muscles, she moved aside a folded blanket, found a pot, added water and vegetables, and began to slice the meat into smaller pieces.

"So where are we?" he asked, turning his blue eyes on her.

"Near Langor. It's the city where the Elders have their retreat." Cael faced him, ready to defend the destination she'd chosen. With her life at risk, she'd wanted to go somewhere safe. "I need to speak with my mentors . . ."

"About?" He arched his eyebrow in that way he had that made her pulse skip a beat.

Damn it. "The Elders advise me about many things."

He glanced at the communicators. "You don't want to call them?"

Call and ask why sharing her blood was taboo? She didn't think so.

"They'll speak more freely in person." And since Lucan hadn't pressed, she shared one of her concerns. "I'm hoping the Elders might tell us more about General Brennon. Perhaps they might even help clear our names."

He stirred the stew with a firm and steady hand. "I thought Elders didn't get involved in worldly matters."

"That's what the general public's supposed to think." She tried not to recall his hands skimming up her body and over her breasts. How good he'd made her feel, but the memory made her tingle. She added the meat to the pot and focused on how well they worked together in the cramped area, easily dividing the chores.

"Will the Elders welcome me to their retreat?" Lucan found two bowls. He blew out the dust, then used his sleeve for a final cleaning. A tiny smudge of dirt smeared his chin.

Without thinking, she reached up and wiped away the streak. He tried and failed to block his emotions. She could feel his desire, but she knew he wanted only sexual gratification and jerked back her hand. "Once I tell the Elders you're telepathic with my dragon form, they'll be elated."

His eyes smoldered. "You don't have a telepathic bond with anyone else?"

"Only with you." She stepped back, unwilling to admit how much their deep mental connection had surprised and unnerved her. She'd thought the telepathy was another sign they were meant to be together, but she'd been wrong. "I don't understand how you were in my head like that."

He folded his arms and his forearms and biceps bulged. "You were in my head, too. When we communicate, can anyone else listen in?"

She would never have thought of that. She'd assumed the mental link was unique to them. But she had to wonder at the odd coincidence that the one man who was not afraid of her also shared this mental link. Was it possible that he didn't fear her *because* of the link? "Have *you* linked your mind with anyone else's?"

"My sister." At the change of subject, he totally blocked her out, but she remained wary, sensing that like sparks amid dry kindling, he could flare up again at any time. "But Marisa lives too far away to reach from here."

Whenever he spoke of his family, his words were sparse and he raised an emotional barrier as solid as stone, making her suspect that he was hiding things.

Were Lucan and his sister's telepathic abilities the reason they lived in such isolation? Even if the siblings had perfect control, people could be cruel to anyone who was different, anyone who had powers they didn't understand. Cael knew all too well that being different could be hurtful. The whispers, the talk behind her back. The isolation of never being included.

"Are you the *only* dragonshaper?" He asked the question innocently enough, but she could feel muted tension beneath his words.

Her mind whirled as she thought about how much to tell him. "Dinner's ready." She divided the stew into two bowls, poured them each some water into mugs, and sat down on a rock ledge.

He carried his bowl and drink to another ledge. "Thanks."

Some information she could share easily enough. "According to ancient legends, there's only one dragonshaper on Pendragon at a time. When I die, the next dragonshaper will be born. Some say it's the same spirit that is reborn, but . . . no one knows."

"So how does a dragon fly?"

She went with the obvious. "Wings."

"Very funny." He smiled, his grin charming. "Your wings aren't big enough to account for flight."

"I also have two massive hearts and a honeycombed bone structure that's strong but light."

"Yeah, but even with a skimmer-sized wing span and light bones, compared to any bird, your mass is proportionally high."

"Are you calling me fat?"

"Your strength's awesome." He spoke with real admiration, his blue eyes bright with wonder, locking with hers. "Without your power of flight, we wouldn't have survived. Beauty comes in many forms, and all of your shapes are beautiful."

Beautiful. She'd never been called beautiful. She shook the traitorous thought from her mind. "I also have a second pair of lungs. Lungs designed to expand with gas."

"Hydrogen gas?" he asked, his spoon stopping halfway to his mouth.

"Exactly. Since hydrogen is lighter than air, when my lungs expand, they help keep me aloft."

"But where does the hydrogen come from?" The curiosity and warmth in his expression amazed her. Despite herself, her hearts fluttered.

Usually she was uncomfortable talking about her biology, but with Lucan she sensed no censure. Instead of disgusted, he looked fascinated, which encouraged her to share more. "Bacteria in my stomach create the hydrogen and funnel it to my lungs." Sometimes she ate pure hydrogen, when she could find it processed properly. "To keep up my hydrogen production and strength, I've always consumed three to four times the amount of calories of a normal woman my size. The more often I dragonshape, the more energy I use and the more food I must eat."

"How long can you go without dragonshaping?"

She became terribly aware that his fascination with her dragonshaping was causing her scales to tingle. "The longest I've ever gone is about one and a half cycles. But since I don't mind the shape change or eating more calories, I frequently do it more often."

His gaze was thoughtful as he dipped his spoon back into the stew. She loved watching him eat. She recalled those lips nipping her ear, her neck, giving her so much pleasure.

"I gather some of your information's from experience, but if there are no written records, where did you learn all the science?"

"I lived a normal life until age five. After I dragon-shaped the first time—"

"What was that like?" His eyes lit with curiosity.

She ignored the sudden warmth flowing through her veins, but she couldn't keep the smile from her face. "It was the best thing that ever happened to me. I was up in the mountains, and my sister Nisco and I slipped off a cliff—"

"You call that the best thing ever?"

"I was terrified. Falling. Nisco was screaming, and the wind whipped through our hair. One moment I was a little girl, frightened and frail, the next I was this powerful dragon with wings. I could fly."

"And you saved your sister?"

"Yes." Her smile faded. "Nisco never treated me the same after that. There was always this awkwardness. Awe. Fear." Was she revealing too much? She didn't know. She only knew that she wanted him to understand who she was, *what* she was. "After that, I was separated from my family and moved into the High Priestess's main residence at Carlane to study the ancient ways. I was trained in my duties."

"Your parents permitted this?"

"My parents died in a skimmer accident when I was five."

"I'm sorry."

She could remember them. Her mother a warm and melodramatic woman, her father loving and scholarly. "Everything changed after they died, but not just because of the accident."

"How so?"

"The Elders raised me and taught me the science of dragonshaping. And that I was not allowed to touch or be touched."

"Why not? And why are the consequences so severe?"

She exhaled a sigh of exasperation. "I suppose it's for everyone's protection. If I lose my temper—"

He wriggled his eyebrows. "I'm still here. Proof you have perfect control."

If she had perfect control, she wouldn't keep recalling how his eyes had raked over her naked body and how hot that had made her feel. She had to remember her feelings were one-sided. She scowled. "Just don't touch me in public . . . not ever."

"I'll make a note." He stared at her mouth, and she could almost feel the intensity of his gaze. "You breathe fire. How does that work?"

Her lips suddenly tingled. Surely not because he was staring at her, as if he wanted to kiss her. "Sometimes I eat platinum."

"You dig it from the mountainside." He didn't sound

surprised. "I could practically taste it myself during our telepathic connection."

She nodded. "I have incisors for ripping meat and molars for grinding the metal. When I eat platinum, it acts like a catalyst and causes the hydrogen to ignite."

"But you don't get burned?"

Again *he* was concerned about *her*. Any other man on this moon would have been worried about his own safety.

"The inner surface of my mouth is practically armor plated. And there's a fleshy valve that prevents a back-draft so I don't set myself on fire."

"And the shapeshifting?"

She shrugged. "No one really understands the process. But I remain warm-blooded. I have a heat-exchanging circulatory system, highly stratified layers of tissue under my scales to minimize heat loss, and a blood protein that prevents the formulation of ice crystals in the blood stream. Even my wings can soak up heat like solar panels."

"You really are a fascinating creature." His voice was low and soft. "So you change shape at will? Whenever the mood strikes?"

"Why do you ask?" She'd told him so much already. She hadn't realized how vulnerable it would make her feel to tell him so much about herself.

He shot her a challenging look. "When we were trapped at the lab, you didn't change shape until after we'd exhausted every other option. Why did you wait so long?"

"I don't like to dragonshape indoors."

"Why? Because you have to be naked?"

"If I dragonshape, my mass expands almost instantly.

If I'm inside a structure, I could easily run out of room and be impaled by a beam or crushed by a concrete ceiling."

Had she revealed too much? The secrets that the Elders had told her to keep to herself were sacred. And now she'd trusted Lucan with knowledge that could be used against her. As a scientist, he could surmise that if she ran out of hydrogen and platinum, she couldn't fly or breathe fire. Was she naive to be so trusting? If he betrayed her to her enemies, they could take advantage.

For all she knew, Lucan, who'd been so closemouthed about his past, could be a spy for the military—although her empathic abilities told her otherwise. And she didn't want to believe that he'd ever put her in danger.

Finishing their meal, Cael and Lucan packed the supplies. If they left now, they could reach Langor well before dark. She was about to slip the pack over her shoulder when her communicator beeped.

Lucan peered at the caller number. "Is it Rion?"

She shook her head. "My sister." Cael opened communications. "Hi, Nisco."

"I heard about the fire." Her sister sounded breathless. "And that the military wants to question you. It's terrible." Nisco sounded close to tears. "And I wouldn't have bothered you except . . ."

Cael broke into a sweat at the raw emotion in her sister's voice. "What is it?"

"It's Jaylon." Nisco sniffled. "He's not responding to his latest treatment. Sonelle's hysterical, and I don't know what to—"

"What are Jaylon's symptoms?" She clutched her communicator so hard, her fingers left indentations on the hard plastic.

"He's vomiting and dehydrated. And he's drifting in and out of consciousness." Nisco let out a sob.

Helplessness and fear stole through Cael. For a moment she cradled her face in her hand and pictured Jaylon in the hospital bed, his eyes wide with fright. If only she could cure Jaylon with her blood. But even if his mother and his doctors would allow her to violate Dragonia taboos, she couldn't in good conscience attempt such an experimental procedure on Jaylon. Curing his cancer was a totally different procedure than closing Lucan's wounds. Still, she should be with him and her sisters at the medical center. She took a deep breath and reminded herself she'd been no more successful treating Jaylon than his regular physician. But if she could find the Grail . . . "I'll call Jaylon's doctors. Maybe we just need to adjust his meds."

"I know you have so much more to worry about. I'm sorry for calling."

"I'm glad you called." Filled with fear and working hard to control it, Cael pulled herself together. "Take a deep breath and calm yourself. We knew the treatments were going to be rough. He's going to have good days and bad. You have to be strong, Nisco. He's a tough little kid."

Lucan came up behind Cael and kneaded her shoulders, offering her comfort. Goddess, she hadn't known her muscles were in knots. While he could hear only her side of the conversation, he could guess the situation wasn't good. But had he guessed she was about to fall apart?

Nisco dragged in a deep breath. "Jaylon looks so pale and listless, lying in that bed. But I didn't call just about him. Is there anything I can do for you?"

Cael had been taught to be the strong one, to stand alone. She'd worried that her independent behavior had pushed her sisters away. But here was Nisco, reaching out to her.

"Actually, I could use your help. Can you meet us at your booth in the market in Langor at sunset?" At her words, Lucan's fingers stopped kneading, but he didn't say a word.

"*Us?*" Nisco asked. "Who's with you?"

"I'll introduce him when I see you."

Nisco was silent for a moment, and Cael knew she must have been shocked that Cael wasn't alone. She was always alone. Finally, Nisco found her voice. "If I leave right now, I'll be there on time."

"Don't tell anyone you're meeting me or that we've spoken."

"Got it."

Cael hung up and could see Lucan was bursting with questions. "Hold on. Jaylon isn't doing well. I need to make a call." She dialed her nephew's room, hoping to ask Sonelle to connect her with the healer in charge.

Her nephew answered. "Hello."

"Jaylon? Is that you, sweetie?"

"Aunt Cael?" He sounded weak but clear-headed. "Have you found the Grail?"

"I'm working on it, baby."

"I'm not a baby."

"Sorry." She wiped a tear from her eye. "I keep forgetting how much you've grown."

"You should come see." He spoke with childish logic.

"I will. Soon. Is your mom there?"

"She's talking to the healer."

"I'd like to talk to the doctor, too." Her hearts were aching, but Cael kept her voice cheerful. "Put her on, please."

"I don't want any more meds. Or shots."

The last time she'd seen him, his arms had been black and blue from intravenous needles. "If you want to get well—"

"The meds make me sick."

He sounded so sad and discouraged. "Don't you dare give up on me. Those meds are killing your cancer."

"No, they aren't. I can tell."

His stubborn little voice put a lump in her throat, but she managed to keep her voice light. "If you don't get better, I can't take you flying."

She'd promised to make him a harness and fly him over the city. His mother wouldn't approve, but it was their special secret.

"You didn't forget?" he said.

"Of course not. Now let me talk to the healer, and I'll see what we can do to make you feel better, sweetie. Love you."

"Love you, too."

Cael spoke to the doctor and then snapped the communicator shut. She couldn't stop trembling. Lucan didn't say a word. He took one look at her face and wrapped his arms around her, and she collapsed against his strength. She hadn't realized she was so cold until he enveloped her in his heat.

Closing her eyes, she rested her cheek against his chest and let the steady pumping of his heart soothe her despair and frazzled nerves.

He held her close, rocking her, caressing her back and shoulders. His clever fingers worked on the tight knots in her neck. And as he smoothed her hair back and kissed her forehead, it was as if through his touch he willed strength into her.

Tilting up her head, she saw the compassion in his gaze. Once again, Lucan was seeing *her.* Seeing Cael as a woman who loved her family.

His breath fanned her forehead and heat sluiced through her.

He cared. She snuggled closer, fitting perfectly in the crook of his arm. She should pull away, shouldn't allow herself to be tempted. But in that moment she could think of nothing she wanted more than his arms around her.

Survival plans are always necessary.

— THE ELDERS

8

Looking for the Grail instead of heading to Jaylon's bedside was the hardest thing she'd ever done. All the delays, the fire, the military takeover of Avalon, and the arson accusation had piled up while Jaylon was losing his battle to live. "I should be there with my family."

"They know you love them." Lucan rocked her against his strong chest while his fingers made gentle circles on her back.

Tears filled her eyes, and she closed them tight so none would escape. "Jaylon's so sick. I want to be there for him."

"Of course you do." His voice was filled with warmth and concern. "But you're with Jaylon in spirit. He knows that."

Lucan was doing his best to put her mind at ease. He was being so nice. Too nice. The last thing she needed was him giving her comfort, making her aware of his strength, his gentle kindness.

He'd wrapped his arms around her so protectively, she had to fight an overwhelming need to get even closer. His heat seeped into her. He smelled so male, and his hands on her back were so tender that she was having difficulty remembering they were friends. Just friends.

She didn't know when her arms had wrapped around his back. Or when her pulse began to pick up speed.

But friends didn't let friends get aroused when they were upset. And even if she was aroused, she couldn't ask more from him. He'd made his feelings clear.

She told herself to pull back. But she couldn't make her body obey her mind.

"Jaylon's going to be okay." His voice was soft and gentle. "We'll find the Grail. We'll save him."

"Suppose we don't ever . . ." She leaned back and their gazes met, his as soft as a caress. He tilted his forehead to hers, until their noses touched and their mouths were a mere inch apart.

"It's going to be okay." His voice was low and sexy, and every time his gaze met hers, her pulse kicked up another notch. "We're going to be okay."

We? "You don't know that," she whispered.

"I know that you'll do your best, and that's all anyone can do." His fingers slid sensuously over her arm.

"But my best—"

"Your best is passionate and strong. Your best is better than anyone else's I know," he insisted, the searing heat in his eyes melting her. Then his mouth closed over hers. She let out a soft gasp and parted her lips. He slipped his tongue between her lips, and while she knew friends didn't kiss like this, she made herself stop thinking. She wasn't going to think about anything painful, not when she could lose herself in his kiss.

Aching deep in her heart and her loins, Cael trailed her hands over his back, his neck, and into his thick hair.

Goddess, she adored kissing this man who could be so tender and hot all at the same time.

Kissing him was oh so much better than any dream she'd ever had. His kisses made her feel cherished, special, and, most of all, for the first time in her life, desired.

Lucan ever so slowly slid his hands under her tunic and onto her waist, and she shivered in anticipation. Tiny flames licked their way from his fingertips, blazing a path of delicious sensations over her flesh. She longed for their clothes to be gone so they could be free to touch every inch of each other. Breathless, she began to tug off her tunic.

"Let me do that." His breath in her ear was enough to persuade her to let him have his way.

He slowly removed her clothes, taking his time, stroking and caressing her hips, then the hollow in the curve of her back and between her shoulders, and the deep ache inside her spread like wildfire.

When he tossed their clothing to the floor and eased her onto her back, his eyes sparkled with tenderness. Excitement coursed through her.

"Let me make this good for you." Without waiting for her reply, he leaned over and kissed her. She opened her arms, expecting another embrace, but he lay on his side. His hand roamed, smoothing her hair back from her face, down her neck, over her collarbone, leaving a delicious trail of heat.

Her nipples tightened in anticipation as he traced a silky trail down the center of her ribs to her belly. Sweet heat seeped between her thighs, and she parted her legs.

His lips left hers to retrace the path his fingers had just taken. He settled between her thighs. When he blew a breath on her curls, she clenched the blankets beneath them. Goddess. She yearned for his mouth.

When he gently parted her folds and lowered his head to taste her, the delicious sensation of his lips on her most sensitive flesh was like nothing she'd ever felt. Every fiber of her being centered on his mouth, the wondrous friction, the lovely sensations. Panting, breath so ragged she couldn't hold still, couldn't take any more of the sweet pleasure, she arched up as he lapped her with his tongue. His tiny flicks against her core sent spirals of heat blazing across her skin.

His hands held her thighs down. And the fire inside her burned hotter. Blazed so bright, she exploded in a fiery barrage of sensations so intense that she screamed.

When she finally regained her senses, he'd covered her with her tunic and moved away. He smiled down at her. "You are amazing."

He hadn't taken his own pleasure. She frowned at him. "What about you?"

"I'm fine." He met her gaze with a level one. Goddess, he'd kept his word. He'd known they were going beyond the limits she'd set. But he'd wanted to comfort her. He'd distracted her from her pain, but at what cost to himself?

She wasn't that selfish. She patted the blanket next to her.

He shook his head, eyes bleak. "When you're ready, we should leave."

He strode away to give her privacy to dress.

LUCAN AND CAEL reached the market about fifteen minutes before sunset. Grateful to be in a crowd where he could look at anything or anyone besides Cael, he realized how close he'd come to breaking his word. He shouldn't have touched her again.

Simply holding her hand now reminded him of tasting her. How the flesh under his lips had been as soft as a flower petal. Even here in the market, he expended all his willpower not to raise her wrist to his lips and nip his way up her arm.

He dropped her hand. Held his breath. He didn't dare breathe in her scent.

Because at that moment, there was nothing he wanted in the entire universe more than this woman. As he recalled the flames flickering in her eyes, her ragged breath, the pulse throbbing in her neck, his need only escalated.

Earlier he'd wanted to comfort Cael, but also to prove to himself that he could stay in control. That he would not let his cravings overcome his good sense. He would not let his burning lust govern the moment.

He'd just barely hung on. Now Lucan had to cool off, and Langor's market was a good distraction. The scents of sugared nuts frying, sweet meats grilling, and corn popping mixed with perfumes, barbecue smoke, and animal odors as they strolled through busy stalls. Vendors sold everything from tools to furniture to pets. Strings of overhead lights and copper lanterns lent a festive atmosphere to the busy market.

Cael had donned large sunglasses, a straw hat with a wide brim, and a scarf wrapped around the lower half of her face. Lucan wore a cap and his regular glasses. So far no one appeared to have recognized either of them as they strolled among Langor's citizens on their way to meet Nisco.

Still, Lucan kept his guard up. He wished Cael had consulted him before arranging this meeting. He didn't believe being out in the open was a good idea. "How much farther?"

"Two aisles over, then once we reach the wharf, another block." She tilted her head toward the river.

Langor sat on a hillside overlooking a midsized waterway. Part of the port was industrial, but much of it had been set aside for restaurants, carriage rides, and clubs.

Two boys ran through the crowd, and he pulled Cael aside so she wouldn't be trampled. After the boys passed, she jerked her arm away. "Be careful," she whispered.

Telling himself he could handle a simple touch once more, he hooked his arm through hers and grinned. "Just think of me as part of your disguise."

A military man on patrol strode by, but his eyes swept over them and moved on. Nevertheless, Lucan angled them the other way.

Cael shook her head. "We have to go to the wharf."

He readjusted their angle and forced the tension from his shoulders as they made their way around a live band. Young girls in clinging green costumes danced to the music and entertained the crowd while a monkey collected tips in a hat.

The aisle of talented street performers led them to the wharf. Here, artists along the boardwalk had set up easels and painted portraits. Others sold glass jewelry and pottery etched with intricate designs. Cael strode through the groups of artisans until she reached a booth filled with sculptures of animals and people carved from a variety of native stones and wood. The sculptress hawked her wares to the passing crowd.

"That's Nisco," Cael said softly.

Lucan suppressed a murmur of surprise. Nisco looked nothing like Cael. The tall woman was a collection of sharp angles—square jaw, knobby elbows, and slanting eyes with slightly hooded lids. Her welcoming smile lacked warmth, and he wondered if Nisco resented not only the prominence, but also the beauty of her famous sister.

Normally, sisters would have hugged, but Nisco and Cael stood awkwardly apart in greeting.

"Nisco"—Cael picked up a sculpture of a dragon—"this is lovely."

"Take it if you want." Nisco gestured for them to enter her booth and turned her curiosity-filled eyes to Lucan.

Cael made introductions, and Nisco frowned. "You know they're still looking for you."

Lucan positioned himself at the front of the booth, stance wide, hands on hips. Several shoppers headed toward Nisco's display, read Lucan's body language, and moved on.

"We have to hide—which is why I need your help." Cael lowered her voice and picked up another piece of sculpture. "Remember your friend Trelan?"

"The private investigator?" Nisco wiped her hands on her apron.

"Can you contact him?"

"I suppose. Why?"

"I want to find out everything there is to know about General Brennon. His family. His friends. His associates. His employees. And most especially anything having to do with Avalon and the Holy Grail."

"General Brennon?" Nisco's voice rose. She raised her palms and backed away. "He's the head—"

"Keep your voice down," Cael muttered. "I know who he is. His military skimmers poured an accelerant on the laboratory fire."

"Why would he do that?"

"I believe Brennon started that fire as an excuse to take control of Avalon, but while they're blaming me for arson, I can't search for the truth. Will you help me?"

Several women shoppers ohhed and ahhed over Nisco's sculptures. Paying no attention to Lucan, they shouldered past him into the booth.

"Yes. I'll help." Nisco looked nervously at Lucan, then at the shoppers, then back at Cael. "I'll contact you if and when we find something."

"Thanks. But *you* stay out of it. Let him do the work, and tell him that it may be dangerous."

"That will make him all the more eager to—"

"Excuse me." One of the shoppers held up a sculpted baby. "How much for—"

Shots rang out. The shopper spun, her eyes wide, a bloody wound in her forehead. She slumped to the ground, and the marketplace erupted with screaming people running for cover.

"Get down." Lucan tackled Cael and Nisco. His sunglasses went flying.

The three of them fell and he rolled under a table, taking Cael with him. Nisco scrambled the other way.

"Let's go." He lifted a tablecloth and urged·Cael to crawl to the next booth.

"Nisco—"

"She's safer on her own than with us." Lucan tugged Cael through one booth, then another. Sirens screamed. More shots were fired as people fled in panic.

When Lucan reached a roadside fountain, he peered into the street. A carriage stopped, and the driver opened a door, gestured for them to get in. Cael started forward, but Lucan tugged her back. He squinted in the dark. Something about the driver looked familiar.

"Get in."

"Rion?" Lucan lunged to the carriage, but he didn't get in. Instead he peered inside, checking it, but it was empty. "What are you doing here?"

"Two soldiers followed you through the market." Rion opened his jacket and revealed a weapon. "I got one of them. The other's still out there. You want a ride or not?"

"Yes, thanks." Cael jumped into the carriage. "Can you take us to the Elders' retreat?"

Lucan followed. "Why are we going to the retreat?"

"The retreat is a sanctuary. General Brennon won't dare come after us there."

Lucan suspected Cael had other reasons for heading to the retreat, but he didn't press her. With the military moving into the city, she would know better where to hide than he.

Rion rode outside, so they had no way to converse. As Rion drove them through the market, Lucan peered out the window, careful not to show his face, especially when he spotted a platoon of soldiers marching in from the opposite direction. "I'd love to know how Rion just happened to show up at the right time and place to offer us a ride."

"If Rion hadn't warned us the military was after us, we would never have made it out of the nest. Now he's rescued us again. Surely that means he's on our side."

Lucan didn't reply. He had a feeling Rion was on Rion's side. Whether he was with them or against them remained to be seen.

Rion turned off the main road into a private driveway. The stately trees and well-trimmed shrubs created an oasis of calm that contrasted with the busy market they'd just left. The splashing sounds of the fountains that lined the drive added to the serenity.

When Rion stopped at an imposing solid steel gate engraved with a dragon, wings unfurled in full flight, Cael looked back and gasped. "Soldiers are violating the sanctuary. They're following us."

Apparently Brennon was daring to risk the Elders' displeasure. Was he growing more desperate? Or did he simply not fear what the public thought?

Rion tipped his hat and gestured for them to exit the carriage. Cael hurried toward a kiosk by the gate and stepped inside. Lucan turned to Rion. "What's happening at Avalon?"

He watched Cael lean into a monitor, give her retinal scan, and return to his side. Reacting to the scan, the gates swung wide.

Rion frowned. "The military have opened a few feet of subterranean tunnel. They've found nothing."

"The sinkhole?" Cael asked.

"Its edges are crumbling faster than ever. We're running out of time."

Behind them, soldiers pounded down the long drive and shouted for them to freeze. Rion clapped Lucan on the shoulder, his expression serious. "Go."

They still had a few seconds before the soldiers were in weapon range. "Who are you working for?" Lucan asked.

Rion grinned. "I'm on General Brennon's payroll." Then his smile faded, and he turned toward Cael. "And Lady Cael, you need to beware of a traitor." He pressed a blaster into Lucan's hand. "Watch out for the Elder."

"HALT." THE APPROACHING soldiers aimed their weapons at Cael and Lucan.

"Go." Lucan shoved her through the gate, slipping in after her seconds before the gate closed behind them.

A white-robed assistant waited on the other side. "Do you seek entrance, my lady?"

"We do." Cael stepped forward, her hearts slamming her rib cage. It wasn't fear of being shot that had her nerves tense, but Rion's warning that an Elder might betray her.

"Please come with me." The assistant led Lucan and Cael over a winding path, the stones worn smooth over the years by the feet of believers who'd come to the retreat seeking prayer or solace. Wind chimes tinkled in the breeze. The tree fronds rustled, and the scent of flowers soothed Cael's ragged nerves. Darkness had fallen, but soft lighting illuminated the landscape, creating an aura of peace and encouraging prayer.

The path ended at an open pavilion. Cael and Lucan followed their guide up the stairs and onto a platform furnished simply with benches and cushions.

"My lady." The assistant bowed. "Please wait here and help yourself to refreshments." He indicated a tray of pastries, meat, and cheese on a nearby bench. In addition, two bottles of blue wine nestled in a silver bucket filled with ice.

"Thank you."

The assistant left, and Cael removed her hat and scarf, tossed her sunglasses onto the table. "The Elders often eat outside, but it's odd we've been left here instead of being ushered to the Great Hall to greet everyone at once."

"Something's wrong," Lucan sighed. After sniffing a pastry, he popped it into his mouth.

"Glad to see your worries haven't affected your appetite."

"I'm starving—all the time." He gazed at her as if she were a tasty morsel and held out the tray. She took a piece of cheese.

Suddenly, Lucan stopped eating and, for no reason she could understand, his lower jaw dropped and his eyes widened.

"What is it?" she asked, looking behind her.

"I see purple marks at your neck."

"Yes?"

"I see your eyelashes. And the tiny mole by your ear."

"And?" She dropped her gaze, her hearts beginning to beat faster as he boldly raked his gaze over her.

"I'm not wearing my prescription glasses." Lucan reached up to his eyes in wonder and stared across the garden. "How is it that I can see tiny lichens growing in the rock crevices over a hundred feet away?" He sniffed. "And not only can I smell the meat in this pastry, I can differentiate the individual ingredients in the sauce, each as distinct as if I'd tasted them one by one."

Her hearts fluttered again, but this time the sensation she felt was dread, not excitement.

He spread his arms and lifted his gaze to the sky. "I can measure the quantity of moisture in the air, feel the texture of every thread in the cloth against my body."

"Maybe you're just exhilarated, your senses height-ened because of the danger."

"My God . . . I can hear Merlin breathe." With one glance he spied the owl, perched in a nearby branch. Lucan pinned her with a hard look. "What's going on?"

"I don't know." But she feared she did, although the thoughts racing through her mind chilled her blood.

"I wish I had a mirror to see if I look as different as I

feel." Lucan narrowed his eyes. "What kind of medicine did you give me while I was unconscious?"

"I didn't give you medicine."

"Then how did I heal so quickly?"

"I cleaned your wounds. I stopped the bleeding. You were very weak. Your body temperature was low. You'd lost so much blood." Stomach churning, she set down her half-eaten slice of cheese. "I gave you a transfusion."

"Your blood?"

She nodded, chewed on her lower lip, and stole a look at him.

The color washed out of his face. "You gave me *dragonblood?*"

She folded her arms across her chest. "I've told you this before."

His face was stony with anger. "But I didn't know then that you could morph into a dragon, and you didn't explain the significance . . . that you've altered my DNA." He clenched his hands into fists. "You could have killed me."

She grimaced. "There wasn't much life left in you to lose. You were dying."

He scowled at her, his frustration evident. "Why didn't you just take me to a medical center?"

She unfolded her arms and stroked her necklace. "Because when I'm a dragon, I think like a dragon. We were being hunted by the military. Shot at. Instinct took over, and I flew to the nest as fast as I could."

He leaned against a tree trunk and crossed his ankles, but there was nothing casual about his smoldering fury. "So what's going to happen to me?"

His anger pounded her until her temples throbbed. "I don't know," she said, her voice a pained whisper.

"You don't know?" He shook his head. "My entire body's changing."

She stepped toward him and spread her hands in entreaty. "Are seeing and smelling better and healing faster such bad things?"

He gave her a long, heated look. "When we made love, I couldn't control myself. Was that because of the dragonblood?"

"It's possible." Goddess help her. She went icy cold, then flushed hot.

At her admission that the dragonblood might have made him lose control, his nostrils flared. She sensed him reining in hard on his anger. "Will I grow wings? Will I breathe fire?"

As far as she was concerned, he was already breathing fire. His anger and sexuality blasted her. Her scales tingled. But after one burst of pulse-jarring emotion, he had snapped up a barrier that blocked her from reading emotions.

"I couldn't let you die." She trembled from the aftereffects of his roiling emotions. "But the Elders never told me what would happen if . . ."

A muscle in his jaw ticked. The cords of his neck tensed. "You really don't have any idea what you did to my genetic code, do you?"

She raised her chin. "As far as I know, no dragonshaper has ever given another person blood. That's one of the reasons I wanted to speak with the Elders. But they aren't going to be happy that I broke their most sacred taboo."

Radiating tension, he advanced on her until they were only inches apart. He lifted her chin with his fingertips, forcing her to look into his unfathomable eyes. "What kind of penalty will you suffer for breaking the taboo?"

"I don't know." He was furious with her. Could he truly be worried about her safety? "This is new territory for me, too." She didn't mention that the Elders had warned her that dragons who broke taboos didn't live long. Too often, believers rose up and killed them.

He smoothed a lock of hair behind her ear. "We don't need to tell anyone that you gave me your blood."

Once again he was protecting her, and his generosity shocked her. "But the Elders might have answers about what's happening to you."

"I don't want to put you at risk to get me answers."

Her communicator hummed. She looked down. "It's Rion."

Rion's voice came over the speaker. "The military's now blaming you and Lucan for Sir Shaw's murder."

"We're being accused of murder?" Cael locked gazes with Lucan, so stunned she felt faint. "That's crazy."

Lucan lifted an eyebrow. "Why are you so surprised?"

Suddenly she grew lightheaded and nearly dropped the communicator from her trembling hand. "People won't believe that I'm a murderer."

Rion spoke quickly. "Brennon has proof. Yours and Lucan's fingerprints are all over the knife they found in Shaw's back."

"We can explain," Cael argued, her stomach queasy. She was a physician. She'd taken sacred vows to cure, to aide, to heal. It was an offense against the Goddess for her to kill.

"Perhaps putting doubts about you into people's minds is Brennon's primary goal," Rion suggested.

"But why would anyone . . ."

"You're a powerful woman," Lucan agreed with Rion. "Discrediting you gives you less respect, less power. If you speak publicly about Avalon or the Grail, no one's going to care about a murderer's opinion."

Cael frowned. "We have to clear our names. And since *we* didn't murder Shaw, we need to find out who did."

Rion spoke fast. "We have to meet and talk."

"What's wrong with right now?" Lucan was clearly frustrated with so many questions and so few answers.

The line went dead. Cael looked at Lucan. "Should I call back?"

Lucan shook his head. "He might have unexpected company. Our call might put him in danger."

"So now you think he's on our side?"

"Although he's admitted to being on Brennon's payroll, I think he's helping us. Why is the question."

Cael slipped her communicator back into her pocket. "We're not murderers. I'll go down fighting before I allow this defamation."

Lucan gave her a long, level look. "Proving our innocence may not be possible."

The Goddess demands punishment for breaking a taboo. And the Elders are the keepers of the law.

—THE ELDERS

9

The Elder's assistant returned. "Elder Benoit will see you now. Come with me, please."

Cael nodded, her face pale, her eyes large and darkly luminous. When she became passionate or upset, the purple in her irises expanded. Right now, only a tiny sliver of white remained.

Her alien biology should have alarmed him, but Lucan found it sexy as hell. He cursed and reminded himself that he'd be leaving Pendragon after he found the Grail. He needed to keep his distance, keep his focus.

After leaving the pavilion, they followed the Elder's assistant along the stone pathway through a stand of ancient evergreens. Dumaro's crescent had risen, and as they left the shadow of the trees, the planet lighted the vista that opened before them. The familiarity of the image took Lucan's breath away. Across a wide meadow in the center of an island in a serene lake stood the main building of the Elders' compound. Constructed of native stone, its high crenellated walls and soaring towers bedecked with dragon pennants could have been Cadbury Castle itself. The trio took the path across the meadow to a stone bridge that crossed the lake and led to the open gates of the castle.

After they passed through the massive gates, Lucan stopped to take in the view before him. The Great Hall stood opposite the gate in a large courtyard that in medieval times on Earth would have housed stables, livestock, and the hovels of peasants. In the Elders' retreat, however, the open space was a well-tended, tranquil garden, constructed around a marble fountain. Small individual dwellings nestled against the interior walls.

The assistant led them into a cozy one-room building nearest the Great Hall. The interior was dimly lighted and sparsely furnished, with an intricate screen hiding what Lucan assumed was a sleeping area.

The assistant withdrew, and a tiny woman with many wrinkles and sharp, sparkling gray eyes motioned Cael and Lucan to cushions before the fireplace, where a blazing fire chased the night chill from the room.

The old woman spoke in a cordial but fragile voice. "Greetings, Lady Cael."

"And you, my favorite Elder." Cael dipped her head. "I'd like to present my friend Lucan Roarke."

He bowed his head.

Elder Benoit walked with a cane, and her hands trembled. Her pale gray skin and physical infirmity indicated she was not long for this world.

"Friends are very dear to a dragonshaper," the Elder instructed him. "See that you don't disappoint my lady."

Benoit acted like a proud grandmamma defending her grandchild. For Cael to inspire that kind of trust, love, and loyalty made him proud. He met Elder Benoit's gaze with deference.

Cael was quick to praise him. "Without Lucan, I'd have

died along with the others in the lab. He convinced me we would survive. But now we've been framed for arson and murder."

"So I've been told," the Elder said. "Have you any idea why?"

"Perhaps the military covet our success." Cael pursed her lips, her eyes thoughtful. "Even if we don't find the Grail, Avalon promises to reveal untold history and possible technological advances. Just the ability to duplicate that shield could change the balance of power on Pendragon."

"How?" the Elder asked.

"It could make the military invincible," Lucan explained. "Right now the military defends this moon and also has police authority, yet it still relies on government funding. But if the military can duplicate the shield, they could sell the technology and become independent of the government."

"And if the Grail is there," Cael added, "can you imagine the wealth and power that could be gained by owning it? Who wouldn't want a shield against death?"

Elder Benoit folded her trembling hands into the sleeves of her tunic. "So whom do you suspect?"

"Everyone," Cael said. "The military, especially General Brennon, and possibly Sir Quentin."

"Everyone?" The Elder contemplated Lucan with a raised eyebrow.

He returned Elder Benoit's steady gaze. "When I went into the lab to look for survivors, I could have killed Shaw—"

"But you didn't," Cael said. "You were with me when the fire started. We watched the military feed the flames together." She frowned at him, and her defense warmed his heart. But if Cael ever found out who he really was and that his real intention was to take the Grail to Earth, she'd have every right to feel betrayed.

"Please," the Elder said warmly. "Let's sit. Have some tea."

"Thank you." Cael helped the older woman onto a cushion, then took her own seat beside a square low table. Lucan sat next to her. The Elder poured the fragrant tea, and a rich aroma filled the air.

"Elder Benoit, why are you greeting us here," Cael asked, "instead of the Great Hall?"

"It shames me to admit that not all the Elders believe in you as I do."

Lucan sat up straighter. The Elder Benoit had couched her words in gentle language, but if there was dissent here, perhaps Rion's prediction of a traitor among the Elders was true.

Cael set down her tea. "Then perhaps it's best we speak in private, esteemed Elder, for I have broken—"

"Don't say anything else," Lucan interrupted. As much as he needed to know if her blood transfusion would have dire consequences, he refused to allow her to put herself at risk for that information. "We agreed—"

"I trust Elder Benoit as much as I trust you," Cael countered, her voice strong and certain.

Lucan couldn't tell her that her trust in him wasn't warranted, not without giving away his cover. And if she was wrong about him, she could be wrong about Elder Benoit. "It's not necessary to—"

"Let me decide what's necessary." Cael turned to Elder Benoit. "The military shot us down. Lucan was badly injured. To save his life, I gave him my blood."

Elder Benoit choked on her tea. Coughing and sputtering, she raised a napkin to her pale lips. "By the Goddess, child, what have you done?"

"That's one reason I came." Cael's voice shook with emotion. "I hoped you could tell us what's going to happen to him."

"You broke our most sacred law." Tears brimmed in Elder Benoit's eyes.

"What's going to happen to Lady Cael?" Lucan asked.

"She ignored a sacred taboo." Agitated, the Elder used her cane to shove to her feet. "I don't know if I can save her."

"Save her?" Stomach knotting, Lucan looked from Cael to the Elder. "What are you talking about?"

A tear traveled through the wrinkles in Elder Benoit's face. "According to ancient law, any dragonshaper who shares blood will be executed. Anyone who accepts that blood will also be executed."

"And I will be the executioner." Another Elder in long robes stepped from behind the screen and raised a weapon at the three of them.

Lucan edged his hand toward the blaster Rion had given him.

"No, Selick." Elder Benoit spoke calmly, like a teacher admonishing a child who had spoken out of turn in class.

Elder Selick's eyes didn't flicker. "They've blasphemed against the Goddess."

Selick adjusted his stance, aimed at Cael. Three things happened simultaneously. Lucan lunged to cover Cael. Selick fired. And Elder Benoit stepped forward, placing her frail body between Lucan and Cael and the blast.

Selick ignored Lady Benoit as she slumped to the floor. Again he targeted Cael. Before he could shoot again, Lucan fired at Selick, and the man dropped.

Cael crawled out from under Lucan and over to Elder Benoit, and her eyes widened in horror. "Esteemed Elder?"

The woman smiled and took Cael's hand. "I'm still here, child."

Cael gently cradled the woman who had been so kind to her. Her wound was massive. "I'm sorry. We'll get you to a medical center."

"I'm dying. I was already dying, child. It's my time to go to the Goddess." Benoit squeezed Cael's hand tight. "Remember to follow the green light."

"Green light?" Lucan asked.

Cael shook her head in confusion, and tears filled her eyes.

"Remember." Elder Benoit closed her eyes.

"Goddess, forgive me." Cael's voice was heavy with grief, and Lucan's heart ached for her.

"She was a very brave lady. And she would want you to flee."

"Flee?"

He pointed to the Elder Benoit and Selick. "You can be sure we'll be blamed for these murders, too." He tugged her to her feet. "We have to go."

"I must say the sacred prayers for her."

"She wouldn't want you captured. Someone's going to investigate those shots. We have to get out of here."

Cael nodded and let out a strangled sob. In the next instant her sob became a roar, and Cael dragonshaped, collapsing the building around them.

Lucan climbed onto her back, pulled the harness out of their pack, and buckled it over her shoulders. Then she spread her huge wings and took to the air.

He expected to see a clear moonlit sky. He expected the

night air and rushing wind to calm his racing heart. What he hadn't expected was a fleet of airships clearing a distant mountaintop, headed directly for the retreat.

The full squad of military ships bearing down on the city was the equivalent of a declaration of war. And Lucan and Cael were the enemy. Fortunately, the ships couldn't get a visual on Cael from such a distance, but their radar might.

Get us out of here.

Merlin flew into position on her wingtip, and Cael beat her wings hard and fast. Lucan hunched his body low against hers and stayed streamlined, clinging to the harness.

Where are you taking us?

Undernest.

She sent an image of a roaring waterfall, which made no sense to Lucan, but he had to trust her, trust her dragon instincts. He had no other choice.

Faster.

Hang on. She headed straight for the mountains, flying into a pass, then spiraling skyward on an updraft. She lost the skimmers in pursuit, and for the next hour, he saw no sign of them.

Then, suddenly, skimmers flew out of a valley below.

Cael banked hard, before nose-diving straight down. His thighs lost contact with her back. His body floated as if defying gravity, but he clung to the spikes on her neck as well as the harness, certain each breath would be his last. At this speed, even landing in a snow bank would be fatal.

They plunged into a deep fog bank, and he didn't dare ask if her dragon eyes could see. Or maybe she had built-in radar. Whatever she used to navigate, she didn't need distractions.

Lucan's left hand slipped off the harness, leaving him dangling by one arm. He gritted his teeth. Reminded himself to breathe. *At least death will be quick.*

I thought you liked speed.

I do when I'm the one flying.

She pulled out of the dive so gently that he floated onto her back, and she leveled out her flight with a skill no starship captain could emulate. Together, Merlin, the dragon, and Lucan spiraled downward.

The fog cleared, and Lucan saw with his new, sharp eyesight that the landscape had changed. Trees actually grew in this desolate place. Bushes and shrubs clung to dark, rocky crevices. And ahead, the mother of all waterfalls cascaded down the mountain, falling to a deep blue-green ribbon of river miles below.

The machines overhead grew louder, and Cael flew toward the waterfall. The airships were about to clear the summit.

Hold on.

That one thought was his only warning before she flew straight toward the thundering waterfall. If she didn't turn aside soon, they would hit the water and the cliff behind it dead-on.

Turn, he demanded.

No. Her answer was serene, as if she were totally unaware of the danger.

There's too much water. That cascade would tear her apart.

She failed to heed him, and the roar of the water matched the roaring in his head. Hunkering down, he plastered his body to her slippery shoulders and hung on for dear life.

To acknowledge ignorance is the beginning of knowledge.

—MERLIN

10

Cael's dragon girth expanded, and Lucan widened his legs. A rumble sounded, and fire shot from her throat. She aimed flames directly at the falling water, and when they struck, it turned to vapor, allowing them to fly straight into an air pocket. The super-heated air might have burned him, except they shot through so quickly that the short blast of heat had little time to register on his cold flesh.

He hadn't even gotten wet. *Amazing.* She'd heated the water to a gas, vaporized it so they could pass through—and flown into an enormous cave. Cael flapped her huge wings, then set down gently. Merlin circled once and flew deeper into the cave.

Lucan slid from Cael's back, surprised to find the rocky floor warm beneath his feet. Yards away, he spied the source of the warmth, bubbling blue thermal pools that puffed steam into the air. Beside him, Cael changed into her human shape, and he unpacked her extra clothing and shoes and handed them to her.

"Did the ships clear the summit before we flew through the water?" she asked.

He shook his head. "They didn't see us, but they might pick us up on their instruments."

"The cave is laced with platinum, and the metal will stop them from finding us. With the steep peaks in this mountain range, they won't set down to search on foot. We should be safe here. At least for a while."

The combination of their near-death experience at the retreat, the reckless dive off the mountain, the wild ride on Cael's back, and the almost fatal collision with the waterfall had his adrenaline pumping, his pulse ratcheted way too high.

And, despite his best efforts, the rush of their near-death experience had shot his libido into overdrive. He wanted to sling her over his shoulder and take her to bed. And since a bed wasn't handy, any surface would do. Oh, yeah, the image of ripping off her clothes, backing her against the cave wall, and pumping into her was almost irresistible.

Thank God, she couldn't read his mind. But she emitted a soft groan of pain. Obviously, she was sensing his sexual hunger. Turning away from Cael, he forced himself to concentrate on their surroundings. Holes in the roof, covered by glacial ice, filtered natural lighting inside the cave, and he saw evidence of an old campfire, ashes surrounded by stones, and an assortment of animal bones in a fire pit. At the back of the cave, steam rose from the heated water.

Lucan removed his fur cloak, attempted to tamp down his dragon-sized desire, and finally risked a glance in Cael's direction. Now dressed, she'd dropped to a sitting position on the stone floor. Her head drooped as if she hadn't the strength to hold it up.

"Are you all right?" She looked so fragile, the polar opposite of her powerful dragon persona. Watching her mentor die had been terrible for her, and he longed to take her into his arms. But he'd comforted her once before, and he'd barely been able to control his desire. He knew if he touched her now, he wouldn't stop.

"Flying here expended a lot of energy. I just need"—she raised her head and looked at him as if she felt the lust coursing through him—"to rest." She spoke slowly and wearily dropped her head onto her knees.

Damn it. Not again. He was hard as a rock. And his need was bombarding her. Cael was exhausted, and guilt stabbed him for battering her with his emotions. He locked them down tight. "There's a price you pay every time you change shape, isn't there?" he guessed. "That takes energy, too."

"Yes." Her voice was barely louder than a whisper.

"How long will it take . . ." He hated to press her. But the idea of staying here alone with her, with nothing to distract him from comforting her again, was already making him break into a sweat.

"Not long. Maybe a day or two."

A day or two. He didn't think he could last the hour. His blood was boiling. He had to get away. He dropped the pack with the thermos beside her. "Eat. Drink some water."

"Thanks." She removed a compass, pen and paper, matches, a knife, and finally the thermos, which she emptied.

He thought she would dig into the pack for food, but instead she pulled it toward her and used it for a pillow. Seconds after closing her eyes, her breathing evened out. She'd fallen asleep, leaving him alone . . . with his lust.

Since the temptation to wake her would be too great if he stayed, Lucan took the thermos, pen, and paper, and set off to explore. He headed for the waterfall, the nearest source of moving water. He drank deeply from the mountain stream, appreciating the cool liquid on his parched throat, refilled the thermos, and moved on, wandering through the cave system, sketching the layout as he went. A large cave like this could go on for miles, and his map would ensure he could find his way back to Cael.

On Earth, prehistoric man had lived in caves like these. Between the fresh water supply, the warmth, and high ceilings, this cave would have made a perfect communal shelter as long as the local food supply could support them. Curious if he might find signs of ancient Dragonians, Lucan walked through the cave, his archeologist's keen eye in search of traces of man.

Merlin swooped down, almost as if keeping him company. The owl flew from ledge to ledge, watching his progress.

When Lucan found no shards of pottery, old bones, or even blackened rocks from prehistoric campfires, he moved deeper into the cave. He chose a wide and level tunnel at random but soon hit a dead end. Turning back, he spied Merlin waiting at the entrance.

Lucan admired the sheer beauty of the cave system, but he was no geologist. Rocks didn't hold the same fascination and mystery as ancient peoples. "Perhaps this cave's too remote from food sources. Or too far from mountain passes or old trade routes," he muttered.

Merlin blinked and flew away. Lucan shrugged the tension out of his shoulders. Riding on Cael's back had strained muscles in his neck and legs. Walking to stretch out the knots did double duty. It took him farther from the temptation of Cael and allowed his abused muscles to recover.

Lucan found another exit in the cave and risked a glance outside. Ships flew overhead, clearly in search mode. Aware the airships might have heat-detection devices that could target his body temperature, he remained close to the rock walls that conducted heat from the hot springs. Taking stock of his surroundings, he spied a ledge that he could walk under for miles and remain mostly hidden if he wound his way out of the canyon.

Turning back into the cave, he caught sight of Merlin flying to a wall. At first Lucan thought the owl had just settled on another ledge. Yet as he turned the corner, he realized Merlin was perched outside a passageway he'd missed earlier.

Unlike most of the cave, which was well lit from above, this area was dim. He was about to turn back when a straight line in the rock caught his eye. In nature, very few configurations were straight. Not layers of rock, not crevices in ice, not trees.

With a kick of excitement, he strode forward, scrutinizing the stone wall. Had he found the Dragonian equivalent of a cave painting?

No. The line was part of an inscription that had been carved into the rock. Years of dust and debris had settled into the ancient image. Wishing he had a soft-bristled brush, he used his palms and then a fingertip to remove sediment. And as the first rune symbols came to light, Lucan's exhilaration grew.

The last bit of debris fell away, and his heart nearly stopped. These Pendragon runes were the exact same twig-like alphabet created by people who'd once lived in what was now Germany, Scandinavia, and Great Britain. On Earth the symbols were often related to the practices of Neolithic magic and shamans. And here on Pendragon, runes were clearly associated with earlier peoples.

"Merlin, look at this." He felt like dancing, pumping his fist.

This find verified his theory. Cael's necklace had been one of many clues suggesting the two planets shared a history, but since neither her necklace's age nor site of origin could be accurately ascertained, it wasn't verifiable, uncontestable scientific proof.

But geologists could date this wall. They could accurately and scientifically estimate the date of carving.

He'd done it. Just made the biggest find of his career. These runes were incontrovertible evidence that Pendragon and Earth shared a history.

Moving back several paces in order to read the runes, he shivered with excitement. Now if only his search would lead him to the Grail.

Merlin settled on a ledge above the inscription as Lucan read out loud.

Welcome, son of Adam.
Here I bequeath to you and your brothers of the
*   Round Table all of my kingdom.*
Beware the tribes and guard well my worlds all the
*   days of your lives.*
Retain for them all the laws that have been extant
*   in my days*
And all the good laws that were in Pendragon's
*   days.*
You have voyaged to Avalon to find the fairest of
*   prizes,*
A prize that will make your kingdom sound,

A prize that will make the world completely whole.
And when you return to your kingdom,
You will dwell among the Britons with surpassing delight.

Lucan rocked back on his heels, his jaw dropping in stunned amazement. Much of this inscription was similar to Layamon's Brut, one of the first major texts written on Earth in Middle English around the year 1200. Or had Layamon plagiarized this message from Pendragon, re-writing some of the words?

"Welcome, son of Adam" must surely refer to Adam and Eve, an Earth legend. It was almost as if this inscription was waiting for someone from Earth to find it. But how could that be?

The reference to "worlds" could be literal and refer to actual planets, or it could be figurative and allude to the physical and spiritual worlds. But the wording about coming to Avalon to find a prize seemed to refer to the Grail, especially with the reference to being "sound," a word the ancients used instead of healthy. But what excited him as much as the promised health was the word "Briton."

As far as Lucan knew, *Briton* was not a word on Pendragon.

Finding the poem sent shivers down his spine. It had been inscribed centuries ago. For *him.*

He shook off the ridiculous thought. Obviously, men had once traveled between Pendragon and Earth. If there were legends about Avalon on Earth, he shouldn't have been so shocked to find references to Briton on Pendragon.

Lucan copied the words to paper, but he also memorized them, branded them into his mind for later analysis. He was about to leave when a mark on the opposite wall caught his attention. Again he wiped away sand and dust to reveal yet another ancient carving. This time he couldn't read the writing, which was similar to Viking runes. Instinct kicked in and he carefully copied the message. Had he found one poem written in two different languages? Or had a second ancient civilization left their own legend?

Peeling off the sheet of paper, he folded it and stuffed it into his back pocket. He wasn't here to research Pendragon history.

He must get back to Avalon. Back to the Grail.

The High Priestess spreads protection over the believers like a dragon's wings.

—THE ELDERS

11

Cael opened her eyes to the crackle of a fire Lucan was building and the shrill sound of her communicator. Exhausted, she fumbled in her pack. "Hello, Nisco."

"Trelan's dead," her sister said.

"The investigator?" Cael hit the speaker button so Lucan could listen, too. "He's dead? What happened?"

Lucan moved away from the fire, and she could see concern—and anger—etched in his face.

"The official reports say he was shot while trespassing at a military installation, but I know he was in the city, with General Brennon."

"You believe that Brennon's involved in a cover-up?"

"Before he was murdered, Trelan sent me papers he'd stolen from Brennon's briefcase. You need to see them."

"Why? What's in them?"

"I'm not sure. It's some kind of formula."

"Brennon may have killed Trelan because of those papers," Lucan said, his eyes worried.

Cael's hand trembled. "Nisco, you need to be careful."

"Don't worry. I doubt Brennon has any idea his papers are even missing. Look, I have to go. Can you meet me at the residence?"

"Tomorrow." Cael shut the communicator and let it fall from her hand. Trelan was dead. And her sister might be in danger.

"It's not your fault that man died."

"I'm worried about Nisco. If Brennon killed Trelan over those papers, they must be important."

"What do you think he found?"

"Nisco mentioned a formula, so it could be a chemical weapon. Or it could be a coded communiqué." She sighed. "It could be about any high-level secret, Avalon, military plans, or their budget."

"Brennon's plan to frame us?"

"I have no idea. But if Brennon knows Nisco has them, he might—"

"None of this is your fault. And tomorrow, after Nisco gives you the papers, she should be safe."

Cael wanted to believe him. She wanted to let Lucan comfort her. But was it fair to ask him to take her into his arms when an embrace incited his lust?

Lucan crouched beside her, and now it was concern she felt radiating off him in waves. "Let me get you some water."

He retrieved the thermos, set it beside her, and then brought her a piece of *jasbit* from the pack. Her fingers touched his, and all the lust he'd repressed came barreling back. He tried to block his need. And failed.

Scalding and sensual, primitive and passionate, his desire cascaded over her. She ached for his touch and his kisses. And there was a hollow ache between her thighs that only he could fill. Between betrayals by the

Elders and the military hunting them, she probably wouldn't live long enough to regret another lapse in judgment.

She ate in silence, appreciating the food that filled her belly, the warmth and crackle of the fire. And the man who was doing his best not to look at her. Firelight played off the angles of Lucan's cheekbones, and the smudge of dirt on his temple only made him more attractive.

Arching her back, she stretched, a not-so-innocent move that lifted her breasts. Lucan followed her silhouette with his gaze like a starving man watching a juicy *jasbit* roast on the hearth. Never in her life had she played the seductress. She hadn't realized that drawing a man's attention could be so exhilarating.

Lucan's bold stare alone had her scales undulating. Her empathic senses picked up cracks in his icy surface. And below the ice was a steaming core.

"Did you eat?" She kept her voice low and husky.

He shook his head, a muscle in his tightly clenched jaws ticking. "You need food more than I do."

She held out a chunk of *jasbit*. "There's no need for either of us to go hungry. I can hunt more prey. In this altitude, fresh meat is plentiful."

"We can't go outside. Those ships are still overhead and flying a search pattern."

"These airships will be out of fuel soon and have to report to their base. Eat." She held a piece out to him again and licked a bit of sauce from her lip.

He stared at her mouth, his eyes fierce. She chewed and swallowed, then licked her finger. Feminine instincts took over, and she licked a second fingertip.

Again he shook his head. "I'm fine." But his voice had grown tense. A muscle pulsed in his neck. Lucan was wound tighter than a compressed spring. When she raised a skeptical eyebrow, he repeated, "I'm fine."

Stubborn man. "There's an ice cave down that tunnel." She pointed toward one side of the cave. "I've stored emergency provisions here, too." Cael had used this cave after she'd pleaded her case to become a healer and had to wait on the government's decision. And she'd come here after she'd learned that Jaylon's last treatment had failed. The cave was a place to rest, to regroup. A place where she could be herself. "We could hole up in this cave for weeks and not go hungry . . . for food."

He frowned as if he couldn't quite believe she'd just made a sexual innuendo. Ah, to think she'd been so stuffy that he couldn't even imagine her as a sensual woman.

That was going to change. Cael was done playing by other people's rules, rules that she now realized had done nothing but keep her isolated. And now, because of that isolation, no one knew her well enough to realize that she'd never set the lab on fire, never kill a human being.

Lucan accepted the food she offered him, but he moved to the other side of the fire. "Why do you store provisions in so many different places?"

She'd let him have his distance for the moment, but not for long.

"Trusted Elders taught me to prepare myself for love or hate."

"Love or hate?" He frowned, stopped eating, and stared into the fire. "Elders taught you to make love?"

"I'm not talking about pairing."

The flames reflected in his blue eyes. "I don't understand."

She twirled a lock of hair around her finger. "During ancient times, dragons weren't understood. People feared the dragon would burn them and eat human flesh. Perhaps some of my ancestors actually resorted to cannibalism. I don't know for certain. Legends tell of hunters stalking the dragon. But every time they killed a dragon, another was born, so it was impossible to rid Pendragon of us."

"This genetic anomaly just pops up at random in the general population?" His gave was riveted on her finger playing with her hair.

"Yes." She took a sip of water and saw his gaze drift back to her lips. "No one knows which family will have a dragon child born into it. It's considered a great honor. In Carlane, a residence has been set aside for me to live in luxury. I'm honored—but separate. But my dragon ancestors—I call them that although they aren't direct genetic links to me—worked hard to gain the people's love and respect. In the past, dragonshapers were blamed for solar eclipses, droughts, wars, and sickness. It's not impossible that war could break out again and modern opinions could revert back to primitive times. So I've prepared for . . . whatever may happen. But I have to tell you that I never thought I would be hunted for murder."

"Your dragon guardians, do they know about this cave?" he asked, his gaze drawn repeatedly to her mouth and fingers.

"No. The Elders instructed me to trust no one. Not even them."

"Why?"

"There was once an ancient king who coveted not only political power, but spiritual power. Knowing that if he could capture the High Priestess, he could force her to do his will, he hatched a terrible plan and married his daughter to an Elder to learn dragonshaper secrets."

"And the Elder betrayed the High Priestess?" he guessed.

"The Elder revealed that the best way to weaken a dragon was to prevent her from feeding on platinum. The king used this ill-gotten knowledge to capture the dragon-shaper, and then he placed her in a cage where she lived many, many years before she died." Cael shuddered at the thought and leaned toward the fire. Her tunic gaped open, revealing the tops of her breasts.

Lucan took in an eyeful. She sensed the desire seething through him, but then he turned away and fed more wood into the fire. "But you've shared your secrets and brought *me* here."

"I like you." She spoke the simple truth. The Dragonian language didn't have a word to define their relationship. Women and men might pair before a marriage ceremony, but since conception of a child often quickly followed the mating, it was accepted custom that the couple would soon formalize their relationship. Men usually took the pairings as seriously as women. But not Lucan.

He held her gaze. "I give you my word that I will never reveal this place to anyone."

From the emotions radiating from him, she sensed that he would keep that word—to the death, if necessary. In his own way, he was a man of honor.

She sighed. "Thank you."

She sipped from the thermos and offered it to him, but he shook his head, stood, and brushed off his hands. "I think I'll take another walk."

"Good idea." Cael shoved to her feet. "I need to work out the kinks." She raised her arms and stretched, rolling her head back, and when his gazed burned into her, she swallowed a smile.

She strolled by him, brushing her hand against him as she passed, and he jerked back as if he'd been burned. She let her gaze become an erotic caress. "Afraid my scales are contagious?"

"I'm not afraid of you," he practically growled.

"Good." She threaded her fingers into his.

He made a strange choking sound in his throat, and for a moment she feared he might pull away. But his fingers squeezed hers tightly, then relaxed. And the scarlet need in him frothed bright as the sun.

He spoke, his voice was calm and careful. Too careful. "I haven't explored this end of the cavern. While you slept, I forayed and refilled the thermos by the main waterfall."

She knew just the place to take him. "The first time I came here, I learned this old cave system has many tunnels carved out by either prehistoric glaciers or sea water from ancient times."

"Have you explored them all?"

She shook her head. "There are too many passages. I did find another smaller waterfall inside." And as its water ran over the rocks for thousands of years, it had carved out a series of pools. Thermal heat warmed the water, making a perfect bathing area. But she'd let him discover that surprise for himself.

She led him around a bend and stopped. Brilliant blue water cascaded from the highest pool before overflowing the stone edges and frothing into a series of seven pools, each one smaller and warmer than the last.

"Wow." His eyes sparkled with pleasure at the sight of the pink marbelite stone framing the glacial blue water. "This is amazing."

She grinned. "You haven't seen the best part." Within a moment, she'd stripped off her clothes.

He raked his eyes over every inch of her flesh, and her hearts flipped over in response. "Are you trying to distract me?"

"Is it working?" She brushed a lock of hair from her shoulder.

He tried to look away, but his eyes kept coming back to scan her naked body. "You're beautiful. But we can't . . ."

"We can."

She turned to reveal the delicate scales on her back, her butt. She'd noticed he liked to caress her there. Then she dived into the pool, letting the warm water sluice over her skin and praying the water would be too inviting for him to resist.

She held her breath, but the pool was too large to discern if he'd joined her. Under normal circumstances the water would have soothed her frazzled nerves and restored her spirits, but not now, not with this impossibly attractive man literally seething to have her—yet still holding himself back.

Undulating her body, she let her bottom surface before ducking back under. While she swam, she wondered if his new DNA required the nutrients the fall's platinum-seeded water would provide. Already the platinum was seeping into her skin, causing her to seethe with energy.

If he jumped in, would he feel it, too?

A sudden disturbance rippled through the water, but she didn't spot Lucan on the surface. Suddenly, she felt hands slide up her ankles. Lucan's hands. He settled his long fingers on her waist and lifted her out of the water. Then dropped her.

Tingling from the combination of his touch and the energizing platinum, she released a playful yelp as she fell back into the water. She plunged deeper, grabbed his ankles, and dragged him down with her. She expected a frisky reaction, but he took her hand and began to nibble up the inside of her arm. The wondrous sensation sizzled up the scales to her shoulder, down her spine, and over the insides of her legs.

She'd never felt anything so delicious, but she had to surface for air. With a kick, she came up and filled her lungs.

Lucan surfaced next to her, his blue eyes sparkling. "Do you know that your scales taste like nectar?"

"You like my taste?" His question shocked her, and she took a stroke backward. She yearned to play the seductress, but the passion burning in his eyes reminded her she was a novice at this game.

"You're exotic. Delicious." He sounded so serious, and she could feel him still trying to fight his attraction.

With the water trickling from his hair, over his brow, and down his cheek, he'd never looked so good. His chest and shoulders glistened, and the heat in his eyes made her stomach tighten in anticipation. "I care too much about you to mislead you. You understand . . . we can't always be together?"

"You've made that very clear." She dived back under the water and lightly nipped his right buttock. At her taunting play, he threw back his head and laughed.

And while she didn't hesitate to pinch and prod and scratch and bite while they frolicked, she wondered if she could truly seduce him.

Pool play was fun, but the water was too deep here to do more than frolic. She swam for the shallow end, hoping he would follow.

When he surged ahead, stood, and grabbed her by the

shoulders like some ancient warrior determined to take what he wanted, anticipation ripped through her.

Between the glint in his eyes, his sensual lips, and the determined jut of his jaw, he was all glistening hard male. Chiseled angles and bronze flesh, his body seemed more powerful than it had been just yesterday.

He lowered his head, and his lips claimed hers. His kiss was hot, hard, heavenly. Possessive.

Need broke over her, and she welcomed his lips, his heat. She needed to feel his skin against hers, but he held her firm, allowing only their mouths to touch. She struggled, but he held her easily, and kissed her thoroughly, maddeningly slowly, until she wanted to scream for him to let her feel his heat.

Each time the water rippled, her scales reacted, as if his mouth were nibbling and caressing them, stroking back and forth over the sensitive insides of her arms and legs.

Jerking back from the kiss, she caught the intensity in his eyes and gasped. "Hurry."

He shot her a charming smile. "As you wish, Priestess."

She expected him to pair with her right there, but he didn't. Instead, he lifted her until her breasts reached the surface and then sucked a nipple into his mouth. Sweet heaven. She thrashed in sheer joy. Between the constant ripple of the water from the swirling pool and his mouth on her breast, she writhed with pleasure.

Lucan's big hands captured her waist easily, and as he swirled his tongue over her nipple, she grew frantic. "Please. I need you now."

"Hush and enjoy."

He tilted her until she floated on her back, then parted her legs as he held on to her bottom. Leaning forward, he nibbled a trail of tiny bites on the inside of her thighs along her sensitive scales. Exquisite sensations tingled up her legs to her core. Tight, panting, tense, she tried to sit up. But his hands gave her bottom a squeeze and he kept her right where he wanted her.

Ah, how she longed for him. Wanted his lips to caress the most intimate folds of her flesh.

He couldn't possibly know how the churning water was teasing her, how his mouth was making her burn, how his fingers increased her need. A soft moan escaped her lips.

He teased his way from her ankle to her calf to her knee to her thigh and rubbed his slight beard over her sensitive flesh. He massaged with his fingertips. He tickled with his tongue. And as he finally closed in on her center, she lifted her hips to encourage him. But, as if he had no idea how much she needed him to touch her, he ignored the heat between her thighs.

"Damn you," she whispered.

He chuckled and nipped her ankle. When she flailed and tried to sit upright, he grabbed her buttocks and squeezed until she stilled.

"I like you like this," he murmured.

"Like what?"

"Needing me." His voice rumbled low and echoed over the water. "You're expecting me to kiss you."

She ground her teeth in frustration. "I'm expecting an entire universe more than a kiss."

He grazed her delicate flesh with the tip of one finger. "Greedy, dragonshaper."

"Why are we talking when I want you inside me?" she gasped.

He laughed, a low, sexy rumble. "I'm just getting started—"

"Just . . . getting . . . started?"

She scowled. He was burning bright with desire and his eagerness fed her own. Yet he was toying with her. Building her up, the delay increasing not just her anticipation, but her need, as if he were kindling a fire, carefully feeding the tiny embers until she burst into flames. And she sensed he would not be satisfied until she burned hotter than a supernova.

When he bit the tender flesh behind her knee, she thrashed. Again he squeezed her bottom, and the sting only drove her into a deeper frenzy. She clenched her fingers. Water rushed over her breasts, and she couldn't help but slip her hand between her thighs to ease the tension.

But his mouth beat her to the spot, and when he caressed her most sensitive place with his lips, she cried out and writhed against him.

His warm tongue thrust into her at the same time as his fingers. Heat radiated from her center outward, along her spine, down her legs and arms to her fingers and toes. But the wondrous sensations didn't stop there. The heat zigged and zagged through her until her muscles clenched, leaving her mindless.

Ready to burst. Just one more second . . . but damn him, he pulled back, leaving her panting.

Instead of giving her the ultimate pleasure, Lucan lifted her from the water and slung her over his shoulder. Trembling, head down, her bottom in the air as he carried her from the pool, she squirmed until his hand slid between her thighs.

His fingers teased and toyed but didn't satisfy her. "I think you've forgotten Jede's lesson, Princess."

"Priestess." Cael scowled. "What lesson?"

Lucan's tone was low and husky. "Be careful what you wish for."

12

I don't want to be careful. I want you inside me." Cael
felt Lucan's heart leap. Apparently he liked her being
so turned on she could barely stand to wait another
moment.

"You don't know what you're asking for."

"I may be inexperienced, but you're forgetting that
I'm a physician and understand fundamental biology."

"Fundamental?" His tone might have sounded amused,
but there was nothing amusing in the sudden coiled tension in his body. He was all sexy, dangerous, and hungry
male. Heat sizzled across her flesh, followed by a rush of
anticipation.

Lucan was taking control, and she found this erotic,
but she knew better than to say so. She realized he wanted
her to fight him—because that would give him the excuse
to demand more, to push harder, to ravish her.

And then she would get what she wanted. Him. Out of
control and totally primal. Totally raw.

So she squirmed again and pounded on his back with
a fist. When his hand slapped her bottom, she had to

swallow a moan of pleasure. Realizing she'd stopped resisting, she tried to bite his back. In response, he slid his fingertips over her clit.

"Oh . . . oh . . . ah," she cooed as he increased the pressure.

She scratched his back. And received another slap. But this time his fingers slipped between her cheeks. At the new sensation, she gasped. "By the . . . Goddess!"

He was touching her everywhere. And his clever fingers were relentless, stroking and teasing her most sensitive flesh, inciting her into a frenzy. She writhed against him, loving him, hating him, needing him inside her, barely aware of what she was saying. "More. More."

But he never gave her quite enough. "Darling, I have a surprise for you."

Before she could lift her head to see where he'd taken her, he tossed her into the air. That she never tightened a muscle was a measure of her trust. She knew instinctively he wouldn't drop her. But as she hit water with a splash, she sputtered and went under. When she surfaced, he'd already jumped into the pool.

She didn't understand him. She slapped her palms on the surface. "What the hell are we doing back here?"

He grinned. "Waiting . . . enhances the pleasure."

Before she could curse him, he was kissing her, heating her with his body.

The feeling of his wet, hot flesh against her skin had her wrapping her arms around his neck, pressing her chest against his, grinding her hips against him. And damn him, the embers burned hotter. His clean male scent, his flesh, his kiss caused a wild need to build higher, stronger, fiercer.

She bit his lip, hard enough to taste blood. He placed

an arm around her back, lifted her onto his hip, and dragged her over to the side. Laying her gently over the marbelite edge of the pool, he raised her bottom into the air, leaned over so his chest pressed against her back.

Finally. He was going to give her completion. She wriggled in anticipation. But he didn't plunge into her with powerful strokes. Instead he did the strangest thing. By the Goddess, he began to vibrate—every part of him.

What in the universe?

She peered over her shoulder. He shook so much that he actually flung the water droplets from his flesh. All of him was vibrating, even his sex.

She arched her back, tipping her bottom to him. "Now, please. Take me now."

"Like this?" he asked as he placed his vibrating sex between her legs. Not inside, where she ached so fiercely to have him, but right against her clit. And then he slid back and forth, the vibrations feeling so damn good. Delicious friction had her arching her back, wriggling.

"Harder," she pleaded.

His touch remained gentle, damn him. But the vibration was making her every muscle clench. Her breath came in deep, raw pants. She tried to squeeze her thighs together to add to the pressure, but he jammed his hips against her buttocks, bit her shoulder, and held her still. Open.

She was panting, writhing, out of her mind. "Lucan. Lucan. Lucan." His name on her lips bought her a nip on her neck. She tried to arch up again, but he denied her even that tiny movement. He kept vibrating, stoking a fire between her legs. And just when she was about to go up in flames, he placed the tip of his vibrating sex inside her.

"Fill me," she cried.

He gave her an inch. She almost sobbed in frustration.

The vibration was ratcheting her up from the inside. He was winding her so tight, she could think of nothing but her need. A need for more. More of *him.*

When he slid his hand around her hip and between her thighs and placed his fingertip on her center, the vibrations ripped through her. She was vibrating everywhere, the pleasure beating through her, thrumming through her blood, clouding her mind.

With a primal roar, he plunged deep into her. But he held perfectly still—except for the vibrations, which rumbled through her and his fingertip on her core that was oh so tender, too tender.

In a frenzy, she tried to lift her hips. The need for movement, for friction, was undeniable. But with his body covering her, his sex inside her, his skilled fingers playing between her thighs, she could do nothing. At his complete mercy, she took the pleasure, and more, then more . . . until she burst.

Her muscles contracted in spasms, and she screamed with the bliss. Wave after wave cascaded through her. Over her. Around her. And through it all, he didn't stop vibrating or stroking with his fingers until after she'd exploded, again and again.

When he lost control, he was fearsome. He seized her hips and plunged into her, the vibrations so intense, he swept her away with him once more.

She must have passed out from the intensity of the multiple pleasures, because when she opened her eyes, she was lying on her back beside the pool. Alone.

LUCAN SUPPOSED HE should have been grateful that he'd finally stopped vibrating. What the hell had happened to him? The sensation had come over him involuntarily, like a sweat breaking out over all his skin. Even now he marveled at the grip of such a powerful force. The intensity had been exquisite. Uncontrollable.

He grinned at the memory, but his smile faded as he wondered if joining with her could be somehow further changing his DNA. Her scent, her sweat glands, her voice, her touch could all serve as catalysts for change.

This time the lovemaking had been mind-blowing. More intense than even the last time. So much so that he wondered if joining with her could be causing him to mutate. He could feel a tingling on the insides of his wrists and arms—the same places Cael bore her scales.

He really shouldn't have made love to her again. But hell, what man could resist Cael? Her body was made for loving. Wild, strong, open to new sensations, she was his match in every way. Never had he made love with such passion. And the sensations . . . had been incredible. *She* had been incredible.

Irresistible.

He shot one longing glance back at the sleeping Cael. He drank in the sight of her, memorized the curve of her neck, the shade of her hair, the sweet hollow on her neck. He would keep those memories. Always.

Lucan picked his way along the pool's edge deep in thought. He had to find a way back to Avalon. But with the military hunting them and framing them for murder, taking Cael with him would only put her in more danger. She'd implied she had more caves to hide in and would surely be safer in these mountains than with him. If he went back to Avalon, he could find a way to clear her name.

Lucan returned to the fire pit, stoked the embers, and

added more wood. He dressed and took the coat she'd given him and sheathed a knife in his belt. He left her the pack and remaining meat.

Cael would be fine. She was better equipped to survive in these mountains than he was. She was familiar with the terrain, could hide out, and could communicate with the outside world if she wished.

Leaving her was a sound decision. He headed from the cave but couldn't stop repeatedly glancing over his shoulder, searching for one last glimpse of Cael.

But once he stood behind the curtain of water that shielded the cave from the world, he refused to look back again. Leaving her was best. For both of them. And if his heart was heavy, he only had to recall the terrible situation on Earth and that it was only a matter of time before the sinkhole swallowed Avalon. No matter the risk, he must head back to Avalon and the Grail.

Only those of good heart can see beyond the veil that separates the worlds.

— THE LADY OF THE LAKE

13

Lucan had been hiking for nearly three hours along the hidden ledge that ran alongside the mountain. The overhead droning of military ships had finally stopped. As Cael had predicted, they'd left the area. He took advantage of their absence to cross an open valley divided by a meandering stream, an offshoot of the waterfall. Game here was plentiful, but he didn't stop to hunt.

He wasn't in the mood to eat. Abandoning Cael was going to hurt her, and the last thing he'd wanted was to add to her pain or loneliness. An owl was no substitute for human companionship. And though she was accustomed to surviving alone in the wilderness, she could fall and turn an ankle or break a bone.

For the hundredth time, he told himself she'd be fine. She was safer out here than where he was going.

He threaded his way along the stream, trying to shake the guilt that gnawed away at him. He would have preferred to follow the main river from the waterfall, since it would likely lead to civilization. But the terrain alongside the waterfall had been too steep to navigate without climbing gear, and he'd needed to hide from pursuit, so he'd used the ledge's cover to head west.

But he should have been going south, straight back to Avalon.

He was debating whether to change direction and leave the stream when his spine quivered. Not the full-fledged vibration he'd felt when he'd made love to Cael, but a flutter that unnerved him.

He kneeled by the stream and drank deeply. At the fluttering whisper of wings fanning air, he spun and drew his knife. Cael in dragon form landed nimbly several feet away, her owl hovering overhead. Despite her bulk, she landed with the grace of a much smaller animal.

She humanshaped and removed the pack from her back. It was impossible for him not to look at her naked beauty, her sculpted curves, her long legs, her graceful neck. She put on her clothes without saying a word, but her actions were too deliberate for him not to recognize her fury.

He sheathed the knife and folded his arms across his chest. "Why did you follow me?"

"Rion called. The military has soldiers stationed between here and Avalon. If you try to get through, they'll catch you."

"And you came to warn me."

"Rion insisted that I tell you," she admitted.

She made it sound as if she'd come after Lucan only because of Rion. That she wanted him to think she cared so little about his safety . . . hurt. Especially after she'd been so honest with him, but he deserved whatever she threw at him. He regretted that he'd violated her trust, wished he could have handled things differently. "I'll head east before going south. Try and slip through one of the border towns."

"Did I ask your plans?" Her icy tone made him feel like a heel.

"Are you all right?" he asked gently.

"You told me we couldn't always be together. But I thought you would at least say good-bye." She couldn't even look at him as she said the words.

Before he could stop himself, he stepped forward and wrapped his arm around her. She allowed him to hold her for a heartbeat, then inched away until they were no longer touching.

"I thought a clean break would be better."

She sighed and spoke sadly. "Believe it or not, the world doesn't revolve around you."

As if he hadn't felt bad enough, she sank to the ground and bowed her head, but not before he glimpsed her tears. "Darling—"

"Don't."

The endearment had slipped from his lips before he could think better of it. He cleared his throat. "What's happened?"

"Nisco called again. She thinks someone's following her."

"She might be mistaken."

"I should never have asked her to help."

"You can't do everything alone. Family help one another."

"I can't even do that." Frustration caused her shoulders to sag. "Nisco also told me that Jaylon . . . he's . . . dying." Sorrow clouded her eyes and made her voice weary. "I promised to bring him the Grail, and I promised to see him. But with Avalon shut down, and me accused of murder . . ."

"Is there anything *I* can do?"

"You can go on your merry way," she said, the fire back in her eyes. "I'll figure out something. I always do."

If anger at him got her through the day, he could live with that. In fact, she could heap all the blame she wanted on him if doing so chased the grief from her eyes.

"Wait. There's more I need to tell you." She spat out the words, making it very clear that she didn't like playing intermediary.

"Another request from Rion?"

She shook her head. "Sir Quentin left a message on my communicator. General Brennon's put him in charge of Avalon. They need your expertise and are willing to talk to the prosecutor about reducing the charges against you if you cooperate." She spoke in a clipped, frigid voice. The brief flicker of anger had left her irises dark, huge and purple, showing just a tiny crescent of white that he still found sexy as hell.

He frowned. "Why would Quentin need my—?"

"Apparently Brennon found another inscription and another shield inside Avalon. With the ground on the verge of collapse, time is of the essence."

"Either Brennon needs me to translate," Lucan replied, "or it's a trap and, if I go, they'll arrest me."

She scowled. "Why are you so suspicious of everyone and everything?"

"Because being falsely accused of murder has that effect on me." Because he hadn't been born on Pendragon. Because he suspected that someone was manipulating them. Because his almost overwhelming need to make love to her scared the hell out of him. Because if the sinkhole swallowed Avalon and he failed to find the Grail, humanity on Earth would become extinct. If he'd been up-front with her, she could have taken her pick—but of course he couldn't tell her the truth.

"I was taught to think of more than one possibility," he said. "It's a practice that works well in the scientific community." And it had kept him alive ten times over. In his experience, things were rarely what they seemed on the surface.

Since the news of another inscription could have been fabricated to bring him out of hiding, he wasn't about to walk back into the military's hands—at least not without investigating first. He hadn't forgotten the fire or being shot out of the sky or the attack from Brennon's men in the market.

Cael braided her hair and clipped the end, a look that emphasized her gorgeous bone structure. "If you still want to meet in secret with Rion, he's willing."

Interesting. Was Rion working with Cael and Lucan, or against them? Or was the astrophysicist suspicious of his superiors, too? Lucan wouldn't know for certain until he talked to Rion, but arranging a meeting created all kinds of complications.

"Rion's allegiance is still an unknown," Lucan began. "While he saved our lives in Langor and warned us about Elder Selick, meeting with him, still, may not be safe. The military could be watching him, hoping he'll lead them to us. Is there anything else you haven't told me?"

"Nisco thinks we're all being watched and warned me not to return to Avalon. I'd love to know what's so damn important in those papers Trelan stole from Brennon that we may all be in danger."

He hoped Cael would stay holed up in the mountains, but she was no longer including him in her planning. He tried to flex the tension out of his neck.

"Are you meeting Nisco at the residence?" he asked.

She shrugged.

"You need to stay hidden. It's too risky for you to meet Nisco."

She glared at him. "I didn't ask your permission."

He threaded his hand through his hair, knowing he owed her some kind of explanation. "I thought you'd be safer in the mountains than with me."

"That was not your decision to make."

Sweat trickled down his neck and, with the back of his hand, he angrily wiped it away. Cael's eyes widened and she gasped.

"What?" he asked. "What's wrong?"

"Your hand."

He glanced at his hand but saw nothing to cause alarm.

"The other side."

Son of a bitch. Purple scales had grown on the inside of his wrist. Dragon scales. No wonder his limbs had been tingling. His cells were mutating.

Dropping to his knees beside the stream, he dipped his hand into the water. The scales didn't wash away. He picked up a handful of gravel to scour the purple scales, scrubbed until his flesh bled. But the scales remained.

Horror seethed through him. "I'm becoming—"

"A male dragon." She whispered the words, awed and shocked.

This couldn't be happening. Not now. But denial wouldn't make the scales vanish. He forced himself to ask, "How long until the transformation's complete?"

"I don't know."

"Is there a way to slow or reverse the process?"

"I have no idea. In all our history, only once has there even been a male dragon."

"Tell me about him." He had to know what he was up against.

"According to the Elders, long ago we had a king who was born with the marks. Legend says he journeyed with his brothers to a foreign realm to make war upon the Tribes."

He jerked up his head, and his voice was sharper than he intended. "Did your king ever return?"

"The myth says he came back to place the Grail inside Avalon, then died in another realm." She shot him a puzzled frown. "That's why we believe the Grail's inside the obelisk."

He asked one last question. "The legendary king. What was his name?"

"Pendragon. His name was Arthur Pendragon—but it's only a legend. We never found any archeological evidence that he existed."

Electric excitement simmered through his veins, and he had to refrain from pumping his fist and tamp down his emotions before Cael realized he was on to something he couldn't explain.

Lucan peered at the bloody scales at his wrists. Cael had told him she must dragonshape at least ten times a year to satisfy her biology. And if he, too, had to periodically change into a dragon, it would take him more than a lifetime to fly home. His ship was too small to hold his dragon form. If his new DNA forced him to shift into a dragon every cycle, it would add incalculable time to his journey.

Damn it. If he had to dragonshape on a regular basis, he'd never be able to fly home in time to help Marisa. Maybe not even in time to save humanity.

"There has to be a way to reverse this process, to take back the dragonblood."

"Why don't you want to be a dragon?" Her voice was filled with pain and disappointment.

"To lose my intellect . . . even part of the time . . ." He raised his head, still unwilling to reveal his mission. "How do you . . ."

"Cope?" She closed her eyes, as if looking inward, then opened them. "I have no choice. But I don't mind the loss of intellect, since there are so many compensations. The gift of flight is awesome."

"But you don't like the isolation," he countered.

"I don't mind *being* different. But I don't like being *treated* differently."

Her words hit him like a knockout blow. Lucan had been her first lover, and he'd walked away.

He'd hurt her with his selfish need to preserve himself. For the sake of his mission.

And, God forgive him, he couldn't stop his growing suspicion that being with her somehow acted as a catalyst for the changes happening to him. The way her scent affected him wasn't normal. Neither was the way his body reacted to her touch. And the tingling up the insides of his arms after their lovemaking, tingling in the same places she had scales, and where *he* now had scales, caused him to question if being close to her was changing him . . . and he couldn't afford to change.

He had to give her up—not just for her sake, but his own. "What else haven't you told me?"

"Excuse me?"

"About legendary male dragons? About being a drag-onshaper?" He tried to keep his voice level, but he knew his anxiety was getting the better of him.

"Let me get this straight." She stood and began removing her clothing, placing it in her backpack. "You paired with me several times but have no intention of ever seeing me again, and you expect me to educate you?"

He reached out to take her hand. With pain and fury in her eyes, Cael jerked back.

She dragonshaped. And then she was gone.

There is a farther unknown world, a world beyond Avalon.

—ANONYMOUS

14

For two days Lucan followed the stream that led him to civilization. He'd tapped into his credit and rented a skimmer. With the military searching for him, he'd be foolhardy to travel straight back to Avalon. Instead, he headed for the remote site where he'd left his spacecraft.

Finally reaching the beach, he walked out to the sea and plunged into the surf. He swam out three hundred strokes, grabbed a deep breath of air, and dived straight down. His spaceship blended with the sea bottom, but since he'd triangulated the position with landmarks, it wasn't hard to spot the craft beside a fan-shaped white coral formation.

He palmed a lock that responded only to his handprint, and the sealed hatch opened. After swimming into the air lock, he pulled a handle and resealed the outer portal.

Water siphoned out, air cycled in, and heat blasted him dry, and Lucan headed straight to the communication center, a circular bridge with giant windows. He keyed in a request for his messages from home.

Since he hadn't been back to the ship in almost a

month, he had video messages from both parents waiting for him. As always, they sent their love, but as he compared the new videos to the pictures of his family on the console, he noticed that worry had added wrinkles to the corners of his parents' eyes.

His sister demanded that he return home immediately, that he was on a fool's mission. Maybe he was. He had yet to enter Avalon, and apparently there were still more inscriptions to decipher to obtain the Grail.

Vivianne Blackstone, CEO of the Vesta Corporation and the woman who'd built this spaceship, had also sent a message. No babies had been born during the last few years. No babies anywhere on Earth.

Lucan used the computer's extensive data bank to bring up Layamon's Brut poem. Just as he'd remembered, many of the lines were similar to those he'd found on the cave wall. The computer couldn't translate the second carving, but it did recognize the language was from the Tribes—Arthur's ancient enemy. And when he logged in the type of rock, the elevation, and the depth of the rune carvings, the computer estimated both of the inscriptions had been made about fifteen hundred years ago—possibly during King Arthur's lifetime.

The legend that Arthur had left the Grail in Avalon before his death seemed even more likely. Now Lucan had to find a way to get back to Avalon and find it.

He had to decide whether he could trust Quentin's offer to intercede with the prosecutor on his behalf in exchange for Lucan's expertise in reading the runes, but first he needed to head for the medical bay. With any luck one of the computer-run diagnostic tools could strain out the dragonshaping blood and restore him to his normal self.

Swinging onto the table, Lucan pulled the diagnostic device over his body. "Full medical scan."

"Processing," the computer answered.

The procedure would take several hours. Lucan should be using those hours to sleep. But he kept wondering about Cael. Had she found her sister? Would she try to meet Rion on her own? Would she return to Avalon?

The computer whirred, then beeped. "Your blood has altered," the male voice spoke in a methodical tone.

"Change me back to normal."

"Processing."

Lucan closed his eyes and tried to let the machine work, but his heart raced as he waited for the results.

He tried to distract himself with work. The King Arthur Pendragon story Cael had told him was yet another fascinating piece of the puzzle. He'd already found abundant proof that there had been contact between their two worlds. And while Arthur had fought under the banner of a dragon and his name meant "master of dragons," Lucan had never believed the dragon to be a genuine being. However, Arthur being a dragonshaper could account for the shapeshifters in old Earth legends.

"I'm detecting an abnormality in your heartbeat."

Considering his thoughts, an elevated pulse was to be expected. "I'm anxious."

"You're growing a second heart."

A second heart? "Reverse the process."

"If I remove your second heart, you won't survive."

"Explain."

"You've *always* had the genetic ability to grow a second heart. Each cell—"

"Just fix me." Lucan ran his hand through his hair. He

understood the theory that in early development any cell could develop into a more specialized one—like a heart.

"I can't. A blood transfusion served as a catalyst, and the process—"

"A catalyst? What do you mean?"

"The blood transfusion speeded up a process that might have happened anyway."

Stunned, he shook his head as if to clear it. "Let me get this straight. You're saying that if Cael had never given me her blood, I'd still be growing a second heart?"

"Possibly."

Lucan snorted. "Have you blown a circuit?"

"Self-diagnostic says that I'm in perfect running order. More than can be said about you."

Lucan rolled his eyes. The computer was wrong. He'd never heard of anyone mutating into a dragon. And dragons were big. Kind of hard to hide. "Look. No one in my family has ever been a dragon."

"This is evolution at work."

"Evolution takes millions of years. It doesn't happen in a week." Lucan held out his hand to the scanner. "These scales weren't on my arms last week."

"But you've always been telepathic—which is tied to the dragon genes."

Lucan swore under his breath. "Are you saying I've always had dragon genes? That Cael and I have a genetic link? But we come from different worlds."

"It's not that rare an occurrence. Many people on Earth share—"

"What's the common denominator among the people on Earth who have this dragon mutation?"

"Processing."

Lucan held his breath and then eased out the air slowly. His own theory was almost too wild to think, never mind say out loud. But if Pendragon and Earth shared a history, perhaps they also shared a blood bond. One that went back over a thousand years.

"Many descendants of Celtic people have some variation of the dragon gene."

"How early?"

"About 1,550 years ago."

King Arthur's time. Coincidence? Lucan no longer believed so.

Lucan almost leapt off the table. The implications were mind-boggling. It was possible, probable even, that King Arthur was his ancestor and a dragonshaper. And somehow his genetic heritage had given him his telepathic ability, as well as an aptitude for dragonshaping. It was even possible that if Lucan and Cael could trace their family trees back far enough, say fifteen or sixteen hundred years, they might share a common ancestor in the distant past.

"So anyone on Earth who also has these genes has the ability to mutate into a dragon?"

"Only Arthur's descendants have the gene."

While King Arthur hadn't had a legitimate child with his queen, Arthur had had a son with the High Priestess of Avalon, the Lady of the Lake. So his genes could have been passed down over the centuries. Arthur likely had thousands of descendants, maybe millions.

For the moment, Lucan put aside his questions about where the dragon mutation had come from and focused on results.

"And what kicked my dragon genes into gear?"

"Your immune system may have reacted to the difference in gravity. Or to something in the air. Or the food.

Anything on Pendragon could have brought about the mutation."

"Alien blood?"

"Maybe. Maybe not. A scent could have triggered the reaction. Or a sound. Or an electromagnetic wave. Or a weapon."

"Could I have reacted to *someone,* not some thing?"

"Most certainly. The trigger could be environmental, physical, or even emotional."

"Emotional?" His feelings when he'd been with other lovers had never been anywhere near as strong as when he'd made love with Cael. Emotions released all kinds of hormones. "Is there a way to slow my physical changes?"

"Not without killing you. And there's nothing I can do to fix you, because you aren't broken."

Lucan left the medical bay much more frustrated than when he'd arrived. He entered the bridge and initiated an investigation. "Search for references to dragonshapers, dragonshifters, and intelligent species of dragons on the worlds we stopped at, as well as Earth."

On the way to Pendragon, he'd downloaded culture, history, science, geography, and religion of the worlds he'd passed through. The knowledge would be precious to Earth, but what good would all that knowledge do if no one was left to utilize it?

"I have 23,425 references to dragons in my data banks."

Lucan scratched his head. "Cross-reference the material to scales like the ones on my arms."

"Do you also have scales on your legs?"

Lucan slid off his pants and swore. Scales ran along the insides of his feet, up his calves and thighs, and over his balls, and joined at the tip of his sex.

"Scales on arms, legs, and genitals verified." The computer had visually scanned him and come to its own conclusion. "Cross-checking."

Lucan opened his eyes, pulled his pants back on, and paced the bridge. Outside, water creatures swam by the giant portals, unmindful of the Earth ship that had become part of their landscape.

Finally the computer spoke. "There's an ancient legend about an alien race seeding the galaxy with dragons. There's one vague reference to purple scales that marked the limbs of the fire-breathers. And there are recent rumors about Honor, an entire planet of dragon-shapers enslaved by the Tribes."

Lucan had difficulty taking in the scope of the drag-onshaping myth.

The computer spoke again. "According to the legends, the male dragon's primary job is to keep the female safe. He'll dragonshape whenever the female needs protection."

"Are you saying the transformation's involuntary?"

"It appears that way, but I'm citing ancient myths."

"What about the female? Why can't she protect herself?" He recalled Cael's fiery breath, her claws, her vicious teeth that ripped through the mountainside.

"There may be limitations on the shapeshifting process. Food, temperature, gravity, atmospheric pressure, hormone fluctuations. It could be anything." The computer beeped. "My communication network's picking up a message, and the sender, Rion, is asking for you by name."

Shit. No one on Pendragon was supposed to know about his ship. "Does Rion know my location?"

"Unknown. His communication's broadband and set to hit a widespread area."

"If I respond, can he trace this call?"

"Pendragon doesn't yet have that technology."

Lucan opened channels. "How's the sinkhole?"

Rion hesitated. "That's not why I called."

"Tell me," Lucan demanded.

"You and I still have much to talk about, but to answer your question, the sinkhole's expanding exponentially."

Lucan frowned. "Any other good news?"

"There's a military buildup in Carlane."

Carlane? Cael lived in Carlane. Had she left the safety of the mountains to search for her sister, after all? Was the military closing in on her? Would they lock her up and try her for murder? At either possibility, Lucan's pulse raced.

The computer confirmed, "Military satellite feeds are picking up unusual troop movements in Carlane around the High Priestess's residence."

Lucan drummed his fingers on the console. "Have you spoken to Cael?"

"That's why I'm calling." Rion's voice was urgent. "I can't reach her."

*He who betrays the will of the Goddess will come to
an evil end.*

—THE ELDERS

15

In dragonshape, Cael flew across the mountains, stopping
several times to eat platinum to restore her strength before crossing the polar cap and soaring over the crowded
continent of her homeland.

Cael yearned to fulfill her promise to visit Jaylon. But
since the military might be watching the medical center in
Feridon, she'd go to the residence first. Nisco and her husband, Depuck, lived next door. Her sister had sounded
frightened during her last call, and it was very odd that
neither Nisco nor Depuck was answering Cael's calls.

No doubt, General Brennon would be watching her
residence, so she had to enter the city in secret. Cael humanshaped and changed into a disguise she'd used before
to hide her identity. With a wig of dirt-brown hair and a
long-sleeved, nondescript gown in a coarse fabric, Cael
drew little attention. She leased a skimmer with a false ID
she'd acquired years ago and kept hidden in the lining of
her backpack, an additional precaution in a life that was
already filled with too many precautions.

But so far those precautions had kept her alive. If she'd

asked the Elders' advice, they would have told Cael to hide. But she needed to make sure Nisco was all right and needed to see Brennon's papers with the formula that the private investigator Trelan had sent to Nisco before he'd died. And Cael was determined to visit Jaylon. Then she was going back to Avalon for the Grail.

She was done hiding out in the mountains.

Cael flew her skimmer toward the green, parklike square of land along the lake and frowned at the lack of activity in Carlane. Where was everyone? Her own home looked deserted, as did the ancient temple next door, which was large enough to hold her dragonshape, if necessary.

Bypassing her own residence, Cael landed next to Nisco's detached garage. After killing the skimmer's engines, Cael heard the roar of several motors that were much too loud to be private vehicles. At the unexplained noise, her hearts began to pump harder.

She hurried around the garage as several military skimmers shot straight up from the front lawn, then poured on the juice toward the capital's center. Alarm shot through her.

Cael turned the corner, and the scent of blood hit her. She spied an injured man lying in the front yard. By the Goddess! Her brother-in-law lay unmoving in a pool of his own blood.

"Depuck." Hurrying across the freshly mowed grass, Cael knelt beside him. Blood gushed from a head wound that required immediate attention, as did a deep gash in his arm.

Cael had to stop the bleeding or her brother-in-law would die. She removed Depuck's belt and made a tourniquet for his arm. As she applied pressure to the head wound, she worried that she'd find her sister in a similar condition. Or worse. Only Cael's medical training allowed her to cage her panic and treat Depuck.

While she applied pressure with one hand, she felt for a pulse. Please, be there. She ached to feel life, the kick of a heartbeat. Yes. Depuck's pulse was weak, but it fluttered wildly.

The head wound concerned her most. She opened his eyelids, and when his pupils narrowed, she deemed he was strong enough for her to move off the lawn. He was heavy, but she dragged him onto the front porch.

Cael dug into her pack for medical supplies. "Nisco! Are you here?"

No one answered. Sickened, scared, fingers shaking, Cael pushed down her fear. She couldn't heal Depuck unless she stopped trembling. Taking a deep breath and letting it out slowly, she sought once again to calm her nerves and set aside her frustration.

She released the belt and applied a pressure bandage to Depuck's arm, then turned her attention to his more severe head wound. With quick, efficient stitches, she sewed up the gash. The jagged injury required two layers of stitches, one deep near the bone, the other on the surface skin. Grateful that Depuck remained unconscious during her ministrations, she sewed with a hand that steadied as she performed the familiar task. As she worked, she prayed he would regain consciousness soon.

Whoever had taken off in those skimmers had left Depuck for dead. Should she call for an ambulance? The military had spies in the city. Before she could make up her mind, Depuck groaned. His eyes opened, and her scales undulated at his panic.

"Where's Nisco?" Cael asked, her voice urgent.

"Not sure. A man . . . grabbed her."

"He took her?" She tipped a flask of water to his lips.

"Don't know. She fought and got away, I think, but he was chasing her again, and then I lost sight of them." Depuck struggled to sit up. "Find her."

"Lie still. Just tell me what happened."

The water seemed to make it easier for him to speak. "I was in the vegetable garden when I heard Nisco scream. I dropped everything. Ran here. Before I reached the house . . . something caught me in the arm and I spun. Then my head burned. Before I blacked out, Nisco was fighting off a man, then she got free and ran away but he kept chasing her."

"Was the man wearing a uniform?" she asked.

Depuck shook his head. "No uniform. That's all I know."

"Don't worry. We'll find her. Maybe she's hiding. She said she had something to show me."

"Before the attack, Nisco was excited about papers a PI had sent her. She said she had to show them to you."

"We were supposed to meet here. Did she say why I had to see them?"

"No. But she's very organized. Perhaps her notes . . ."

"Notes? Did she leave them on the computer?"

Depuck tried to sit up. "Don't you care about *her?* They might hurt her . . . or worse."

"Easy." She placed a hand on his shoulder and he lay back down. "Of course I care about her. The information she received from the investigator may be our best lead to find her. I'll look inside."

"Try her desk. Her computer password is *oregimo*."

Cael stepped through the open front door and winced. Nisco's house looked as if an earthquake had shaken it. Not one picture remained on the walls. Every drawer was opened, smashed, and tossed aside. They'd slashed the couch and pulled the stuffing out of the cushions. Knocked over lamps. Broken cabinet doors, which hung at crazy angles. The intruders had definitely been searching for something.

Stomach churning, already suspecting the entire house had been ransacked, Cael checked the study, stepping over debris. Just as she suspected, the computer's memory hardware was gone, the monitor shattered along with the message machine. When she turned over a smashed bulletin board, she saw that every handwritten note had been ripped away. But when she went into Nisco's studio, she found her sister's most recent sculpture, a figure of the Goddess, sitting on the table, the clay still wet. Cael picked it up. Scratched into the base's bottom were the words "Go to the Kisster."

Sweet Goddess. *Kisster* was Nisco and Cael's secret childhood name for Sonelle. When Sonelle was little, to get her way, she'd go around kissing her teachers, her parents, and her sisters.

Nisco obviously had left that note for Cael, and she'd wanted Cael to join Sonelle in Feridon. But had Nisco left the message before the attack? Or after?

If Nisco had eluded the man chasing her, it was possible she might still meet Cael at the medical center. But if he'd caught her, she might be a hostage. Without another clue to Nisco's whereabouts, Cael decided to head to the medical center. If Nisco wasn't there, Cael would move mountains to find her.

Still very worried about Nisco's disappearance, Cael returned to Depuck, who was lying where she'd left him. "Did Nisco say anything else?"

"She was close-mouthed, even with me." Depuck's

angry eyes bored into hers. "You're wanted for murder. The military came here because of you. You should turn yourself in. This is your fault—"

"I'm sorry. So sorry. I didn't know I was putting you both in danger."

"Your ignorance won't save her." His eyes closed but at least his breathing remained shallow.

Depuck was right. She had to set aside her worry and guilt. She had to do something. "I'll find her."

On the off chance her sister might answer, Cael flipped open her communicator and called Nisco. Her sister didn't reply, but Cael left a message. "Nisco, Depuck's suffered no permanent injury, but he's been hurt. Call me."

Standing, she gripped the rug he lay on with two hands. Slowly, carefully, she dragged the rug and Depuck inside, knocking aside a broken table, a shattered urn, and a toppled potted plant.

Suddenly, she felt her necklace slip away and cold steel bite into her neck. She couldn't breathe. A noose of steel chain was cutting off her air. Her captor yanked the chain, pulling her upright, forcing her to release the blanket.

Holy Goddess.

Her thoughts spun wildly. Even if she'd had the ability to dragonshape, if she tried with the chain around her neck, her head would be severed.

Her attacker yanked tight on the chain, forcing her to straighten or risk a broken neck. Lungs burning for air, she clawed at her neck, trying to ease the metal noose.

From behind, her attacker looped another chain over her wrist, then captured the other, clamping her arms behind her back. Her ankles received the same treatment. She stood on tiptoe, and only then did the chain around her neck ease slightly, enough for her to drag in a painful breath.

"What do you want?" she gasped.

"We'll start with Nisco. Where is she?"

"She was supposed to meet me here." Cael's stomach knotted, and she prayed Nisco wasn't being held captive, that somehow she'd gotten safely away. "Nisco's husband saw someone take her away before I arrived." It was a lie, but she needed to keep this villain from going after her sister.

"And the linguist? Tell me where he is, and as I promised Elder Selick, your death will be merciful."

"Elder Selick?" she gasped, unable to keep the dismay from her voice. No wonder her captor had known exactly how to contain her powers by surprising and immobilizing her. The Elders knew her vulnerabilities.

Rion had warned her, but she'd assumed Elder Selick had attacked her at the retreat after hearing Cael admit she'd shared her dragonblood. Yet her assumption had been wrong. Selick had been hiding in that room, planning to attack her *before* she'd mentioned one word about sharing her dragonblood.

"Where's the linguist?" her captor repeated. Sword drawn, the masked man walked in front of her and held her sacred dragon necklace like a trophy. He was large and muscular, and yet his movements were surprisingly stealthy and agile.

Openly, he wore the uniform of the Division of Lost Artifacts, and General Brennon's audacity rocked her. But was this conspiracy to find the Grail widespread or confined to only General Brennon, his men, and Elder Selick? It sickened her to think other Elders and military leaders might be involved, too. For all she knew, the conspiracy reached into the highest levels of society and extended into the very heart of their culture.

Her keen hearing picked up the rumble of ships heading their way. If she could stall, maybe she could survive.

Ignoring her aching toes and seeking to ease the fiery pain in her throat, she lifted her chin. "If I'm going to die, at least tell me why. Why do you want the linguist?"

He placed her necklace around his own neck, and his contempt sent icy fear down her spine. He had no respect. No honor. And behind the mask, his calculating, cold eyes held no mercy. "The linguist can read the inscriptions and knows how to bring down the shields. Avalon is sinking. He may be our last chance to find the Grail."

"We don't really know that Lucan brought down the first shield. It's possible—"

He placed the tip of the weapon to her throat. "You were with the linguist at the Elders' retreat."

"And then we split up."

He slashed her arm and she screamed.

"A lie! You were seen flying him above the city."

"True, but then he left me." By now, her captor had to hear the ships approaching, but he gave no indication of it. Hoping to keep his attention on her, hoping the ships were rescuers and not his co-conspirators, she asked, "If you needed Lucan's help, why did you try to kill him in the fire? And blame him for Shaw's murder."

"Quentin assured us he could bring down the interior shield, but he overestimated his ability."

Quentin? Was he a traitor, too? "I know nothing that can help you."

Her captor brandished his sword. "Tell me where he is."

"Quentin?" She raised an eyebrow. "I have no idea."

He slashed out again, slicing deep into her shoulder. She screamed at the searing pain.

"Not Quentin. The linguist. Tell me where he is. *Now.*"

"I've already told you. I don't know."

"You will tell me—"

"I don't—"

"Or die from a hundred cuts." He slashed her again, this time drawing blood on her thigh.

Drowning in a quicksand of agony, she had to swim through the hurt, no matter how thick or deep. She had to stop the pain from pulling her under. Help might be coming.

He raised his sword just as men entered the house. More masked men.

Through a haze of anguish, she realized they weren't here to rescue her.

A burly man strode through the door. Through his mask, his eyes flicked over her wounds. "Have you found the linguist?"

"I'm working on it." The swordsman raised his sword. When he struck again, she braced for more agony. Tried to be stoic. But as the metal sliced through her, as if of its own accord, her mouth opened and she screamed. She lost her balance, and the chain around her neck tightened, choking off her cry.

The masked man whipped the sword near her face, his cruel blade hissing by her cheek. "I'm skilled at missing vital veins, arteries, and organs. Tell me where the linguist is and your death will be swift."

"I . . . don't . . . know."

Goddess help her. She was going to die a brutal and barbaric death. A hideous death.

But even as the pain took her under, she was glad she couldn't give away Lucan's whereabouts. Perhaps he would live.

When the magic of the Great Ones is committed to human hands, those hands serve the will of the Goddess.

—THE LADY OF THE LAKE

16

*P*ain.

What the hell? The message ripped through Lucan's head, the thought so intense he doubled over in the skimmer. Sweat broke out all over his body.

Pain. Had he been injured? Twisting, he looked down, expecting to see a wound. But he didn't have a mark on him. Yet the sharp, searing pain in his mind continued despite the fact that he saw no blood.

Was this mental shout in his head, this pounding agony, a side effect of his dragonshaping evolution? Swearing under his breath, he braced against the nauseating torture.

Luckily, the skimmer's autopilot had no difficulty finding Carlane and Cael's residence. He'd come west, across the sea and the volcanic mountains that slid into foothills before the pain had struck. Now that he neared Carlane, a marbelite and glass city sparkling in the harsh midday sunlight, the brutal shout of pain made it impossible for him to think clearly. If not for the autopilot, he might have crashed into soaring skyscrapers, aerial maglev tracks, or the traffic flowing past or moving walkways. Through a haze of agony, he spied the parklike setting in the city center that held the dragonshaper's ancestral residence. Spectacular in size and color, Cael's home sparkled like an emerald beacon amid ancient trees and flowering gardens bisected with pathways and tumbling streams. The verdant, luxurious landscape contrasted with the hard surfaces of the city that surrounded it.

Pain. He clapped his hands to his temples as another mental scream ripped through him, but this time he recognized the pain was coming from Cael. It was *Cael's* scream ricocheting through him.

Holy Hell. Cael was in trouble. Terrible trouble.

His horror rising, awful comprehension set in. She was broadcasting her pain through their telepathic link, her screams so loud and deafening he clamped his hands over his ears, certain his head was about to explode. Her beautiful face came to his mind, and he focused on it. He could not let her suffer. No one could take this kind of pain and survive.

When Lucan spied military ships flying from the dragonshaper's home, he barely retained the presence of mind to change his landing site. Instinct made him cautious. Pain made him frantic to find Cael. Anger that anyone would hurt her drove him on.

After landing at a public garage, he exited the skimmer and fought down the pain, trapping it in a corner of his mind. Heading straight for the park and Cael's spectacular sanctum, he expected perhaps fences or guards, but nothing stopped him from crossing the immaculate grounds.

The passersby, a few couples walking hand in hand, a child on some kind of rolling wind vehicle, and a traffic cop, gave him perfunctory nods. No one seemed to think it odd that he was jogging onto sacred ground and into dragon territory. Into Cael's home.

Through the mental link he felt her scream of pain, and his shoulder seemed to catch fire. The blaze seared down his torso and burned his guts. He began to shake with the depth of his fear for her.

As another, then another, even more horrible agony ripped through him, his ears picked up Cael's raw scream, and Lucan's hearts didn't just elevate, they rumbled like a starship engine.

In response, a strange and powerful energy flooded through him.

An owl swooped out of the trees, dipped by his head, and swerved across his path. Lucan swore. "Merlin. Take me to Cael."

As if the bird understood, it veered right and Lucan sprinted after him. The bird was leading him away from Cael's residence to a mansion that bordered the parklands.

Sweat poured down Lucan's back, and he prayed Cael was dragonshaping right now, breathing fire and scorching anyone who hurt her. He leapt over a metal bench, dodged around a lavender fountain, and stumbled over a loose stone. But he didn't go down.

Merlin led the way, staying low and a few paces ahead. Thankful for good balance and the peculiar spikes in his metabolism that seemed to be urging him faster, Lucan ran at full speed, appreciating the raw energy pouring into his body.

Cael screamed once more. Pain hit Lucan, but he braced, building a mental shield to protect him from the worst of her raw agony. Despite his newfound pain filter, despite his extra strength and power, he wasn't moving fast enough. He tried to force his legs into a quicker run, but oddly, his pace was laborious. He looked down and the sidewalk was too far away, as if he'd tripled in height. But his eyesight was much sharper than ever before. Tattered clothing and a torn shoe, his spaceship-supplied multi-tool and laser poking through the sole, littered the ground.

What the hell?

His mind was slow to process. His human legs had turned into mountain-sized limbs. He was tall, heavy. Huge.

A dragon.

And his mate was crying out in agony, calling for him on the mental plane. Pure instinct, rage, and dragon power took over. Lucan flapped arms that had grown into wings and flew, soaring into the air without effort, without thought.

He had only one goal.

Protect Cael.

Guard his mate.

Save her.

Lucan banked right. He spied men. Flying machines that spat fire. And they turned those weapons on him.

Without hesitation, without a plan, he flew in fast and hard, curving, diving, and swatting. With a whack from his powerful wing, he knocked one machine into another. The crash and flying debris on the front lawn of the house made the other machines swarm like flies.

The scent of gunpowder singed his nostrils. Blasters stung his flesh and incited his fury. These men were keeping Cael from him.

Hurting Cael.

She screamed again, and her distress set off his primal rage.

He roared his fury and breathed fire, catching two men in the flames. The next time he roared, he'd aim better. Kill more. Flames took precious energy, energy he couldn't waste.

A machine flew in close to his wing, and he batted it down near the front porch. Metal fragments flew, exploding in every direction. Men guarding the door dropped to the ground, injured or dead.

Lucan landed by the porch and his legs buckled. He rolled and managed to shove back to his feet. He was weak. So weak. But Cael was inside this building. He could smell her blood. Her pain.

She needed him, and he had to go to her. But his wings had grown so heavy he could barely lift them. In frustration, he rammed against the portal.

And then once again he was human. Naked and human.

Move. His human brain kicked in. He took in the battlefield, the downed skimmers, the dead bodies and realized that he had caused this devastation. Killing by instinct with fire and mighty wings, he'd fought with a primal and alien savagery he hadn't known he'd possessed.

These men wore the uniform of the Division of Lost Artifacts, but since they were all masked he suspected they weren't here on official business.

He peered inside the building, and his gaze slammed to . . . Oh, God. Cael.

She hung by her neck from a chain, so bloody she must be dead. His knees buckled and he staggered forward. "Cael."

He should never have left her.

"Cael," he whispered.

Shocked, horrified, he shook with nausea as the heavy

weight of loss assailed him. She had to be dead. Not even Cael could survive so many wounds. Blood trickled down her scalp, matting her beautiful hair and flowing onto the chain that had prevented her from dragonshaping.

"Cael?" Perhaps, just perhaps, she still breathed.

She raised her head. "Run," she whispered, her eyes hopeless with misery. "Save yourself."

After all she'd suffered, she was worried about him? A roar of fury surged up his throat, but for her, he kept his tone gentle. "Who did this to you?"

A masked swordsman, thickly built and in his prime, stepped from behind Cael. To get to her, Lucan would have to go through him. He hoped the bastard was ready to die.

"Hold on, Cael. Just hold on," he said softly, sick in his soul at what she'd suffered. "Soon, I'll have you free."

Lucan breathed hard, preparing for battle. With a war cry of fierce fury, he advanced, his hands itching to choke the life from the swordsman who'd dared to hurt Cael. So what if he had no weapon save his wits?

Scooping up a broken pot, Lucan tossed it at the man's head. The man ducked, and Lucan picked up a broken chair.

His opponent lifted his sword, no doubt expecting Lucan to raise the chair to protect himself. Instead, Lucan hurled the chair at the man's feet. But weak from dragon-shaping, he couldn't toss hard enough. The man didn't go down, just lost his balance.

Lucan staggered forward a half step, but the man cut his advance short with a swing of his sword. Lucan leaped back, but not in time to avoid a slice across his middle. A mere flesh wound was a small price to pay to learn the man was skilled. An amateur stabbed, a master sliced and diced.

And Lucan was about to be shredded to pieces if he didn't find a weapon long and strong enough to block that lethal blade. Dodging the swordsman's advance, Lucan retreated and kicked a broken shelf right into the guy's knees. The man grunted in pain, lost his balance, and retreated a step.

But Lucan was running out of room. His back was almost against the wall.

As if reading his mind, Cael spoke, her voice raw, "Pipe."

He followed her frantic gaze to a wall heater and the pipe beneath it, almost hidden by decorative molding.

The swordsman swung, and Lucan ducked and lunged, skidding over the side of a toppled couch. He landed by the wall, yanked the pipe from the heater.

The swordsman picked that moment to attack. The sword sliced toward his neck. Lucan raised the pipe to block a glancing blow and scrambled sideways, stumbling to his feet.

The pipe was lightweight. Some kind of aluminum alloy. Nowhere near hard enough to stand up to a direct sword blow. He'd have to make do.

Eyes gleaming, his opponent advanced. He slashed, once. Lucan shifted right. He slashed again. Lucan spun left.

Lucan had to wait for the right moment. His opponent had the better weapon. The advantage.

Wait.

He might get only one shot.

Wait.

Sweat rolled into his eyes.

Wait.

When his opponent tripped over a lamp, Lucan attacked,

lunging with the pipe. The man recovered his balance and sliced the pipe in two.

Moving lightly from foot to foot, half a length of pipe in each hand, he balanced on the balls of his feet.

Watch the eyes.

He expected the man to feint, then attack. But the swordsman retreated, pivoted, and swung his sword tip.

At Cael's throat.

Eyes wide with terror, she tried to pull back. But the chains held her fast. She couldn't do more than flinch. One thrust and she'd be dead.

Rage poured adrenaline into his system. He'd been too slow. He'd waited too long. Now Lucan had only an instant. And even if his muscles weren't trembling with fatigue, no way could he cover that much distance in time to save her.

From out of nowhere, Merlin flew at the swordsman, his talons raking the man's face. With a howl of pain, the man stepped back from Cael to protect his eyes.

Hefting the pipe like a spear, Lucan heaved it at the swordsman. The rod sailed through the air, aimed straight for the man's chest and vital organs.

At the last instant, the attacker spied the oncoming danger and shifted. Instead of striking his chest, the rod struck a hard blow to his sword shoulder. With a yowl of pain, he dropped his weapon, and it skidded out of reach.

Lucan closed in on his opponent, and Merlin flew to a high windowsill.

The man swung a wild punch and Lucan took a hard fist to the jaw. Shaking off the blow, Lucan lunged for the guy's knees and tackled him to the floor. Lucan crawled on top, hammering the guy's face with his fists.

His opponent twisted and turned away from the facial

blows, giving Lucan his back. A fatal error. Lucan snapped the man's neck, and the clasp of Cael's necklace loosened. The heirloom fell into his hands.

With a final heave, Lucan tossed aside the body. Fearing the worst, shoving to his feet, he stumbled to Cael's limp body.

Oh . . . God. She didn't appear to be breathing.

Sick with dread and terrified the noose had cut off her air supply for too long, he fought to free her. Her blood drenched the chains and made the task a slippery nightmare. His hands shaking with the fear he'd injure her further, he finally released Cael from the noose. As she toppled to the floor, he broke her fall and carried her to the overturned couch. Stomach churning, sickened by how much she'd suffered, he tried to be gentle. Kicking the couch upright, he placed her on the cushions. Her chest rose and fell.

She was breathing, and a measure of relief filled him. But when she whimpered, rage sliced through him. He wanted to kill the son of a bitch all over again.

Carefully, he liberated Cael's wrists and ankles from the chains. As he tended the nasty cuts, she didn't open her eyes. Amazingly, thanks to her dragon constitution, her bleeding stopped and within just a few minutes her wounds began to close. Gently he replaced the necklace around her neck.

She opened eyes still clouded with pain. "Lucan? Why are you naked?" She frowned in confusion. "Are you really here?" Lifting her hand to him, she stroked his cheek.

"I'm really here." He placed his hand over hers and held it against his face. "Are you okay?"

"I will be." Her eyes softened. "Why aren't you in Avalon?"

"I felt your pain."

She caressed his cheek. He abruptly stood. "Let's see to your wounds. Where's your pack?"

She sagged back onto the sofa. "I'm not sure."

"I'll find it." Every step was a huge effort. He had to force his legs to move with willpower alone. When he searched the living area, he saw a body he hadn't noticed before. This man was injured but alive. On his feet, he would have been a tall man, well built. His current complexion was pale, his breathing ragged. Blood seeped from a bandage on his brow and matted his dark hair. From the looks of him, someone had patched him up. Since he wasn't dressed in a military uniform or masked, Lucan left him alone. But if the injured man tried to hurt Cael, he wouldn't live to take another breath.

Lucan found her pack by the window and glanced outside. Smoke from the downed skimmers curled into the blue sky. The dead lay scattered across the lawn like broken toys. Reinforcements might already be on the way, but Cael was in no condition to flee.

Neither was he. He could barely walk. Forget running.

Returning with the pack, he kneeled beside her and opened it. "What do you need?"

"Green tube."

He found three and held them out to her, but when she tried to take them, her fingers trembled. She was playing tough. Brushing aside her hand, he sat beside her, scooted over until her head rested on his lap. "Still hurting?"

"I'm better." She watched him, her eyes glazed with residual pain.

"What can I do for you? Smooth this over your wounds?" he asked.

She groaned. "It's not medicine, it's food. Platinum."

He smiled. "Then open up."

He squeezed out a line of green paste onto his finger, and she parted her lips, then slowly and delicately licked the paste from his finger. She sighed, and the sound whispered between them, a warm pulse against his fingertip.

He squeezed out more food, and this time her lips closed around his finger, sucking him in, drawing the nutrients in eagerly. She was clearly gaining strength.

Then suddenly she was taking the tube from him and pushing his hands away. "You need to eat, too. Platinum helps the healing process."

Her voice was a throaty whisper. As she grew stronger titanic relief filled him.

After squeezing a line of platinum from the tube, she pressed her fingertips to his mouth. He could taste the tang of the platinum combined with the salt of her skin, a tantalizing combination.

"See." Through half-shuttered eyes, she gazed down at his stomach, where he was surprised to find his wound already healing.

"Your turn." He fed her more platinum, enjoying the moment.

He peered out the window, then back at her. "How long until someone arrives to investigate?"

She frowned. "I don't understand."

"There are five crashed skimmers on the front lawn, as well as about thirty charred bodies. I dragonshaped. I killed them all."

Her eyes narrowed. "You dragonshaped. *Here?*"

He nodded, liking the fact that he'd surprised her. "I know you've been through a lot, Cael, but I need to keep you safe. Are more of those military guys going to show up?"

"I don't know." She shrugged and winced as a wound

opened, then slowly rehealed. "The guy was following Brennon's orders and was in league with Elder Selick." She raised her hand to stroke her necklace.

At the thought of how close he'd come to losing her, his throat tightened and he had to clear a lump before he could speak. "You should replace that flimsy clasp."

"Thanks."

He forced himself to look anyplace but into her eyes. "We can't trust anyone. As soon as you're fit to travel, we should leave." Somehow he'd summon the energy, but from where, he didn't know.

She motioned to the other tubes. "You need to eat more."

Before he had a chance to protest, she pressed more platinum to his lips. "You've dragonshaped. Used platinum, too. I need your strength. Please. Eat."

He did as she directed, because she was right. He needed to keep up his strength to protect her. But he couldn't deny that he liked how much she was worried about him. "Did you find your sister?"

"I haven't seen her. Her husband, Depuck, told me a man grabbed her during the attack. She fought and got loose. Then the man chased after her. We don't know if she escaped . . . or if he caught her again." She held up her hand to forestall him. "That's all Depuck knew."

Lucan swallowed the food, and energy surged through him. This was a new kind of hunger—for platinum—that he would have to feed to keep up his strength. The platinum tasted delicious, but despite his craving, he ate only one tube.

"Don't conserve. Your body just dragonshaped for the first time, right?" she asked, her gaze full of wonder.

"Yes."

"You had an initial supply of platinum and hydrogen—"

"From where?"

She cocked her head and smiled. "Your skin probably absorbed it when we swam in the pool."

In the pool? Had swimming there started his physical changes? He recalled them playing in the water, making love.

"But you can't get enough nutrients through skin absorption. You're weak."

As much as he yearned for the energy, he shook his head. "You need food more than I do."

"My wounds are surface cuts. My organs are whole and fully formed. Yours are still developing. Trust me. You need to eat." She dropped another tube into his lap.

He ate the second tube and could have downed a dozen more. He made a mental note: don't run out of platinum. "How long before you'll be well enough to leave?"

"I can't abandon Depuck." She swung into a sitting position and moved toward the wounded man lying on the floor. "I must see that he's safe."

Lucan held her gaze. "What do you want to do?"

As if their voices had awakened Depuck, he groaned, sat up, and stumbled to his feet. Although she'd barely recovered from her own wounds, Cael hurried to him, wedged a shoulder beneath his arm to support him, and staggered under his weight.

"Here. Let me help." Lucan supported the man's other side, and together he and Cael helped him to the couch.

The man spoke in a croak. "I'll recover. You must find Nisco."

"Depuck. You need more rest." Cael placed two fingers on his neck, but he pulled back before she could take a reading.

"When you have Nisco back safe, I'll rest. Please. Go after her."

Cael shook her head. "We won't leave you—"

"You must." Depuck removed a communicator from a broken drawer. "I'll hide and call for help if I need it."

"He'll be all right." Lucan placed an arm over Cael's shoulder. "Let's find your sister."

Depuck looked at Lucan as if noticing his nudity for the first time. "You need clothes. Mine are in the master closet. Help yourself."

"Thanks." Perhaps once he dressed he would feel more like himself. Because the emotions roaring to life inside him were . . . alien.

Cael led him through a maze of hallways, through a triple-door entrance, and into a master suite. Inside was a private apartment with music and meditation rooms, a media area filled with monitors and windows, an exercise zone that included a swirling lap pool, and finally a closet, brimming with clothing.

If Nisco lived like a queen, then what did Cael's residence, the home of the High Priestess of Avalon, look like?

Only one thing was missing in this luxurious residence—servants. People who lived this well didn't clean and cook and garden, they employed others to do the menial chores.

Perhaps the workers had run away at the time of the attack. Or maybe they'd deliberately stayed away, allowing the atrocity to occur.

Lucan grabbed a tunic and pants from the master closet and dressed, grateful the clothes fit, covering the scales on his arms and legs. "Where are the caretakers?"

"Caretakers?"

"Cooks, maids, butlers?" he asked.

"Nanobots clean. Nisco likes to do the cooking herself. The gardeners come in at night." Cael helped herself to her sister's clothes from another part of the closet and removed her own bloody garments.

Cael's wounds had already closed. At the sight of her flawless skin, he sucked in a deep, steadying breath. And forced himself to look away.

"What about alarm systems?" He found boots and shoved his feet into them. Too small. He strapped on a pair of rugged open-toed sandals that worked just fine.

She frowned. "I already hear ships coming. We don't have much time. They want you really badly."

"Me?"

"Yeah, apparently they think you're the only guy on this moon who knows how to bring down the rest of the shields before Avalon falls into the sinkhole."

"We need to leave Carlane. Now."

"*I* need to leave. *You* could make a deal with them."

"Like I would trust them after they just tortured you?" Did she think so little of him that she believed he'd abandon her to those bastards? "When I go back to Avalon, it'll be under my own terms."

At the roar of the skimmers approaching, she trembled and increased her pace. "Let's go."

"Tell me there's a secret tunnel out of here."

"I've got something even better."

The Round Table was constructed by a strange carpenter from beyond the mist.

—ARTHUR PENDRAGON

17

A cannon?" Lucan took Cael's arm and led her out of the master suite.

She shuddered. "If there was another way to flee—"

"If you hate the cannon, we can take a skimmer." He must have sensed her dread. For a man who could walk away without saying good-bye, he could be amazingly perceptive.

"The military's got to be tracking every skimmer that flies in and out of the city." She hurried back to where they'd left Depuck.

"He's gone. He said he was going to hide." Lucan tugged her through the room. "Come on. Let's go."

"This way." She turned down another wing, and they ran down the hallway.

She still couldn't believe Lucan was here. If he hadn't shown up, she would have died. Hideously. She'd needed him, and Lucan had come for her. He'd saved her life. He cared about her. She'd seen it in his horrified expression, in his raging blue eyes and gentle hands. Even more astonishing, he had dragonshaped.

It was all too much information to process, especially on top of her injuries and healing, which had sapped precious energy. Still, Cael held on to the comforting fact that they were a team again, and for now, she let the rest go.

"Tell me about the cannon. Why so reluctant?" he asked, matching her jogging run.

She wished she could sprint, but her body had yet to fully recover. As they ran, she appreciated that he let her set the pace.

Cael also appreciated that he didn't question her courage, only her reluctance. And she wished she could give him a better reason than childhood terror.

Cael had to rest a little and slowed to a fast walk. "It's always frightened me. I'm not exactly sure why. Perhaps because I don't understand how it works."

"That makes sense." He took her hand. "Does anyone in the military know about the cannon?"

"It's possible." She sighed. Elder Selick had betrayed her, and there was no telling what sacred information he had revealed. "But since the military probably believes I'm dead, I doubt anyone will consider that we're going to use the ancient escape route."

"We can't make assumptions. Your captor's probably already late reporting to his superiors. Those reinforcements we hear could be routine, or they could suspect we've gotten away."

"If we weren't so weak, we could fly out," she said, "but flying's not an option. This way." She led Lucan out a side door and into the back compound, looking over her shoulder at the sky, her pulse skipping in dread. "The ships are closer."

"I hear them."

Hand in hand, Cael and Lucan sprinted across the grass. They raced past sculpted hedges, beds of blooming flowers, and several tropical fish ponds. Panting, she headed straight for the expanse of wide stairs that led into the ancient temple, built in honor of dragonshapers. By dragon standards, the shrine was cozy. Mammoth columns, separated by a distance wide enough for her to pass through in dragon form, supported the domed roof.

As they ran up the worn stone steps, she breathed in the familiar scents of incense, wax, and old dust that had settled into ancient cracks on the stronghold's thick walls. The chamber's wide entrance narrowed and Lucan slowed, craning back his head to read the inscriptions that wrapped around the graceful columns.

"No time for that." She tugged him through the corridor with its magnificent stained-glass windows. Usually she stopped to light ceremonial tapers and ring bells, a tribute to her dragon ancestors, but today, ritual was abandoned for urgency. She hurried directly for the temple's center.

Lucan had slowed again to peer at the vaulted roof. Natural light filtered through the upper windows, flowed over the walls, flickered over the golden floor. He let out a low, appreciative whistle. "Wow."

She'd spent so much time here, she sometimes forgot how mesmerizing the platinum pictures on the ceiling could be. Quadruple spires carved in tiers of marbelite depicted Dragonian life, the Goddess, and the esoteric realm of reincarnation. The Elders had used those carved and gilded images, messages from her ancestors, to teach her what it meant to be a dragonshaper.

"Come on, Lucan. I need help." Hurrying into the next chamber, she headed straight for a lever in the wall that engaged an ancient device built with gears and machine parts and metals from meteors that had crashed into their moon millions of years ago. The antiquated floor trembled, the massive weight rumbling as the stone slabs slid open to reveal another archaic device. Smelling old and dusty, the intimidating cannon perched on a plain black pedestal that rose high above the base.

"Oh, my God." Lucan's eyes widened in awe. "That's the Round Table."

"Table?" She looked from him to the round platform.

"Nothing," he muttered, but his eyes had taken on a wild gleam.

Cael had used the cannon only once, and that memory made her go cold. Could they both fit inside the structure? Was the device powerful enough to blast the two of them through the opening in the roof?

While she set coordinates, Lucan leaped onto the round base and inspected the cannon. Tubular in shape, about a body length wide, the cannon looked like a huge pipe, the mouth pointed at the open dome. He skimmed his palm over the surface.

He looked impressed, but he didn't understand that this device might very well kill them both. Cael could point out a pictograph that depicted a dragon who'd failed at her attempt to clear the sanctuary's circular opening. Her blood had stained the roof for two decades. But Cael didn't want to think about the gruesome story, never mind repeat it.

She gestured for Lucan to walk around the cannon to the other side. "Climb in."

"And then what?"

Her hearing keen, Cael picked up the drone of military skimmers closing in. "Ships are almost here. Get in."

She pulled another lever, and several large, rough-hewn stones rose from the edges of the platform. At the sight of the stones, Lucan's gaze flew to hers in surprise and excitement. "This is unbelievable."

"It's very old."

He stared at the pillars that powered the cannon. He was mumbling under his breath, something about Stonehenge and Knights of the Round Table.

She gave him an odd look. "What's Stonehenge?"

He shook his head in amazement. "This place reminds me of another . . . it doesn't matter right now." He gestured to the large circular stones. "What are these ring stones for?"

"Those power the cannon."

She pulled a second lever, and steep stone steps rose out of the floor. "Climb over the lip and slide to the bottom."

She had to give Lucan credit. He didn't hesitate. Taking the steps two at a time, he climbed over the edge and slid into the cannon's mouth. He landed on the bottom with a thud, then held up his arms, ready to catch her.

She scooted over the lip and slid down the polished stone into his welcoming arms. "I've only done this once. It's not . . . fun."

Lucan cocked his head, questions in his eyes. "It's going to shoot us into the air, right?"

"Sort of."

"And then what?"

"We dragonshape or we die."

"Then why do we need the cannon? Why can't we just dragonshape and fly out of here?"

"We're too weak. Besides, the cannon can shoot us faster than we can fly."

"Can it shoot us all the way to Avalon?"

She nodded. At the roar of skimmers overhead, she had to shout. "But I need to find Nisco."

"How?" he asked, eyes bleak.

"She left me a message to meet her at the medical center. I have to believe she got away." She bit her bottom lip. "I'll find her."

Outside the temple, commanders shouted orders to soldiers. Cael fingered her necklace. "You ready?"

He nodded.

She pushed a series of dark spots in the stone control panel, then turned to wrap her arm around Lucan. "Hold me."

He complied, his touch gentle. He smelled musky, and to her, it was the most beautiful scent ever. She was alive. In his arms.

Soldiers stomped through the temple.

"Tighter. Hold me tighter. And remember to follow me after we dragonshape."

Beneath their feet, the ancient stones began to rumble, the cannon's engines beginning to fire. Heat from the rocks engulfed them. The large ring of stones drew in energy from the cosmos, and bolts of electricity arced around them.

Lucan held her tight. One moment they were standing inside the cannon, the next they were in midair. Above Feridon. Just as quickly, they began to fall. Wind rushed through her hair and cooled her flesh.

They'd made it through the ceiling, into the cloud cover over the outskirts of the city, not far from Jaylon's medical center. But the speed of their plunging descent had made holding on to Lucan impossible. Flung from her arms, he tumbled. But even as he fell, he craned his head to look for her.

She reached for him with her wings. She'd dragon-shaped.

He hadn't.

Cael. His mind called to her.

Lucan was plunging like a skimmercraft diver with no parachute, tumbling through the air, plummeting toward Pendragon. In moments he would smash into the ground.

I'm coming. Without hesitation, Cael dived, tucking her wings in tight, streamlining her body. She caught up to him, adjusted her speed, and then flew under him, matching their rate of descent. *Climb on.*

Lucan grasped her back. And slipped. She stabilized, felt him seize her neck. For a moment, Lucan remained airborne, then pulled himself over, straddled her shoulders, and clung—not an easy task.

Got you. Lucan's mind linked with hers as he wrapped his arms around her neck.

Hold on.

She needed to climb into the clouds before Feridon's citizens spotted her in the sky.

"Hurry." Lucan's words conveyed an urgency she shared. They flew over the city, and she picked up a thermal current and spiraled, climbing high into the cloud cover. She didn't need a clear view to find the medical center. Jaylon had been sick for several years, and she'd visited often.

But Cael was finding flying an effort. Her injuries and healing had depleted her platinum reserves. Hunger drove her forward. She must feed soon—or fall out of the sky from exhaustion.

No.

If she did, her mate would die. And she would be alone.

Her wings ached. Her lungs heaved with effort.

She had to reach the medical center. Her wings felt so heavy, the man on her back like lead.

She couldn't stay high enough or level. *We aren't going to make it.*

We will. You can do this.

She tried to relax, tried to make her limited energy last. But it was no good. She corkscrewed downward, dived through the traffic streams, barely avoided a building's canopy, fought the wind shear and vortices whipping around the skyscrapers.

Set down on that rooftop, he instructed.

He'd picked a building large enough to support her weight. Saving every drop of energy for the rooftop landing, she tensed, dropped. Her feet touched and she collapsed.

LUCAN REMOVED HIS tunic, wrapped a naked and unconscious Cael in it, and carried her from the rooftop. He opened a door, followed a stairway down to a hallway. She needed clothing, hydrogen, platinum, and time to recuperate.

He needed recovery time, too—not so much from physical exhaustion as the enormity of what he'd seen. A round table with names of knights engraved around the rim. Twelve knights, plus Arthur Pendragon. And the round table was motored by a device that looked like a miniature Stonehenge. The concept blew his mind.

Lucan tried several locked doors along the long corridor before one opened. After peering into an unoccupied room, he slipped inside, placed Cael in the only chair, and looked around. Cleaning supplies, brooms, chemicals, and a mop surrounded him.

No handy uniforms hung inside. He had two choices, stay and hope she recovered, or leave and search for platinum and clothing. He didn't like either option. The idea of leaving her unprotected tied his gut into knots.

When the storage-room door suddenly opened, Lucan grabbed the intruder, a woman, by the wrist and dragged her inside. Tall, busty, and with sharp brown eyes, the woman didn't resist or call out for help. She didn't seem particularly surprised by their presence, either.

She carried clothing in her free hand and thrust it at him. "Here. These should fit the High Priestess if you roll up the pant cuffs. I'm Lady Barena. I came to serve."

Was this some kind of trick? "Who knows we're here?"

Barena raised her eyebrows. "I don't know about any others. I saw my lady land on the roof. Her loyal followers know that she often needs clothing after she lands. All who help clothe her . . . are blessed. Do you require . . ." Barena peered at Cael. "Is the lady . . . ill?"

"Exhausted."

"Yes, of course." Barena was clearly relieved.

"What city is this?"

"Feridon."

So the cannon had blasted them to their target. And Cael had flown them the rest of the way. "Can we expect others who wish to serve the High Priestess?" he asked.

Barena frowned. "Is there a problem?"

"There was an attack on Lady Cael at her home. Until she learns who was behind—"

"An attack? That cannot be."

"It's true." Cael opened her eyes. Weary but alert, she gestured to the woman. "Come to me. Don't be afraid."

She lifted her hand and touched the stone necklace, then beckoned the wary Barena forward again. Finally, Barena took one step, then another. Cael held out her hand and placed her finger above the woman's pulse at her neck. "Blessed are those who serve the dragonshaper."

"Thank you." Barena glowed but moved back quickly, exhibiting that duality of fear and reverence Lucan had noted before. Barena hesitated, then spoke again. "Is there anything else I can do to help you?"

"Say nothing to anyone about our meeting. Secrecy is for your own safety. Those that seek to do harm have hurt my family. They might harm you, also."

"I understand, my lady." Barena backed away. "I will say nothing."

Lucan stopped her before she backed out the door. "Can you tell us more about this building?"

Barena frowned. "It's a gambling enterprise. The premises include private rooms, many restaurants, and a shopping area."

"Thank you." Lucan held open the door, and the woman left. He turned to Cael, who still looked pale, and helped her into her clothes. "Is there somewhere we can get you some platinum? And how far is it to the medical center?"

"It's not far. We can walk."

Cael shoved to her feet, then swayed. She hadn't answered his question about the platinum.

He stopped and turned to face her. He raised her chin with his fingertips and looked into her eyes. An undeniable connection flared.

His voice was soft, husky. "We could be walking into a trap."

"Nisco wouldn't do that—not if she had a choice."

"Still . . . there's something I want you to know." He slipped his hand from her chin to her neck. He could feel her pulse beating wildly.

"Yes?"

She waited for him to say more. But he couldn't tell her he was from Earth, that she meant so much to him that he hoped she'd return with him. She wanted the Grail for Pendragon, and he wouldn't make her choose.

Yanking her to him, he kissed her with the desperation of a drowning man sucking down air. Like a man who couldn't bear to think beyond this moment. This place. This kiss.

*Pendragon is the banner of Briton under one great
dragon and stands in token of all folk, Briton, Chris-
tian, Druid, Old People, and all believers of Avalon.*
—ARTHUR PENDRAGON

18

Finally, Lucan had kissed her. And she melted into his
arms, surged into his kiss. Having him there with her
meant everything. Instead of going to Avalon for the
Grail, he'd come to help *her*. Even now she could feel his
worry for her, as well as the constant thread of desire.
Wrapping her arms around his shoulders, she wove her
fingers into his hair, stood on tiptoes, and pressed against
him chest to chest, hips to hips.

He'd gathered her into his arms with all the urgency
she could have wished for. For a moment Cael allowed
her own emotions to sweep her away, but then her empathic skills kicked into gear. She read deeper, and the
conflict raging in Lucan disturbed her. She sensed his
real concern for her. But even as she tasted his intensity,
beneath the surface, he was taut, tense, torn.

He broke their embrace too soon. She felt him bank
his desire, and he reached up to tuck a loose strand of her
hair behind her ear.

Disguised in a scavenged hat and clothes that covered

her scales, Cael was finally going to fulfill one of her promises to Jaylon. And hopefully meet with Nisco. Cael still hadn't replenished her platinum stores, but her anticipation of seeing her family helped buoy her energy.

The freedom of moving through the medical center without anyone recognizing her was liberating, but the restful pink walls reminded Cael of all her failures as a healer. Although medical science had made steady advances during the last few centuries, too many of her people came here and never went home. Many diseases had no cures. And she'd tired of waiting for a scientific breakthrough, tired of hoping that medical researchers would find cures.

The moment Cael opened Jaylon's door, Sonelle gasped in recognition. Behind the attending nurse's back, Cael raised a finger to her lips and Sonelle nodded.

Her sister's hair had grayed since Cael had last seen her. She'd lost weight, and her pretty blue eyes were bloodshot and shadowed. In her sorrow, her sister wasn't eating properly. Or sleeping. A good mother, she lived at Jaylon's beside, but she was neglecting her own health.

The nurse gave Lucan and Cael a professional nod. "Don't stay too long and tire our patient."

Cael noted the little guy's color. Too pale. Jaylon's eyes looked huge in his sunken face. Tubes went into his stomach. An oxygen tube was strapped beneath his nose. She automatically checked his monitors and suppressed her dismay at the readings.

Cael sat beside him on the bed. "How're you feeling, Jaylon?"

Jaylon looked up, finally recognizing her through the disguise. "Did you find the Grail?"

At his weak whisper, a lump clogged her throat, and

she shook her head. The dark circles around his eyes and his paper-thin skin told her Jaylon's cancer was no longer in remission.

Jaylon's stoic gaze moved on to Lucan. "Are you a friend of Lady Cael?"

"I am."

"Good." Jaylon sighed. "She'll need a friend when I'm gone."

Sonelle sobbed. "I told you not to talk like that."

"Lying doesn't change the truth." Jaylon licked his lip, and Cael held a water glass with a drinking straw to his mouth and wished she held the Grail. This brave child had rarely complained. Not when he couldn't play with the other children. Not when his stomach rejected all food.

He sipped, swallowed, and peered at her. Illness seemed to have made him much wiser than his years. "Tell me about the Grail."

When Cael didn't respond, not trusting her voice to remain even, Lucan spoke up. "We believe the Grail's inside Avalon. We're making progress. The first shield's down."

"There are more?"

Lucan nodded. "Those will come down, too, when we decipher the code."

Bless Lucan for giving the child hope.

"When you find the Grail, you'll bring it to me and cure my cancer?" Jaylon asked, his soulful eyes staring straight into Lucan's.

"That's the plan." Lucan took Jaylon's hand, and it looked so fragile in his large one. "So you hold on. You fight, okay?"

Seeing him so honest and tender with the little boy

tore at Cael. The child's own father refused to visit anymore. He found it too painful. He'd abandoned Sonelle, too. Lucan would never be that weak. If he committed, he would be there for his wife, his son. Funny how Cael was so certain of that.

Jaylon closed his eyes, and Sonelle gestured for them to come to her by the window. Her eyes brimmed with tears. "We're losing him."

Cael reached out to hug her sister, but Sonelle jerked away. "Don't touch me. I don't need more trouble."

Cael ducked her head and bit her lower lip. After spending time with Lucan, she'd let down her guard. A mistake she couldn't repeat. "No one recognizes me dressed like this."

"You know I can't take that chance." Sonelle raised her head and squared her shoulders. "Jaylon needs me. I can't risk . . ."

"I understand," Cael said. When Lucan slipped his hand into hers, she clutched him so hard his knuckle cracked, but he didn't pull away, and she relaxed just a little. "Have you heard from Nisco?" Cael didn't mention the attack at the residence or her fear that Nisco might be a prisoner or dead. Sonelle didn't need any more on her shoulders.

"By the Goddess. I forgot." Sonelle reached into her pocket and pulled out a sealed note. "She sent this by messenger. It's addressed to you."

"Thanks." Cael took the envelope.

Sonelle eyed her disguise. "Are you in danger?"

"No," Cael lied, then remembered their lack of funds. "Just in a hurry to return to find the Grail. Could you lend me some credits? I'll pay you back."

Sonelle dug into her pocket and handed her sister a

card. "Take all you need, especially if it will help Jaylon."

"Thanks." Cael said good-bye to her sister and Jaylon, exited the medical center with Lucan, and steadied her nerves before she opened the envelope Nisco had sent her.

Cael unfolded a piece of computer paper and quickly scanned the printed words. "Nisco says after the attack at the residence it was too dangerous to meet at the medical center as she'd planned. She claims she's hiding nearby. In the Feridon nest."

"So she got away from the man who was chasing her?" Lucan asked.

"She didn't mention him. Goddess knows if this note's genuine and really from Nisco." Worry weakened her knees, and she trembled at the idea of another of the general's men grabbing her sister. "She's also enclosed a copy of the formula the private investigator found in General Brennon's briefcase."

Cael headed to a bench, sat down, and broke the seal of the inner envelope. She pulled out another sheet of paper and shook her head in confusion. "I don't understand what this is."

She handed the paper filled with scientific equations to Lucan. He held it up, then let out a low whistle. "These are specs to build a device that tracks communicator calls."

"I don't . . ."

"That's how the military knew where we were. They've been tracking your calls."

"But . . ." She stared at the paper. "I oversee all military funding. I should have heard about . . ."

"Obviously, they have secrets. And if Nisco knows them, it explains why she isn't answering your calls."

"Goddess. These specs are why the swordsman wanted Nisco as well as you. They need to keep this device a secret. Because once the technology is revealed, no one who's hiding from them will make any calls. I need to fly to the Feridon cave so Nisco can give me the original document to take to the government. With proof that Brennon's been developing an illegal device, the government should lock him up."

"It could be a trap." Lucan placed an arm over her shoulders, giving comfort but also making her feel as if they were a team.

"I have to go. If not for me, Nisco wouldn't be in this mess." She shuddered. "I can't let General Brennon get to her."

"And I'm not letting you go up against them alone." He shot her a warm glance, protective heat flaring from his eyes. "Are there other cannons in other shrines that we can use?"

She shook her head. "There's only one sacred cannon. We were lucky the ancient technology worked—"

"There's a limit on how often you can use it?"

"No, but—"

His eyes sparkled with interest. "That device was amazing. I saw the ring stones charging up. And we seemed to travel instantaneously from the ground into space. Do the Elders know how it works?"

She shook her head and sighed. "The cannon is as old as Avalon. Our ancestors were more technologically advanced than we are. We have yet to figure out all their mysteries."

"Are there ancient stories about the cannon and the ring stones?"

"Why are you so curious?" she asked. Her scales

itched, and she was picking up that mental-emotional barrier he erected so often.

"I saw ancient symbols on the stones in your shrine. Ones like those at Avalon. Seems to me that the people who built your residence may have been the same ones who built Avalon."

"You're probably right. We've never understood how Avalon's shield or the High Priestess's cannon works. But enough about the past. Right now I'm too weak to fly. We need to buy platinum without casting suspicion on ourselves, then fly to the nest." She stood from the bench and strolled toward the city center.

Lucan followed. "Platinum's available in the city?"

"It's used to make jewelry, but expensive."

"And if you eat enough hydrogen and platinum, you'll be able to change shape at will?"

"What's with all the questions?" she asked.

"I need to understand my biology." His tone was even, but she could sense the intensity beyond his words.

"I'm not an expert in male—"

"I need to know the advantages and limitations of my dragonshaping."

Frustration simmered within her. "Is that why you came back? You think I have the answers you seek?"

His mouth twisted wryly. "Of course not. I was worried about you."

He did care for her. Just not enough to give her what she wanted. And that was why the damned man had her so on edge. One moment he was sincere and caring, the next passionate. And yet . . . he was holding back. She wanted to know why.

They strode past stores and restaurants. Traffic passed,

and the sidewalks were filled with strolling shoppers, workers on lunch breaks, and teens holding hands. When a skimmer pulled out of traffic, screeching to a stop at the curb, Cael's instincts kicked in. She tugged Lucan into a knitting store.

Pulse skittish, she glanced over her shoulder through the store's front window to see two men in military uniforms spring out of the skimmer, hands nervously fingering their holstered weapons.

"Out the back." Lucan hurried her past skeins of yarn and knitting needles. They ended up in an alley. Weary to the bone, so fatigued she could barely move, she stumbled, trying to keep up.

"Run," Lucan urged.

"I can't." She waved him off. "It's you they want. Leave me."

She expected him to argue. Instead, he gave her a quick kiss and ran down the alley.

He'd left her.

Shocked, she slid against the wall to her butt. Numb, aching, and wondering where Lucan had gone to, she waited for the soldiers. No way had Lucan abandoned her for good. Deep in her hearts she knew he hadn't saved her from torture to abandon her to this new threat.

She might not know his plan, but she believed he was doing his best to help her. She'd seen the horror in his eyes when he'd found her chained and bloody. He'd stayed with her to search for Nisco—even when he'd wanted to return to Avalon. She might not have been experienced with relationships, but she knew him. He cared about her. If he had a choice, such an honorable man would never leave her in danger.

Her nerves ragged, she didn't wait long. The soldiers

raced out of the store like fire was nipping at their heels. For a moment they debated whether to go right or left, their gazes passing right by her.

If she was lucky, they'd run the other way. Not even notice her.

Cael wasn't lucky.

"There she is!" A soldier shouted, his voice fearful. He yanked his blaster from his holster. "Don't move."

If she could have moved, she might have laughed, but she didn't have the energy. If they wanted her, they were going to have to carry her. But no one touched a dragonshaper.

They'd probably shoot her.

She was going to die. And as much as that thought upset her, she wished she knew Lucan was safe. She wished he could know that she went to her death without blaming him. Whatever he was, he would do his best to help her. She feared he'd been cornered, too.

Cael closed her eyes and prayed for the blaster to take her out in one clean shot.

She heard a loud thud, a grunt, and two shots fired. But she felt no pain. At first she thought she was dead. According to the Elders, the Goddess promised there would be no pain in the afterlife.

With her last ounce of energy, she opened her eyes. She wasn't dead, but the soldiers were, or, at the least, they were unconscious.

Lucan stood over them, trussing their hands behind them with their belts. He'd leaped off the roof onto her assailants. He'd saved her. Again.

Lucan insisted that Cael eat all the platinum they'd bought in the city. With her strength renewed, she flew him to the cave outside Feridon and humanshaped. Lucan removed her clothes from where he'd stored them inside his tunic and handed them to her. Cael dressed, hoping that the computer message Sonelle had given her from Nisco was genuine. But if Nisco was here, why hadn't she greeted them? Her sister knew the way well and would not have gotten lost, yet Merlin was the only living creature in sight.

When Cael and Lucan entered the dark cavern, Nisco wasn't inside.

"Where do you think she is?" Lucan peered over Cael's shoulder into the empty space, his breath warm on her neck.

"She could be taking a longer route to make sure she isn't followed." Cael prayed that she was right.

"Then all we can do for now is wait." Lucan gestured to the sacks of supplies stored on open shelves. "You said there's food here?"

She was still hungry, but he must be starving. She gestured to the stalactites and stalagmites. "Help yourself. This cave is rich in platinum."

"I can eat this in human form?" He broke off an icicle-shaped piece.

"Your teeth are stronger, and your digestive system has adapted."

He sniffed, raised an eyebrow, and began to gnaw. She did the same, replenishing the nutrients she needed so badly.

"What about him?" Lucan's gaze went to Merlin. "Aren't you going to feed him?"

"Most of the time he hunts for himself."

"Merlin helped save your life back at the residence. If he hadn't attacked . . ."

"He's a good friend."

Merlin perched over the entrance as if standing watch. Every once in a while he turned his head and blinked.

"How did he find us here?" Lucan asked.

She shrugged. "I have no idea."

"When those men captured you at the residence, Merlin led me straight to your location." Lucan glanced from the owl to her, his gaze bright, blue intensity simmering beneath the surface. "Did he follow you to Avalon, too?"

Cael remembered thinking she'd seen him in the cooling conduit. "I'm not sure. Why?"

"Just curious. How long has he been a pet?"

"Merlin's not a pet. He's wild and free."

"But he happens to show up when . . ."

"When he feels like it." She floated a blanket over the floor, then sat and scooted over to give Lucan room. "The very first time I dragonshaped, Merlin was there. He often escorts me. I'm glad for his company."

She poured them juice from the supplies and shared a few honey cakes from one of the airtight canisters. Lucan's questions seemed odd, almost as if he was skirting around other issues—like the feelings that were obviously growing between them.

She trailed her fingers over his palm. She toyed with his sleeve and his wrist where his sensitive scales fluttered.

He jerked. Not away. But in surprise. His eyes widened, and he unbuttoned the tunic's cuff, turned his palm up, and stared. The scales had elevated and were vibrating.

He sucked in a breath. "What else will happen?"

"You'll grow stronger. Your human flesh will become

denser, tougher. When injured, you'll recover quickly. You'll age more slowly."

"How slowly?"

She leaned over and kissed his scales, and they undulated in response. "Dragonshapers can live for several centuries. But since you weren't born of the blood—"

"Several centuries?" He whistled. "And there's no reversing the process?"

"Why would you want to?" She shot him a seductive grin and watched his scales ripple, his lust build. His irises darkened and grew, until the whites of his eyes vanished.

He was a beautiful man. When she'd first seen him, he'd been larger than most Dragonian men. Stronger and more fit, too. But with his dragonblood, he was honed, his cheekbones sharper, his muscles more defined. He'd put on mass, all of it muscle.

No longer just a man—he was a force unto himself. A very male, very attractive force.

He lay back on the blanket, and she snuggled against his side, her cheek pressed to his chest. And heard his heartbeats—both of them. Goddess. His human physiology was evolving, making him her perfect mate in every way save one.

She could see that he could no more deny the pull of their attraction than she could. She could hear the increase in his pulse, his ragged breathing.

"I want you," she murmured. Cael was way past denying she wanted him. Way past holding back. She was going to fight for herself and what she wanted.

And she wanted him. She desperately wanted to show him how she felt. After that, the decision was out of her hands.

She'd live with the consequences. Because Lucan Roarke was worth fighting for, and if she fought and lost—that was way more honorable than retreating from a losing battle.

Desire flared in his eyes. "Thank the universe. I wasn't sure if I could hold back much longer." He dropped the shield that had blocked her from feeling his emotions. The blast of lust might have knocked her over if she'd been on her feet.

Merlin fluttered his wings and flew out of the cave.

Lucan tugged her shirt over her head. She slid his off, taking the opportunity to curl her fingertips over his massive shoulders. His flesh was so warm, so firm. And his scent set her on fire.

She tugged at his pants, but he brushed aside her trembling fingers. She opened her mouth to protest, and he placed one finger over her lips.

"Shh. Let me."

Forget that. She was done waiting. Teasing his finger with her tongue, she sucked it into her mouth and then bit him. And when he slipped away, she leaned forward and licked her way over his chest to his nipple.

His body quivered in anticipation. She continued teasing him with her tongue as she let her hands wander over his flat stomach, to his hips, to his straining sex. He sucked in a breath, and she grinned with satisfaction, ever so slowly sliding her lips over the path her fingers had just taken.

When she took his pulsing sex into her mouth, she explored, she nibbled and nipped and teased. He radiated pleasure, bathing her in it, until she was trembling with his desire. She took him to the brink. His muscles tensed. His thighs quivered.

She slowed down, giving him just a little breathing

room, and then once again she amped up the urgency, loving the way he responded. His fingers in her hair massaged her scalp and she prickled all the way to her toes.

"Damn, you feel good." He wound his fingers into her hair. "Too good."

He tugged her up and into his arms. In moments they lay naked on the blanket. He swooped down on her, covering her forehead, her nose, her cheeks, and finally her lips with swift, sensual kisses.

Sliding her arms around his back, she attempted to draw him closer. She might as well have tried to move a mountain. Rock-hard, he didn't budge. Instead, he continued to brush his lips over her flesh, tickling her earlobe, nuzzling her neck.

"Is that all you can do?" She wriggled her hips.

His eyes burned with a golden flame in a sea of blue. "I'm just warming up."

She pursed her lips into a pout. "But I'm already . . . hot."

"To me"—his lips brushed her along the tender spot behind her ear—"you're always hot."

With his words came a fiery burn, a sizzling heat that blazed to her core.

Arching her back, she slid her breasts teasingly against his chest, eager to feel more of him. She twined her fingers into his thick hair, clasped his head, and nipped his shoulder—not enough to draw blood, just enough to sting.

"No, darling. I'm not permitting those kinds of distractions." With a grin, he rolled her to her belly with gentle but firm hands.

He'd called her darling. Heat filled her belly, and moisture seeped between her soft, private folds.

When she tried to roll back, he swatted her bottom. The sting raised the heat. Her blood caught fire, kindling a blaze between her thighs.

Squirming, she tried to press her legs together to create the friction she craved, but his hands thwarted her. Ever inventive, he was sensuously drawing tiny circles up the insides of her thighs along her scales. "What are you doing?" she gasped.

He chuckled. "What I do best." One hand slipped under her belly. He'd placed a rolled blanket under her hips, almost bringing her to her hands and knees. "Relax."

Relax? Every cell screamed for his touch. Her scales writhed. She tried to squirm but with a firm palm on the small of her back, he pinned her in place.

Then he slipped his hands around her and found her breasts. At the same time, his hips pinned hers to the blanket. His fingers plucked at her nipples, and his breath fanned her ear. "You like this, don't you, sweetheart?"

"Yes." She quivered with the need to have him. Her tone was an open invitation to hurry, but he didn't seem to notice. He was too centered on slowly caressing her breasts, slowly tugging and teasing her nipples.

She tried to arch into his hands, but since he'd pinned her with his weight, he held her exactly where he wanted. And his tender, leisurely teasing was sweet torture. She needed more of him. Ached for him inside her, under her, over her. Why wasn't he filling her?

"I want this to be good for you," he murmured.

She groaned. "It's already good. It would be better if you'd—"

"Touch you here." Gently he lowered his hand to her hip, traced a path around to her belly, then dipped into her curls.

She quivered in anticipation. "Yes. There."

Ever so slowly, he parted her folds. She wanted to scream at him to get on with it. To touch her where she wanted. To give her what she needed.

She tried to lift her bottom, to guide his fingers where she needed them most. But he kept her still, his fingertips teasing the insides of her thighs, the outer edges of her moist folds. And yet he, too, trembled with fierce need. His holding back was foolish. She wanted him without the chivalry. She wanted him raw. She ached for primitive and primal.

She bit back a moan, her cells screaming for release. Every atom of her being demanded he set them free.

She couldn't bear another second of his light, gentle touch, not with the rushing sensations almost overwhelming her. "Please, Lucan."

His fingers stroked their own rhythm on her clit, slowly wrapping her in a sensual haze. His ragged breath fanned her ear. His hard sex nestled against her bottom. His clever fingers never ceased taunting and stroking. Occasionally he slipped inside her wet heat, the motion a hint of what he would eventually give her.

"Does it feel good, sweetheart?" he murmured.

"Yes. Oh, yes."

"We're . . . going . . . to . . . go . . . slow and easy. Right until the end."

"By the Goddess, why?"

"Because I'm a man." His fingers moved in a slow, sensual circle. "Because I'm not . . . a beast."

She could barely think, but this was important. She fought to suppress her lust so she could speak. "Fighting our natures is wrong. Giving in is expected. It's right. It's what's supposed to be."

"Not for me."

She felt his determination thunder through her. She didn't know how he could hold back. Frantic to move, to wrap her arms around him, to pump her hips, she burned for him, and his tender, slow friction brought her ever higher. Then a warm explosion blessed her with sweet, merciful release. As she spiraled into her pleasure, he finally, finally entered her, finally filled her.

He gave her no time to recuperate, no time to catch her breath. At first he thrust slowly, his pace gentle. His hands slipped over her breasts and his fingertips teased her nipples.

Then he was like a dam finally breaking after too much rain. And the moment he lost control of his emotions, she felt his desire, showering her, drenching her. There was no more denying their true needs. He clamped his hands on her waist. His hips moved as if with a will of their own. Moved with power. He began to pound into her, his hands demanding, his lips greedy on her neck, her ear, her shoulder.

He spilled into her with a heady groan, his hearts thundering, his breathing ragged. And still he held her tight, his fingertips caressing her hips, his warm breath on her neck.

Thank the Goddess. He'd stopped fighting himself and given her what she most wanted—his real self. His essence. The man she loved.

Yes. She loved him. With her spirit, with her heart and with her soul.

Pleasure washed over her once more, this time his feelings flooded her, too. Defiance, protectiveness, lust, and something else . . . something indefinable that she was afraid to name, something that made this bonding of body and spirit extraordinary and special.

As she recovered in his arms, she was certain he'd felt it, too. A moment when they weren't High Priestess and linguist, not man and woman, but together as one.

Resting in his arms, at peace, she started to doze and noted in a haze of bliss that he hadn't vibrated this time. That earlier peculiarity must have been a result of his ongoing transformation. She started to mention it but heard footsteps outside the cave.

"Did you hear that?" She sat up and grabbed her clothes.

A man shouted, "Are you here, son of Adam?"

He who sheds blood for me shall I call brother.
—ARTHUR PENDRAGON

19

Lucan recognized Rion's voice immediately. When Avalon's astrophysicist called out "son of Adam," using words from Layamon's poem, which Lucan had read on the cave wall, his every sense sharpened. "What the hell's Rion doing here?"

Beside him, Cael quickly dressed. "By the Goddess. Maybe Nisco's with him."

Lucan hoped he would have an opportunity to talk to Rion alone and find out what the man knew about the "son of Adam" reference. Doing so in front of Cael would be too dangerous. Perhaps Cael and her sister would want some private time, too.

But when they met Rion at the entrance, Nisco was nowhere in sight. Cael went forward and greeted Rion.

Uncertain whether he could trust Rion, Lucan edged protectively closer to Cael. Rion's gray eyes were clear and he wore a welcoming smile, but the dark circles under his eyes and the shadow of his beard hinted at hard times, as did his torn and filthy clothes. He looked rough, tough, and dangerous.

Lucan was thankful for his dragon blood, which made

him stronger than normal in human form. Without it, he might not have been able to take Rion down in a fight. Rion was bigger, broader, his muscles honed. It was good to know he could do whatever was necessary to protect Cael.

"Have you seen Nisco?" Cael asked.

Rion nodded. "After I intercepted General Brennon's orders to attack your home, I got there as soon as I could." Rion hung his head. "They'd already beaten your brother-in-law. She fought me at first, but I was able to convince your sister to let me take her out of harm's way."

"Thank the Goddess." Cael looked stricken by the thought of what might have happened if Rion hadn't arrived. "So where *did* you take my sister?"

"She wanted to go to the medical center, but it was too dangerous. I talked her into hiding at a hotel in Feridon. From the hotel, we sent a messenger to the medical center with the note asking you to meet us here instead."

"So where is she?"

"My lady, when Nisco heard your message about Depuck's injuries, she insisted on going to his side."

"But he's not at the residence, he's hiding."

"She seemed certain he would go to a cousin and planned to meet him there. She said you'd understand."

"I do." If Cael was disappointed, she didn't let it show.

Lucan searched for a skimmer and frowned. "How did you get here?"

"Nisco flew me partway in a skimmer. I walked the rest."

"Please, come inside." Cael gestured to Rion. "We were just about to eat."

"No, we weren't." Lucan blocked Rion from following Cael into the cave. "Why are you here?"

"Such suspicion." Rion looked puzzled and annoyed.

"You haven't been accused of murder as we have. And I haven't forgotten you're on General Brennon's payroll."

Rion folded his arms over his chest. "And I've been working with Quentin at Avalon. So what?"

"Seems to me you're very cozy with the people who are hunting us."

Rion held his stare. "Working there, brother, is how I've kept you informed of their activities."

"I'm not your brother."

Rion grinned. "So you're still fighting."

Lucan frowned. "I'm not fighting anyone."

"Except yourself."

Cael stepped back outside the cave. "What do you mean?"

"Cael, please go inside." Lucan spoke softly.

She rolled her eyes in irritation. "I'm not going anywhere."

"This man may be dangerous."

Her voice was calm but threaded with steel. "Rion saved Nisco. How can you doubt—"

"We don't know where his allegiance lies," Lucan countered.

"Look, let's just speak the truth." Rion sat, leaned against a rock, tipped his face to the sun, and for a moment closed his eyes. When he reopened them, his gaze locked with Lucan's. "I'm a son of Gerwain. You are a son of Adam. And it is written that together we shall uphold the laws of Uther and the laws of Arthur."

Cael stepped beside Lucan. "I don't understand."

Lucan did. Since Rion knew about Arthur and Gerwain and Adam, he probably knew about Earth, as well. But how would Rion know Earth's history unless he was from Earth? And if he was from Earth, why hadn't he said so sooner?

Rion bowed his head to Cael. "Lady, fear not. Our hearts are true to this quest to find the Grail before the Tribes can steal it."

"The Tribes?" Stomach in knots, Lucan folded his arms across his chest. On Earth, the Tribes had been the enemies of King Arthur. Most historians believed the Tribes were Saxons and Vikings. With the help of the Knights of the Round Table, King Arthur had kept law in his land by keeping the Tribes at bay. But Rion was speaking as if the Tribes sill existed.

Rion pulled a thermos from his tunic and sipped, appearing as weary as if he'd just completed a long and difficult journey and was stealing himself to gear up for yet another. "For centuries the Tribes have sought the Grail. If they find it, their darkness will snuff out our light."

Lucan snorted. "You aren't speaking like an astrophysicist, but like some religious—"

"Like someone," Rion interrupted, "who has read the ancient legends and has seen into the future."

Lucan scowled. "What are you saying?"

"I get flashes." Rion's gaze challenged him to listen with care. "They're a form of clairvoyance. Bits and pieces of history, as well as of the present and future, come to me in waking dreams. It's a family gift. Or curse," he said with a shrug, "depending on how you look at it."

"He believes what he says." Cael looked at Rion intently, as if searching for what the man wasn't saying.

"I'd like more proof," Lucan muttered but recalled

how Rion had seemed certain the shield was about to come down—right before it had vanished.

Rion pulled out a note and handed it to Cael. She shook her head in confusion. "This is Nisco's writing. She says that Rion warned her that Depuck would be injured and she didn't believe him—but it happened. She also says Rion told her she'd be in danger, and she didn't believe him, but that came true, also."

"I knew I had to save her," Rion admitted. "I've been following your sister ever since I learned Brennon suspected she was involved in the theft of top-secret papers from his briefcase. But I didn't know exactly when Brennon would make his move on Nisco." Rion reached into his pocket. "Nisco gave me this, too."

Lucan frowned. "That looks like the copy of the specs Nisco left for us at the medical center."

Rion nodded. "This is the original from General Brennon's briefcase." He turned over the paper to expose writing on the back. The script had similarities to early Viking symbols. "Can you read that?"

"No. But I recognize it," Lucan said. He'd seen markings exactly like these on the cave wall across from the Layamon Brut's inscription.

Rion nodded. "You must not underestimate Brennon. The Tribes can be ruthless."

"The Tribes?" Lucan asked.

"Are you saying General Brennon is in league with the Tribes?" Cael asked.

"He may work for them or with them. Or be one of them." Rion grimaced. "Evil is not always overt. The Tribes are expert at infiltrating a society and permeating the current government. Often those who do the Tribes' bidding have no idea whom they really work for."

"What do the Tribes want?" Lucan asked.

"They seek world domination, the death of all beings of the light and the law," Rion said. "By lowering Avalon's shield, we tempt—"

"So you don't want us to enter Avalon because the military might follow us in and steal the Grail?" Lucan asked.

"I'm merely pointing out possible repercussions of what we're going to attempt."

"We?" Lucan stood and tugged Cael to her feet.

"You need my help," Rion insisted. "And we've already delayed too long."

Cael frowned. "Where do the Tribes come from?"

"Other worlds." Rion held Lucan's gaze.

Cael's voice rose an octave. "The Tribes are not of this moon?"

Talk of other worlds shot Lucan into motion. He placed his arm around Cael and pulled her toward the cave. "Cael, don't encourage him. If he fears these mythological Tribes, that's his problem. Jaylon needs you to find the Grail. This conversation is over."

He stepped toward the cave, but Cael slipped from under his arm. She brushed dirt from her clothing, in no apparent hurry to leave.

Rion continued, "Legends say the Tribes spread across the Milky Way Galaxy about fifteen hundred years ago. For a time, the Tribes coveted a world called Earth, a land called Briton."

As Rion spoke, his gaze pierced Lucan's. At the mention of his home world, Lucan's muscles knotted.

Rion told his tale, his words almost hypnotic. "Gerwain, a great seer and my ancestor, predicted that if Briton and Earth succumbed to the Tribes, the entire galaxy would fall into total darkness. So centuries ago, the best warriors from many worlds, Knights of the Round Table, united with King Arthur Pendragon. Together they pledged to protect the Britons from darkness and took on a secret mission to find the Grail. They believed that possession of the Grail would protect their soldiers in battle. After a long search, the knights presented the Grail to Arthur, who, before he died, supposedly left the Grail in Avalon."

"How did King Arthur travel from Earth to Pendragon?" Lucan asked.

"That's just one of many things that the legends don't explain," Rion replied.

"The Grail isn't doing any good behind Avalon's shield," Cael spoke firmly. "But in any case, why have I never heard these tales that you speak?"

"The tales are common in the land of my birth. It's a world called Honor."

"You come from another world?" Cael stared at Rion, as if caught between awe and disbelief.

Damn it. Honor was the planet the computer had told Lucan about, a planet of Dragonshapers who'd fallen into savagery and slavery. But Rion was no dragonshaper. He didn't have the telltale scales on the insides of his arms.

Lucan wasn't an empath or a seer, but his instincts told him danger was brewing. He tried to tug Cael away. "Don't believe him."

"Truth radiates from him like sunlight." She rooted her feet to the rock. "How did you get to Pendragon?"

"I stole an ancient spaceship. I barely made it here and then crashed. My ship's pieces are scattered over the southern mountain range."

Cael stared, eyes wide. "How did you survive?"

"I ejected. My chute left me dangling in a tree with broken bones."

"That must have been painful."

Rion's eyes darkened. "It took me a year to make it to civilization."

"How long have you been here?" Lucan asked.

"About three years." Rion stared at Lucan as if he knew that was how long Lucan had been here, too. But he hadn't said anything to indicate he knew Lucan wasn't from Pendragon.

"Are there any other visitors here from your world?" Cael asked

"I'm not the only offworlder. Lucan comes—"

"Silence," Lucan ordered, too late.

Cael stiffened beside him.

Rion's gaze locked with Cael's, his face sincere and honest, practically willing her to believe him. "Lucan's not from Pendragon."

Cael's eyes widened in shock. "You weren't born on this moon?"

"No." There was no longer any point in denying the truth.

She raised her fist to her mouth and glared at him as if he had three heads. "You came here for the Grail."

"Yes."

Cael jerked away from Lucan. For a moment her irises went dragon dark. "You're the enemy? *You* come from the Tribes for the Grail?"

Saddened that she would accuse him of belonging to such an evil race, Lucan shook his head. "I'm from Earth. And on my world, Arthur defeated the Tribes fifteen hundred years ago. Since then, the Tribes have been relegated to history."

His truth may have registered with her, but her eyes flashed outrage as comprehension set in. "But you came from Earth to steal Pendragon's Grail."

Lucan spoke resolutely. "It's not theft to take back what's yours."

"The Grail's inside Avalon." Cael stood ramrod straight. "By what right do you lay claim to my world's heritage?"

"According to *our* legends, King Arthur was from Earth, and he left the Grail in Avalon. Our worlds share a history—"

"Now who's making up outrageous stories?" Cael's shock was evident in her trembling voice.

"Our three worlds are connected by history, honor, and the light," Rion interceded. "Centuries ago, we all banded together on Earth to protect the Grail. Arthur believed it would be safest here and left it on Avalon. Now, if we fail to join together once again, the Tribes will defeat us."

Cael's eyes narrowed. "From which world did the Grail originally come?"

Rion shook his head. "There are myths across the galaxy with many worlds claiming this honor."

"You're saying other worlds besides Earth will contest ownership?" Cael asked tersely, in frustration.

"I believe you're missing the point," Lucan said, "that our three worlds once banded together to fight an ancient enemy—the Tribes."

"Yes, my brother," Rion stood and held out his hand.

Lucan went still. "Your story's compelling, but why should I trust you?"

Rion simply smiled. "You must never speak of what I am about to do."

Before Lucan or Cael agreed, Rion dragonshaped. One moment he was a man, then he morphed, his skin changing to scales, his legs thickening, his arms extending into giant wings.

Cael gasped. "I never gave him my blood. I swear it."

Rion morphed back into human shape. "I was born a dragonshaper. On Honor, all my people are dragonshapers."

"You don't have scales on the insides of your arms," Cael noted.

"My chromosomes are slightly different. I'm from another world." Rion turned to Lucan. "The Tribes cannot dragonshape, but they seek to dominate us with their military superiority. We must all stand against them. Our dragon blood makes us allies. Brothers." Again he held out his hand. "Together we must protect the Grail. If you'll accept my help—"

"Glad to have it." Lucan shook his hand.

"And I have your promise not to speak of what you just saw?" Rion pressed.

Lucan nodded. "You have my word."

"Mine, too," Cael agreed. "But why the need for secrecy?"

"We can't risk changing the future."

Lucan wasn't certain he understood. But Rion was entitled to keep his secret.

"But who are the Tribes today?" Cael frowned at the men. She'd donned her authoritative mantle and sounded calm, but Lucan sensed her churning fury beneath her cool exterior.

Rion shrugged, his eyes bleak. "No one really knows. Once they claim a world, they destroy it. No one is left to tell the tales."

That the Tribes were still their enemy seemed impossible, but Lucan had traveled too far and seen too much not to believe Rion. Right now Lucan was Earth's only representative, and he could use an ally. Who better than Gerwain's son, a descendent of one of Arthur's most trusted knights? The military's hostility and the murder accusations, plus the High Priestess herself being tortured, indicated that other offworlders might already be here. And the Tribe inscriptions on the paper from Brennon's briefcase troubled him deeply. The Tribes . . . King Arthur's ancient enemy had survived.

The Tribes wanted the Grail.

If Lucan succeeded, if he took the Grail to Earth, the Tribes might follow. It was a gamble, but he had no choice but to accept the risk.

CAEL SHOOK WITH an anger so fierce that it took every iota of her willpower not to shout, shake her fist and curse the Goddess. Lucan had deceived her. Used her. There was no telling how many things he'd lied about. She'd trusted him and betrayed her people. She felt like a fool. She felt as if her heart were breaking. But worst of all, in giving him her dragonblood, she'd created a most formidable enemy.

Holy Goddess! For the first time in her life, she wanted to roast someone alive. She stomped into the cave before she vented her anguish and pain.

But even as she fled down the passageway in a terrible temper, she knew she wasn't prepared to kill the man who'd made love to her so skillfully. She didn't want to kill him, but she did want revenge. She wanted him to fail. She wanted to make certain he never took the Grail to Earth. She wanted him to hurt as he'd hurt her.

Her thoughts weren't appropriate for a spiritual leader, but she was human, too. And what he'd done was despicable.

How easily she'd fallen into his trap. She should have been more suspicious. No wonder he hadn't known their customs and their religion. No wonder he hadn't feared her. He wasn't from her world—but an enemy who'd come to Pendragon to steal their greatest treasure.

"I'm sorry I lied." Lucan had followed her into the cave, but in her anger she hadn't noticed until he spoke.

He wasn't lying: she could feel his remorse coming off him in waves and spun around to face him. "You're sorry you got caught."

"That, too." He nodded, his eyes calm and steady.

"Do you even have a sister?" she snarled.

"Yes. And on my world there are billions more like her. We're all sterile."

She gasped. No wonder he hadn't gotten her pregnant— thank the Goddess. All she needed was to bear this traitor's baby. At least she'd be spared that dishonor.

His face was somber. "Without the Grail, my people will become extinct."

"Why? What happened?"

"By the time we realized free radicals from pollution had damaged our bodies, it was too late to reverse the problem. If I take the Grail home, Marisa can have a baby. Many women will have babies. My people will not die."

When she said nothing, he continued in a quiet and reasonable tone. "The Grail is our last hope. Without the Grail's healing properties, all my people will be dead within two generations. Out of desperation, I came here hoping the Grail would cure us."

She nailed him with a hard look. "And your promise to Jaylon, was that, too, a lie?"

"Of—"

"How could you look into that dying boy's eyes and steal his only chance to live?"

"I—"

"You're contemptible."

"That's enough." Lucan sharpened his voice, his eyes furious. "Before I leave with the Grail, I will return to Jaylon's bedside. I don't break my promises."

She fisted her hands on her hips. "Like I'm going to believe that after how you twist your words? Jaylon isn't the only Dragonian dying of an incurable—"

"On Earth, my *entire* race is dying. Our need is far greater."

"That's your opinion."

"According to Rion, if Earth dies, then Pendragon and other worlds will fall to the Tribes."

"Thieves always justify their need to take what is not theirs."

He raised an eyebrow. "Are you angry about my mission, or because I didn't tell you the truth?"

Goddess help her. She didn't know. She'd never been so confused. She hadn't ever expected to meet a man she could love. She'd certainly never dreamed that man would be an alien. Or that they'd work at cross-purposes.

She glared at him. "I don't owe you any explanations."

He held out a hand palm up, then slowly let it drop to his side. "When I could, I told you the truth. I do share mental communication with my twin. She did suffer two miscarriages. I am a linguist who specializes in ancient languages."

"From Earth."

"From Earth," he nodded. "What I didn't tell you is that my people are sterile. If I do take home the Grail, I'm fairly certain the Tribes will follow. But I have no choice. And now, even if we find the Grail, it may take me so long to get home, I'll be too late."

At his bitter words, her gaze narrowed. "What are you talking about?"

"My spaceship isn't large enough to hold a dragon."

No wonder he'd struggled with his dragonblood. She'd never understood his conflict—until now. Perhaps she had stopped him from leaving with the Grail, after all.

"Then you'll have to stay on Pendragon—where the Grail can be of great use."

"I can't give up. It's true that if I stop on other worlds to change shape, I will add years to an already long journey. By the time I return, my sister and everyone else may be too old to have children. But while there's still a chance, I must try. I was hoping you would want to come with me."

With him?

Rion ducked into the cave and cleared his throat. "There is more at stake here than the survival of Lucan's people. Every knight sworn to King Arthur came from a different world. If Earth falls, all of us fall. Not just Pendragon and Honor. There are twelve worlds in Arthur's alliance."

"Why is Earth the key?" Lucan asked.

"I don't know. But we can't fight among ourselves. We can't let the Tribes rise again."

Cael stared at Rion, horror churning her gut. "You can't know this."

"My father saw it. So did my father's father and his before that. So did I."

"Do all your visions come true?" Cael asked, her empathic ability telling her the warrior in him was conflicted, but whether it was about his abilities or his mission, she couldn't be sure.

"It's complicated, my lady. The flashes come true . . . unless we act and change the future. We should leave for Avalon as soon as possible. The cavity beneath the obelisk is widening. Avalon has sunk a full inch in the last two days. Besides, I don't trust Sir Quentin."

"You think he's of the Tribes, too?" Cael asked.

"It's possible. Quentin and General Brennon have grown close, and they *are* up to no good. And Quentin's claiming he can bring down the inner shield with a dyno blast."

Cael frowned. "Even I know that a dyno blast set off inside Avalon will weaken the ground."

Lucan added, "Quentin might be setting a trap for us, threatening to blow up Avalon if we don't return to help him bring down the inner shield."

"Rion's right," Cael said. "We need to head straight for Avalon. But bear in mind, we may be arrested for murder."

Although they'd reached an agreement, Cael remained angry and uneasy. Feeling as if she were swimming upstream against a raging current and had lost her footing, she struggled for balance. Cael didn't trust either man. For all she knew, Rion and Lucan both came from Earth, and this legend Rion spoke of was yet another lie. Earlier, she'd sensed Rion's truthfulness, but after Lucan's betrayal, how could she trust her empathic abilities?

Worse than not trusting either man, she no longer

trusted her own judgment. To think the High Priestess could have a real relationship with a man went against every law the Elders had taught her. Dragonian society had good reasons for the laws they'd enacted and honed for thousands of years. For her to hope she knew best was arrogant, and now she was paying for her arrogance.

She didn't want to think about Lucan's suggestion that she accompany him to Earth. She was the only High Priestess on Avalon. Her world might already be under attack from the Tribes. With General Brennon and Sir Quentin and maybe some of the Elders already under enemy influence, she couldn't even consider leaving Pendragon.

The Grail is made from metal that fell to Earth from a falling star and tis forged in the blood of a land where the ring stones were first raised.

—MERLIN

20

Lucan barely recognized Cael as the warm, friendly, and compassionate woman he'd come to know. Since learning he was from Earth, she'd wrapped herself in High Priestess formality, building a wall between them that he couldn't breach. Right now he was giving her space, giving her time to heal from the wounds he'd caused, hoping she wouldn't have permanent scars.

At least Lucan and Rion had talked Cael into bypassing the authorities and sneaking into the laboratory building at night. If not for Cael's knowledge of a secret underground administrative tunnel, fortunately untouched by the flames, they'd never have made it inside the building undetected. After they'd helped themselves to supplies from the research team's storage unit and assembled a bag of flashlights, picks, and other gear, they were back at the main entrance of Avalon.

The structure's exterior, massive and dark, looked exactly as Lucan remembered—except the front doors stood wide open and the building sat lower in the ground.

"Don't turn on the light until we're deeper inside," Lucan instructed.

"We're not idiots," Cael muttered.

Aware she was still nursing hurt feelings, he kept his tone gentle. "You're also not accustomed to sneaking around."

Cael stiffened. "I may not be a thief and a spy, but you don't need to tell me—"

"Please." Lucan cut her off. "Hush. I hear something."

"Me, too." Rion agreed, his presence helping to diffuse the awkward tension between Cael and Lucan. "It sounds like . . . wings beating the air."

"It's Merlin." With a look of impatience, Cael strode forward into the dark chamber.

Sure enough, Merlin was there. But how had he flown all the way from the mountains? Surely a bird couldn't keep up with a skimmer. And how had he found them? Perhaps he was attuned to Cael through some kind of internal radar.

Lucan pulled a flashlight from his belt and resettled his heavy pack. He carried an empty duffel for the Grail, pickaxes and shovels, and minor explosives, brushes, and trowels. He had no idea how far into the structure they would have to go before they encountered the next shield.

"Hurry," Cael said, walking quickly. "We have only eight hours before Quentin's team returns to work and discovers us."

"I'm surprised they're not working 'round the clock," Lucan said.

"They stopped out of exhaustion and frustration," Rion explained, "and they were out of options. Quentin thought a rest might result in new ideas."

Cael had packed food and drink, but she'd been extremely quiet until now, letting Rion and Lucan make the plans. Lucan was glad to hear her speaking up again. He missed her voice: he missed her common sense. Most of all he regretted he'd hurt her so badly.

Shining his light on the interior walls, looking for more ancient glyphs, Lucan expected sophisticated building materials, because whoever had constructed Avalon's shield had a high level of technology at their disposal. But the passageway reminded him of corridors inside Egyptian pyramids, dark and solid stone. The floor ran level for as far as his flashlight could reach.

"How's our air?" Lucan asked.

Rion raised his wrist meter to his flashlight. "We're fine. But I don't understand why. I haven't seen a ventilation system."

"There isn't one." Lucan shined his light along the ceiling, noting joints so tight a piece of paper wouldn't fit between the cracks. Talk about precision building. Whoever had constructed Avalon had been master craftsmen, and ghosts of the past had his imagination firing.

Had King Arthur and his trusted knights once walked through this same corridor? Had the counselor Merlin been at their side, giving sage advice?

"Quentin must have aired out this corridor," Cael remarked, her voice once again level.

Lucan would rather have an angry Cael with him than no Cael. She was so good at teamwork and possessed keen powers of observation. He longed to hold her and share his thoughts. Now that his secret was out, he wanted to tell her about Earth. Tell her how much she meant to him.

Rion stepped next to Lucan. "Rumors in the city are running rampant that Quentin's new team has experienced several deaths."

"Avalon may be booby-trapped." Lucan moved ahead,

keeping his eyes peeled for anything out of the ordinary. Ancient builders often added death traps to guard their prizes. At the pyramids in Egypt, the builders used many lethal traps to prevent thieves from stealing gold and jewels. Since the Grail was one of the most famous and valuable treasures in the galaxy, and since Avalon had likely been constructed to safeguard the Grail from the Tribes, it made sense that booby traps might be inside. "Don't touch the walls. And don't step on anything suspicious."

"Suspicious how?" Cael asked.

"A loose stone. Or a hole in the rock that doesn't look natural. Anything that doesn't belong."

Cael fingered her necklace. "Maybe coming here at night wasn't such a good idea."

"Daylight won't penetrate these walls," Lucan said. "I'm surprised Quentin hasn't posted guards. Maybe they're farther inside."

Lucan hoped she didn't ask to return to the entrance. He didn't like the idea of her going alone, couldn't be certain she'd be safe. He wanted her beside him, where he could watch out for her.

Lucan turned to Rion. "You have any psychic flashes on where we might find the Grail?"

"Nope."

"Have you seen what it looks like?"

"Nope."

"That power of yours—"

"More of a frustration than a power." Rion sighed. "Do you have any idea how disconcerting it is to see part of the future and not know how or when or where the event will take place?"

"Look at this." Cael shined her light on a darker area of the stone wall.

"Is that heat discoloration?" Rion stepped back to allow Lucan a better look. Although the rest of the stone was sandy brown, this spot, about as wide as his hand, was a darker pigmentation.

Lucan took a pick from his supply bag and scraped at the spot. The outer rock flaked, and beneath was soft, fine sand. "It could be water damage, or . . ."

"What?" Rion prodded.

"There's something here." Gently, Lucan swept away the sand, letting the grains fall to the floor. Cael and Rion edged closer. "Stand back."

"I'm not going anywhere," Cael argued.

"If I set off an explosion, I don't want you in the line of fire."

Cael took a step back. "I don't believe Avalon's builders are trying to kill us."

She'd no sooner finished her comment than Lucan's fingers grazed a metal panel embedded behind the rock. A loud report behind them sent them all diving for cover. Instinctively Lucan lunged on top of Cael, protecting her from . . . a blast of air?

No debris or dust or even a grain of sand fell on them. Lifting his head, he saw that a shimmering copper shield had risen behind them. Slowly he shoved to his feet, half expecting the shield to blast down the hallway and rip them to shreds.

He turned and offered Cael a hand to help her to her feet. Pain flickered in her eyes, and she hesitated, but then she placed her hand in his. Progress. Lucan told himself not to put much store in such a tiny gesture, but he couldn't stop his hopes from rising.

"The shield appears to be stable. Let's see how it reacts to an inanimate object." Rion hefted a pick.

"Don't throw—" Lucan warned. Too late.

Rion had already tossed the tool. Lucan held his breath. Would it bounce off the shield? Would the shield retaliate in some way?

The pick disappeared, without a sound. There was no clink of metal hitting rock on the other side.

Rion walked toward the shield. "I'd love to know how this baby works."

"Later." Lucan grabbed his tunic and yanked him back. "The Grail's our first priority."

Cael turned away from the shield. "I wonder how far inside Brennon's team got."

"Far enough to find a glyph they couldn't read." Lucan shifted the pack and took the lead. With the passage behind them blocked, they had no choice but to go onward. "At least no one's going to sneak up on our backs."

"Let's hope there's another way out," Cael said.

"Of course there is." Rion sounded almost cheerful.

Lucan wished he could be as certain.

CAEL TRIED TO keep her mind on the current situation. She was trying so hard to keep her thoughts on finding the Grail and returning to heal Jaylon, but she'd just allowed Lucan to hold her hand. And at his touch, memories threatened to overwhelm her. Memories that she'd been trying to repress. Lucan swimming with her in the cave. His rescuing her at the residence. Her hearts ached. Yes, he'd lied to her, but he'd also shared so much of himself.

Ahead, Merlin flapped his wings, soaring through the stone passageway as if Avalon were fresh mountain air instead of a massive stone cage. She'd never been a fan of closed-in places, and the knowledge that her dragonshaping in a corridor this narrow would kill them all didn't help. She supposed feeling vulnerable was normal when the option of changing shape was denied her. The men seemed to have no trouble breathing, but Cael was certain the air was thinner here.

Stop it. She was fine. But her neck prickled, and the scales on the insides of her wrists undulated. Nerves unsettled, she focused on the glow of Lucan's flashlight, shining ahead of them. The monotony of the stone corridor should have soothed her, but she felt as if the men who'd built Avalon were watching and expecting her to make noble and honorable choices.

"Look." Lucan aimed his light at a glowing copper-colored shield ahead.

"One in front, one behind," Rion said, his voice amazingly calm. "We're trapped."

"Are those marks on the ceiling arch?" Cael asked.

Lucan nodded. "Those must be the glyphs Quentin's team wanted me to read."

Lucan sounded eager to go forward, but she hung back a step, then two. Couldn't the men feel the stillness, as if the building was holding its breath? Couldn't they sense the souls of those who'd walked these corridors in ancient times?

Feeling like a trespasser, she reminded herself how badly Jaylon needed the Grail. She shoved aside her doubts and pressed forward.

The glyphs helped distract her. Straight-lined symbols written in a row across the ceiling arch, the glyphs were similar to the ones outside Avalon, yet different from those on her necklace. "Can you read them?"

Lucan, his forehead creased with concentration, read, "When dragon breath mingles, the Grail shall be freed."

"What does that mean?" Rion asked.

Lucan frowned. "I don't know. But the wording implies that the Grail's here."

Cael stepped forward. "When dragon breath mingles. Mingles with what? The air? The shield?" She sighed. "But how can there be dragon's breath here? There's not enough room to shift. Do you think my human breath is considered dragon breath?"

"Why don't you try breathing on the shield?" Rion suggested.

"All right." She advanced another step, warily eyeing the shimmering shield.

Lucan blocked her. "Let me approach first."

Even now he spoke with care not to give away the secret of his dragonblood. Obviously, Lucan didn't want Rion to know—indicating he didn't have total trust in the other man.

Rion's muscles bulged as he crossed his arms over his broad chest and he eyed Lucan with curiosity. "So the legend's coming true?"

"What legend?" Lucan focused his attention on the glyphs, but Cael's scales tingled, and she sensed his wariness.

Rion cocked his head, his square jaw dusted with a day-old beard. "On Honor it is written that a man who is of King Arthur's blood shall return for the Grail. A male dragonshaper."

She spun and stared at Lucan. "You're a direct descendant of King Arthur?"

"One of many. It's not a big deal."

Cael raised her eyebrows. "You two are the first *male* dragonshapers on Pendragon in over a thousand years."

Rion grinned a charming smile. "So my flash was right."

Lucan frowned at him. "How come you don't have any useful flashes?"

Rion winked at Cael with manly charm. "Then I'd be perfect." He shrugged at Lucan. "Perfect is boring."

Cael smiled and wondered how many other secrets Lucan was keeping. She lost her line of thought as he stepped up to the shield and blew on it.

"Nothing." Lucan shook his head and removed the heavy pack.

Rion hauled it away from the shield. "Maybe you misread the symbols?"

Lucan stepped back and perused the runes once more, then repeated, "When dragon breath mingles, the Grail shall be freed."

"Maybe your breath and my breath must mingle together on the shield," Cael suggested.

Rion retreated a few steps to allow her room to approach the shield. Lucan held out his hand, and she hesitated. She knew how his touch would feel, warm, strong, and familiar. Despite his lies. Despite his traitorous plans for the Grail.

But when he gazed into her eyes and said, "Let's try it," Cael couldn't resist.

Hand in hand, they approached the shield. Almost cheek to cheek, they breathed onto the flickering copper surface.

"Still nothing." Lucan's mouth tensed into a thin line. "We're obviously not—"

The floor beneath their feet rumbled, reminding Cael of the ancient machinery inside her temple. She gripped Lucan's hand tightly. "We did something."

"What the hell?" Rion yelled. The floor had cracked between them and Rion.

Then a force of enormous power yanked Cael and Lucan forward. She should have been frightened, but for some reason she had no fear. One moment they were in the same corridor with Rion. The next, they were standing inside a stone fortress.

Cael craned her neck. "What is this place?"

Surrounded by hundred-foot-high walls of stone, a large circular platform dominated the room. Stone steps led to the platform's plateau. The ceiling appeared to be yet another shimmering force field.

"Wow." Lucan's eyes lit as he took in the structure. "I expected internal bracing, crossbeams, columns. But force fields must keep this tremendous mass in place. Otherwise it would collapse upon itself."

When the stones beneath their feet began to heat, Lucan tugged her toward the steps. "Come on."

"Something is herding us."

"Or directing us." Lucan didn't sound the least bit rattled.

"You think intelligent beings are here?"

"I don't know." Lucan reached the steps and leaned down to touch one. "The stairs are cool, but I suspect if we delay too long, they'll begin to heat, too."

"Where's the Grail?" Cael stepped onto the first step and halted. She didn't like the idea of some unknown entity urging her forward. They could be walking straight into a trap.

Lucan climbed the next two steps. "This place reminds me of—"

Once again, a force like a giant, invisible hand picked them up and deposited them at the top of the stairs.

Cael had prayed they'd find the Grail, but she'd never really expected to see it. Until now, the healing cup had seemed unattainable. A hope. A dream. An ancient legend.

"By the Goddess." Her jaw dropped as she advanced toward the sparkling copper object that sat on a marble pedestal. "Is that—?"

"Stay back."

An urn, about the size of a human head, rested dead center in the middle of a carved marbelite pillar. The Grail glowed with an inner light.

Cael had to remind herself to breathe. "It's beautiful."

Still holding hands, they stepped toward the Grail. And the solid rock disintegrated beneath their feet. They were falling.

Plunging into a giant bluish abyss.

Wind rushing in her hair, Cael took one look at the giant cavern within Avalon and knew she had room to dragonshape. Within moments, her clothes shredded and she lost touch with Lucan's hand.

Her arms grew into wings. Her sight sharpened.

In dragon form, her keen eyes picked out distant walls that glowed with an eerie blue light. Spreading her wings, she slowed her descent and craned her neck to look below for Lucan. But the flap of a wing beside her made her realize that he, too, was in dragon form.

Huge, powerful, he spread his wings and slowed his descent. He smelled primal, alluring, seductive. A rough trilling in his throat made her blood thrum, and her hearts beat faster. Hormones flooded her. Here was a mate.

Her mate.

Her true mate.

Her life mate.

He flew in fast, nipped her neck. Joy flooded her, and she spiraled downward, her body trembling in anticipation. Sharp and primal, his male dragon need cascaded over her, claiming her, branding her as his own.

Without effort, he matched her flight pattern, his enormous body hovering over her, under her, beside her. Lazily they circled the giant cavern, taking their time to explore the space and each other.

His wing occasionally brushed her back, her tail. His teeth nibbled her neck, her spine.

His touch caused her pulse to rush. She wanted him. She would have him. But first, he must prove he could catch her. Tipping back her head, she issued a trumpeting challenge and skyrocketed straight for the roof.

Up for the chase, he followed with a roar that shot sparks of heat down her spine. When they both reached the zenith, his talons clasped hers and tipped her upside down. Blood rushed to her head. Her talons prickled with warmth. And her scales rioted with heat.

Together, they spiraled downward, and during their crazy plunge, he mated with her swiftly, madly, deeply, his hardness filling her. His talons held her fast and hard as the wind rippled over her scales. Tension gathered in her core as he stroked and pumped inside her. Arching her neck back with a throaty roar, she spasmed and shot fire as she took his seed deep into her body.

Their breath mingled. Their fire entwined. Their spirits and life forces joined.

At the last moment, they separated. And Cael felt beautiful, whole.

Cael landed on the bottom of the cavern next to the east wall and humanshaped. Lucan landed beside her. Naked and languid, she faced her dragon. Her lover.

Damn, he looked ferocious. Eyes dark with dragon passion, he nuzzled her with his hot breath. Her gorgeous lover had matched her fire in every way. Her dragon didn't care about Lucan's deception. Her dragon side recognized what she didn't want to acknowledge. Lucan was her perfect mate.

Then he humanshaped.

Lucan stood before her, his breath ragged, his chest glistening with sweat. His eyes pierced hers with a possessive fire, and she recalled the way his body had locked with hers. Heat rose up her neck. Their pairing had been primitive and animalistic. Savage. Good and right.

She wondered if he'd ever acknowledge that although they were from different worlds, they were meant to be together. Not just this once. But for always.

He stared at her, the pulse in his neck ticking, once again his emotional barrier solidly in place.

Lucan drew her into his arms. "That was crazy."

"Insane." She snuggled against his chest, satiated and exhausted, not from their dragon mating, but from the hours she'd spent as a human, fighting with herself. The truth was that she'd always wanted Lucan. She wanted him still.

He tipped up her chin and peered into her eyes. "I wouldn't have lied for anything less than the fate of my world."

She swallowed hard. He meant every word.

"Lucan!" A voice echoed down.

They both looked up. She could see someone holding a glowing object. "Is that Rion? Does he have the Grail?"

"How did he get through the shield?"

"Rion?" Lucan shouted. "What's wrong?"

Rion tucked the Grail under his arm. "We have company. And they have guns."

Because we are few in number, the Tribes will descend from the heavens and ravish us unless we have the blessing of the Goddess.
                              —THE LADY OF THE LAKE

21

Blaster bursts streaked past Rion. The pops of gunfire echoed through the chamber. Had the dragons' pairing somehow disabled the shields?

Cael tilted her head back. "They're shooting at Rion. He should dragonshape."

"He won't. He thinks it will change history." Lucan had dragonshaped only twice, and both times Cael's life had been in danger. He had yet to morph at will, and now, with time so short, was not the moment to practice. He grabbed Cael by the shoulders. "We need to go back up there for Rion and the Grail."

"Agreed." She dragonshaped, and their mental connection snapped into place. *Climb on.*

Lucan held on to the spikes on Cael's neck and hoped there would be enough room for her to land and change shape. She hadn't hesitated to shift and fly into danger. As they rose, the blaster fire echoing above them increased in intensity, and he lost sight of Rion.

Drop me off on the ridge and fly to safety. Lucan prepared to leap from Cael's back as she rose through the hole in the floor. But the moment she flew high enough for him to attempt a jump, he spied Rion.

The other man leaped from a prone position to his feet, the Grail in hand.

Blaster fire flared all around him. Rion paid no attention.

Behind him, General Brennon shouted at his men. "You idiots, don't fire at the Grail!"

The shooting stopped. Armed men in military uniforms moved in on Rion. One man aimed his blaster, and Merlin dived down and attacked. The man let out a screech of pain, and his shot went wild.

Rion glanced over his shoulder. Men with weapons advanced, too many men for him to fight, even with Merlin's help. Rion spun and ran toward the rim where Cael hovered, Lucan straddling her back.

"Jump," Lucan shouted, holding out his hand.

For a moment, Lucan thought Rion was going to fling himself into midair. But he slid to a halt, teetering on the edge, the Grail in hand.

"Catch." Rion tossed the cup into the void—just as Brennon, Quentin, and a squad of men moved in and forced Rion to the ground. Rion was down, but that didn't stop him from yelling, "Go. Go. Go."

Why hadn't he jumped? An armed man smashed the butt of a blaster into Rion's skull, and he crumpled to the ground. The Grail fell through the air, and Lucan reached for it, leaned as far sideways as he dared. His fingers grazed the handle. He tilted a little farther, slipping sideways, wind whipping him.

Then his fingers closed on the handle and he reeled in the surprisingly light artifact. *Got it.*

Your brother? Cael asked.

Brother? Lucan instantly knew she meant Rion. Had Rion stayed behind to split the enemy forces? To buy them time? Had Rion given his life to throw the Grail to him? He prayed not.

Obviously Quentin had teamed up with Brennon, but was the entire military against them, or just a faction? Lucan supposed it no longer mattered. He had the Grail.

He glanced over his shoulder. Quentin, Brennon, and their armed men were carrying Rion away. Rion grabbed at but failed to reach his weapon. Not even his dragon strength could free him from so many men.

Rion's alive.

Should they go back for him? If they did, they wouldn't stand a chance. They'd likely lose the Grail, too, and Rion's sacrifice would be in vain.

The man from Honor had proved a noble and trusted brother, sacrificing his own safety and risking his life by refusing to dragonshape—all to ensure the future of the Grail.

Lucan wished he could do something for Rion, but right now they had to find a way out of Avalon. The massive walls and ceiling trapped them. It was only a matter of time before Brennon and Quentin returned with reinforcements.

Cael's fire-breathing trick to evaporate water wouldn't work on stone. Unless they found a way out, they'd have to surrender the Grail. Cael circled down to the floor, making a clean sweep of the interior. Lucan saw no exits. No passageways. No stairs or tunnels.

Cael humanshaped and wearily leaned against a stone wall. Obviously so many shifts in such a short time had taken a toll on her energy reserves. But she didn't complain.

Instead she peered at the Grail, gently touching the burnished coppery cup. "How old do you think it is?"

"I have no idea." Once, he would have been certain that the Grail had originated on Earth around the time of Christ. But Rion had claimed it was far older and may have originated on another world. "This metal is an unusual composition. I suppose that's why drinking from the cup is a shield against death and what gives it healing properties."

Cael grinned. "I don't care if it works by magic, as long as it does work."

"It's going to work. Avalon's builders wouldn't have gone to this much trouble to protect the Grail unless it was special."

"You think the Grail will save Jaylon?"

"Before we can help your nephew, we have to find a way out."

Exhaustion in her eyes and the sagging of her shoulders indicated she was close to collapse. Even her voice was weary. "Any suggestions?"

He frowned. "While we were flying, I saw nothing to indicate an exit. Avalon's builders may not have put in a back door—especially if they built this place to keep the Grail from the Tribes."

"If their *only* goal was to keep the Grail from the Tribes, they could have destroyed it. But they didn't. My people went to great effort and expense to build Avalon—so we would have the Grail."

Her words made sense. "Then we must be smart enough to figure out the clues they left for us."

"Clues?" Cael sighed and studied the bluish walls.

"Maybe we have to *do* something. Or find something."

"There's nothing here. Nothing but us and the Grail."

"That's it." Lucan leaned down and kissed her lips. "You're a genius."

"Me? What did I say?" Cael frowned and brushed a lock of hair from her eyes.

"The answer must be *in* the Grail." Lucan lifted the Grail by the handles and turned it around. Beautifully sculpted, the Grail was light and easy to hold, perfectly balanced in his hands. He tipped it upside down, inspected the lip, the handles, the base. And found nothing.

He peered inside the cup. Nothing there, either.

Slowly he inserted his hand into the cup, but his fingers were too big to reach the narrow bottom. "You try." He held the Grail out to Cael.

She ran a finger over the lip. "Did you feel warmth in the metal?"

He hadn't felt a thing. "Is the Grail reacting to you?"

"I'm not sure. But I have this compulsion to drink from the cup. Isn't that odd?"

"There was a small spring among these rocks." Lucan took the Grail, rushed to the spring he'd sighted earlier, and dipped water into the cup. He returned to Cael and handed her the artifact. "Don't fight it."

"You're sure?"

He shrugged. "What have we got to lose?"

Cael lifted the cup and sipped the water. "This metal's part platinum. Concentrated platinum." She stood up straighter. "I feel stronger, but not strong enough to dragonshape yet."

Where her mouth had touched the cup, the Grail had changed from copper to smoky scarlet. Then slowly the scarlet faded back to copper. He peered at her. "Is your compulsion gone?"

"I just want to caress it now."

"Go ahead."

She ran the tips of her fingers along the rim. And wherever she touched, the cup changed to scarlet, then slowly faded back to burnished copper. "This is interesting, but I don't think—"

"Wow." He blinked. "Did you see that?"

"What?"

"The scarlet parts have moving pictures in them, but they fade quickly."

Cael leaned forward, touched the Grail with her palm, and released it to peer at a square with two tiny stars at the bottom. "What's that?"

Lucan rubbed his forehead. "I think the rectangle is an image of Avalon. These two blinking lights . . ." He pointed to the bottom. "That's us." A faint but glowing green line formed between the two blinking lights and a wall.

"Sweet Goddess." Cael's voice rose in excitement. "Elder Benoit, right before she died, told me to follow the green light. I thought she was hallucinating, or seeing her final pathway to the Goddess. But she was talking about the Grail."

Green light pulsed along the line, and a thrill flowed through him. "It's a map," Lucan said.

She narrowed her eyes. "We need to follow the green line."

The Grail led them across the stone floor. After several minutes, they had crossed about one tenth of the space, and the green trail on the Grail ended.

"We're here." Lucan glanced around.

"This can't be right." Cael looked right, left and overhead. "There's nothing here."

Lucan handed her the Grail and searched the stone floor. He saw no discoloration. No loose stones. No switches or levers. "What's it trying to tell us?" He peered at Cael. "You have any more impulses?"

"It's more like an instinct."

He eyed her with a calculating expression. "What?"

She set down the Grail and wrapped her arms around his neck. "When Dragon breath mingles, the Grail shall be freed." She repeated the rune message back to him. "Kiss me."

He slid his arms around her, threaded one hand into her hair, and cupped the small of her back with the other. The moment his lips touched hers, the Grail trilled. Startled, they pulled apart.

Cael tilted her head back to look at him and then she looked past him, her eyes widening. "By the Goddess."

Lucan followed her gaze. Avalon's roof . . . was gone. They could see the night sky, stars, and Dumaro's crescent in the heavens.

Cael sucked in her breath. "Are we hallucinating?"

"Can you shift?"

She shook her head. "I'm still too weak."

Lucan would have to find a way to dragonshape. "I'll fly up there, test to see if the ceiling's still there and transparent or if it's really gone, and then I'll come back for you."

Avalon began to tremble. Cracks opened in the floor. Lucan frowned at them. "The ground is giving way."

Cael stumbled. "Avalon's going to collapse. Hurry."

He closed his eyes, tried to shift. "It's not happening." Frustrated, he frowned. "Surely I haven't depleted my platinum yet?"

"You just haven't practiced enough."

"Tell me what to do."

"Urgency helps. Try thinking about how much the Grail means to you and what will happen if you fail." Cael said. The floor under her foot cracked, and she jumped aside. "Think about falling into the sinkhole."

Lucan concentrated. Sweat poured down his forehead. He closed his eyes and thought about Marisa. He recalled her pain after that last miscarriage. How she'd forced herself to go to work. How she'd forced herself to laugh. And then he thought about ten Marisas, tens of thousands of Marisas, none of them able to bear children.

Nothing happened. And the cracks widened until the floor buckled.

Lucan focused on the danger Cael would be in if he didn't shift. If the soldiers returned, they might kill Cael. Lucan would lose the Grail to earth's ancient enemy— the Tribes. His mission would be over if Avalon fell into the sinkhole.

His worry was real, but he still didn't shift.

Someone above fired three shots. The ancient edifice slid sideways. A rock tumbled from above, the crash deafening. His pulse leaped. His muscles bunched. Before the fourth shot echoed against the stones, Lucan shifted, and Cael, holding the Grail, climbed onto his back. *Fly.*

A blaster burst hit his side, but the sting only increased his urgency. With a flap of his wings, Lucan lifted into the air.

Shots from the brim above enraged him, and he spiraled upward. Rocks from Avalon's walls tumbled around them. Soldiers clung to columns and fired more shots.

Cael cried out softly. *Pain.*

How dare they hurt his mate?

I am . . . all right.

Furious energy and dragon power surged through him, pumping him with a white-hot rage. Lucan roared, summoning fire to blast up his throat. And with one throw of flames he wiped out the squad, banked into a turn, and flew out of Avalon, the owl on his wing.

Behind him, the ancient edifice tumbled into the sinkhole, sucking in rocks, machines, and men. The collapse made the ground rumble and shot a giant mushrooming dust cloud into the sky.

Take us to Jaylon, Cael pleaded. *Fly to Feridon.*

A man of honor does swiftly that which must be done.

—ARTHUR PENDRAGON

22

Cael gripped Lucan's back with her legs and prayed he remembered to fly level. She could hold on to his spine with only one hand. The other gripped the Grail. Riding another dragon was a new and exhilarating experience. In human form, she could appreciate the power of Lucan's dragon wings, the force of the wind in her face.

Avalon collapsed into the sinkhole, and she expected Lucan to spiral upward to avoid the dust cloud. Instead, he circled the ground destruction that had sent men scrambling in every direction. Giant aerial lights illuminated the surviving soldiers, and their armored vehicles revealed their formidable numbers. The troops had a menacing air, an on-the-march momentum.

Dawn approached, and the sun rose on the horizon. Lucan flew lower. *I don't see Rion.*

She squinted through the dust that coated her skin and tasted like grit. *We'll keep looking.*

With the prize in hand, a ruthless and selfish man would have kept going, but Lucan was risking their freedom as he searched for Rion.

Suddenly, between two vehicles directly below, a squad of military men thrust another man forward and closed in around him.

Cael gasped. *To the right. There's Rion.*

Angling to the right, Lucan flew in low and hard. As they dived, his giant shadow announced his presence. Most soldiers scattered. A few used Rion as a shield. One or two fired at the dragonshaper.

Lucan roared his fury, and flames swept over the military vehicles, but he took care not to harm his friend. Those who fled lived. Those who tried to shoot down the dragon died.

Cael focused on keeping her grip on the Grail without sliding off Lucan's back. Her thighs trembled with the effort.

Below, soldiers slammed Rion against a truck, and one aimed a weapon at him. She held her breath, knowing she and Lucan wouldn't reach him before the soldier pulled the trigger.

Hands tied behind his back, Rion bounced off the truck and rammed his shoulder into the soldier, who fell to his knees. Merlin flew in and attacked a second man, ripping a bloody gash in his throat. Meanwhile, Rion kicked the weapon out of the downed soldier's hand. But another soldier attacked with his fists. Rion ducked under a punch and leaped sideways, his legs scissoring around the man's neck, snapping it.

Cael had never seen a man fight like that. So fast. Deadly.

Fly level. Slow. I'll haul Rion in.

But she had only one free hand, since the other held the Grail. Cael didn't know if she could lift Rion. He was a large man. Even if she found the strength, his weight might unseat her.

"Rion!" She yelled to get his attention. More soldiers closed in, but Rion dodged, ducked, and eluded capture. Despite Lucan's constant flame-throwing, the soldiers advanced. One grabbed Rion's arm, but he twisted free and raced toward the spot where Cael and Lucan were descending. At the last moment, Rion leapt into the air.

Cael grabbed his belt. She squeezed her legs tight and somehow hauled Rion onto Lucan's back without losing her seat. *I've got him.*

"Why didn't you leap the first time, back on the ridge?" she asked Rion.

"I didn't know if you had the strength to carry the weight of two men," he admitted.

In truth, she didn't know, either. Her platinum was so depleted she might have fallen out of the air and killed them all. But she was aware she was holding on to a man of extraordinary courage. At the least he'd taken a beating to give them a chance to get away. His refusal to dragon-shape and save himself to avoid changing history was no less than heroic.

Soldiers below had taken cover. Again they fired upward.

She gripped Rion's belt tighter. *Fly us out, Lucan.*

The added weight didn't seem to faze him. His huge wings flapped smoothly, and he rose on a warm air current.

They'd made it out, Rion, Lucan, and Cael. Merlin joined them on their wing, and Cael grinned. They were alive.

And they had the Grail.

*   *   *

LUCAN LANDED IN FERIDON, directly on the roof of the medical center. He humanshaped and saw that Rion had given Cael his tunic. Rion offered Lucan his robe, and the group made their way to the rooftop.

"So what's your plan?" Rion opened a doorway that led down a flight of stairs.

Lucan strategized as they headed down. "We go in fast. We come out faster."

Rion rolled his eyes. "That's it?"

"Is there a way to reach Jaylon's room without going through public areas?" Lucan asked Cael.

The fact that Cael had never hidden her concern over her nephew might help their enemies predict their next move and pinpoint their location. Lucan hoped Brennon and Quentin, if they'd survived the collapse, were still trying to figure out what had happened at Avalon rather than organizing a raid on the medical center.

Cael led them down a second flight of stairs. "We have to take public corridors. I just hope Jaylon's still hanging on, that the Grail will save him. But . . ."

"We don't know how to use the Grail," Lucan finished for her.

"Maybe Jaylon just needs to drink from it," she said. "Or maybe if he holds it, the Grail will give his body whatever he needs to heal."

"We'll have to try everything." Lucan wished the Earth legends had explained exactly how the Grail healed.

"On my world," Rion said, "the legends say only that soldiers who possess the Grail won't die in battle."

Cael frowned. "That almost implies the Grail can heal from a distance. But we had to touch it to see the map."

"I want Jaylon to see it," Lucan added, "to give him hope."

"He needs a universe more than hope," she said, tension and worry radiating off her. "The Grail is amazingly light, but the last time we saw Jaylon, he was so weak that—"

A door burst open. Several patients visiting with their families walked by. Showing respect for the High Priestess, the Dragonians moved aside to let Cael pass, their happy chatter dying on their lips. They lowered their eyes and bowed their heads, whether in deference or fear, Lucan couldn't discern.

Had news of their arrival preceded them? Or were the patients at this medical center so accustomed to Cael's presence that seeing her didn't come as a surprise?

Most of the patients and visitors moved down the corridor, but a woman with a newborn baby in her arms approached Cael with a shy smile and only a little wariness. "My Lady, would you bless my baby?"

Cael's impatience to reach Jaylon flickered across her face briefly before she smiled and held out her arms. "This is my favorite part of the High Priestess's duties." She didn't actually touch the child's flesh, since the baby was wrapped in blankets. Still, she took the baby from the woman with a smooth ease that revealed she'd held many babies.

Lucan couldn't stop staring. He hadn't seen a real baby since his youth. He couldn't recall seeing any woman hold a baby, but watching Cael with the child stole his breath. The baby was so tiny, so fragile, so perfect. Its head was large and out of proportion to its frail body—and yet it looked healthy. Perfect. The infant's wide eyes looked back into Cael's with curiosity, and a lump lodged in Lucan's throat.

Cael looked . . . lovely. She wasn't merely at ease,

she looked happy. And he realized that although she'd never spoken of children, she longed for them. But no High Priestess on Pendragon was allowed to have a mate—thus no children. And yet, as she cuddled the baby against her breast, Cael couldn't hide the yearning in her eyes.

He wanted that infant to be theirs—his and Cael's. He wanted to have lots of babies with this woman. He watched her smile at the child and his hearts swelled. He'd told himself he was leaving this world and Cael behind. That he couldn't let himself love her.

But despite his best efforts, he'd fallen in love with her.

Cael blessed the child, then kissed the air over the baby's forehead. She tucked the blanket tighter around the child's shoulder, then handed the infant back to her mother, still careful not to touch her flesh. "She's beautiful."

"Thank you, my lady." The young mother's eyes sparkled. Clearly this was a moment she would tell her grandchildren about.

The proud young mother left the corridor and headed back to her quarters, and Lucan wished he had some privacy. But now was not the time to tell Cael his feelings.

Some moments were not to be shared. Besides, with his flashes, Rion might have already seen some of Lucan's future. Lucan refused to ask. If he and Cael couldn't work out the difficult situation and find a way to be together, he didn't want to hear about it. Better to savor how much he loved her right now in this moment. The future was impossible. And they'd already delayed too long.

Jaylon's room was crowded. And silent—except for beeping monitors and the labored sound of a breathing machine. Although flowers decorated the room, it had the overclean smell of bleached sheets, medicines, and antiseptics.

Jaylon's mother looked up as they entered the room. Sonelle's eyes were swollen and red-rimmed, but she wasn't crying now. Lucan suspected she had no tears left. Still and silent, she held the little boy's hand tightly clenched in her own.

Jaylon's skin was pale, his eyes closed, and his breathing shallow. Depuck, mostly recovered from the beating he'd suffered at the residence, stood beside Nisco.

Several solemn healers moved around the room, monitoring instruments. A nurse fluffed a pillow. But clearly, they were all helpless as Jaylon struggled to breathe.

When the sisters spied Cael, they didn't utter a greeting. They didn't smile. Their gazes slowly moved to the Grail she held in her hands. Sonelle released her son's hand and gestured for Cael to take her place at his side. "You came."

"With the Grail?" Nisco's voice rose in hope. "Is that the Grail?"

Cael nodded. "Are you all right?"

Nisco shrugged. "I sent a copy of those specs to the press. Since it hit the airwaves and the secret's out, there's no longer a reason for the military to come after me."

"And you, Depuck?" Cael asked.

"He's healing." Nisco stepped away from Jaylon and gestured Cael forward.

Cael leaned over her nephew and kissed his forehead.

One of the physicians gasped.

"I'm allowed to touch the boy to heal him," Cael said

with quiet dignity. Jaylon's eyes didn't flutter, and she took his hand and squeezed. "Is he conscious?"

Sonelle shook her head. "Do something. Anything. Please."

Cael wrapped the boy's fingers on the Grail's handle. Unlike when Cael had touched the Grail, the coppery shimmer didn't turn to scarlet. Lucan didn't know if this was because the child didn't have dragonblood or because the life in him was too weak to register. Cael waited a full minute.

No one spoke. Tension escalated.

The monitors didn't change. Jaylon didn't open his eyes. His color remained pale.

Cael looked at Lucan, her gaze frustrated and filled with haunting pain.

Lucan picked up a glass and poured water into the Grail. Cael tilted the cup to the child, and water trickled between his bluish lips. Most of the liquid dribbled onto the pillow. But a few drops entered his mouth.

Jaylon coughed and opened his eyes. Cael smiled, a smile that lit up her entire face. "Jaylon, I brought you the Grail like I promised. Sweetie, can you drink a little more for me?"

When Jaylon didn't answer, Sonelle climbed onto the bed, sat behind her son, and propped him upright. "You can do this, baby, after all you've been through. Just do one more thing. Drink."

Again Cael held the cup to his mouth. And Jaylon sipped. He swallowed once. Twice. Then his head lolled to the side. The buzzers and alarms on the medical equipment shrieked in shrill beeps.

"By the Goddess." Sonelle, her face racked with grief, scowled at Cael. "What have you done?"

Lucan didn't understand how Sonelle could be so cruel. Couldn't Sonelle see how badly Cael wanted to cure Jaylon? Didn't she comprehend that Cael was risking her own life to come here?

At her sister's question, Cael's lips tightened and pain thundered in her eyes. But she kept her silence with a strength that astounded him.

Still, he ached to comfort her. Leaning over the bed and Jaylon, Lucan squeezed Cael's hand. "You did what you could."

"Is he . . . gone?" Nisco whimpered, her gaze also turning on Cael in horror.

More pain filled Cael's eyes, but she held her chin high. How much could her sisters expect her to take? Clenching the Grail tightly to her chest, Cael again let the insult go. She smoothed Jaylon's hair from his face. "Come on, little guy. Fight."

Healers clustered around Jaylon. They shook their heads and stepped back. "He still has a pulse," one observed. "He still breathes."

Everyone knew from the healer's tone that he didn't expect Jaylon to live much longer.

Sonelle shuddered and pointed at Cael. "You've weakened him."

Cael shook with anger. "I risked my life to bring the Grail here. Jaylon's illness . . . is not my fault."

Sonelle and Nisco didn't look the least bit ashamed. In fact, Cael's words didn't even seem to register.

Lucan placed an arm over Cael's shoulders. "You've done everything you could."

"Not everything." Cael removed Jaylon's blanket and sheet, then raised his gown to reveal his chest. Next she picked up a sharp instrument from a suturing kit.

"What are you doing?" Sonelle screamed and lunged at Cael.

Lucan stepped between Sonelle and Cael, giving her room to proceed.

"No." Nisco lunged to grab Cael's hand. "Let him go in peace."

"Let the High Priestess do her work." Rion wrapped his arms around Nisco, pulling her back.

Cael's mouth tightened in determination. She clenched the sharp instrument. Then she pierced Jaylon between his ribs.

"Are you mad?" Sonelle screamed, struggling, tears streaming down her face, but Lucan held her back. "You've stabbed him in the heart."

"No," Cael corrected her. "His lung."

Whatever she'd hit, blood spurted, covering Cael's hands, her neck, her clothing. The monitors shrieked. Her sisters cursed and sobbed. More healers rushed in, but when they saw the High Priestess, they shuffled back from the bed.

Cael paid them no attention. As if in a queenly trance, she poured the rest of the Grail's water over Jaylon's wound. Beside her, Lucan saw the agony in her eyes, the tremble in her hands.

Was this a mercy killing?

"Why?" he asked, still stunned, his heart aching for her. She'd gone through so much. To fail Jaylon would haunt her the rest of her days.

"Legend says whoever possesses the Grail, their armies won't die in battle," Cael intoned.

"But Jaylon isn't a soldier. He's ill," Rion said.

"Exactly." Cael nodded. "So I gave him a battle wound."

Sonelle's face crumpled with grief, and tears ravaged her cheeks. "I will never, ever forgive you. I don't care if you are the High Priestess. You've killed my son."

"Sonelle, Jaylon was dying. I may have robbed him of his last painful breaths, but . . ." Cael wiped the boy's blood from her hands, and then she froze.

Lucan followed her gaze. Jaylon's bloody chest wound had stopped bleeding. The wound was closing. Healing.

"Oh . . . my . . . God." Lucan squeezed her hand. "The Grail—"

"Is closing his wound. But will it heal his illness?" Cael peered at the monitors, and then she raised teary eyes to Lucan's. "He's growing stronger." Her voice broke with relief. "His white cell count's approaching normal. His cells are repairing themselves."

Her words sent his thoughts spinning. "If the Grail can repair cell damage—"

"What are you saying? Tell me," Sonelle demanded.

Lucan caught the woman's gaze, had to stop himself from shaking her. Keeping his temper, he said with careful deliberation, "Cael has cured your son. He's going to live. And you, my lady, owe your sister an apology."

Sonelle ignored him and lunged toward Jaylon. This time, Lucan let her go. "Jaylon. Jaylon, baby. Mom's here. You're going to be well."

Jaylon opened his eyes and peered over his mother's shoulder. His gaze went from the Grail to Cael, still covered in his blood. "Thank you." He reached out to Cael, and they hugged. When she straightened, tears of happiness streamed from her eyes.

Jaylon took his mother's hands. "Mom, you need to thank her, too."

Sonelle shook her head and broke down into heart-wrenching sobs, but she wouldn't look at Cael. "She stabbed you."

Cael smiled at Jaylon over his mother's shoulder. "It's all right."

"But—"

"Remember what I told you when you first got sick and the other children made fun of you?"

"That some people can't see beyond their own past."

"Exactly." She nodded approval. "That doesn't mean we love them any less."

By the Goddess. That she could forgive her sister floored Lucan. But no one else seemed surprised, as if they expected this kind of sacrifice, nobility, and honor from her. But she was human. She had feelings. And after she'd saved Jaylon's life, the least her sister could do was—

The woman whose baby Cael had blessed earlier barged into the room. "My lady, soldiers are in the lobby, demanding that you give yourself up to them. A Sir Quentin is with them."

Lucan suppressed a curse. Coming to the medical center had been a too-predictable move. But they'd saved Jaylon's life. He couldn't regret their decision.

"Thank you." Cael turned from the young mother to Jaylon and again kissed him on the forehead. "We must go, sweetie."

"Is there anything we can do?" Depuck asked.

"Trade clothes with us," Lucan said. "Rion, find us some weapons. We need to get up to the roof."

Sometimes only a good heart can save the world.
　　　　　　　　　　　　　　— ARTHUR PENDRAGON

23

Forget the weapons." Cael turned from the window, picked up the Grail, and thrust it at Lucan. Hundreds of soldiers were converging on the medical center. Armored skimmers had lifted into the air from hidden positions behind warehouses, hovered around the building, and were landing on the rooftop. Even more reinforcements poured in by air and ground. The three were clearly outnumbered. Cael had to shout to make herself heard over the skimmer engines. "We can't get away."

"They were waiting for us," Lucan said.

They couldn't all get away, but perhaps Cael could help Lucan and Rion escape. She knew in her hearts that Lucan would never agree to leave her behind. Not if he was conscious.

While Lucan was distracted by the sight outside the window, Cael handed Rion a syringe, jerked her thumb at Lucan, and lowered her voice to a whisper so only Rion could hear. "You might have to use this on him."

Rion palmed the syringe and kept his voice low. "What's it do?"

"It'll put him to sleep."

Rion nodded and didn't ask questions, bless him.

With a nod good-bye to her family, she led the men from Jaylon's bedroom. She didn't want her sisters privy to their plans or blamed for their actions.

Before she changed her mind, she spoke with all the authority she could muster, "You two should hide while I go talk to Quentin."

"No." Lucan's gaze pierced hers. "I'm not letting you—"

"You're not in charge." Cael drew her High Priestess aura around her like armor. Later she would allow herself to feel the pain of losing him, but not now. "You and Rion must escape with the Grail while I draw their attention to me."

Rion remained silent.

Lucan scowled and blocked her from leaving. "You aren't sacrificing yourself for us. Splitting up is not an option."

"We don't have time to argue."

He didn't move. Eyes hard, arms crossed over his chest, hip cocked, he radiated a charged dominance. "And what happens when they discover you don't have the Grail?"

"By then, you'll be long gone." She forced herself to meet Lucan's eyes with a serenity she was far from feeling. This was good-bye. She swallowed hard. For Cael and Lucan, there would be no tomorrow. "You have the Grail. Go save your people so they can save us all from the Tribes."

"I can't let you do this." Lucan placed a gentle hand on her shoulder.

She wanted to lean into him. Instead, already feeling an acute sense of loss, she stepped back. "Most of my people are decent, and I may yet clear my name of the murder charges. Even if I can't, I got what I wanted. Jaylon's well."

"So now you're throwing your life away?"

Pulse pounding, she knew what she had to do. She threw a pleading glance at Rion. "You have a world to save, and I might buy you the time to escape."

Rion placed his hand in his pocket.

There was no hesitation in Lucan. "We'll all escape together." His eyes burned with determination. "I won't let you martyr yourself for us."

"Either they get *all* of us, or they just get *me*. Either way, I'm caught. So go." She spun on her heel, dismissing his concerns, but she didn't have to be an empath to feel Lucan's resolve harden.

She glanced over her shoulder at Rion. Good man. He was fingering the syringe.

Lucan's sadness blasted her, and he stepped forward, again blocking her escape. "What about *us?*"

"We don't have a future together. You've always known that. I've finally accepted what must be." She sounded cool, composed. Yet inside, her hearts were shattering into tiny pieces. But she held herself together and forced back the pain. She couldn't let him know exactly how much she cared, or she might falter. And faltering would cost his life. "You and I, and Rion," she swallowed roughly, "we have no choice."

The military had the medical center surrounded. She'd much rather go on, or die if need be, without Lucan, knowing he was safe on his world, a hero to his people, than try to keep him here, where the military would use the Grail for their own devious reasons, possibly even hand it over to the Tribes.

"We always have a choice." Lucan's voice turned to ice. A muscle ticked in his jaw, and the veins on his neck and forehead looked ready to explode. "I won't run away while you give yourself over to them."

She'd never seen him so furious, but she refused to back down. "You aren't thinking straight. How will getting yourself killed help your world?" Again she stepped around him.

Lucan grabbed her arm. "The last time they caught you, they tortured you. You aren't going out there."

She pulled back and to one side, drawing Lucan's eyes toward her, away from Rion.

With a quick thrust, Rion shoved the needle into Lucan's neck and depressed the plunger. Startled, Lucan flailed once, then collapsed, the Grail still in his hands. Rion caught him and eased Lucan to the floor.

"When he wakes up, he won't thank you," Cael muttered, but she recalled Rion fighting with his hands tied behind his back and thought if any man could match Lucan's strength and determination, it would be Rion.

Rion nodded, his eyes bleak. "I'll be fine, my lady. But what about you?"

She ignored his concern. "Find an attendant and take his uniform. Place Lucan in a casket and take him out through the morgue's back doors."

"Don't worry. I'll see to him. But what will you tell Sir Quentin?" Rion asked.

"I'll think of something. I can be very convincing." Especially with Lucan and Rion's lives at stake. "By the time I'm through with them, you and Lucan will be long gone."

"You're very brave, my lady."

She wasn't. Her stomach had turned into a hard knot.

And she couldn't draw enough air into her lungs. Faint, queasy, she stepped around Lucan. "I must go. When he wakes up, tell him . . . tell him that I did what I had to do."

"I will."

She kneeled and kissed Lucan's warm lips, then stood. "And Rion?"

"Yes, my lady."

"Tell him that I will always miss him." Cael fled before her eyes filled.

Trying to breathe normally, Cael strode outside the medical center toward General Brennon and Sir Quentin and a bustling group of military men, their weapons at the ready. She kept her face composed, her head high, and refused to think about how she'd never see Lucan again. If she did, she'd fall apart. And to save him, she had to keep calm. What she said next might make the difference between Lucan and Rion's survival and their deaths.

She had to stall. Use her status to make these men listen. Because if they searched the medical center from top to bottom, Lucan and Rion would never escape.

"Where's the Grail?" Sir Quentin asked. From the smirk on his face, he believed he held the upper hand. She intended for him to continue to think that way.

"Don't worry." She made her voice happy, as if they were on the same side and she was glad to see him. "I hid the Grail."

"In the medical center?" Quentin peered at the building behind her.

"Of course not." She kept her back straight, her shoulders squared, and ignored the weapons aimed at her chest. "After we left Avalon—"

"You mean after you stole the Grail and helped Rion get away—"

"You twist my words and misunderstand my actions, Sir Quentin." She paused, hoping he'd believe her performance as she placed resentment into her tone. "Rion and Lucan planned to keep the Grail for themselves. I stayed with them to make sure Avalon's prize would be put to the highest use."

Brennon nodded to a man who slipped a metal chain around Cael's waist. She could no longer dragonshape. The steel chilled her, but she would not let them see her cower, and she tossed her head with disdain. "As High Priestess, my duty is to do what's best for Pendragon."

"You're a traitor." Quentin scowled. "Where's the Grail?"

"I told you, I did what's best for Pendragon." Giving the Grail to Earth so Lucan's people could live was the right thing to do. Their need was great. But she hadn't betrayed her responsibilities. According to Rion, helping Earth would help her people. She'd believed in Rion's flashes of the future. She believed the Tribes would come to Pendragon, if they weren't already here.

"We won't ask again. Where's the Grail?" Quentin demanded.

Lying to these men didn't faze her. She would do whatever she must to protect her people and keep Lucan and Rion safe. "On the way here, I hid the Grail in the mountains between Avalon and Feridon."

"You lie." Quentin growled. He looked to Brennon, who was clearly in charge, even if Quentin was asking most of the questions.

Cael shrugged and held Quentin's gaze. "While the men answered a call of nature, I buried the Grail."

Sir Quentin raised his eyebrows. "And after they returned, they didn't notice the Grail was gone?"

"They knew the military was chasing us. They feared for their lives and were in a great hurry."

"But the boy, Jaylon, you cured him. And witnesses saw you use—"

"Witnesses saw me pour holy water into Jaylon's wound. The water cured him. That healing water originally came from the Holy Grail, not the common urn they saw me use."

Quentin tried to punch holes in her story. "You're saying you outwitted brilliant scientists. Rion and Lucan are geniuses and had the most innovative minds on my team."

The team Brennon had destroyed. Almost all of them were dead.

While her pulse thudded with anxiety, she managed to curl her lip in a satisfied smile. "Smart men always believe they're superior. Fooling them wasn't difficult." She'd set the bait. Now she had to reel them in. "I'll take you to the Grail, but I want something in return."

Brennon raised his weapon and pointed it at her. "You're in no position to bargain."

"The only reason this chain's around my waist is because I allowed you to put it there."

Quentin gestured to the military. "You're surrounded by men and weapons, Lady Cael."

"I came to you of my own free will. Nothing prevented me from flying away to safety." Except they would have shot her down, but she ignored that truth. Better to perpetuate the aura that she was invincible. She raised a haughty eyebrow. "And I told Lucan and Rion that I wouldn't give up the Grail's location until they helped me save Jaylon. So we came here." She smiled. "It worked. The boy's well, and I expect him to make a full recovery. Thank you for your concern."

"Enough talking," Quentin said gruffly. "Take us to the Grail."

"Of course. But in return, I want the murder charges against me dropped."

"Done." Brennon had agreed too easily. He had no intention of keeping his word. But she sensed that they now believed her story—because she'd acted in a way they understood. If they'd been in her position, *they* would have bargained for their lives.

"I can't fly to the mountains with this noose around my waist."

"We're not letting you out of eyesight. We'll take a skimmer." Brennon gestured to one of his men. "Search the medical center. I want Lucan and Rion captured."

Cael did her best stoic imitation. And she prayed to the Goddess that she'd bought Rion and Lucan enough time to escape.

I shall not hand over my kingdom—for you have failed to heed the laws that have stood all my days.
— ARTHUR PENDRAGON

24

Lucan awakened with a pounding head and a tongue so dry he couldn't speak. He heard the sound of waves hitting a beach. When he opened his eyes, bright sunlight pierced his corneas and pain washed over him. He fell back to the ground, and someone placed a damp cloth on his forehead.

The dampness felt good, and for a moment he allowed the coolness to soothe his fiery headache. What the hell had happened? Where was Cael? He recalled that they'd found the Grail. His fingers reached out and touched the artifact.

Lucan clutched the Grail to his chest. Some healing cup. The seven lower hells of the universe had taken up residence in his skull. He held his breath and risked cracking one eyelid.

Rion raised water to his lips, and Lucan drank. Every cell in his body craved water, and as his thirst was quenched, memories came flooding back. Cael's sacrifice. Rion stabbing the needle into his neck. The man had betrayed him.

Even as anger filled him, Lucan forced himself to sip slowly. "Cael?"

"Her plan worked—at least on our end." Rion placed the water beside Lucan. "We're safe."

Lucan recalled saving Jaylon and the medical center surrounded by troops. With a groan he also remembered Cael's plan to give herself up to Quentin and Brennon like some holy martyr. What had she been thinking?

Damn Rion for helping her.

Fury simmered through his veins "*You* got us out?"

"Yeah. I borrowed an orderly's tunic and pushed you out in a coffin."

"How long . . . ?"

"Were you out? A little over six hours."

Lucan cursed. He shoved himself upright. Pain stabbed his temples, and he swore again. Grabbing his head to make the world stop spinning, he tried to open his eyes. The resulting light set off fireworks in his brain. "Son of a bitch. What was in that shot?"

"I don't know."

"If I felt better, I'd knock your teeth down your throat."

Rion laughed. "And here I thought you'd be thanking me for saving your miserable life."

"Cael—"

Rion's laughter faded. "Without her help, I'd never have gotten us out of there. I'm not sure what she said to Quentin and Brennon, but she bought me time to sneak you out."

"Where is she?"

"What do you care? You have the Grail. You're free to go save Earth."

Is that what Rion thought? That he cared only about

Earth and the Grail? That he wasn't worried sick over
Cael in the hands of those bastards? "Damn, I'm not that
cold."

"Hey." Rion shrugged. "I'm just helping you get what
you wanted."

Lucan grabbed the thermos, gritted his teeth, and
poured the rest of the water over his head. The sunlight
was frying him, and no wonder. They were on a beach. A
very *familiar* beach.

Damn it. "How did you know . . ."

"My instruments picked up your spaceship when you
landed."

"And you never said anything."

"You wouldn't have trusted me. But I've been trying
to help you ever since."

"Why?"

"The Tribes have already invaded my world," he said
with obvious bitterness. "I've been trying to get home
since I crashed. I hoped you'd give me a ride."

Lucan could see pain and a longing for home in Rion's
eyes. "What was your plan if I said no?"

Rion shrugged. "I'd wait until the Tribes landed. Steal
one of their ships."

"How come you didn't try to steal mine?"

"I would have considered it," Rion said, his tone bru-
tally honest, "but I cannot allow Earth to fall, or my
world falls, too."

"Perhaps we'll find a way to help your people. You've
been planning for me to take you to Earth since—"

"The day you landed," Rion admitted. "Honor's on your
way to Earth. And since your ship is sitting a few hundred
yards off this beach"—Rion pointed out to sea—"all we
have to do is take the Grail aboard and fly home."

When Lucan remained silent, Rion clapped him on the shoulder. "You'll be a hero. You'll save your people. The victory will keep the Tribes at bay. Isn't that what you wanted?"

Lucan didn't answer. He'd accomplished the first part of his mission. Swimming the Grail out to his ship and flying home was the next step. It should have been a piece of cake.

All he had to do was forget he'd ever met Cael.

AFTER FLYING IN the skimmer craft for an hour, Cael peered out the window over the mountain range, careful to keep a puzzled expression in her eyes. Quentin, Brennon, and a squad of armed soldiers had already landed on three separate ridges, but each time after surveying the terrain, she'd told them it was the wrong place. "I'm sorry. We must have set down on the tall ridge over there." She pointed east to a steep, forbidding pinnacle where the skimmers couldn't land. It would take hours to climb on foot.

Quentin's communicator buzzed. "Yes?" He paused and looked over to Brennon's skimmer, which flew alongside theirs. "No, I don't have the Grail yet. But I promise, I'll bring it to you soon."

"Why does the general want the Grail so badly?" she asked.

"He doesn't."

"I don't understand."

"He's afraid that if anyone else has indestructibility, his military will lose their effectiveness."

Cael was surprised Quentin bought the general's explanation. She certainly didn't. The general didn't just want to keep his enemies from the Grail. He was obsessed with finding it for himself. And Quentin had played right into Brennon's hands.

Quentin's eyes glittered, and his greed sickened her. "Brennon's right. Once *I* have the Grail, I'll live . . . forever."

"You aren't working together?"

"Brennon thinks I'm working for him—the fool. But I wouldn't risk my reputation or smear my good name just to give up such a prize to him."

"You started that fire? You killed Sir Shaw and all the others?"

"For a prize I still don't have." Quentin glared at the mountain, his face darkening, his patience ending. Being out of his sterile laboratory was testing his composure. A quiet madness flickered in his eyes.

Quentin pointed out the window. "You're certain that this time, we're in the right place?"

"I'm sorry, but I'm not certain at all. My dragon sight is sharper than my human sight, and the geography appears different."

Quentin raised his hand to strike her, but one of his men blocked the blow. "Sir, please. The lady's cooperating."

"Is she?" Quentin spat the words in her face.

Cael turned to the man who'd come to her rescue. "Thank you." She nodded, and the man bowed his head. Even though she was chained, he feared her. And once Quentin learned she'd misled them, she doubted anyone would help her again.

She was alone, with no one to count on but herself.

These last few weeks, being with Lucan had made her feel as if she wasn't alone. And now that he was gone, she missed knowing he would watch out for her and protect her. But most of all she missed his company. The look in his sparkling blue eyes as their gazes met across the campfire. The touch of his fingers as he smoothed hair from her face. The special telepathic connection they shared.

Cael had her memories and more. She would never think of herself in the same way again. He'd changed her in ways she hadn't expected. And she would never be as alone as she'd been before she'd met him.

She hadn't known how much it would hurt to lose him. Because even though she was trying to assure his survival, she'd lost him—if not to death, then to his mission.

Cael longed to breathe the cold mountain air. This altitude soothed her aching hearts. Those stark, snow-covered peaks were home. If only she could lunge out of the aircraft and escape. She edged sideways, leaned toward the open door.

Quentin seized the chain at her waist and yanked her back, then slammed his elbow into her guard. "Fool. Don't forget she can fly. You let her leap out and she'll remove the chain and dragonshape."

Cael's hip burned where the chain bit into her tender flesh. But she kept her head raised, her back straight. Quentin was in charge of this squad, but, Goddess willing, she had an ally or two on this skimmer.

In any case, Cael needed a plan. She could take Quentin over the side of a cliff with her. That would be satisfying. She had no use for the man who had murdered Shaw and wanted the Grail for his own greedy ends.

The pilot set the skimmer down as close as possible to the remote site she'd indicated, and the men broke out climbing gear. Quentin held on to her chain, and she exited the vehicle with him.

She climbed outside and shivered. One of the soldiers thrust a heavy cloak into her arms. "My lady, you're coming with us."

Cael accepted the cloak and donned it, then tilted back her head and gazed at the icy cliff. Was her continued deceit necessary? Had Lucan already fired up his ship and headed for Earth? Was she endangering Quentin's squad for no reason?

She felt light-headed, a bit queasy. Not knowing about Lucan had her insides in knots. Even as she wished him a speedy journey, her spirit wept.

She remembered his sensual kisses, his determination to treat her with respect. She'd never met a man like him. There wasn't another man like him.

Her mate.

When she spied a dark speck flying against the gray rock, she kept her face blank, although a bit of hope lifted her spirits. At least Merlin had stuck by her side.

LUCAN AND RION had no difficulty swimming back to his ship with the Grail. Lucan had yet to give Rion an answer about dropping him off on Honor on the way home, but he was considering it and appreciated that Rion didn't press him. Mostly he was worried about Cael. He didn't trust her people to treat her well.

Once inside, Lucan headed straight to the bridge and plugged into the communications network. Rion stared out the portals, seemingly fascinated by the fish. Or maybe he was just reading Lucan's mood—angry, frustrated, and missing Cael like hell.

Striding to the command center, Lucan set the Grail down and ignored messages from home. He should send a reply, then power up and leave. He'd done what he'd come to do. He'd found the Grail. Taken it back to his ship. He should be celebrating.

But how could he?

Cael.

God. He'd been prepared for one hell of a journey. He'd expected to get lost, suffer mechanical breakdowns, or run into vicious aliens, but never had he imagined a woman would sacrifice herself for him.

She'd broken Dragonian taboos and given her own blood to save him. And now she'd gifted him with the Grail and sacrificed her life to keep him and his mission alive.

He thought about how she had stood up to him with fire in her eyes. How she'd wept with happiness at Jaylon's recovery. How she'd responded to his touch. How she'd shared her hopes and her secrets and her sweet body.

How could he leave?

He burned to know what was happening and booted up the computer's language circuits. "Where's Lady Cael, High Priestess of Avalon?"

The computer replied, "Six hours ago I picked up the High Priestess on a traffic camera outside Feridon's medical center."

Eager for a glimpse of her, Lucan ordered, "Let me see."

He watched the image of Cael bravely striding up to Quentin, Brennon and his armed men as if those guns couldn't hurt her. Her face looked brave, her eyes sad. And when her lips moved, he burned to hear the conversation. "Don't we have audio?"

"It's encrypted."

"Decode it."

Rion joined him and stared at the screen. "I thought we were leaving."

"We are." Lucan watched as Cael stood her ground, ignoring the weapons like some high-born queen. She was so brave. So lovely. And she'd faced those armed men—for him. Tightness in his chest had him swallowing hard. Every dragon cell in him longed to fly to her side, but this event had taken place hours ago. She might already be . . .

He couldn't finish the thought. He closed his hands into fists recalling how those bastards had chained her. Tortured her. Surely after all they'd shared, he'd know if she was . . .

When a man placed a chain around her waist and she did nothing to stop him, Lucan swore. Now she could no longer dragonshape and fly free. She'd surrendered her freedom so she could stall their search and give Lucan and Rion time to escape.

"If we don't go," Rion said, "her sacrifice will be in vain."

"This happened hours ago. A lot could have happened since then. Computer—"

"Captain, I've broken the code. You should hear this," the computer said. "It's coming live from Quentin's private audio feed to General Brennon."

Quentin's voice piped in through the speaker. "Once we have the Grail, we execute her as a murderer. In public."

"It'll be my pleasure," Brennon answered. "But what if we don't find the Grail?"

"We'll torture the truth out of her, then execute her at sunset. The bitch is too much trouble."

Slamming his fist into the console, Lucan swore again, the pain in his hand nowhere near the agony in his hearts. "Does Quentin have the power to authorize her execution?"

"General Brennon has that authority," the computer answered.

"Where are they holding Cael?"

Rion clapped him on the shoulder. "We're going after her?"

Lucan speared him with a hard look. "You approve?"

Rion's gaze glinted steel. "I'll support whatever decision you make."

But Lucan could see from the kindling rage in Rion's eyes that the man was ready, perhaps as eager to do battle as Lucan was.

The computer reported, "Quentin's holding Cael at the High Priestess's residence. An army surrounds her. Approach by ground is impossible. The Division of Lost Artifacts' troops are everywhere. No skimmer can slip past the air-defense system."

"What about a dragon?" Lucan asked.

"You wouldn't arrive before sunset."

Lucan frowned. "Can this ship get past their missiles?"

"Uncertain."

"Give me a probability."

"I can't estimate without more data."

"But with your speed and shielding, there's a chance we could get to her?"

"A small chance."

Rion stared at him, his gaze level. "How far are you willing to go to save her?"

Lucan clenched his fingers into fists. "I don't know."

"You're willing to risk the Grail for her life?"

Heart pounding with dread, he spoke between teeth clenched tight. "I . . . don't . . . know." That was one decision Lucan didn't want to ever have to make. Losing Cael would tear him apart. He would give his life for hers. He would give anything to protect her. But the Grail was not his. It belonged to Earth. So how could he measure her sacrifice or his pain against the survival of an entire world?

"Dragonian justice is swift," Rion said. "We don't have much time."

They had only about an hour. Lucan paced, barely containing the pain of having to make such an agonizing choice.

"What do you want to do?" Rion asked gently.

God help him, he didn't know. By going after her, he was risking the Grail and humanity's future.

But how could he live with himself if he left her to die? If he didn't try to save her?

His choices had consequences. Terrible, catastrophic consequences. He could either abandon the woman he loved to torture and certain death—or allow humanity to become extinct on Earth. The rational part of him told him he had to forget her, that somehow he had to move on.

But the dragonblood pounding through him reminded him she was his life mate. That life without her would be pure misery. With his mind battling his heart, he felt as if he was being ripped apart.

"Have you seen my future? Are Cael and I reunited?" He hadn't wanted to know the truth earlier, but now he couldn't bear *not* knowing what the future held.

"I've seen nothing helpful. Just bits and pieces. Us fighting together." Rion sighed, his face compassionate.

"I'm not even sure if we're battling on Pendragon or some other world." Rion clasped his forearm. "I would give you more if I could."

Lucan spoke to the computer. "Get me every detail on Dragonian weapons and detection systems and a schematic of the residence." Lucan gestured to Rion and led him toward his own shipboard locker. "Come with me. I want to get you up to speed on our weapons."

"So if the computer finds us a rescue angle . . ."

"It won't hurt to prepare for a fight." He handed Rion a laser pistol. "Notch one is stun. Two is injure. Three is kill."

Rion slammed the setting to kill. "What else have you got?"

*For a time, the veil will thin, the worlds shall touch,
and mankind will reach into the heavens.*

—THE LADY OF THE LAKE

25

A few hours ago, Quentin had flown Cael back from the mountains to Carlane. He'd ordered his men to chain her to a chair in a lower room of the residence. Now she was trying to smile at Jaylon, who stood shifting from foot to foot in front of her. Quentin, the bastard, wasn't above using her family, even a small boy, to get her to give up the Grail. But even if Cael wanted to tell him the Grail's location—and she didn't—she had no idea where Lucan and the artifact were now.

She only had a short time—time to reflect, Quentin had said—before his men resorted to torture. If she revealed the Grail's location, Quentin had promised her a painless death at sundown. With the murder accusation and her fingerprints on the knife in Shaw's back, she couldn't prove she was innocent.

Even if the Elders or some of the believers wanted to try to rescue her, the residence was built like a fortress. Over the years these ancient stone walls had been upgraded with modern security systems and would be impossible to penetrate.

For Jaylon's sake, Cael pretended the chains and the guards around her didn't exist. She pretended that the threat of being tortured to death wasn't making her head light-headed with fear. "You look better."

"I am." Jaylon puffed up his chest with pride. "The healers said I'm a miracle. But I know the truth. You healed me." Jaylon bit his lower lip, and his eyes grew round with worry. "They say you're a murderer."

"Just because they say a thing doesn't make it true."

"Why won't you give them the Grail to heal other sick children?" Jaylon asked.

Funny how a small boy was the first one to ask *why* she'd acted as she had. No one else had had the sense to do more than make demands. Even her sisters, huddled together on the opposite side of the room, had urged her to take the easy way out and give Quentin the Grail.

How could she explain the stakes to this precious child so he could understand? She thought for a moment and then spoke gently. "Suppose everyone was sick with a fever and there wasn't enough medicine to go around. Some people would be very sick, but many would just be a little sick. Whom should we give the medicine to?"

Jaylon looked down and scowled, then looked her straight in the eyes. "Those who are very sick?"

"But suppose those who are very sick needed lots of medicine. And those who are only a little sick needed only a little medicine."

"Then it would come down to which choice would save more lives."

Proud tears came to her eyes. "That is what I have done. By giving the Grail away, I have saved more lives than would be saved if I gave it to those who keep me here."

"It's not fair." Jaylon advanced another step.

He was close enough for her to breathe in the sweet baby scent of him, but a wise soul looked back at her from those childish eyes. She'd never lied to him and wouldn't do so now. "Life isn't fair. But the Goddess doesn't ask more from us than we are able to give."

"I don't want them to kill you." His eyes filled with tears.

Her stomach clenched. She didn't want to die. She especially didn't want to die in terrible pain. This dear child, who had been through so much, must have recognized her trembling. Jaylon slipped his tiny hand into hers.

Sonelle gasped. "Don't touch her."

Jaylon pretended he hadn't heard.

Cael's voice sharpened. "Tonight I'll face my own mortality and you'd deny me a bit of comfort?" She lifted her head, but Sonelle would not meet her eyes.

"Why must you be so stubborn?" Sonelle's words, proud and resentful, cut Cael to the bone.

Hurt that even now her sister chastised her, Cael lashed out. "Yes, I'm stubborn. Stubborn enough to have gone after the Grail to save your son."

Sonelle's neck reddened. "For that I will always be grateful. Thank you for saving him." The words came out stiff, formal.

But Sonelle's thanks shocked Cael almost as much as the sorrow she heard in her sister's voice. Apparently, it took Cael's impending death to win Sonelle's sympathy. Still, it was an unexpected gift to know her sister would mourn her. Cael swallowed hard. "Take good care of Jaylon."

Sonelle nodded. "I'm sorry your life . . . has come to

this." She held out her hand to her son. "Jaylon, let her go."

"No."

"Jaylon, you will obey me."

"It's all right." Cael nodded to Jaylon. "Do what your mother says."

His lower lip quivered. "I'm staying right here." To his mother's horror, he crawled into Cael's lap, flung his arms around her neck, and sobbed.

Sonelle shook her head and rejoined Nisco.

Meanwhile, Jaylon cried himself to sleep on Cael's lap. His presence, his touch, his tender affection were a most cherished gift. Cael wished her arms were free to hold him. But she could nuzzle his hair, breathe in his innocent scent, and take comfort in his weight and his body heat.

Nisco wrung her hands and sighed. "I'm so sorry this is happening to you. To us."

"Have they threatened you again?"

Nisco shook her head. "But once you're gone, we'll lose everything. Our home on the sacred grounds. I don't know what we'll—" She drew herself up straight. "I'm sorry. Here I am going on about a silly house when you . . ."

"Isn't this what you always wanted? To be free of me?"

Nisco shook her head, her eyes tearing. "I didn't want this. Not for you. Not for me. Not for Jaylon." Her gaze swept over the sleeping child and softened. "Is there anything I can do?"

Nisco's offer touched Cael. She was about to answer when she yelped at a sudden pain in her hand. Still on her lap, Jaylon held a small sharp knife. There was blood on her palm. Blood on Jaylon's palm. He was placing his palm to hers, letting their blood mix.

"By the Goddess, Jaylon, no!"

"Yes." He lifted his face to hers, his eyes calm.

"Why would you do such a thing?" Cael demanded, struggling against the chains, unable to move.

"I saw the *male* dragon fly you to the medical center. I want to be like him."

Sonelle looked from Cael to Jaylon, her expression confused. Her gaze dropped to their bloody hands. And she fainted. Nisco rushed to her.

"Jaylon," Cael said, "why do you think mixing our blood will turn you into a dragon?"

"The healers at the medical center saw the male dragon, too. They said you'd broken a taboo and must have given Lucan your dragonblood. Were the healers right? Will your blood make me—"

"I don't know. Do you understand that if you change into a dragonshaper that you'll be feared?"

"I'll be fine."

"Sweetie, you'll likely live out your life alone." Of course, he hadn't thought this through. He was a child. "Why, Jaylon? Why do you want to be a dragon?"

He answered without hesitation. "Because I want to be strong and brave like you."

I rode forth to war, and part of me prayed that I would return no more to hopeless love.

—Arthur Pendragon

26

Nisco patted Sonelle's cheeks. "Open your eyes. Wake up."

Sonelle moaned softly and regained consciousness.

"There's something I must tell you," Cael said.

Sonelle struggled to her elbows. "About the Grail?"

"About your son."

"Jaylon?"

"He may have dragonblood."

Sonelle turned even paler. "What?"

Cael kept her words calm. "Don't faint again. There's no time. Quentin and his henchmen will be back soon." Goddess help her, they would torture her. Breathing hard, mouth dry, she forced down the panic. Pain would come soon enough.

"What does having dragonblood mean?" Sonelle asked, as if afraid of the answer.

"Jaylon may become like me."

"A dragonshaper?" Sonelle backed away.

"Lady Cael is more than a dragonshaper," Jaylon cried.

Nisco pulled him to a far corner of the room, away from the discussion.

"How could you?" Sonelle said to Cael. "Not my Jaylon." Her eyes were wild with panic. "You're lying. There are no male dragons."

"There are now."

"It's not possible."

"Later Jaylon can tell you about what happened. Be gentle with him. Be patient—"

"Don't tell me how to bring up my son." Her face twisted in fear and horror. "How could you do this to him?"

Cael sighed. "Jaylon will need your help and your love."

"No one loves a dragonshaper. You know that."

Her sister's words sliced like a knife. Lucan had loved her, but he was lost to her. Somehow Cael stifled her pain. "You're his mother. Sonelle, please, for the love of the Goddess, listen to me for once. Being High Priestess or High Priest is lonely."

"I'm not stupid. I understand that it isn't always wonderful. But you live in a palace. People adore you."

"People fear me. It's taboo to touch me. I would not wish that for Jaylon—"

Outside, the scream of an engine unlike any Cael had ever heard screeched across the heavens. As if renting the air, the terrible sounds thundered through the residence.

Was the Goddess showing her displeasure by shaking the moon with a giant quake? A deafening clamor filled the air, like the cries of a thousand wounded birds of prey.

Quentin burst through the door, his eyes black and demonic, his weapon in hand.

Cael spied the open door at his back. She flicked her gaze to Nisco in the corner and, with a jerk of her head, indicated she should take Jaylon and run.

Sonelle started to bolt but froze. Quentin aimed his weapon at her. With his attention on Sonelle, he didn't notice when Jaylon and Nisco made their escape.

Sonelle finally managed to move, but before she could reach the door, Quentin fired. Soundlessly, Sonelle dropped at his feet, her blank eyes staring sightlessly at Cael.

Stunned, horror-struck, Cael blinked. One moment her sister had been alive, the next she'd passed into the Goddess's realm. Now Quentin was aiming his weapon at Cael.

"Last chance." Quentin spoke over the screeching metal that sounded like a hundred crashing skimmers. "Tell me where the Grail is or I'll burn off your toes, then your feet, then your hands. Inch by inch, you'll die."

The floor shook. Stones separated and cracked. Bursts of light shot into the room. Quentin scrambled for cover behind a row of shelves.

Flying debris filled the room as a huge metal machine crashed through the far wall, the thunder so loud her ears pounded in pain. Mortar and stone tumbled, and one wall of the residence toppled and shot up a dust cloud. Cael stared in shocked silence as a foreign metal object the size of a skimmer slid across the stone of the storage room floor, engines screaming, sparks flying.

The object was round, black metal, shiny. Alien. Some kind of transport? A spaceship?

By the Goddess. Was this Lucan's ship? If so, could anyone inside have survived the crash?

She expected Quentin to call for his men, but he

strode straight to her and placed his weapon against her forehead.

She closed her eyes and prepared to meet the Goddess. At least there should be little pain.

Still, she shook with terror.

"Fire that weapon and I'll destroy the Grail." Lucan spoke softly, his voice edged with fury.

Cael opened her eyes. Lucan was exiting a hatch in the side of the smoking ship with the Grail held firmly in his grasp. Rion covered his back, firing at soldiers who were attempting to pour through holes in the damaged building.

Firing a strange weapon, Lucan wiped out the guards in one swiveling burst of white light.

Lucan had come. He had come to save her.

She didn't know whether to laugh or sob or curse. But her eyes drank him in like a starving dragon in need of platinum. He had a long cut over his forehead, a bruise under one eye. His tunic was shredded, matted with dirt and soot and blood.

He'd come for her.

But he shouldn't have. His ship was smoking, sparking. Smashed. The brave fool was going to get himself killed or blow them all up. And now how would he get back to Earth? Yet she was so happy to see him her pulse raced, her hearts danced.

"Let her go," Lucan demanded, hefting the Grail over his head, "and I'll give you the Grail."

Keeping the gun to her head, Quentin reached into his pocket and pulled out the key to the lock that kept her chained. "Hand over the Grail and I'll give you the key."

"Don't believe him," Cael said. "He killed Sonelle."

"She was a means to an end," Quentin boasted. "Unimportant."

"Not to her son," Cael argued, hoping to distract Quentin as Lucan edged forward.

Rion took up a position by the door and cut down all who entered. But it was only a matter of time until the military brought in heavy armor and more soldiers swarmed inside. Even with superior firepower, Rion and Lucan couldn't hold off an entire army.

Lucan stopped advancing on Quentin when the two men were at arm's length. He held out the Grail with one hand, reached for the key with the other. Then he tossed the Grail straight at Quentin's face.

Quentin dropped the key and the gun. His fingertips touched the Grail. And Lucan lunged and tackled the man to the floor. The Grail went flying, clanging as it rolled. Wrestling, the men tumbled, arms and legs punching, jabbing and kicking.

Rion grabbed the fallen key and freed Cael. "We have to get out of here."

Cael kneeled and scooped up Quentin's weapon. She rammed home the energy clip and turned to see what she could do to help Lucan.

She peered through the dust. Quentin had pulled another weapon from somewhere. Lucan backhanded the other man's wrist and Quentin yowled in pain, then kneed Lucan in the kidney.

Soldiers broke into the building through a damaged area and another wall crumbled. Cael fired, pushing them back as they dived for cover, wishing she had a clear shot at Quentin. But with the men rolling across the floor, she might hit Lucan by mistake.

Rion kept firing steadily. Outside, the military forces

were unifying and coming closer. Merlin suddenly flew in through the open ceiling, and for a moment the owl appeared to dive right at Rion.

What in the universe? The bird had an uncanny ability to tell friend from foe. Why did he look as if he was about to attack Rion?

Cael searched for a reason, peered into the smoke, and her throat closed with fear. "Jaylon."

The boy was running toward the residence, past soldiers who were firing at Rion from behind overturned vehicles, downed trees, and rubble. Ducking and weaving, the boy stayed low. But he'd been running straight into Rion's line of fire until Merlin swooped down and flew straight at the barrel of Rion's weapon.

Terror for the boy slamming through her, Cael shouted, "Rion, don't shoot the bird. Or Jaylon."

"Jaylon?" Rion frowned, lowered his weapon, and peered through the smoke and haze. "The kid's here?"

Jaylon tried to run straight past Rion toward his mother's body, but thankfully, Rion scooped him up, placed him in a protected corner, and kept firing. "I can't hold much longer."

Lucan killed Quentin with a kick to the head just as the military, wearing uniforms that identified them as serving the Division of Lost Artifacts, broke through on three sides. The scientist was dead, but General Brennon's troops were overrunning the residence.

"Retreat to the ship," Lucan ordered above the smoke and noise.

"It's on fire," Rion yelled back.

They had mere seconds before the soldiers converged on them. Lucan rammed another energy clip into his gun. Rion grabbed Jaylon and pushed the boy behind him, then used his body to shield Jaylon as they both retreated to the center of the room.

More men poured into the residence.

"Follow me." Adrenaline pumping, Cael ran to Jaylon, picked him up, and raced out of the lower room and up the stairs. Merlin flew overhead. Rion and Lucan followed, taking turns to stop and lay down covering fire.

Cael led them out of the residence and up the temple's stairs. Again Lucan and Rion took turns firing shots that halted their closest pursuers, then followed Cael into the temple.

"Everyone," Cael said. "Get in the cannon." Her fingers flew over the controls, and she pulled a lever to warm up the ancient machine. Before she thought too hard and changed her mind, she tapped in the destination code. "Hurry."

While Lucan held off the soldiers, she motioned for Rion to leap over the rim. "Get inside. I'll hand Jaylon to you."

"You first." Rion hoisted Cael over the lip. She slid down and immediately turned to catch Jaylon. "Are you all right?" she asked the trembling boy.

Tears trailed down his smudged cheeks. "My mother—"

She hugged him. "I'm sorry."

Under her feet, the ancient machine rumbled. "Lucan, Rion, get down here."

The men leaped into the cannon. In the tight confines, Lucan slid down her front, Rion slid down her back. She could barely draw a breath. Merlin flew in, too, and perched on her shoulder.

The old stones around them began to heat. Soldiers were searching for them. She heard Brennon giving orders. "Find them."

Rion's elbow was shoved into her side. Lucan had his arms around her and Jaylon. "Rion, tell me you have the Grail?"

Rion shook his head. "I thought you had it."

"I'll go back." Lucan reached for the lip.

Cael tugged him down. "It's too late."

Rion agreed. "By now the whole army must be inside the residence."

Lucan's muscles tensed. She had to stop him.

"Even if you could climb out"—Cael leaned her cheek into his chest—"when the second wall caved, rubble buried the Grail. You'd need heavy equipment—"

"The High Priestess couldn't have disappeared into smoke," Brennon shouted. "Find her!"

The searchers drew closer, but as the cannon fired up, fear entered their voices. "Sir, the floor—"

"Look out, General."

Suddenly Brennon screamed. "Help me. That's an order."

"I can't, sir. The stones are too hot."

Brennon cursed.

"Get back or you'll burn," another soldier shouted. "We can't save him."

Brennon's screams of terror and pain echoed from the rafters.

Men pulled back. When they spoke, their voices were filled with awe. "What in the Universe?"

"Holy Goddess."

"Get out. Get out. Get out!"

Ancient engines hummed, and their pitch rose to a whine. Jaylon sobbed and held Cael tight, his little body trembling.

She said softly, "It'll be all right. We'll be safe."

"Nowhere's safe." Jaylon closed his eyes.

Lucan had lost his ship. He'd lost the Grail. Never had she seen his face this dark and grim, but his whisper remained calm. "Where *are* we going?"

"Where we'll be safe."

"Not without the Grail."

"It's too late."

He strained his arms overhead to reach the lip. But not even Lucan was that tall.

"It's all right. You don't need the Grail."

"Why not?" He looked down and gave her a puzzled frown.

"Because you have me." She grinned, a secret grin. And then the cannon blasted them through space.

Life is sustained by the flow of subtle energy called love.

—HIGH PRIESTESS OF AVALON

27

One instant Lucan, Cael, Jaylon, Rion, and Merlin were in the cannon. The next they were tumbling across grass. Lucan had tried to break Cael's fall and Rion protected Jaylon. Lucan had landed on his back on a hillside with Cael sprawled on top of him. With a flap of wings, Merlin soared into a hazy gray sky that smelled like rain. The owl settled on a huge circle of towering rocks, some with cross braces across the tops.

From the crowd gathered around them, Cael picked up astonishment at their sudden appearance amid the center of the ring of huge stones. These gray-haired people wore a style of clothing she didn't recognize and spoke in a language she didn't understand.

"Stonehenge!" Lucan grinned, and from his smile she knew the cannon had delivered them where she'd intended even before he said, "Welcome to Earth."

Nearby, Jaylon bounded to his feet with the enthusiasm of youth, but to Cael's surprise, the Earth people pointed square boxes at him. Their flashes were almost blinding.

"Is Jaylon under fire?" she asked, unsure, for she sensed no hostility.

"He's fine." Lucan chuckled and squirmed out from under her. "They're taking his picture."

"Why?"

"No one on this planet has seen a child for several decades."

Cael peered at the photographers and sensed excitement and hope in the crowd. "I don't understand what they're saying."

Rion and Jaylon joined them. Rion pulled a tiny device from his tunic's pocket. "Here's a universal translator." He pressed the chip into her forearm, where it disappeared beneath her skin.

She expected it to hurt but didn't even feel a sting. "Thanks."

"Give it a moment and you'll understand and speak like a native." Rion also gave one to Jaylon, who stood wide-eyed, clearly a bit overwhelmed, but at least he'd stopped sobbing.

Cael took his hand. "We're safe."

"Yes, we are." Lucan borrowed a phone and called Vivianne Blackstone, the woman who'd funded his mission. Apparently she'd been away on a business trip and was on her way back here. In the meantime, the woman had graciously arranged for a vehicle to take everyone to her residence in London.

Jaylon pressed his nose to the glass during the ride, and Cael was as eager as he to get her first look at Lucan's world. While the buildings in the city were spectacular and the scents enticing, everyone seemed so old. And sadness permeated these people.

But their welcome was warm, and two hours later,

after they'd dined on fish and chips and Jaylon's new favorite, three-cheese toast, they were shown to private quarters. Rion was ensconced in Vivianne's guest room. Cael and Lucan shared a suite, and Lucan jumped in the shower while she put an exhausted Jaylon to bed across the hall.

Cael hoped the dark circles under his eyes would go away as he recovered his strength. He'd been through so much. But he was strong, he was healthy, and he would be safe here. She'd make certain of it.

After pulling back the bedcovers, she patted the soft pillow. "Come here, little guy. I know you're tired."

Jaylon yawned and rubbed his eyes. "Are we staying on this planet?"

She smoothed his hair and smiled a reassuring smile. "For now." Cael and Lucan hadn't had a chance to talk since they'd landed on Earth. "Is that all right with you?"

He nodded, but she could see the lingering fear in his eyes, and sadness. Cael sat on the bed. She lifted the child into her arms, rested her cheek on his head. "No one can ever take the place of your mother, but you and I can be a family. Would you like that?"

Jaylon was quiet for a while. Then his arms tightened around her. "You'll teach me to fly?"

"Of course I'll try." She laughed. She helped settle him in the warm bed, tucked the covers around him. She kissed his forehead, feeling the responsibility of her newfound motherhood. "I love you. Now go to sleep, sweetie."

He closed his eyes and before long fell into a deep sleep. Her hearts ached for him. Swallowing the lump in her throat, she made a silent vow to Sonelle that she would love the boy as her own.

When Cael returned to their suite, Lucan was on the

phone. He covered the mouthpiece for a moment. "I'm talking to my family. There's a hot bath waiting for you." He pointed to the bathing area.

"A bath would be heavenly."

"Take your time."

He went back to his phone call, and she could feel the joyous emotions flooding through him and imagined everyone talking at once as Lucan assured his parents and sister he was back safely on Earth. She left him making plans to meet them in London tomorrow and followed the steam to the large tub.

He and his family had years of catching up to do. She was happy for him, but she'd gotten spoiled having him all to herself. The thought brought a smile to her lips.

She and Lucan had never spoken about a future. He'd never planned beyond his mission. But now with her here with him on Earth, they had all kinds of options. And she couldn't wait to talk to him. This might be her last night alone with him for a while.

She was too on edge to relax in the luxurious bath, scented with oils. Still, she took her time, enjoying the fresh citrus soap that made her feel refreshed. After drying in a thick terry towel, she slipped into a belted robe and padded over the thick carpeting into their suite.

Lucan was sitting in front of a computer. His desk overlooked a manicured garden lit up at night for a romantic effect. But he was staring resolutely at his monitor, his excitement visibly gone.

She came up behind him and placed her hands on his shoulders. He kept typing but spoke at the same time. "Remember the paper Rion gave me?"

"The one Nisco's PI stole from General Brennon's briefcase?" she asked.

"We thought they wanted it back so badly because of the tracking technology. But we were wrong."

She peered at the symbols on the screen. "It was the writing on the back they wanted to keep secret?"

"Yes." He glanced up at her, and her hearts sank to see those eyes dark with worry. "I've seen that writing before. Inside the cave with the giant waterfall. While you slept, I explored and found a poem about Arthur carved in the wall. Beside it was another poem in a different language. My notes are back on Pendragon, but I have a pretty good memory. I typed both poems into the computer on my spaceship, and luckily for us, it's the same poem in two languages."

She tensed. "Which means you can translate the writing on Brennon's paper?"

"Some of it." Lucan's tone was grim. "Enough to know that after the Tribes secure the Grail, they're planning a huge invasion."

"Where?"

"I don't know." Lucan exhaled heavily. She kneaded the muscles in his neck, found him so tense, so worried. This was no homecoming. He had lost the Grail because he'd saved her. She could feel him hurting with frustration and guilt, wanted to ease the turmoil of a situation that hadn't left him any choices. Any good ones, anyway.

As if realizing she could read him, he rose from his chair and took her into his arms. "I'm glad you're here."

And he was. She could feel him pouring fierce joy and bittersweet happiness into his kiss. A kiss that was downright possessive, demanding and sexy as hell.

She'd wanted to be wanted by this man, but who could have foreseen such love coming out of such danger, for his world, for her world? No. She could never have imagined this. Not when the future before her on Pendragon had been one of isolation and loneliness. Now she adored the way he wanted her. The way she no longer felt alone.

Arching into him, she let her robe slide to the floor. She ripped off his shirt, unfastened his slacks, all the while dragging her palms along his hard flesh. He'd always been fit. But now his muscles were denser, harder, more powerful and honed.

Without breaking their kiss, he easily lifted her and carried her to the bed. The heat in his eyes melted her. No matter what planet they were on, he desired her and she desired him. That much hadn't changed.

Already she ached to have him inside her. Reaching between their bodies, she used her fingertips to tease the ridge along the knob of his sex. He jerked in her hand, and she stroked him where he was hard, cupped him where he was soft, all the while enjoying the blast of tension radiating from him.

With a groan of need, he dipped his head, took her nipple between his lips, and laved the tip with his tongue. The swirling sensation set her mind spinning. Her breath rasped. But when she caught the fire in his gaze, the mischievous glint in his eyes, she suspected that this would be a night of all nights to remember.

Lucan sucked on one nipple, then the other, then licked his way down to her belly. Gently he parted her legs and kneeled between them. Slowly he opened her moist folds. And then he dipped the tip of his sex into her moisture, using her wetness to make his flesh slick.

Expecting him to press in further, she lifted her hips, but instead of filling her, he slid his sex over her folds, back and forth over her clit. The delicious friction had her writhing against him.

"More," she demanded.

"You like?" He gave her slow and easy, each stroke enticing and exciting.

She didn't know she could pulse with such need. She didn't know that her whole world had been reduced to waiting for his next caress. And with his hard flesh stroking back and forth against her moist folds, she was clutching his thighs, urging him to go faster, the coos coming from the back of her throat, urgent and needy.

She exploded, the wave of pleasure breaking over her in a long, smooth crest. Lucan kept caressing her with his sex, his momentum never changing, his pace never slowing. Her spasm kept going, like she was riding a tidal wave ripping along the shore.

"Easy," she murmured, thrashing. Her nerve endings were so sensitive, his slightest touch had her trembling.

Lucan leaned down and kissed her mouth. And when he did, she rolled until she was on top. In one smooth motion, she took him deep inside her—and then held perfectly still.

His satisfaction and need blasted her. He was desperate for her to move, but instead she experimented and tightened the muscles around his sex.

He hissed out a breath. "You . . . feel . . . good."

She squeezed harder, released him, then squeezed again, finding a rhythm that pleased her and that caused the irises in his eyes to darken to dragon purple. Sensing he was barely hanging on, she lifted her hips and began to ride him. His hand sneaked back between her moist folds. He placed a fingertip on her clit, drawing her taut with tension. Her head began to spin. Her hearts pumped so fast that all her blood seemed to rush to where his finger tapped a dance and his sex plunged in and out.

She exploded again and collapsed on top of him. He gave her only a few seconds to recover, stroking the back on her head, before he rolled and she ended up on her back, realizing he still hadn't finished.

Again, he kneeled between her thighs. She was so sensitive she could barely stand the pleasure. And yet she was already gathering, her body tensing under his touch. Light-headed, toes curled, she reached down and tugged his hips, bringing him into her. Then she wound her legs around his back, crossed her ankles, and reached down beneath his sex. While his hips thrust into her and pulled back out, she held on to his balls, teasing, cupping, tugging. And when they tightened and his breath rasped harsh in his chest, when she felt him gathering to explode, she slammed her hips up at him, tugged with her hands, and felt his seed pour into her.

His excitement took her right over the edge again. And the intensity of her pleasure left her numb. Satiated. Languid. She had no idea what the future would hold for them, but for the first time Cael was able to hope, dream, and imagine.

She may have slept for a few moments or even hours. When she opened her eyes again, he'd pulled the sheets over them. She lay snuggled against his warm chest, surprised to find him tense, worried.

She rolled onto her side and rested her cheek in her palm. Lucan reached over and held her hand. "I just checked on Jaylon, he's fine."

"Sonelle always said he's a heavy sleeper and never wakes up during the night."

"I don't know anything about children."

Cael grinned at Lucan. "You and your people had better get used to children." She dropped her hand to her stomach and covered it protectively. "We're going to be parents."

He stared at her with skeptical eyes. "Without the Grail . . . it's not possible."

"We don't need the Grail."

He scowled. "Cael, I'm sterile. All of Earth is sterile."

She placed his hand low on her belly. "I can already feel our babies."

"You're pregnant?" His gaze lifted to hers in wonder.

"With twins."

"How do you know?"

She laughed. "I'm an empath, remember? I can feel their emotions."

Clearly stunned, he rubbed his forehead. "I touched the Grail and now you're pregnant?"

She shook her head. "Jaylon required a battle wound for the Grail to heal him, remember?"

He raised an eyebrow. "So how did I get you pregnant?"

Cael chuckled. "Surely you haven't forgotten how we paired—"

"I remember." His voice was husky. "If the Grail didn't cure my infertility, then what did?"

"My dragonblood healed you."

"Sweet Lord. Of course. Your dragonblood set off all kinds of changes in my biology."

"First your vision sharpened, and you no longer needed your glasses. Then you became stronger. Grew scales. Shapeshifted into a dragon. *And* now you're fertile. Now we're going to have twins."

He grinned so broadly she couldn't doubt his excitement.

Cael nodded. "If your people can synthesize my blood—"

"You think we can cure everyone? Or only those who are related to King Arthur?"

"Dragonshaping and infertility involve different genes. A cure should work for everyone."

Lucan whooped and hugged her. "Earth will have the mother of all baby booms. I can't wait to tell my sister. Lady, do you know I love you?"

"How do you feel about Jaylon?"

"He's a great kid. Why?"

"I intend to raise him as my son."

"You think he'd accept me for his father?"

"His own father abandoned him and he's always longed for him. He'll be delighted." Cael snuggled happily against Lucan, loving that he was worried about the boy accepting him.

Lucan placed a hand on her belly. "How long does it take a baby dragonshaper to be born?"

"I don't know." She placed her hand over his. "But if they grow as fast as I heal, we're going to be parents quite soon."

"Are they empathic, too?" he asked.

"I'm not sure." She squeezed his hand. "This is new territory for me, too."

"It's going to be new for everyone on Earth. Those of my people in Arthur's bloodline will turn into dragonshapers."

"Will that be so terrible?"

He laughed. "I'm looking forward to adding to the Pendragon legacy." He caressed the back of her hand with his thumb. "How do you feel about staying here and having a large family?"

"So do you have marriages on Earth?"

Lucan rolled away from Cael, and immediately she missed his heat.

He sank onto one knee. "Cael, my love, will you do me the honor of spending the rest of your life with me?"

Cael scooted out of bed and kneeled, too. "I will." Heat rose to her cheeks. "Are we married now?"

He threw back his head and laughed. "Not yet. We'll have a huge ceremony and a feast. You'll wear a beautiful white dress. My mother and sister will never forgive me if we don't have a celebration."

"They won't mind that I'm a dragonshaper?"

"Are you kidding? They have my blood. They're going to be dragonshapers, too."

"With so many dragonshapers on Earth, even if the Tribes do invade, we should be strong enough to protect our children."

Merlin flew in through a window and hooted. How the owl had gotten in, Cael didn't know. Or care.

She was too busy kissing her future husband.

LOOK FOR THE NEXT
SEXY ROMANCE
IN THE
PENDRAGON LEGACY
SERIES!

•

Please turn this page
for a preview of

Rion

Available in mass market December 2009

1

London, the near future

"You call that relaxing?" A deep male voice reverberated through the exercise room, and Marisa Roarke opened her eyes. "Meditation is so overrated."

Rion Jaqard stalked with predatory zeal across the Trafalgar Hotel's workout room, flung a towel onto a chair, and whipped off his shirt before sliding onto the weight bench.

The few times Marisa had run into Rion at her brother Lucan's apartment, she'd noticed Rion was built. But she hadn't realized he was so solid. Talk about walking testosterone. She'd bet even his sweat had muscles.

Trying to ignore the size of Rion's very broad, very muscular chest, she frowned. "These days I find relaxing pretty much like trying to fly with only one wing."

Conversation over. She shut her eyes again, trusting he'd take the hint, and attempted to banish the image of his ripped chest and totally toned, totally etched abs.

Damn it. It wasn't like her to be so aware of a man's

physique—even if he was half naked, and a very yummy half at that.

Rion was from the planet Honor, and if all Honorians were built like Rion, Earth's women would be rioting for interplanetary travel visas. Of course, no such documents existed. Not since the United Nations had shut down travel from Earth to the rest of the galaxy.

Still—she sneaked another glance. All that maleness was dazzling. From the manly wisps of black chest hair to his rugged profile to his sharp and confident movements, he was drawing her attention like a London tourist attraction.

Stop. Just look somewhere else. Anywhere else.

Marisa had thought herself past the age of ogling men. Her atypical reaction had to be caused by a fifteen-hour shift, exhaustion, and her not-so-successful attempt to erase the emotional aftereffects of dealing with her over-sexed clients.

She closed her eyes. *Out. Out. Out.* Rounding up the stray emotions, she corralled them into a tiny corner of her mind, then squashed down hard.

But she couldn't block out the man across the room. The weights clinked as Rion raised and lowered them, and Marisa peeked again through her lowered lashes. The guy was gorgeous.

"Hard day?" he asked.

"Uh-huh." The one-on-one telepathy she'd signed up for wouldn't have been this taxing, but after Marisa had begun her new job, she'd discovered her ability to communicate with an entire group, which meant she was exposed to all of their emotions at once.

Don't think about work.

Unclenching her teeth, she forced her lips to part,

breathed deeply through her nose, and told the muscles in her aching neck to loosen. Or at least to stop throbbing so she could go up to her hotel room and sleep.

"Maybe lifting would relax you. If you need help, I could spot you."

"No, thanks."

Why couldn't he just leave her alone? Surely by now even his oversized biceps had to be burning, his lungs aching for oxygen. But he didn't sound out of breath.

"Let me know if you change your mind."

"Meditation works better in silence," she said calmly, pleased that her voice didn't give away how aware she was of the way his buttocks tightened and relaxed in a fascinating rhythm that made her mouth go dry.

"Seems to me your meditation isn't working."

He was right. She couldn't keep her eyes off him. A light gleam of sweat glistened on his skin, emphasizing his muscles as he set the weights down, then perused her with a raking gaze. "Your pulse rate's over one thirty."

Hell. Any women within ten meters of him would have an elevated pulse. "Are you deliberately trying to annoy me, or do you come by it naturally?"

She expected him to take off, but he grabbed his towel, slung it over his shoulders, and wiped the sweat from his brow. And gave her a look brazen enough to heat every flat in London—for the entire winter. "There are better ways to relax."

"Like?" Marisa couldn't prevent a tiny smile raising the corners of her lips.

He took that for an opening. Of course, he would. She doubted anyone had ever told him no. Approaching with pantherlike movements, he sat on the mat behind her and placed his palms on her shoulders.

She should have pulled away. Should have told him to keep his hands to himself.

But she couldn't. Not when he felt so damn good.

Gently, ever so slowly, he kneaded her neck and caressed her shoulders with a sensual thoroughness that melted away the tension. Circling in on the tight spots with soothing caresses, he feathered his fingertips over her sore muscles.

Her pulse leapt. She swallowed hard.

Rion eased the heels of his palms into her tight shoulders with lingering, luscious strokes. After several wondrous minutes, he leaned forward and his breath fanned her ear. "You carry tension in the neck."

"I do?" She sighed and leaned into his hands, grateful for the relief.

He kneaded gently, gradually going deeper, until her muscles melted, until she felt as warm and pliable as taffy. His fingers were so clever, but as he released one kind of tension, a sensuous anticipation began to build.

She was relaxed. Yet filled with expectation. She jerked upright.

"Am I too hard for you?" he asked, almost sounding innocent.

She made a choking sound. He was sitting behind her, but she could see his chiseled face reflected in the mirrors and caught a gleam in his eyes. "My hands. Am I pushing too hard?"

"You feel great. And you damn well know it." She lifted an eyebrow and shot him an I-know-what-you're-up-to look.

But she really had no idea what his intentions were. He may have been a first-class flirt with other women, but he'd always treated her like a pesky sister. What was going on here?

Even if he was only being friendly, she shouldn't be encouraging him. For one thing, Rion was her brother's friend. And for another, perhaps more importantly, she wasn't into one-nighters.

"I'm glad you like my touch," he murmured.

Was his voice a bit too husky, or was she so starved for male attention that she didn't know when a man was simply being kind? She cast him a suspicious glance. "From what I hear, you've had lots of practice."

Rion rubbed a knot next to her spine, applying tension until the tightness ebbed, and for a moment she wished he could rub away the old psychological wounds. Ever since her divorce seven years earlier, Marisa hadn't trusted any man who wasn't related to her by blood.

She had to give Rion credit, though, when he didn't deny his active social life. "You have an Earth saying, 'Practice makes perfect.' But I'm not certain if a massage can ever be perfect. After all, there are so many variations of where to touch . . . how to touch . . . when to touch . . ."

Surely no one could accidentally be *that* suggestive—not even a man from another planet. No doubt when she fell asleep, she'd dream about where and how and when he would touch her next.

Leaning forward, he whispered into her ear, "Did you know you have a very sexy neck?" His gray eyes met hers in the mirror, and she could have sworn they smoldered. When he brushed a wispy tendril from her nape, heat shimmied down her spine.

Okay. They'd gone at least two steps beyond

awkward, she scooted from under his hands and stood. "Thanks. It's been a long day. I need to hit the sack."

"Good night, Marisa." He stood, too, and grabbed his shirt. As she left the workout room, he called out to her. "Pleasant dreams."

Pleasant was out of the question. Sizzling hot was more like it.

AND THE LEGEND
CONTINUES
IN THE STUNNING
THIRD ROMANCE OF THE
PENDRAGON LEGACY
SERIES!

·

Please turn this page
for a preview of

Jordan

Available in mass market March 2010

1

"Damn it, Jordan. You lied to me." Vivianne Blackstone, CEO of the Vesta Corporation, tapped the incriminating report against her leg and restrained her urge to fling it at Jordan McArthur, her chief engineer. The world was in a total meltdown after learning an ancient enemy had infiltrated Earth's governments and major industries, and Vivianne was determined to keep her *Draco* project safe.

Head throbbing, she stared at the spaceship's complex wiring. The *Draco* had to fly as planned. It had to work out. So much was riding on this venture to find the lost and legendary Holy Grail. Vesta's future. Earth's future. Her future. Everything she'd ever wanted, everyone she'd ever loved, might be lost if this project didn't succeed.

When Jordan didn't respond, she nudged his foot with her shoe. "I'm talking to you."

Lying on the deck with his head halfway through a hatch, Jordan shifted until she could just see his intense golden brown eyes.

"I heard. How did I lie to you?"

She dropped the papers, but she'd already lost his attention to the ship. He'd wriggled back inside the compartment, pulling another wire to hook into the circuits, no doubt following an electrical schematic that existed only inside his head.

He threaded a wire into a panel box of delicately networked circuits. "Hand me a screwdriver."

Scowling at his back, she slapped the tool into his hand. "Tell me these findings are wrong," Vivianne demanded.

"What findings?" His profile, rugged and somber, remained utterly still, except for a tiny tick in his jaw that told her he was unhappy she'd interrupted his work. He wouldn't even have a job if not for her—and he would lose it, if he didn't come up with a satisfactory explanation for why his entire résumé had been one big, fat lie.

"You've never attended Harvard. Never got your PhD at MIT. Never taught at Cambridge."

"The Phillips head." He held out his hand again, and this time his voice was laced with impatience. "It's the screwdriver with an X on the tip."

Like she didn't know a Phillips head when she saw one? While her specialty was communications technology, she'd designed and built her first hydrogen rocket by age twelve. However, when it came to spaceship design, Jordan was the go-to guy.

Despite his doctored résumé, the man knew his aeronautical engineering. From hull design to antigrav wiring, no detail on the *Draco* was too small for Jordan to re-engineer and make more efficient.

One of Jordan's engineers spoke over the ship's intercom. "These voltage converter equations can't be right."

"They are," Jordan answered evenly.

"They're frying the circuits." The man's frustration was evident in his tone.

"Sean, you'll find a way to keep them humming. You always do."

"I'm stumped."

"I'll give you a hand as soon as I can."

"Thanks, boss."

"But I'm sure you'll figure it out before then."

Sean chuckled. "I'll do my best."

While this was a side of Jordan she hadn't seen, his encouragement didn't surprise her. But it wasn't his leadership skills she questioned. Vivianne's gut churned. "Jordan, we really need to talk."

"So talk."

Vivianne paused and considered precisely what to say. She'd already made one mistake by hiring Jordan before he'd been properly vetted. She couldn't afford to make another—like accusing him outright of being a spy.

"As the first hyperspace ship to carry a full crew, the *Draco* has caught the imagination and attention of the masses. Everything we do is headline news, and when the press finds out that my chief engineer falsified his employment application—"

"Damn it, Vivianne, I know what I'm doing."

"To the public, a liar is a liar. And if you lied to get a job, they'll think you've lied about the *Draco* during our press conferences."

"So we don't tell anyone. Problem solved."

Vivianne pinched the bridge of her nose to ease her headache. "But if your lies come to light, you don't just lose your job, you ruin my credibility. My company's reputation. It could crash Vesta's stock."

Jordan threaded one of myriad wires into a nexus of circuitry. "As long as this ship doesn't crash, your stock will be fine."

She could handle the business end. Hell, if she put his picture on the news, the female half of the planet would fall in love at first sight and forgive him anything. The gorgeous face of Mr. Dark, Tough, and Brilliant might just sway the general population and perhaps her stockholders, as well.

What she couldn't handle was a traitor.

"What other lies have you told me?" she asked.

"Whatever would get me this job."

"Real inspiring. Why didn't you respond to the memo I sent last week?"

"If I spent all my time reading your memos, how would I get anything done?"

"You've installed miles of wiring that isn't in the specs."

"We're ahead of schedule, so why are you concerned?"

"I suppose you'll say the same about the cancellation of the prototype cosmic-energy converter?"

He merely arched a brow.

She frowned. Before she'd known about his lies, she'd shrugged off his changes to necessary modifications. But could it be more?

In a desperate attempt to suppress her frustration, Vivianne reminded herself how far she'd come. Peering at the *Draco*'s shiny metal, she had difficulty believing they'd built this ship in just over three months. Almost every system was a new design, and although the number of things that could go wrong was almost infinite, she had high hopes for success.

"If the story of your doctored credentials leaks, our client may get cold feet," she explained.

"Chen won't back out." Jordan sounded completely certain.

She didn't bother to keep the exasperation from her voice. "Billionaires willing to buy a spaceship in order to search the galaxy for the Holy Grail aren't a dime a dozen."

Jordan grunted.

"If Chen does back out, I'll have to refund his investment. And with the way you've been spending, not even I have that much credit."

"Down to your last few billion, are you?" Jordan teased without glancing in her direction.

She clenched her fists in irritation. "That's not the point. Maybe we can break the news, spin it in our favor." She pictured an advantageous story. Something like, 'Genius engineer discovered.' "Then the article could go on to praise you and some little-known college. I'll have my PR department put together a package."

"Not a good idea."

His golden eyes glittered dangerously, and his response made her uneasy. Something wasn't right. He should be grateful that she was willing to fix the publicity nightmare he'd created. Instead he was acting like a man with something else to hide. But what?

"Do you always make contingencies for contingencies?" he asked.

She snorted. Orphaned at age ten, Vivianne had become a ward of the state. Control became her lifeline. She planned her days from start to finish. She arranged her appointments, both business and personal, to the minute, and any disruption was cause to work twice as hard to get back on schedule. She'd used her obsession to earn herself a first-class education and to build a successful small business into a worldwide conglomerate.

The downside of running a huge company, however,

was that she had to rely on others. Brilliant engineers like Jordan didn't give a damn about her minute-to-minute expectations. Jordan got the job done—but he certainly didn't do things her way.

"In your case, I haven't planned enough."

Jordan rubbed his ear and stood, reminding her just how tall and broad he was. But if he was attempting to use his size to intimidate her, he'd learn she didn't back down. He was, after all, her employee.

"What do you want me to do?" he asked. "You have someone else who can build the *Draco* on budget and under deadline?" He didn't wait for her reply. They both knew the answer was no.

"Where *did* you go to school?"

Jordan shrugged. "Here and there."

Her blood pressure shot up ten points, but she did her best to keep her temper under control. "Could you be a little more specific?"

He shot her a nonapologetic smile that was way too charming. "I'm pretty much self-taught."

Hell. She needed more than a damn charming smile to convince her he hadn't been educated on another planet. That he wasn't a spy.

"You don't have a PhD?"

He didn't answer.

How could Jordan have fooled her so easily? More importantly, what was he hiding? What else hadn't he told her?

"What about job experience?"

"Nothing verifiable."

"I suppose you fudged the glowing recommendations, too?" Her pulse pounded and she massaged her aching temple. "Who the hell are you?"

"You might want to take an aspirin—"

"Thank you, *doctor*." Her sarcasm escaped unchecked. "Oh, excuse me, you aren't a doctor of anything, are you?"

"I don't need a medical degree to see that your head hurts and you're taking it out on me." His tone was calm, low, and husky, and she found it sexy, which irked her even more.

"So now you're a shrink."

He'd barely glanced at her before turning to work on his beloved circuits, but it was so like him to notice details, even her wincing in pain.

Vivianne willed Jordan to turn around. "How did you do it? It's as if you appeared in Barcelona six months ago. Until then, you had no credit. You attended no schools. Even your birth records are fake. I can't find anyone who knew you before you walked into my office to apply for a job."

"And you've never regretted it."

"Until now." Damn him.

"You don't mean that." Jordan shrugged. "You don't regret letting me build you this ship."

Vivianne hadn't developed her company by allowing handsome men to sweet-talk her into trusting them or by ignoring urgent government warnings. Both Vivianne and the Tribes were after the same goal—both wanted the Grail. So it was very possible that the reason her chief engineer had faked his past was because he was a spy—for the Tribes.

She felt sick to her stomach, but her tone snapped with authority. "Jordan, put down your tools. You can't work on the *Draco* until security clears you."

In typical Jordan fashion, he kept right on working.

"Don't you want to see if the new engine's going to work?"

"We'll straighten that out later." Her temper flared, because Jordan knew just how to pique her interest. From the get-go, the engines had been a major issue. It almost broke her heart to know that the *Draco* might never fly now that she was pulling him off the project.

"I'm about ready to test a new power source."

"What are you talking about? What new power source?"

"The Ancient Staff." Jordan reached to a sheath he wore on his belt and drew out an object that resembled a tree branch with symbols carved into the bark. When he flicked his wrist, the rod telescoped and expanded with a metallic click. Extended to five feet, the Ancient Staff gave off an otherworldly shimmer unlike anything Vivianne had ever seen.

The air around the staff glittered like heat reflecting off hot pavement. It was as if the staff folded and compressed the space around it, the eerie effect and haze continuously rippling outward.

She peered at Jordan. The cords in his neck were tight, his broad shoulders tense, as if he were bracing for her reaction. She tried to tamp down a pinch of panic. "Don't move."

He moved to place the staff into position. "The Ancient Staff will supply far more power to the *Draco*'s engines than a cosmic converter."

That staff wasn't in the plans. It hadn't ever been discussed. For all she knew, once he attached the strange power source to the *Draco*, they'd all blow up. Unnerved, she reached for her handheld communicator to call security, but there was no time. It would take only a second for him to snap the Ancient Staff into the housing.

She'd have to stop him herself. "Turn it off."

"The staff doesn't have an off switch."

Vivianne jerked backward a step. "Don't attach that thing to my ship."

"It's meant to—"

"I said no." Mouth dry with suspicion, she clamped her hand on his shoulder.

Before she could yank him back, Jordan snapped the rod into place. The anxiety she'd been holding back knotted in her stomach.

But controlling her fear was the least of her worries as the air around the rod shimmered, then spread up his arm.

"What type of energy is this?" she asked.

"The powerful kind."

"The engines can deal with that kind of power?"

"I hope so."

The energy crawled all the way up his arm and stretched toward her hand. She tried to jerk back, but her body refused to obey her mind. Her feet wouldn't move. Her fingers might as well have been frozen.

Panicked, she watched the glow of energy flow over Jordan's shoulder to her hand. Every hair on the back of her neck standing on end, she braced for pain. But when the glowing energy engulfed her fingers and washed up her arm, then sluiced over her body, the tingling sensation somehow banished her headache and expelled her fear.

The effect was instantaneous and undeniable. Her breasts tingled. Her skin flamed as if she and Jordan had spent the past fifteen minutes engaging in foreplay rather than arguing over his nonexistent past. She'd always found him attractive, but now it was as if the staff had turned on a switch inside her. She swallowed thickly. If he felt the same effects, he wasn't showing it.

Every centimeter of her skin now was demanding to be stroked. Unwarranted sensations exploded all over her erogenous zones. Her nipples tightened, exquisitely sensitized. The scales on the insides of her arms and legs fluttered. Sweet juice seeped between her thighs.

Drenched in pure lust, she shook her head, trying to clear it. "What the hell is going on?"

"Don't know." Jordan practically growled, as if it took superhuman effort just to speak.

So he felt as totally, inexplicably aroused as she did. Obviously, he wasn't handling it well, either, but that didn't stop desire from rushing through all her senses.

She craved him like a starving dragon needs platinum, yet this could not be. Not without an emotional connection. She didn't do chemistry. She didn't do one-nighters. She wouldn't crave a man she barely knew.

But there was no fighting or denying the potent passion slamming her. Sexual need burned into her flesh, blazed in her bones, smoldered through her blood, the sensations fiery hot.

If she didn't have sex in the next few seconds, she was certain she would spontaneously combust.

THE DISH

Where authors give you the inside scoop!

♥ ♥ ♥ ♥ ♥ ♥ ♥ ♥ ♥ ♥ ♥ ♥ ♥ ♥ ♥

From the desk of Susan Kearney

Dear Reader,

I came up with my idea for LUCAN (on sale now), the first book in the Pendragon Legacy Trilogy, in the usual way. A time machine landed in my backyard early one morning, and I forgot all about sleeping in—especially after a hunky alien sauntered right up to my back porch and knocked.

Scrambling from bed, I yanked on a cami and jeans, stashed a tape recorder in my back pocket and ran my fingers through my hair. Like any working writer worth her publisher's advance, I was willing to forego sleep for the sake of research.

I yanked open the back door.

Did I mention the guy was hot? No way would I have guessed he was an archeologist back from a mission to a planet named Pendragon. But I'm getting ahead of myself. From his squared jaw to the intelligent gleam in his eyes to his ripped chest, Lucan was all macho male.

And for the next few hours he was all mine.

"I understand you're interested in love stories written in the future," Lucan said, his lips widening into a charming grin.

"I am." Heart pounding with excitement, I joined him on the porch. We each took a chair.

Lucan steepled his hands under his chin. "In the future, global pollution will cause worldwide sterility."

Uh-oh. "Humanity is going to die?" I asked.

"Our best hope will be a star map I found in King Arthur's castle."

"A star map . . ." Oh, that sounded exciting. "You followed the map to the stars?"

"To find the Holy Grail."

"Because the Holy Grail will cure Earth's infertility problem?"

He nodded and I was pleased. I was a writer for a reason. I could put clues together. But I wanted more. "You mentioned a love story?"

Lucan's face softened. "Lady Cael, High Priestess of Avalon."

"She helped you?"

His full lips twisted into a handsome grin. "First, she almost killed me."

"But you're still alive," I prodded, settling back in my chair. There was nothing I liked better than a good adventure story about saving the world, especially when it involved romance and love.

If you'd like to read the story Lucan told me, the

book is in stores now. And if you'd like to contact me, you can do so at www.susankearney.com.

Enjoy!

Susan Kearney

♥ ♥ ♥ ♥ ♥ ♥ ♥ ♥ ♥ ♥ ♥ ♥ ♥ ♥ ♥ ♥

From the desk of Marliss Melton

Dear Readers,

"What inspires your stories?" my readers ask. I tell them *everything*—news stories, movies, dreams, but most especially personal experience. "Write what you know" is wise advice, especially when it comes to painting a vivid setting. Though I've never visited the jungles of Colombia the way my characters do in my latest book SHOW NO FEAR (on sale now), I did get to experience the jungle as a child living in Thailand. During my family's three-year tour there, we often vacationed at a game reserve called Kao Yai.

Children are wonderfully impressionable. I will

never forget the moist coolness of the jungle air or the ruckus of the gibbons, swinging in the canopy at dawn and again at sunset. And the birds! There was a great white hornbill named Sam, hand-raised by the park rangers, that liked to frighten unsuspecting tourists by dive-bombing them! One morning, I fed her Fruit Loops off my bungalow deck. By day, my parents would drag all five of us kids on mile-long hikes, an experience stamped indelibly into my mind, providing inspiration for Gus and Lucy's perilous hikes. Our labors were always rewarded by a swim in the basin of a thirty-foot waterfall. Behind the waterfall, I discovered a secret cave, just like Gus and Lucy's. On one hike in particular, we stumbled into a set of huge tiger tracks. Who knew how close a tiger was lurking? Luckily, it left us alone.

Without a doubt, my childhood adventures have provided me with tons of material for my writing. I hope you enjoyed Gus and Lucy's adventures in SHOW NO FEAR. To read more about my adventurous childhood and what inspires my writing, visit my Web site at www.marlissmelton.com.

Sincerely,

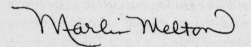

♥ ♥ ♥ ♥ ♥ ♥ ♥ ♥ ♥ ♥ ♥ ♥ ♥ ♥ ♥ ♥

From the desk of Michelle Rowen

Dear Reader,

In my Immortality Bites series, I've put fledgling vampire Sarah Dearly through a great many trials and tribulations, and she's weathered them all with her trademark sarcasm (her greatest weapon against nasty vampire hunters), grace, and charm (although this is usually mixed with a whole lot of anxiety and paranoia).

In TALL, DARK & FANGSOME (on sale now), the fifth and final book in the series, Sarah finds all of her vampire-related issues coming to a head. Her nightwalker curse seems likely to turn her permanently into an evil, bloodsucking vamp; she's being blackmailed into helping Gideon Chase, the leader of the vampire hunters, become the strongest vamp ever created; and her romance with master vamp Thierry seems destined to break both of their hearts.

Life sure ain't easy for a vamp.

How will it all work out? Will Sarah get the happily ever after she's been hoping for?

I wish I knew!

(Ha. I *do* know. I wrote it! But I can't just give away the ending so easily, can I?)

What I know for sure is that writing these crazy characters for the past five-plus years has been a pleasure and I'm going to miss them very much! I hope you've enjoyed the journey and that you're as pleased as I am with the ending to Sarah's story . . .

Happy Reading!

Michelle Rowen

www.michellerowen.com

Want to know more about romances at Grand Central Publishing and Forever? Get the scoop online!

GRAND CENTRAL PUBLISHING'S ROMANCE HOME PAGE

Visit us at www.hachettebookgroup.com/romance for all the latest news, reviews, and chapter excerpts!

NEW AND UPCOMING TITLES

Each month we feature our new titles and reader favorites.

CONTESTS AND GIVEAWAYS

We give away galleys, autographed copies, and all kinds of fun stuff.

AUTHOR INFO

You'll find bios, articles, and links to personal Web sites for all your favorite authors—and so much more!

THE BUZZ

Sign up for our monthly romance newsletter, and be the first to read all about it!

VISIT US ONLINE

@ WWW.HACHETTEBOOKGROUP.COM

AT THE HACHETTE BOOK GROUP WEB SITE YOU'LL FIND:

CHAPTER EXCERPTS FROM SELECTED NEW RELEASES

•

ORIGINAL AUTHOR AND EDITOR ARTICLES

•

AUDIO EXCERPTS

•

BESTSELLER NEWS

•

ELECTRONIC NEWSLETTERS

•

AUTHOR TOUR INFORMATION

•

CONTESTS, QUIZZES, AND POLLS

•

FUN, QUIRKY RECOMMENDATION CENTER

•

PLUS MUCH MORE!

Bookmark Hachette Book Group
@ www.HachetteBookGroup.com.

If you or someone you know
wants to improve their reading skills,
call the Literacy Help Line.

WORDS ARE YOUR WHEELS
1-800-228-8813